The fiery brilliance ...... *which you see on* ...... *holography.*" This is ...... *which a powerful las...... diamond-like facets ...... a square inch. No print or photog...... ...e vibrant colors and radiant glow of a hologram.*

So look for the Zebra Hologram Heart whenever you buy a historical romance. It is a shimmering reflection of our guarantee that you'll find consistent quality between the covers!

A CHERISHED PRIZE

"You're crazy," shouted Leigh. "You don't own me. I'm not a piece of property. You have no right . . ."

"Oh, yes I do have the right," Matt said in a low steely voice. "You're mine, kitten. I was the first — and by my word I'll be the only man in your life!"

His mouth swooped down on hers. Leigh struggled, but he pushed them both against the wall behind him, pinning her with his big body as his lips assaulted hers. Leigh tried to fight the sensations he was causing, her mind screaming. But her body, denied for so long, betrayed her. She turned soft and yielding in his arms, a low moan rising from her throat.

Matt felt her response and released her arms, slipping a hand behind her back and molding her body to his. His lips left hers to rain fiery kisses over her brow, down her temple, across her chin, lingering at the sensitive spot just below her ear.

"Oh, Leigh, I've missed you. Let me show you how much . . ."

FIERY PASSION
In every Zebra Historical Romance

WILD FURY   (1987, $3.95)
by Gina Delaney

Jessica Aylesbury was the beauty of the settled Australian Out-back. She had one love; her childhood friend Eric. But she could never let him know how she felt — and she could never let anyone but him teach her the smouldering pleasures of womanhood . . .

CAPTIVE SURRENDER   (1986, $3.95)
by Michalan Perry

Gentle Fawn vows revenge for the deaths of her father and hus-band. Yet once she gazes into the blue eyes of her enemy, she knows she can never kill him. She must sate the wild desires he kindled or forever be a prisoner of his love.

DEFIANT SURRENDER   (1966, $3.95)
by Barbara Dawson Smith

Elsie d'Evereaux was horrified when she spilled wine on the pants of the tall, handsome stranger — and even more shocked when the bold Englishman made her clean it up. Fate drew them together in love and passion.

ECSTASY'S TRAIL   (1964, $3.95)
Elaine Barbieri

Disguised as a man, Billie Winslow hires on as a drover on a trail herd to escape a murder. When trail boss, Rand Pierce, discovers that the young tough is a nubile wench, he promises to punish her for lying — and keep her for his loving.

PROUD CAPTIVE   (1925, $3.95)
by Dianne Price

Certain that her flawless good looks would snare her a rich hus-band, the amber-eyed lass fled her master — only to be captured by a marauding Spanish privateer. The hot-blooded young woman had gone too far to escape the prison of his arms.

Rapture's Revenge

Lauren Wilde

ZEBRA BOOKS
KENSINGTON PUBLISHING CORP.

For my sister, Dolores, whose warm sense of humor brightens the lives of all those around her.

ZEBRA BOOKS

are published by

Kensington Publishing Corp.
475 Park Avenue South
New York, NY 10016

First printing: May 1987

Printed in the United States of America

Chapter 1

Leigh O'Neal paced the small hotel room restlessly back and forth across the worn, faded carpeting, her long skirts swishing about her slim, shapely legs as she walked with quick, agitated steps. She stopped and shoved a wave of thick, mahogany hair back from her high forehead, then glared at the door that led to the hallway, her eyes, usually a seductive smoky gray, darkening like angry storm clouds.

"Where is he?" she muttered irritably.

Her Uncle Sean had left hours ago after promising to hurry back. Surely, it wouldn't take that long to find sailor's clothing that would fit her. Now, it was dark outside and way past her mealtime. She was hungry and bored to tears from being locked in this stuffy, small room with nothing to do.

Leigh flounced on the bed, and the springs squeaked loudly in protest. She looked about her, her small nose wrinkling in distaste. Her uncle had said many sea captains stayed here while waiting for their ships to be refitted and reloaded before sailing back out to sea, but the hotel had obviously seen better days. Situated on the border between downtown Charleston and Cooper River, it was neither as luxurious as the better hotels in the city or as seedy as those that squatted beside the river harbor, but now Leigh wished her uncle had taken her to one of the hotels nearer the port, even if they were less respectable and surrounded by grogshops and brothels. At least she would have been able to pass her time watching the activity of the harbor from the window.

She glanced at the window across from her, wondering if she would be able to catch a glimpse of the ships riding anchor since she was on the third floor. Quickly, she rose and walked to the window to push the heavy, faded drapes to the side. She peered through the glass pane, barely able to see the brick wall across from her in the darkness. Then, spying something from the corner of her eye, she turned her head and craned her neck, seeing the lamplight on the street.

She recalled that the hall ran toward the street. If there was a window at the end of it, she would be able to look out from there. Even if she couldn't see the harbor, at least she would be able to look out over the street.

She whirled, and went to the door and unlocked it. Then she hesitated, remembering that her uncle had sternly cautioned her to stay in the room and keep her door locked until he returned. But it was obvious he hadn't rushed back. No, she knew her Uncle Sean's love of gab and ale. He had probably stopped at some grogshop to pass the time with some of his sailing cronies, completely forgetting about her.

Well, she would be damned if she would sit here one minute more and stare at the walls while he had a grand old time swapping sea tales and ribald jokes with his buddies. Besides, what harm could possibly come to her in the hallway of this dull hotel?

Leigh opened the door and peeked out into the darkened hallway. Seeing that it was totally deserted, she stepped out, closed the door softly behind her, and hurried to the window at the end of the narrow corridor. Looking out the window to both sides, she frowned, for she could see nothing of the harbor from there. Disappointed, she dropped her eyes to the street below.

Fortunately, there was a lamplight just outside the window, and she could see people leisurely strolling on the sidewalk below her. She watched as a carriage drove up to the hotel, its metal-rimmed wheels clattering on the cobblestones, and a young, red-headed, voluptuous woman emerged from it. As the driver closed the door behind her and the woman paid him, Leigh frowned, wondering where the woman's escort was, for, from her expensive-looking clothing and haughty carriage, she appeared to be a lady of quality. Did respectable young women in Charleston venture out into the night without a male escort? Well, they certainly didn't in Boston, Leigh thought with disapproval.

Preoccupied with watching the woman below her, Leigh didn't notice a door opening in the hall behind her and a man dressed in a white shirt, with long, flowing sleeves, and dark breeches stepping into the corridor, his tall, muscular frame outlined by the light coming from the room behind him. Had she turned at that moment and seen him, she would have been more than surprised, for women always remembered their first arresting sight of Captain Matthew Blake. Broad-shouldered, slim-hipped, superbly muscled, his long legs encased in skin-tight breeches and knee-high boots, the ruggedly handsome captain, with his golden hair, flashing dark eyes, and sensuous smile, had a devastating effect on women of all ages. It wasn't just his rugged male beauty that attracted women. No, it was something much more elemental that drew them. Even if his looks had been quite common, women would have still found him compelling. There was a presence about him, an aura of danger, of unleashed power, of savage maleness that radiated from him, drawing women to him like a powerful magnet. He wasn't simply all male. No, every fiber of his being bespoke his masculinity, and every woman, to one degree or another, answered that primitive call.

Matt's dark eyes narrowed as he peered down the narrow, darkened corridor. He swayed slightly, and only those who knew him well would have realized he was well on the way to becoming intoxicated. He had been drinking steadily all afternoon, waiting for Monique to arrive. Was she playing games with him, thinking by making him wait he would be all the more eager for her lush body, he wondered. He scoffed at the idea. If anyone was eager, it was Monique. She had been chasing him like a bitch in heat ever since he had returned to Charleston, arranging these assignations at this out-of-the-way hotel where no one would recognize her as the respectable daughter of one of the wealthiest bankers in town. Respectable? He scoffed again. Why, Monique was as much a whore as any common street doxy or more so, and he strongly suspected she was entertaining ideas of his proposing marriage. The little fool. No woman would ever trap him into marriage. He would never give up his freedom for any woman!

He frowned, spying a figure at the end of the hallway. Monique? Somehow the figure seemed smaller and slimmer. He glanced at the young woman's hair and saw its reddish highlights in the lamp-light coming from outside. Yes, it was her. Who else could it be with that red hair? But what was she doing staring out the window and acting as though she didn't know he was standing here? More games? He grinned and walked toward Leigh with feet as quiet as a cat's.

Suddenly Leigh felt herself being spun around and enfolded in a pair of steely arms. All she could manage was a gasp of surprise before a man's mouth swooped down on hers, his tongue taking quick advantage of her open mouth to slip inside. A hard male body pressed against her, his strong arms almost squeezing the breath out of her.

Leigh had been kissed before, but never like this. She turned rigid with shock as Matt's tongue explored her mouth, his tongue swirling around hers. Then indignation replaced her shock, and she struggled, pushing against his rock-hard chest, and finally managed to tear her mouth away.

She glared at the audacious stranger, her breath catching in her throat at the sight of his rugged, golden good looks revealed to her in the soft lamp-light. Then, quickly regaining her senses, she sputtered, "How—how dare you!"

Matt looked down at her in puzzlement. What in hell was wrong with her, he wondered through his alcoholic haze. Why, she was acting as though she was some innocent virgin. More of her games?

He scowled and jerked her closer, nuzzling the soft crook of her neck and growling, "Cut it out, Monique. I'm not in the mood for your silly games tonight."

Monique? Who was Monique, Leigh wondered wildly. Then, as Matt's warm lips sensuously nibbled at her neck, slowly inching upward, a tingle of

9

pleasure ran up her spine, and when his tongue circled her ear, then flicked inside like a fiery dart, her legs turned to water. Fearing she would collapse, she caught his broad shoulders, her body melting into his long, hard length.

Matt groaned and pulled her into a tighter embrace, muttering, "That's better."

As Matt's lips blazed a trail of fiery kisses across her jawline, Leigh cried out weakly, "No, wait!"

"For what?" Matt mumbled, teasing the corner of her mouth with his tongue.

My God, Leigh thought, where did he learn to use his tongue like that? She shivered, muttering, "You don't understand. I'm not . . ." She stopped in midsentence as Matt's hand cupped one of her breasts, his slender fingers massaging the soft flesh, his thumb stroking the sensitive peak through her clothing. And then, as his sensuous lips closed over hers in a long, searching kiss that seemed to suck the air from her lungs, she was swimming dizzily in a sea of pure tactile sensation.

God, Matt thought, his own senses reeling as he molded Leigh's body to his long, hard one. Monique had never excited him this much before. He didn't remember her being so soft, her scent so intoxicating, the taste of her skin and mouth so sweet. He shifted his weight and ground his hips into hers, then trembled as he felt his aching need press against her softness.

"Matthew? What is the meaning of this?" a sharp female voice cried out from behind him.

Matt's golden head snapped up, jerking his lips from Leigh's. He whirled and saw Monique standing in the shaft of light coming from his room, her hands on her broad hips, a furious look on her face. He shook his head, trying to clear the alcoholic haze that befuddled his brain, and then glanced quickly from one woman to the other. If that was Monique, then who was this delectable creature? He peered down at Leigh's face, but was unable to recognize any of her features.

Leigh was still whirling from Matt's fiery, passionate kiss when Monique swooped down on them, demanding, "Who is this woman?"

"I'm afraid I don't know," Matt replied with a frown, strangely irritated that Monique had shown up on the scene. "I found her standing out here in the hall and in the dark mistook her for you."

"For me?" Monique asked in an indignant voice. "You mistook this little trollop for me?" She shot Leigh a look of pure disgust.

Leigh felt the ugly accusation like a slap in the face, shocking her back to reality. "Trollop!" she gasped.

Monique shoved Matt aside and thrust herself between him and Leigh. Glaring down at the dainty girl, she spat, "Yes, trollop! Don't you think I know what you are? You're nothing but a doxy, a common streetwalker, wandering through this hotel in the hope of finding a man for the night."

Was that what she was, Matt wondered. Some cheap whore seeking some business for the night? With all the sea captains staying in this hotel, he imagined the place would offer good pickings. But she had seemed so innocent. There for a minute, when he had felt her body go rigid when his tongue had touched hers, he could have sworn she had never been kissed like that before. And then her indignation. Had it all been a clever act? Then he remembered her capitulation, how she had melted into him, pressing her soft curves against him. Yes, like all whores, she was a consummate actress, undoubtedly

11

hoping to make some poor fool think she was a virgin so she could charge him more. Monique was right in her estimation of the girl. After all, Monique should know. It took one to know one. A strange sense of disappointment filled him.

Leigh watched the expression on Matt's face harden and the warm glow in his dark eyes disappear. Why, he believes Monique, she thought in horror. Furious at both his brazen treatment of her and the woman's base accusation, Leigh sputtered impotently, her eyes flashing.

Ignoring her, Monique took Matt's arm possessively and all but dragged him back down the hallway, saying, "Come on, Matt. Leave the little whore to her business."

Matt allowed Monique to lead him away. As they walked into his hotel room, he disengaged his arm and turned to close the door. Despite himself, he couldn't resist looking back down the hallway at the figure still standing in the darkness, and wishing it was her, instead of Monique, that he was taking to bed. He still tingled where she had pressed against him; her sweet scent still lingered in his nostrils. And God, the taste of her—like nectar from the gods!

"Matthew!" Monique shrieked from behind him.

He flinched at the sharp rebuke, then scowled. Damn the little bitch, he thought angrily. Why did she have to show up? If only . . .

"Matthew?" Monique, changing her tactics, muttered in a low, seductive voice and pressed her lush curves to his muscular back, her arms encircling his trim waist.

Matt shook his head, still trying to clear the alcoholic haze from his brain. What in hell is wrong with you, he asked himself in self-disgust. What difference does it make which woman you take to bed? One woman's as good as another between the sheets.

But still, he couldn't help but wonder what making love to *her* would have been like.

Chapter 2

The fog was coming in, rolling silently and persistently over the harbor, sneaking across the pier, and lifting gray, ghostly fingers to the lamplights that dotted the long lines of wharves with faint circles of yellow light. Somewhere in the harbor, a foghorn blew, the eerie sound echoing over the water, deep and mournful.

Leigh, crouching behind a pile of rotting bales of cotton on the pier, peered through the dense, swirling fog at the sleek schooner that rode anchor beside her, her eyes glued to the name painted on the ship's hull, *Avenger*. She knew this was her uncle's ship. It was the only one with furled canvas and would soon set sail. The other ships in the harbor were bare masted and looked like skeletons rising from their graves.

Leigh shivered, but not from the cold, damp air or the ghostly appearance of the almost deserted harbor. The tremor of fear that ran through her small body stemmed from her realization of the audacity of what she was about to do. Stowing away on a ship was a serious offense.

Offense! Leigh scoffed to herself. Crime was a more accurate word, a crime punishable by law or, worse yet, punishable at the discretion of the captain of the ship. And if caught, what would the punishment be? A whipping with a cat-o'-nine-tails? Imprisonment? Hanging? She shivered again.

Stowing away was reckless enough, but the *Avenger* was no ordinary ship, nor were these ordinary times. The *Avenger* was a privateer, a "fighting ship" her uncle had called it, and her country was at war with Great Britain. She could be killed in a battle!

Faced with the realization of this added danger, Leigh was assailed with sudden doubts. Perhaps she should have waited until the war was over to go to England as her uncle had begged her to do. Her eyes drifted over the stripped ships rocking in the harbor, ships idled by the British naval blockade that was slowly strangling her country's economy. How much longer would the war last, she wondered. If it lasted as long as the War for Independence, that would be another five years. No, she couldn't wait that long. If stowing away on a privateer was the only way she could sneak past the British blockade, then she would do it — and damn the consequences. She couldn't wait any longer to find her father. She had already waited her whole life.

Leigh remembered her shock when her dying mother had revealed to her the truth of her birth. She had always thought her father had been an Irish sailor, lost at sea before she was born. To learn suddenly that she was the illegitimate daughter of an English lord, a man who had no knowledge of her existence, had stunned her. Leigh had not condemned her mother for her illicit love affair with the nobleman she was in service to, a married man no less, for her mother had impressed upon Leigh that their love had been no casual encounter, but a deep, profound love. No, at the time of the startling revelation, Leigh had felt only a deep poignancy. All her life, she had hungered for a father, had always felt cheated that she did not have two parents as her friends did. To discover that she had a father in all probability still alive at a time when she lost her mother had seemed a cruel twist of fate.

Only after her mother died had Leigh been besieged by a hundred questions about her father, questions that her uncle, for some unknown reason, had stubbornly refused to answer. She didn't even know her father's name, for her mother had referred to him as "his lordship," and Leigh had not thought to ask at the time. So armed only with the knowledge that her father was an English lord and with his signet ring that her mother had given her before she died, Leigh was leaving the country in search of the man who had fathered her, a total stranger.

No, Leigh remembered, she had one more weapon at her disposal—her uncle's promise to her mother that he would slip her out of the country on his privateer and take her to England to her father. And she had not hesitated to wield this weapon against her uncle. She knew he regretted the rash vow, a hasty promise to a desperate, dying woman. He had begged Leigh to release him from it, pointing out all the dangers and promising to take her as soon as the war was over. But Leigh had held him to his solemn word, playing on his conviction that to break a deathbed promise was a mortal sin, a sin that would damn him to hell. Leigh felt a twinge of guilt, knowing that her determination was motivated by her compulsion to find the man who had fathered her as much as by her wish to keep the pledge made to her mother.

The sound of boisterous male laughter startled Leigh from her thoughts. She crouched lower, watching as two sailors swaggered down the pier, walked up

17

the gangplank to the *Avenger*, and disappeared into the darkness and fog.

She glanced apprehensively down the pier, wondering what was keeping her uncle, then saw him hiding behind another bale of cotton not ten feet from her. The bush of fiery red hair on his head and chin stood out like a flame even in the dim light.

She watched as he darted to where she hid, then crouched beside her. "Can we go on board now, Uncle Sean?" she asked.

"Aye, lass," her uncle answered. "Willy's on watch tonight, and I'll have no trouble lurin' him away for a drink." He bent lower, placing one big hand on her small shoulder, saying, "Now, listen carefully, lass. When you see me and Willy walk to the back of the ship, ye scurry up the gangplank and hide behind those crates at the front of the ship. Do ye understand?"

Leigh nodded.

"Now, let's have a last look at ye," Sean said, pulling her up to stand before him.

Leigh stood patiently while her uncle carefully scrutinized her appearance. The baggy sailor's pants and bulky sweater thoroughly concealed her womanly curves. Sean looked at her forehead and, noticing the rich mahogany hair there, frowned. Tugging on her sweater cap, he said, "Here now, keep yer stockin' pulled down."

"It's too tight," Leigh replied. "You should have let me cut my hair."

"Nay, lass. I couldn't do that. As 'tis, the devil will have me soul for dressin' ye like a lad. Nay, ye'll not be cuttin' yer hair. Just keep it braided and pinned tight to yer head." A roughened finger hooked under her chin. "Now, let me see yer face."

Obediently, Leigh lifted her head. Sean gazed at

18

the heart-shaped face with its small tilted nose, sensuous full lips, and dimpled chin. He shook his head sadly. She's the spittin' image of her mother, he thought. His eyes drifted to her wide, smoky-gray eyes, her father's eyes. Aye, Sean thought, 'tis his lordship's stamp on her.

His anger at the man who had fathered his niece flared, an anger that had simmered for twenty years, despite his sister's insistence that the lord had not seduced her, that theirs had been a deep, mutually shared love. Damn the booger, he thought.

Sean seriously doubted that the lord would acknowledge Leigh as his daughter. He knew the ways of the gentry too well. And twenty years was a long time. The Englishman had probably forgotten the whole affair long ago. Well, the lord had hurt his sister, Meagan, but he would be damned if he would let him hurt Leigh too. No, when they reached London, he would approach the lord first. If the man refused to acknowledge Leigh, then he would tell his niece her father had died. Better that she be disappointed than hurt by the knowledge that her father had denied her. For that reason, Sean had stubbornly refused to tell Leigh anything about the man who had fathered her, even the man's name.

Sean gazed down at the pretty face before him. No one was going to mistake that face for a boy's, he thought. Jesus, Mary, and Joseph! Why had he made that rash promise to Meagan? He was daft to be taking a beautiful young woman on board ship with two hundred sailors—two hundred men hungry for women. The thought sent ice water running through his veins.

Roughly, Sean grabbed Leigh's shoulders, his fingers biting into the soft flesh. "Nay, lass! I can't do it. Please, tell me ye'll change yer mind."

Leigh was stunned. Certainly, at this late date, her uncle wouldn't back out. She stuck her small chin out stubbornly, saying, "You promised!"

" 'Tis too dangerous, lass," Sean cried in an anguished voice. "I'd never forgive meself if anythin' happened to ye. Neither would yer mother, God rest her soul."

Leigh's voice was hard and coldly determined. "The only thing my mother wouldn't forgive you is breaking your word to her. You promised her on her deathbed, Uncle Sean."

Sean sighed in resignation. I'm damned if I do, and I'm damned if I don't, he thought with despair. "Aye, and I'll be regrettin' it to me death!"

Leigh felt another twinge of guilt at his words. Then, lifting her head with renewed determination, she said, "Can we go on board now? It's cold out here."

Sean glanced up and down the darkened pier before answering, "Aye, lass. Now remember, as soon as ye see me and Willy disappear, ye scurry aboard."

Leigh watched as her uncle walked up the gangplank to the *Avenger*. As soon as he and the sailor standing at the head of the gangplank disappeared, she picked up her sea bag and moved across the pier. She hurried up the precariously swaying plank, almost slipping on the wet wood, and quickly hid behind the crates her uncle had pointed out to her.

She waited, shivering in the cold, damp air and wishing that her uncle would hurry. As if hearing her thought, Sean ambled toward her and then crouched beside her, whispering, "Now, let's get ye below, lass."

Sean took Leigh's arm and started to lead her away, but the sound of an approaching carriage on the pier forced them to cower back into the concealing shadows. They watched in silence as the carriage

20

stopped beneath the lamplight right next to the *Avenger*.

The door to the carriage opened, and a man dressed in elegant evening wear backed out of it. As he stood, Leigh could see he was tall, broad-shouldered, and slim-hipped, but with his back to her, she could see nothing of his face.

A minute later, a beautiful, dark-haired woman emerged from the carriage, but instead of taking the man's offered hand, she threw herself into his arms, locking her arms tightly around his neck and kissing him deeply. For a second, Leigh watched the passionate kiss with a mixture of curiosity and awe. Then she became acutely aware of something else. She found herself staring in fascination at the bunched muscles in the man's arms, at his broad shoulders straining against his dark coat, at his firm buttocks and long whipcord legs enclosed in his tight-fitting breeches. She glanced at his golden hair, curling lightly where it touched the back of his coat collar. A glimmer of recognition teased at the back of her brain.

"Who is he?" she asked her uncle.

"Why, 'tis the cap'n, lass. Captain Matthew Blake."

Matthew? Of course! She recognized him! She would never forget the feel of those broad shoulders and that soft hair at the nape of his neck beneath her fingers, nor that tall, muscular body pressing against hers so closely, so intimately. He was the same man who had kissed her so passionately in the hotel hallway last night. She flushed hotly, both in anger at his boldness and in shame at her own reaction to his heated kiss and tantalizing caresses.

She glanced quickly at the dark-headed woman, realizing, for the first time, that she wasn't the same woman Leigh had seen in the hallway last night. No, that one had been a redhead, a voluptuous redhead.

21

Then who was this woman? Had the handsome captain been cheating on his wife? "Who is she? His wife?"

Sean squirmed, embarrassed by the open display of passion. "Nay, lass. The cap'n's not married."

Leigh wondered briefly at the satisfaction this bit of information brought her. She peered closer, thinking that the captain was quite a busy man, what with entertaining a different woman every night. But as the dark-haired woman pressed herself even closer to his tall frame, Leigh felt a twinge of jealousy. She frowned. What's wrong with you, she asked herself in self-disgust. Why should you care how many women the captain beds?

Sean didn't think it at all appropriate for Leigh to be viewing the passionate scene taking place on the pier below them. Besides, knowing how uncommonly curious the lass was, she might ask who the woman was, and a man didn't discuss that kind of woman with his innocent niece. Hoping to draw her attention away from the couple, he tugged at her arm and said, "Here now, lass. Step back before the cap'n sees ye."

See you? My God, Leigh thought in horror, what if the captain recognized her? She stepped quickly back into the shadows and glanced nervously down at her bulky sweater and baggy pants. But surely he would never guess she was a woman in this disguise, she assured herself. And she was positive he hadn't seen her face in the dark hallway. Well, almost positive. She wondered if she should tell her uncle what had happened at the hotel, warn him that once she was discovered as a stowaway, as they knew she eventually would be, the captain might recognize her face. That would ruin all their carefully laid plans. The captain might not turn the ship back to deposit a male stowaway, but he surely would a female. She decided

22

against telling her uncle what had happened. He would be furious if he knew she had disobeyed him and left the room. No, she would just have to take her chances and hope the captain wouldn't be able to recognize her.

The sound of the carriage driving off roused Leigh from her musing. A minute later, she heard the sound of the captain's firm steps on the gangplank and the watch saying, "Evenin', Cap'n."

"Good evening, Willy," Matt answered in a deep baritone voice. "Are all hands on board?"

"Aye, Cap'n. You're the last to board, sir."

"Good. Then pull up the gangplank and rouse the crew. The tide's going out and we're sailing immediately."

"Devil take it!" Sean muttered in frustration. "I was hopin' to get ye safely below and hidden before we sailed, but in a few minutes this whole deck will be swarmin' with men. Now I'll have to find someplace to hide ye topside until we're out to sea." Pulling Leigh toward the bow of the ship, he said, "Come on, lass. Hurry now."

Sean led her to the front of the ship and tucked her behind a stack of crates that sat in one corner. "Stay here, lass. Once we're safely out to sea and things calm down a bit, I'll be back for ye."

Leigh looked around the foggy harbor in disbelief. "He's not going to sail now?" she asked in alarm.

"Aye, lass."

"In this fog? Why, you can't see your hand before your face. He'll run us aground!"

Sean chuckled, then said, "Nay, lass, not Cap'n Blake. He was born and raised here in Charleston, and has been sailin' this harbor since he was a wee lad. He knows it like the back of his hand. He could sail it blindfolded, if he had a mind to."

23

"But . . ."

"Nay, lass," Sean interjected. "Don't ye fret now. Just keep down so no one can see ye."

Before Leigh could object, her uncle was gone, and within minutes the deck was swarming with men and activity. Voices and commands rang through the humid night air.

Leigh heard the deep, commanding voice of Captain Blake calling, "Release the shores lines!" then, "Give me staysails and jibs!" and then, "Hoist the anchor!" and finally, "Loose the sails!"

Leigh jumped in surprise as the sails above her unfurled and then caught the wind with a brisk snap. She looked at them as they filled and felt a thrill run through her, for she had always thought that a ship, with all sails set and filled with wind, was the most beautiful sight in the world.

Then she felt the ship moving. Her heart raced with excitement. I'm sailing, she thought. I'm actually sailing. I'm really going to England to find my father.

But an hour later, Leigh's excitement had disappeared. She knew from the deep roll of the ship that they were in open sea now. She was shivering from the cold, damp air; her legs were cramped from sitting in the limited space of her hiding spot. The ship was absolutely quiet now; the only thing she could hear was the faint humming of the rigging above her. The total silence and ghostly fog swirling around her gave her an eerie feeling, a feeling that she was all alone on the ship and, any minute, would sail off the end of the earth and into the dark abyss beyond.

And then she saw it—a light, looming right in front of the hull of the ship. That must be a running light of a British ship, she thought. She froze in silent terror; her breath caught in her throat. My God, we're going to ram it. Then the *Avenger* veered ever so slightly, and Leigh watched in disbelief as the bobbing light floated right past her, so close she could have sworn she could have reached out and touched it.

The perilously close brush with death left Leigh feeling weak and giddy. She was trembling so badly that she was forced to lie down, for fear of fainting. She curled herself into a tight ball on the cold, damp deck, thinking, Oh, God, what have I gotten myself into?

Several hours later, Leigh was awakened by her uncle. He led her below deck and through a maze of passageways. Finally, he opened a door and motioned her inside.

As the door closed, Sean said, " 'Tis where we keep our extra canvas, lass. 'Tis the safest place I could find for ye. No one should be comin' down here. At least not for a few days."

As Sean lifted his lantern, Leigh could see the small cabin in the flickering light, cluttered with piles of folded canvas and coiled ropes. One corner was crowded with pulleys, tackles, swabs, and scrubbers.

Leigh turned to see her uncle opening the door and gasped, saying, "You're not going to take the lamp with you?"

He turned, saying, "I'm sorry, lass, but ye can't burn a lamp down here. If anyone were to see a light comin' from under the door, they'd investigate for sure. Then ye'd be discovered. Come mornin', ye'll get a bit of light from that porthole over there."

Sean saw the look of fear that came over his niece's face. "Now, lass, there's nothing to be afraid of down here. And I'll be coming back now and then, bringin' ye fresh water and food."

She felt ashamed of herself. She had begged, no, browbeaten her uncle into bringing her along, and now she was acting like a big baby. She managed a weak smile, "All right, Uncle Sean."

Sean grinned, saying, "That's me brave lass."

As the door closed behind her uncle and the cabin was plunged into total darkness, she felt another pang of fear. Then she took herself firmly in hand, reminding herself her uncle had said it was a perfectly safe place. She lay down on a pile of canvas and, being totally exhausted, fell asleep.

It was afternoon when Leigh awakened. She looked around the dim, musty cabin in disgust. Struggling to her feet, she stumbled to the small porthole and peered out, but all she could see was the gray sea and a small streak of blue horizon. Somewhere over her head, a sea gull cried.

She found the water and food that her uncle had left for her. She gulped most of the water down but, because of her queasy stomach, could only nibble at the sea biscuits and salt pork. When she had finished eating, she rummaged through her sea bag and pulled out her small book of poems. But when she opened the book, she found that the light was far too dim for reading. Disgusted, she tossed the book aside. She spent the rest of the afternoon restlessly pacing the small cabin.

Trying to pass the time of the day in the dim light was bad enough, but at night it was an impossibility. From her small porthole, she couldn't even see the stars. Deciding that the best way to pass the time was sleeping, she lay down on a pile of canvas. But sleep was elusive that night, and she lay tossing and turning for a long time before slumber finally claimed her.

She was awakened in the middle of the night by a noise. She strained her ears and heard a scratching

26

noise, followed by the distinct sound of tiny feet pattering across the wooden floor. A few seconds later, a warm, furry object brushed her foot.

Rats, her mind screeched. She barely muffled her scream as she frantically scampered to the top of the pile of canvas. There she cowered, terrified, cold sweat beading her brow and her heart racing in fear. Her eyes searched the darkness. She gasped when she saw two beady eyes glowing in the dark across from her. A minute later, they were joined by another pair.

"Get away," she hissed.

The eyes glittered in the dark.

"Get out, damn you!"

Still the rats did not move.

I need a weapon, Leigh thought. Then she remembered the book she had tossed away that afternoon. Frantically, she searched the pile of canvas until she found it. She threw the book with all her might at the pair of rats. The book skittered across the pile of canvas where they perched and bounced off the wall with a loud thump. A split second later, the two sets of eyes disappeared.

Leigh exhaled a ragged sob of relief, but she didn't relax. The rest of the night, she huddled on the pile of canvas, her eyes darting in quick searching looks from one side of the cabin to the other. That morning, as soon as it was light enough to see, she cautiously crept to one corner of the cabin, picked up a long swab, and dragged it back to her perch. Then she waited, fully prepared for battle.

This was how Sean found her when he opened the door the next morning, crouched on the pile of canvas, cannon swab raised and ready to strike, a wild look in her eyes. "Me God, lass! What in the devil is wrong with ye?"

In a split second, the swab was dropped, and Leigh

27

was in her uncle's arms, her head buried in his massive chest, sobbing, "I can't stay down here, Uncle Sean." She looked up, her eyes glittering with fear. "There are rats down here!" she screeched.

"Sssh, lass," Sean cautioned and kicked the door shut behind him. Pity for the pale, trembling girl filled him. Gently, he said, "Now, lass, 'tis all right. A few little mice won't hurt ye."

Leigh's head snapped up. "Not mice. Rats!"

Sean squirmed, then shrugged, saying, "Aye, well, so they're rats. But still, they won't bother ye."

"They might bite me!"

"Nay, lass, I don't think so. With the ship newly stocked, they'll find plenty to eat without nibblin' on ye." He looked down at her frightened face and sighed. "Ah, lass, I wish I didn't have to leave ye alone like this, but, 'tis still the safest place to hide ye."

Leigh looked at her uncle's face, his eyes filled with distress. Again, she was ashamed of her cowardice. She forced a smile and said, "All right, Uncle Sean. Whatever you say."

After her uncle had left, Leigh made a decision. Knowing that rats were nocturnal animals, she decided to sleep during the daytime and stay awake at night to keep watch. Exhausted from her ordeal the night before, she had no trouble falling asleep.

When she awakened a few hours later, she was lying on her side. She opened her eyes to see the biggest black rat she had ever seen. Still groggy, she thought she had never seen such long legs on a rat before. Suddenly, it dawned on her. This was no rat. It was a cat.

She sat up slowly, afraid any sudden move would frighten the animal off. "Here, kitty, kitty," she called softly.

The cat eyed her suspiciously and stepped back.

"Goodness, fella, you have no idea how glad I am to see you. I'll bet you're a good mouser, aren't you?"

The cat's yellow eyes narrowed, his black tail twitched in agitation.

"But how in the world did you get in here?" Leigh asked half to herself, looking at the closed door.

The cat was bored with the conversation. He turned and leaped to the top of the pile of canvas across from Leigh. Settling himself in and totally ignoring her, he began to bathe himself meticulously.

How lucky could she be, Leigh thought. This cat was the answer to her prayers. Certainly with a cat in the room, the rats would stay away. How had he gotten in? There must be a crack in the wall somewhere. But if he could get in, he could just as easily get out. Somehow, she had to find some way to keep him with her.

She crumbled a small portion of sea biscuit left over from her breakfast and cautiously approached the wary cat. Holding out her hand, she whispered, "Are you hungry, fella? Would you like a bit to eat?"

The cat rose, hesitated, and then sniffed at the crumbs in Leigh's hand. His nose wrinkled with distaste. He turned and lay back down.

"Not good enough for you, huh?" Leigh mumbled.

Somehow or another, she had to make friends with this cat, she thought. But how? He wasn't the least bit interested in her pitiful offering of food, and he was too distrustful to let her pet him. Maybe he was lonesome and, if she talked to him, he would stay.

So Leigh commenced to tell the cat her whole life story, and then, when that was finished, she carried on a make-believe conversation with the cat, taking both of their roles. The cat lay during this long, drawn-out oration, his yellow eyes ever alert, his long

29

black tail swishing occasionally.

When she heard her uncle at the door, Leigh jumped up to greet him. "Oh, Uncle Sean, look what I found." Then she laughed, saying, "Or rather he found me." She turned, but the cat had disappeared.

"What was that, lass?"

"A cat. A big black tomcat. He was right here, but now he's gone," Leigh answered, looking about her in disappointment.

"Aye, lass, that's Lucifer. He's the cap'n's cat. But I'm not surprised he disappeared. He's a bit skittish."

After Leigh's uncle had left and as darkness fell, Leigh climbed back up on her mountain of canvas, wearily dragging her cannon swab with her. Despite her resolve to stay awake and watch for rats, her eyelids kept dropping shut. She finally lay down, thinking that she would only take a short nap.

She was awakened by the feel of fur on her feet. She lay in utter terror for a minute and then heard the faint purr. Her heart raced with excitement as she exhaled deeply.

"Lucifer? Is that you?" she cried softly.

The cat purred louder, rubbing his soft fur against her legs as he walked up toward her head. When he reached her side, he plopped down beside her and snuggled closer to her stomach. Tentatively, Leigh reached out to pet him, and the cat rubbed his silky head against the palm of her hand. She sighed in relief. Now, she could sleep in peace. Lucifer would protect her from the rats. Her knight in shining armor was back.

The big black cat stayed with her for the better part of the time from then on, but he always disappeared when her uncle came to visit. He made other trips from the room also, hunting forays, and Leigh never tried to stop him. She knew he would be back by nightfall.

One morning, Leigh and Lucifer slept unusually late. Neither awakened when the door to the storeroom opened and two sailors walked in.

"If this doesn't beat all!" the first sailor said in disgust, "You'd think the cap'n could find better things for us to than look all over this damned ship for a fool cat."

"Aye," his companion answered, "but the cap'n is worried about him, I guess. No one has seen hide or hair of him since we set sail."

"I don't know why that's worryin' the cap'n. That goddamned cat is always disappearin'. Sometimes, for days at a time."

"Aye, but never this long. No one has seen him for over a week now. The cap'n is afraid he may be sick and has slipped off somewhere to die."

"Well, what in the hell are we goin' to do even if we find him?" the first sailor grumbled. "That black devil won't let anyone but the cap'n touch him. Never saw such an unfriendly animal!"

The failure of his companion to answer prompted the first sailor to turn around. He saw his crewmate holding the lantern high in his hand and staring down at something lying on the canvas at his feet. "Did ye find him?"

"Aye, I found him," the astonished sailor answered. "Him and something else . . . a stowaway!"

Chapter 3

Matt stared at the map that lay on the desk before him, trying to force himself to concentrate on it. Then he shoved the paper aside irritably and sat back in his chair.

These damned nights of interrupted sleep were beginning to get to him, he thought, rubbing his forehead wearily. Ever since that night he had held the mystery woman in his arms and kissed her in the hotel hallway, he had dreamed of her—vivid dreams. He had felt every soft, warm curve of her, smelled her intoxicating scent, tasted her sweetness. Only her face had remained hidden from him, clothed in shadows, taunting him, haunting him. Each time he had awakened, aroused and aching, then had lain awake for hours, wondering what her face looked like, what her name was, what she was doing just then? The last question had always disturbed him deeply. For some unknown reason, he couldn't stand the thought of her being in another man's arms and sharing intimacies with him.

A knock at the door interrupted his thoughts. Looking up, he frowned, then called, "Yes?"

"Bennington and Jones reportin', Cap'n," a voice

answered.

"Come in," Matt called back with an irritated voice, his eyes dropping back down to the map and studying it.

The door opened, followed by the sound of shuffling feet and the door closing. Without lifting his head, Matt asked, "Well? Did you find the cat?"

"Aye, sir, we found him," one of the sailors answered in a gruff voice. "And this, too!"

Roughly, the sailor pushed Leigh forward. She stumbled into the desk, falling halfway across it. She raised her eyes to find herself just inches from the captain's face and looking into a pair of black eyes.

For a long minute, Matt and Leigh stared at each other, the captain in surprise and Leigh in fear of his recognizing her. Then Matt muttered, "What the hell!"

The oath had the same effect on Leigh as a slap on the face. Her head snapped up, and she staggered back from the desk. She stood before the captain, her heart racing and her legs trembling.

Matt rose slowly from the desk and towered over her, his black eyes boring into her. "Where did *he* come from?"

Leigh let out a long, silent sigh as a wave of relief washed over her. Thank God, he hadn't recognized her, and her disguise had stood her in good stead.

"We found him in the canvas storage room, Cap'n," the sailor who had shoved Leigh forward explained. "Him and the cat."

Matt, glaring down at the small, dirt-streaked face before him, demanded, "What are you doing on my ship, lad?"

Leigh trembled under that hot, angry look. This man is dangerous, she thought.

34

"Well?"

Leigh didn't answer. She couldn't! Her tongue seemed to be glued to the top of her mouth.

"I asked you a question!" Matt barked. "Now what in the hell are you doing on my ship?"

Leigh struggled to find her tongue, but discovered, to her dismay, that she no longer had any control over it.

Matt leaned across the desk, hovering over her, his dark eyes glittering dangerously. "Do you know what you are? A stowaway!" He paused to let this sink in, then said, "Do you know what happens to stowaways?"

Leigh gulped nervously, then shook her head dumbly, her gray eyes wide with fright.

"Cap'n, sir," one of the sailors interrupted. "Excuse me, sir, but I don't think the lad sneaked himself on board. I think someone on this ship helped him."

Matt's golden head snapped up. Now the dark eyes bored into the sailor. "Why do you think that?"

Under those black, piercing eyes, the sailor was beginning to feel uneasy himself. He squirmed and said nervously, "Well, you see, sir, we found a jug of fresh water and a little food down there with the lad." He shuffled his feet and cleared his throat before continuing, "Sir, I could swear that food looked like leftovers from last night's supper."

The dark eyes narrowed, looking even more dangerous. Matt swung back to Leigh, saying, "Is that true, lad? Did someone on this ship help you?"

Leigh had been frightened before, but now her fear was for her uncle. After all he had done for her, she couldn't betray him—wouldn't betray him. She lifted her small chin defiantly, her jaws clamped stubbornly shut.

"If you know what's good for you, you'd better answer me," Matt said, his voice low and menacing. "Did one of my men help you?"

Leigh's chin rose an inch higher. She glared at the captain.

Matt looked at the glaring boy in disbelief. Impudent, little devil, he thought, infuriated by the boy's stubbornness. Why, not even his crew, hardened, tough seamen that they were, dared to look at him like that. His control broke as his hand came down on the desk with a hard, ear-spitting slap. "Goddammit!" he roared. "Answer me!"

Leigh and both of the seamen flinched but, despite her knocking knees, Leigh stood firm in her resolve, her smoky-gray eyes meeting the captain's dangerously glittering ones levelly. The two glared at each other, eyeball to eyeball, in a silent contest of wills.

At that minute, the captain's door flung open, and Sean rushed into the cabin, stumbling in his haste. He shot a quick, apprehensive look at his niece. News traveled fast in the small confines of a ship, and as soon as he had heard a stowaway had been discovered, he had hurried to the captain's cabin, fearing what the captain might do to Leigh and thinking, poor little lass. He's probably got her in tears by now. Instead, he found four pairs of surprised eyes on him.

Matt recovered quickly, snapping, "What in the hell are you doing here, O'Neal? I didn't give you permission to enter my quarters."

For the first time, Sean realized the audacity of his rash behavior. He, like every other man on the ship, stood in awe and, if truth be known, a little in fear of the captain. And here he had come barreling into the captain's personal quarters without a thought. He looked about him in embarrassment.

"Well, O'Neal?" Matt demanded.

Sean flushed and stammered, "Well, sir, when—when I heard about the—the lad . . ." He stopped, suddenly aware of the two sailors' curious stares. Sean was a fiercely proud and private man. He didn't want what he had to say to the captain spread all over the ship. He shot the two seamen a hard look and said, "Can I speak to ye alone, Cap'n?"

"Does it have something to do with this lad?" Matt asked.

"Aye, it does that, sir," Sean answered tightly.

Matt studied the rugged Irishman standing stiffly before him and then looked at the small bundle of defiance standing beside him. He glanced at the two grinning sailors. "Dismissed!" he barked to the two seamen.

The sailors' looks turned to disappointment. They turned and reluctantly left the cabin, sneaking curious glances over their shoulders.

After the cabin door had shut, Matt turned to Sean, saying in a hard voice, "All right, O'Neal, what do you know about this?" He motioned to Leigh.

"I brought the—the lad aboard ship, sir," Sean admitted.

"You what?" Matt asked in disbelief.

"Aye, sir. I'm the one responsible for him bein' here."

"But why, for God's sake?"

Sean placed his arm around Leigh's shoulder protectively. "Ye see, Cap'n, this here is me nephew, Leigh."

"That still doesn't explain what he's doing on my ship!" Matt said in an exasperated voice.

"Aye, sir," Sean mumbled. His mind searched frantically for a reasonable explanation.

"Well? Speak up, man!"

Sean flushed, feeling like a five year old being reprimanded by his father. "Well, ye see, sir, when I reached Boston, I found me sister dying."

Matt frowned. "Your sister? Didn't you tell me she was a widow woman?"

"Aye, sir. The lad's pa died at sea before he was born."

"All right, O'Neal," Matt said, "go on."

"Well, sir, ye see, I promised me sister I'd take care of the lad. He has no other family, ye see. And ever since he was a wee mite, the lad's been wantin' to go to sea." Sean threw up his hands and finished in a rush of words. "So I brought him with me."

"And you sneaked him on board, without my knowledge or permission?" Matt asked in an accusing voice.

Sean shuffled his feet, muttering nervously. "Aye, well —"

"Knowing full well my rule about no boys on my ship?" Matt added in a hard voice.

Sean hung his shaggy head, mumbling, "Aye, sir." Then he raised his head, his eyes imploring, saying, "Ah, Cap'n, I couldn't bring meself to leave him behind. Ye know how bad things are now. No jobs to be had, not even for grown men. The poor lad would have starved to death."

Matt sighed deeply. O'Neal had a valid point there. The British blockade was strangling the American economy. Unemployment ran rampant; people were starving. Even the rich were feeling the pinch and tightening their belts. A young lad, like the one standing before him, would be forced to steal for survival, and as frail as this lad looked, Matt was sure he wouldn't survive for long. But still, he wouldn't have the boy on his ship. No boys. It was his ironclad rule. He would be damned if he would have another lad's death on his conscience.

"Dammit, O'Neal!" Matt said in an exasperated voice. "How long have I known you?"

The unexpected question stunned Sean. "Why— why since ye were a lad," he stammered. "I sailed under yer father before he retired from sea, and then under ye."

"Then, after having known me all of these years, why didn't you come to me with this before we sailed? I would have found a safe place for you to leave the lad while you were at sea."

Guilt for having lied to the captain washed over Sean, but he didn't dare tell him the truth. The captain was angry enough at him for slipping the lad aboard, but if he knew Leigh was really a woman, he would have his hide—in little pieces!

" 'Tis sorry I am, Cap'n," Sean replied. "I've not been thinkin' too clear." He plowed on, saying, "But, Cap'n, Leigh's a good lad. He won't be in the way, I promise ye. I'll keep him by me side and teach him meself."

"He's not staying," Matt replied in a hard voice.

Both Leigh's and Sean's faces blanched. "Ye'll be turnin' back to Charleston?" Sean asked in a weak voice.

"Hell no!" Matt spat. "It was just sheer luck we made it through that blockade the other night. I'm not about to turn back and try to run it again. But the lad goes back to port on the first prize we take."

Sean covered his relief quickly and hid a smug smile. The captain was playing right into his hand. That had been his plan all along, to volunteer for the crew that took the first prize in. Once in a French port, it would be a simple matter to catch a ship sailing to England.

"Trying to look appropriately disappointed, the big Irishman said, "Aye, Cap'n, if you say so. And I'll be goin' along with the prize meself. To get the lad settled in some place."

"Well, you can go if you want to, but it won't be necessary," Matt replied.

Sean looked at the captain in confusion. "What do you mean, sir?"

"I mean, I have relatives in New Orleans," Matt answered. "I'm sure any one of them wouldn't mind looking out for the lad until he's old enough to go to sea. All the lad would need would be a letter of introduction from me."

"New Orleans?" Sean questioned, still confused.

"Yes, that's where we'll be taking our prizes from now on," Matt answered calmly.

"Ye mean, we won't be takin' our prizes to France any more?" Sean asked, barely able to contain his panic.

"No, we won't," Matt answered. "Since England and France are no longer at war, all the European ports are closed to us now. No one wants to take the risk of breaking the uneasy peace by violating their neutrality acts."

"We'll be runnin' our prizes all the way from the English Channel to New Orleans?" Sean asked in disbelief.

Matt frowned, saying, "No, that would be too far. I'm afraid we're going to have to look for newer, less lucrative hunting grounds. We'll try the Caribbean and off the coast of South America."

Matt had been pacing while he talked. He stopped beside Leigh, looking down at her with a deep scowl on his face. "But enough of that!" he said in a stern voice. He whirled and faced Sean, saying, "Dammit, O'Neal! Do you realize the position you've put me in? Even if I didn't have a rule about no boys on my ship, you've aided a stowaway. You realize you've got to be punished, don't you?"

Sean had already prepared himself for this. "Aye, I know."

Matt glanced at the frightened face of the lad. A brief twinge of pity ran through him. Dammit, he guessed if he had been in O'Neal's place he would have done the same thing. This realization prompted him to temper his punishment. "All right, O'Neal. Three days in the brig with bread and water."

Sean gasped, shocked at the captain's leniency. Why, it was only a token punishment. Aye, here was a good, compassionate man. Sean felt even more remorse for having lied to him. Then he remembered Leigh and asked, "And the lad, sir?"

"He'll stay up here. I'll turn him over to Cookie until you're topside again.

Leigh's head shot up. "Nay!" she cried.

Matt turned to Leigh in surprise. He chuckled, saying, "So, lad, you do have a tongue in your head after all?"

"Aye, I've a tongue, for sure, Cap'n," Leigh replied hotly. "But I'll not be staying with anyone else. I go with me uncle."

Sean looked at his niece in shock, both at her bold announcement and her sudden Irish brogue. Why, he hadn't heard her talk like that since his sister had sent her off to the fancy school for ladies. Seeing the look of anger on the captain's face, he quickly recovered and said, "Nay, lad, ye'll do what the cap'n says. Ye'll stay in the galley with the cook. Ye'll be safe with

41

him."

Leigh lifted her head stubbornly and said, "If ye go to the brig, so do I." She shot Matt a hot, resentful look. "If he sends ye to jail, 'tis only fair I share in the punishment. I'm just as guilty as ye."

Sean caught his niece's arm and shook her roughly, saying, "Now you listen to me, lad—"

"Just a minute!" Matt interjected. He had been watching the argument with raised eyebrows. He admired spirit, but the lad was far too cocky. If he wanted to be a sailor, he would have to learn to obey orders. As much as he hated to do it, Matt thought a few days in the brig might teach the lad a well-needed lesson in discipline. "On second thought, you both go to the brig."

Sean looked aghast. "But, sir—" Then, seeing the steely look in the captain's eyes, he ducked his head, mumbling, "Aye, Cap'n."

From the corner of his eye, Matt saw the smug look on Leigh's face. Well, let him think he got the best of us for the time being, he thought. After three days in that hellhole, he'll know to keep his mouth shut the next time.

Matt strode to the door and opened it, calling, "Mr. Kelly!"

A big man, his craggy, windburnt face framed by a pair of muttonchops, stepped forward, "Aye, Cap'n?"

"Take O'Neal and this boy down to the brig," Matt said.

Kelly's eyes filled with disbelief. "Surely not the lad, too, Cap'n?"

"You heard my orders, Mr. Kelly," Matt said tersely.

Kelly snapped to attention, saying stiffly, "Aye,

sir."

Matt watched as Kelly led the big Irishman and the lad away. Damn that stubborn, little mule, he thought. He knew his first mate didn't approve of locking a mere boy in the brig, but the lad had forced him into it. Now, he would probably have to put up with Kelly's sullenness. Well, the sooner he got the boy off his ship, the better. Obviously, the lad was a troublemaker, and the last thing he needed right now was more problems.

Leigh was having a problem of her own at the time, trying to keep up with the long strides of the two men she was walking between, almost running to keep up. She glanced up at her uncle and the first mate, both silent, staring straight ahead, their mouths tight set. She knew her uncle was angry with her, but she wasn't quite sure whom the first mate was angry with, her and her uncle or the captain.

Her eyes settled on the first mate. In many ways, he was much like her uncle, big and brawny, red-faced with bushy eyebrows and a seaman's squint. But there the resemblance ended, for Sean's chin was covered with a full beard and the hair on his head was a thick bush, whereas the first mate was clean-shaven and virtually bald, except for a thin band of gray hair that circled the back of his head. In fact, most of his hair seemed to be in his thick muttonchops. She also thought him older than her uncle, not because of his gray hair, but rather because the lines that fanned his eyes and mouth were etched more deeply into his weathered face. Scrutinizing him, Leigh decided he looked more like her idea of what a sea captain should look like than the young, handsome, arrogant man she had just left.

The first mate led Leigh and Sean down a ladder

43

and through a maze of passageways, then down another ladder, and another. When they stepped from the last ladder and into the bowels of the ship, an overpowering odor assaulted her nostrils, not just a stale musty smell, but a strong sour stench that made her gag.

After the first mate had led them to a small cell, locked them in, and left, Leigh looked around the room in shock. The cell was completely empty except for the filthy straw that littered the floor. She realized, with disgust, that the sour stench she smelled came from that straw.

Her shock and disgust were quickly replaced with anger. "This is horrible! Why, it's an outrage!" she cried.

"I tried to warn ye, lass, but ye wouldn't listen to me!" Sean snapped back. Then he sighed, shaking his shaggy head, saying, "Ah, lass, why did ye have to be so stubborn? 'Tis no place for a little lass like ye."

Too late, Leigh realized her mistake. She should have kept her mouth shut. But complaining about it now would only increase her uncle's anguish. Besides, it was because of her that he was in this predicament, and it was only fair that she share it with him. She lifted her head proudly, saying, "Don't worry about it, Uncle Sean. If you can stand it, so can I."

"Nay, lass, I'm used to cold and wet, but ye're not. If ye should get sick—"

"Nonsense," Leigh interjected. "I've never been sick a day in my life. I'm as healthy as a horse." She plopped down on the straw. "At least here I have you to keep me company."

Sean settled his big body down beside her, then stared at her, a worried look on his rugged face.

Leigh leaned forward and patted his hand reassuringly, saying softly, "Please, don't worry about me, Uncle Sean. I'm much tougher than I look. Honestly!"

She leaned back into a more comfortable position. For the first time, she realized the straw was not only filthy, but soggy, too. She dug down into the straw, hoping to find a drier layer on the bottom. She froze. The floor was covered with a good inch of water.

Trying to sound calm, she asked, "Where did all this water come from?"

Sean shrugged and said indifferently, "from the leaks."

"Leaks?" Leigh asked in a high, squeaky voice. "This ship leaks?"

Seeing her pale face, Sean said, "Now, don't be frettin', lass. All ships have some leaks. The *Avenger* leaks less than most. There's no danger of us sinkin'."

Soon, Leigh was much too busy to worry about the leaks, for the dirty straw held more than water. It was full of vermin. She sat squirming and scratching, muttering curses under her breath. The vicious little devils seemed to be everywhere.

Despite her vow not to complain, Leigh burst out, "I think the captain is horrible to punish you this way. Locking someone in a pigpen like this. It's inhumane!"

"Nay, lass. Bringin' a stowaway on ship is serious business."

"But it's not like I'm just any stowaway. You explained it to him. If he had any compassion at all in him . . . Why, he's just a big brute! A hard, cruel man!"

"Aye, he's a hard man, 'tis true. He has to be hard and tough to handle a rough crew like this one. But he's not cruel. Me God, lass! Don't you realize what

45

he could have done to me? He could have put me to the lash, or put me over in a boat."

"Put you to sea in an open boat?" Leigh gasped.

"Aye, lass, an' many a captain would have, too. Nay, he's not cruel."

Despite what her uncle said, Leigh still thought the punishment unduly harsh. And perhaps they would have been better off in an open boat, she thought. Right now, it certainly looked more appealing than sitting in this stinking, wet straw, being slowly eaten alive by vermin. She wondered if their punishment would have been less severe if she had been a full-grown man? And why did the captain have a rule about no boys on his ship?

"Why doesn't Captain Blake allow any boys on his ship?" she asked. "I know merchantmen have cabin boys. I've even heard the navy hires powder boys."

"Aye, that's true. But the cap'n has his reasons for not wantin' any boys on his ship." He shook his head sadly, saying, " 'Tis the devil ridin' his back."

Leigh frowned. "What do you mean, a devil riding his back?"

"Well, lass, 'tis like this. The cap'n's family owns a shipyard and a shippin' company. About four or five years ago, the cap'n took his younger brother to sea with him. He was goin' to start teachin' him the ropes, being as he'd be a cap'n one day himself. The cap'n's brother was just a lad. Couldn't have been over twelve years old at the time."

"And something happened to him?" Leigh quickly surmised.

"Aye, lass, that it did," he replied in an ominous voice. "We were stopped by a British man-o'-war and searched. When they left, they took three of the cap'n's crew with 'em. Claimed they were British

46

deserters that had jumped ship. The cap'n's brother was one of 'em."

"But why would they take a boy? You'd think if they were going to take anyone, they'd want full-grown, experienced seamen."

"Well, lass, ye see, the cap'n's brother was a healthy, strappin' lad. Big for his age, he was. The British navy likes 'em big an' healthy. And young. 'Tis easier to break a younger man's spirit than an older, more experienced man's."

"And Captain Blake let them take him?" Leigh asked in an outraged voice.

"Nay, lass. He was furious. Like a demon, he was. He grabbed a cutlass and attacked the boardin' officer. Sliced him up a bit, too, before they shot the cap'n."

"They shot Captain Blake?"

"Aye, lass. Ye see, we were all pretty mad about being stopped and boarded. The British crew had muskets trained on us the whole time. For a few days, 'twas nip and tuck with the cap'n. He almost died."

Leigh thought the whole story horrendous. "What happened to the captain's brother?"

"We don't know, lass. Haven't heard hide nor hair of him. Cap'n Blake's father went to London himself. As I said, he owns a shippin' company and he had several offices in England at the time. So you see, he was a man of considerable influence, with powerful friends. But it didn't do any good. No one is as high and mighty as the British Admiralty. They denied it, bold and brazen as you please. The cap'n thinks the lad is dead, and he blames himself. That's why he has the rule about no lads on his ship. Like I said, 'tis the devil ridin' his back."

"But it's so sad," Leigh sighed. "And so unjust."

47

"Aye, 'tis that. But now Cap'n Blake has his own brand of justice he's dealin' the British navy. That's why he's in privateerin', to get his revenge. That's why he named his ship the *Avenger*. He knew, sooner or later, there'd be war with England. When war was declared, he was ready." He smiled, saying in a proud voice, "We were one of the first American privateers to set sail."

Leigh frowned, saying, "Captain Blake owns this ship? I thought it was a naval ship. You said it was a fighting ship."

"Aye, lass, the *Avenger* is a fightin' ship. But we're not part of the American navy. And we don't fight the British navy, not if we can help it. The *Avenger* is a privateer."

Leigh was confused and frustrated. "Then what does a privateer do if it doesn't fight the British navy?" she snapped.

"Why we capture British merchantmen, lass. Then we take our prizes to port, and after they're sold, we all get a cut of the profits. Of course, the owner and cap'n get the biggest share." He grinned, saying in a proud voice, "Aye, I've done right well for meself. Sure beats the wages on a merchantman."

"Why, that's horrible!" Leigh cried in an outraged voice. "You attack unarmed merchant ships, capture them, and then sell them. That's piracy!"

"Nay, lass, 'tis not the same thing. The cap'n holds a letter of marque from Congress commissionin' his ship and authorizin' him to attack British shippin'. Besides, lass, those merchantmen aren't unarmed. They carry a few guns 'emselves. And some of 'em put up a good fight."

"But you sell the ships for personal profit!" Leigh retorted. "If you gave them to the government to sell

48

and the profits went into the treasury—"

"Give 'em to the government?" Sean interjected in astonishment. "Nay, lass, not even the American navy does that. Like us, the prize money goes to the cap'ns and crews."

"Well, the whole thing sounds illegal to me!" Leigh snapped.

"Nay, 'tis legal. All nations do it, England included. Our eastern seaboard is just crawlin' with British privateers."

"But how can Captain Blake sell private property that's been virtually stolen?"

"Actually, lass, the cap'n doesn't sell the prizes himself. They have to be taken to a port where there's a court of the admiralty. The prize court condemns 'em, appraises 'em, and does the actual sellin'."

Leigh sat back, feeling disgusted with the whole thing. Despite her uncle's assurance that privateering was legal, to her, it still smacked of piracy. And to think that only a few minutes ago she was actually feeling sorry for Captain Blake and admiring him for taking revenge on the British navy. Well, if he was so noble, why hadn't he joined the American navy? Then he could have fought the British navy honestly. Instead, he was taking his hatred out on the poor innocent merchantmen and, undoubtedly, getting rich in the process. Her opinion of the captain fell to new depths.

Another thought crossed her mind. What would happen to her uncle if the *Avenger* was captured by the British navy? She knew the crews of captured naval ships were considered prisoners of war. But what happened to the crews of privateers? Were they hanged? "Uncle Sean," she said in a trembling voice, "what would happen to you if the *Avenger* was captured by the British navy?"

"Ah, lass, we'd all go to prison. All except the cap'n, that is. Aye, if the British ever caught him, they'd hang him for sure."

"See?" Leigh cried. "I told you he's a pirate!"

Sean shook his head in exasperation. "Nay, they'd not hang him for bein' the cap'n of a privateer. Why, they'd just throw him in prison, like the rest of us prisoners of war. Nay, lass 'tis not for the privateering they'd hang him for. 'Tis for the spyin'."

"Spying!" Leigh gasped. "Captain Blake is a spy?"

"Well, that's what the British call it." He frowned and scratched his beard thoughtfully. "But to me way of thinkin', 'twas just plain stealin'."

"Spying? Stealing? What in the devil are you talking about?" Leigh cried in frustration.

"Well, 'twas like this. The first prize we took was an English fishin' boat, and the cap'n sailed it right up the Thames to London. Now, the cap'n knows London like the back of his hand, and he headed straight for the Admiralty buildin'. That night, he broke into their offices and stole certain top-secret papers. That's why the British navy wants him for spying."

"But how did they know it was him?"

"Aye, that's the bad part of it, lass. Right in the middle of it, a British officer walked in and caught the cap'n red-handed. And unfortunately, the officer recognized him. Seems the cap'n and the officer once attended the same dinner party before the war, and they had had a heated argument about impressment. At any rate, that's where the cap'n made his mistake."

"What mistake?"

"Well, lass, the cap'n should have killed the man, instead of knockin' him out."

Leigh gasped at her uncle's cold-blooded words,

50

but Sean ignored her reaction and continued. "The cap'n got back to the boat right before dawn, and we sailed right back down the Thames, as pretty as you please, with the whole river just crawlin' with British ships of war. It turned out that the papers the cap'n stole were sailin' orders, orders goin' to the naval escorts assigned to the convoys supplyin' Wellington in Portugal." Sean grinned. "We knew the dates, sailin' times, number and type of escorts, what the convoy was carryin'—everythin'!"

"But if the British knew the papers were stolen, why didn't they change the orders?"

Sean laughed. "Ah, lass, that's just it. They didn't know which papers had been stolen. The cap'n left their offices in such a mess, they had a devil of a time tryin' to figure out what was missin'." His eyes twinkled with remembered excitement. "We took fourteen prizes that month. We captured troop ships, ammunition ships, food shipments, packets." He chuckled, saying, "Aye, 'twas a grand month!"

"Strange," Leigh muttered, "I've never heard any story about an American spy breaking into the Admiralty and stealing top-secret orders."

"Nay, lass, an' ye can be sure the British people haven't heard about it either. Ye don't think the almighty Admiralty is goin' to let anyone know that an American sailed right up the Thames, past half the British navy, then broke into the Admiralty offices and stole secret papers, and then sailed away, scot-free, do ye? Nay, ye can be sure the Admiralty kept that one under close wraps. But they did put out a warrant for the cap'n's arrest and a sizable reward on his head. Aye, lass, there's not a British naval cap'n that wouldn't give his eyeteeth to capture the Sea Wolf."

"The Sea Wolf?"

"Aye, that's the Admiralty's code word for the cap'n. Ye see, 'twas bad enough the cap'n stole secret orders from 'em. That was downright embarrassin'. But what really infuriates 'em, is that he's taken more prizes than any other American privateer. An' he continues to elude 'em, despite their determination to catch him. He keeps takin' one prize after another. That's why they call him the Sea Wolf, because he's so crafty in sneakin' up on his prey and snatchin' it right from underneath their noses."

Once again, Leigh was forced to alter her opinion of Captain Matthew Blake. While she could never approve of privateering, she had to admit the captain was extracting his pound of flesh from the British navy after all. But instead of fighting the navy, he was harassing them, irritating them, waging a much more subtle, yet damaging war on them — a war of nerves.

Their last day in the brig, Sean was preoccupied. Leigh sat across from him wondering why he looked so worried. She finally asked, "Is something troubling you, Uncle Sean?"

"Nay, lass, I was just thinkin'. If we'll be takin' our prizes to New Orleans from now on, we'll have to catch a neutral ship sailin' to England from there. Aye, now, I'm mighty glad yer mother gave us that money she saved. We're goin' to need it."

"That's why she saved it. Remember, she said to use it to buy our passage with, once we reached a neutral port. Where is it, by the way?"

" 'Tis right here in me pocket," Sean answered, thumping his chest. "An' I'm tellin' ye, 'tis makin' me nervous carryin' around all this money on me. I think I'll turn it over to the cap'n to lock in his safe for me. I'd feel a lot safer."

"You'd turn our money over to that pirate for safekeeping?" Leigh asked in an outraged voice.

"Stop it now, will ye? I've told ye over and over, the cap'n is not a pirate. He's a privateer! An' I'd trust him with me life!"

Leigh sat back, a sullen look on her face. She didn't share her uncle's high estimation of the captain. For some reason she couldn't explain, she didn't like the idea of his holding her money.

The last night in the brig was an agony for Leigh. She lay in the wet straw, scratching the vermin's bites, her stomach cramping from lack of food, cursing the man who had forced her to endure these miseries and indignities. "Mark my words, Captain Matthew Blake," she whispered into the dark, "just as you will have your revenge on the British navy, someday, I'll have mine on you."

Chapter 4

Leigh and Sean were released from the brig the next morning. It was Kelly, the first mate, who came, unlocked the bars at the door, and led them back to the top deck of the ship.

When they stepped onto the sunwashed deck, Kelly said to Sean, "The cap'n wants to see you and the lad in his cabin as soon as you've cleaned up and eaten something."

"Aye, sir," Sean replied.

An hour later, Leigh and Sean entered the captain's cabin. Again, the captain sat at his desk, the light from the porthole behind him playing over his thick golden hair. He looks like a king sitting on his throne, Leigh thought, with a strange mixture of admiration and bitterness.

The captain looked up and smiled, saying, "Well, I see you two survived your ordeal."

Leigh caught the flash of sparkling white teeth against the captain's darkly tanned face; a deep dimple creased one cheek. The smile had a devastating effect on Leigh. She stared, feeling suddenly weak-kneed. What in the world is wrong with you, she thought in disgust. One little smile and you melt like so much butter.

Matt rose from his desk, walked to the front of it, and perched on one corner, swinging one leg casually.

Despite herself, Leigh couldn't keep her eyes off his muscular thigh, the hardened muscles rippling under the skin-tight breeches.

Crossing his arms over his broad chest, Matt said, "I've been thinking about the lad, O'Neal. I've decided he can be my cabin boy until we take our first prize."

Sean's normally florid face turned deathly white. This was the last thing he wanted. If the captain should discover Leigh's true identity . . .

Matt, unaware of Sean's reaction, continued, "I don't want him on the gun deck with you. He's not used to those big guns and you know yourself those carronades have a mean recoil on them. I don't want to take any chances of his being injured."

Sean frowned, finding it hard to argue with the captain's reasoning. Those thirty-two-pound carronades were dangerous. Besides the recoil, he had seen more than one man mangled when his foot got tangled in the ropes of the tackle. Then there were the powder burns, too. No, he didn't want to take any chance of Leigh's being hurt either. "Aye, Cap'n," he agreed.

Matt nodded, then rose, saying, "Also, he can sleep in here with me. You know how rowdy the men can get in the forecastle at times. Besides, it's crowded in there already. I doubt if you could find room to hang one more hammock."

Sean didn't like the idea of his niece sleeping in the same cabin with the captain, but for the love of him, he couldn't think of a plausible reason to object. "Aye, Cap'n," he muttered reluctantly

Leigh's head had snapped up at Matt's words,

"sleep in here with me." When she heard her uncle agreeing, she couldn't believe her ears. Her knees buckled and she gasped, "Nay, I go with me uncle!"

Matt whirled, his black eyes flashing dangerously. "That stay in the brig didn't teach you a damned thing, did it, lad?"

Sean saw the angry look on Matt's face. Saints preserve us, he thought in alarm. She'll keep it up until the cap'n throws us back in the brig. And Sean had no intention of staying in that pesthole until the first prize was taken. Sean stepped forward, his own face flushed with anger, and said in a stern voice, "Now you listen to me, lad! I'll be havin' no more of your foolishness. Ye'll do exactly what the cap'n says and no back-talk." Sean grabbed her arm and shook her lightly to emphasize his next words. "Remember, lad, ye begged me to come along."

Sean's taunt hit home. She had made her bed and now she would have to lie in it. But oh, how it galled her to have to play the meek and humble role to the arrogant man standing next to her. And was that a smirk on his handsome face she saw from the corner of her eye? "Aye, Uncle Sean," she managed to say in a tight, sullen voice.

Matt nodded in approval of Sean's stern tactics, then said, "I'm going on deck for a few hours." He walked to the cabin door, then turned, saying to Leigh, "When I come back, I expect this cabin to be shipshape, lad. Do you understand?"

"Aye, sir," Leigh mumbled.

Matt looked down at the lad. He hadn't missed the resentful look in the boy's eyes. But at least he wasn't out and out refusing. It was a start. He turned to Sean, saying, "O'Neal, show the lad how to hang his hammock. He can use that chest," he pointed to one corner, "for his things."

After her uncle had shown her where the cleaning supplies were kept and she had transferred her meager possessions from her sea bag to the sea chest, Sean showed her how to hang her hammock, placing one end on a hook in a corner of the cabin, and pointing out the other hook set at right angles.

"I'm supposed to sleep in that?" Leigh asked, eyeing the hammock with disgust.

"Aye, lass, once you get used to it, 'tis right comfortable."

Yes, Leigh thought ruefully, if you're a baby possum and used to sleeping in a pouch.

After her uncle had left, Leigh set to work cleaning the captain's cabin, determined not to give Matt any excuse to humiliate her again. She scrubbed and polished until the cabin sparkled. Then she stood back, looking at the cabin proudly and thinking, We'll just see what he has to say about this.

But when Matt returned to the cabin that evening, Leigh was disappointed. He walked straight to his desk, completely ignoring her and the room, and sat behind it, his full attention on the papers that lay there.

Leigh frowned with disappointment, then walked to her sea chest and sat on it, watching the captain warily. After what seemed an eternity to Leigh, she felt fur rubbing against her ankle and heard a soft purr. She glanced down and saw Lucifer at her feet. Delighted at seeing her friend, she bent down to pick him up.

"I wouldn't try to pet him, if I were you," Matt said. "He might scratch you. The only person he will let touch him is me."

Leigh shot the captain a defiant look and squatted beside the cat, petting his sleek fur. Lucifer purred even more loudly, rubbing against her feet and legs, begging for more.

Seeing the surprised look on the captain's face, Leigh smiled smugly and said, "He and me are old friends."

A brief frown crossed the captain's handsome face. Then he said, "That's right. They did say they found him in the sail room with you."

"Aye," Leigh answered, bending to pick up Lucifer. Then she sat back on her sea chest, the cat snuggling into her lap and purring with contentment. Both she and Lucifer totally ignored Matt.

Matt watched in astonishment. Lucifer hadn't let him pick him up since he was a kitten. What did the big, fiercely independent cat find so special about this lad that he tolerated, no, welcomed his familiarities? For a few minutes, he puzzled over the cat's unusual behavior; then he looked back down, his attention once more on the papers on his desk.

An hour later, Leigh still sat on her sea chest with the big cat in her lap, her head thrown back against the wall behind her, both dozing.

Matt glanced up and, seeing them, frowned. He said, "What did you say your name was, lad?"

Leigh's head bobbed up. "Leigh . . . 'tis Leigh, sir," she stammered.

Matt nodded curtly, saying, "All right, Leigh. You can go to bed if you want to. I won't be needing you for anything else tonight."

Go to bed? Suddenly, Leigh was wide awake, her heart hammering in her chest. This was what she had been dreading all day. Did he expect her to undress?

On trembling legs, she rose and gently put the sleeping cat on the floor. She picked up her hammock and hung it from the second hook, trying to ignore the captain's penetrating gaze on her. Carefully, she sat down on the precariously swaying hammock and

59

started to lie down.

"Don't you think you'd be more comfortable without your boots on?" Matt asked, an amused smile on his lips.

"Oh, aye, sir," Leigh answered, quickly unlacing the heavy boots and pulling them off. Then, giving the captain a quick defiant look as if daring him to say anything else, she lay back.

The hammock swayed, and Leigh was tossed to the floor with a loud thump. Matt threw his golden head back and roared.

"I was afraid that was going to happen," he said, still chuckling.

Leigh glared up at him, then scampered to her feet, having never felt so humiliated in her life.

"Didn't your uncle show you how to lie down in a hammock?"

"Nay, Cap'n," Leigh replied sullenly.

Matt rose and walked toward her, saying, "Well, there's a trick to it. You have to swing your feet up at the same time you lie back. Sort of roll into it." He sat on the hammock. "Now, watch me."

In one smooth, graceful moment, he reclined, so quickly the motion was a mere blur to Leigh's eyes. He lay on the hammock, hands folded behind his head, grinning up at her.

He rose, saying, "Now see if you can do it."

Leigh sat on the hammock again. As she swung her feet up, one foot tangled in the hammock, and again Leigh hit the floor. The fall knocked the wind out her. She looked up, her vision blurred, to see Matt frowning down at her.

Pulling her to her feet, he said irritably, "You're not swinging your feet up fast enough. Try again."

Gathering her courage and taking a deep breath to steady herself, Leigh repeated the procedure. This time she was successful in getting into a prone position, but the hammock swung from side to side violently. She lay in it, white-faced, holding onto each side for dear life. Finally the rocking subsided and the hammock stilled.

Leigh lay rigidly in the hammock, afraid to make the slightest move for fear of sending the hammock rocking again. She watched as Matt yawned, stretched his long arms, and then blew out the lamp. Moonlight from the porthole bathed the cabin in a soft subdued light.

Leigh's eyes trailed after Matt as he walked across the cabin and sat on his bunk. She watched mutely while he removed his boots and socks, then his shirt. He stood, his hand at his belt buckle. My God, Leigh thought in shock, he's going to strip completely naked. Quickly, she rolled to her side to put her back to him. The movement was too abrupt. The hammock swung, tilted, and for the third time, Leigh was slammed hard to the wooden deck, this time banging her elbow painfully.

Lying spread-eagled and face down on the floor, she heard a muttered "goddamn" and then the strike of a match before the lamp was relit. She lay on the floor, afraid to look up as Matt padded softly across the cabin.

"Are you hurt?" he asked in a gruff voice.

"Nay," Leigh lied, resisting the urge to rub her throbbing elbow. Then she became aware of staring at a pair of calves and the bottoms of his breeches. She sighed, thinking, thank God, he hadn't had time to strip them off before she fell. Gamely, she struggled to her feet and glared at the hammock.

"What in the hell did you do, anyway?" Matt asked.

Leigh shot him a hot, oblique look, saying, "Rolled

over too fast."

"Well, you'd better not make any more sudden moves until you're more accustomed to the hammock." Matt turned and walked back to his bunk, throwing over his shoulder, "Now get back into your hammock and see if you can manage to stay in this time. I've got to get some sleep tonight. I have to be back on watch in three hours."

Leigh lay in the hammock, staring at the ceiling and afraid to even breathe long after the light was doused. Even after she heard Matt's deep, rhythmic breathing and knew that he was asleep, she lay rigid, her elbow aching painfully. She blinked back tears of frustration, wondering why he always managed to humiliate her. It wasn't until she heard him rise, dress, and leave the cabin that she finally allowed herself to fall asleep.

Leigh was sleeping deeply when Matt returned that night. He glanced at the boy in the hammock, then walked up and looked closer, hardly believing his eyes. Leigh lay on her side, the big cat curled into the warmth of her stomach. Thinking that the cat would disturb the boy's slumber, Matt reached down to pick him up. Lucifer spat, a big paw lashed out, one long claw raking the back of Matt's hand.

Matt swore softly, then stood staring down at the jagged scratch on his hand in disbelief.

During the following week, Leigh's life at sea fell into a comfortable pattern. After cleaning the captain's cabin every morning, she joined Cookie in the galley to help prepare the noonday meal.

The cook was a crusty, old sea dog, and it took Leigh a day or two to realize his bark was worse than his bite. But it wasn't the snappish old man that

Leigh dreaded facing, but rather the chore itself. She was amazed at how much work was involved in feeding the big crew of the *Avenger* and wondered how the little old man managed such an awesome task all by himself.

The first day, Leigh had been dismayed when the crew constantly harassed the cook about the food, griping about the size of their servings and making derogatory remarks about his cooking skills. Of course, the old man gave the crew tit for tat; for every barbed remark they made about him, he threw back one equally insulting.

It wasn't until the third day that Leigh realized that the crew's harassment was just good-natured teasing, hidden under a rough exterior. Even more amazing was the realization that Cookie enjoyed these exchanges, even anticipated them, as they were his only social contact with the crew. And when the crew began including Leigh in their rough ribbing, making remarks about her small size, Leigh was secretly pleased. She knew that it meant they had accepted her as part of the crew.

Leigh's favorite time of the day was the afternoon, for this was her free time of the day, a time she always spent on deck. She loved standing on the quarter-deck, with the wind rushing past her, the feel of salt spray on her face and the smell of the sea in her nostrils, the sound of the sails snapping at her back and the rigging humming in her ears. It was an exhilarating, exciting feeling.

She passed her time sitting on the quarter-deck and watching the sailors at their chores, men who were surprisingly friendly and patient with her, despite their rough exteriors. At other times, she visited with First Mate Kelly, her favorite among the crew next to her uncle. For hours, she would listen as he entertained her with sea tales. Leigh thought if she could choose a man she would like to be her father, she would choose Kelly, a man who despite his toughness and strength was amazingly sensitive and gentle.

The only person Leigh wasn't friendly with on the *Avenger* was the captain, and him, she went out of her way to avoid. That didn't mean she wasn't aware of him. No, that was impossible, for his presence dominated the entire ship. She was acutely conscious of him standing on the quarter-deck, the wind ruffling his golden hair and molding his clothes to his tall, muscular body, of his powerful thighs straining against his skin-tight breeches as he walked across the deck, of his deep, authoritative voice as he called commands. Just being on the same ship with him was enough to make her nervous and tense. Every time she looked at him, she was reminded of the night he had held her in his arms and kissed her so intimately, a memory that always made her heart race and her knees turn weak, which only irritated her the more. When she was alone with him in the cabin, his overpowering maleness seemed to suffocate her, so that she was defensive, her answers to his efforts at friendly conversation curt and biting.

This uncomfortable awareness of the captain only added to her anxiety to be off the *Avenger* and on her way to her father. Thus, as the first week blended into the second and the only ships sighted were two merchantmen, one flying the French tricolor and the other an American that had braved the blockade, Leigh was just as disappointed as the crew.

The weather grew warmer as the *Avenger* sailed farther south, and Leigh was forced to give up her bulky sweater in favor of the coarse cotton shirt her uncle had bought for her. The shirt was deliberately oversized to hide her breasts and hips, the tail of the

64

huge shirt flapping about her knees and the sleeves rolled up several times to bare her hands.

The first time Matt saw her in her shirt, he laughed and said, "My God, lad, couldn't your uncle find something to fit you better than that? You look like you're wearing a tent."

"Nay, Cap'n, 'twas the only size they had," Leigh replied curtly, ducking her head to avoid those dark, penetrating eyes.

Matt glanced up at the stocking cap on Leigh's head. The cap was none too clean, and he doubted that it had ever been washed. The lad even slept in it! He asked in a friendly voice, "Don't you think you can shed your cap now? It must be getting damned hot under there."

Leigh's head shot up. A brief look of horror crossed her face. Then she reached up and tugged the cap even lower, snapping, "Nay, I'll not take it off. I like me cap!" Then, giving the captain a go-to-hell look, she turned and flounced away.

Dammit, Matt thought irritably as he stared at Leigh's retreating back. Just once he wished he could say something to the lad without Leigh snapping his head off. He frowned, wondering why this lad was so friendly with everyone else on the ship except him. He had even been aware of Leigh watching him, as if he, Matt, were some predatory animal about to pounce on him. Why did the lad dislike him so much? Was Leigh still resentful because he had locked him in the brig? No, Matt doubted that. If it was just resentment of his authority, it would have showed up in the lad's work. And Leigh did his chores well. No, he sensed it was something other than just simple resentment.

And what do you care what he thinks, Matt asked himself. Since when does a captain concern himself with the opinions of a mere cabin boy? Don't you have enough worries to occupy your thoughts?

Even more puzzling to Matt was why the lad reminded him of his mystery woman, so that now he was haunted by her ghostly specter both day and night. Was it because the boy was young and innocent, and he still thought of her in that way, regardless of what Monique had said? He shook his head in self-disgust. You must be going crazy, worrying over the opinions of a dirty-faced cabin boy and mooning over some faceless, nameless whore. Angrily, he turned and walked from the quarter-deck.

The next day, Leigh was sitting on the quarter-deck, only half listening to several of the crew as they talked. During the first several weeks on the *Avenger*, she had been embarrassed by these overheard conversations, both by the seamen's language, coarse and liberally spiced with curse words, and by their favorite topic of discussion, women and sex. But despite her shock, Leigh had been amused when the men related their exploits to each other, each story more exaggerated than the last. To her, they had sounded much like little boys, each trying to top the other's tale. After a few days, when the conversation began to get repetitious, she learned to tune them out. But now, when she realized they were talking about the captain, her ears perked up.

"Dammit, I wish I had all the women the cap'n has," one sailor said.

Another laughed, saying, "Aye, a regular fuckin' harem, he has."

A wave of coarse laughter followed.

"Say, do you remember that countess he had back in France?" one crewman asked. "Now she was some looker."

"Well, that one in Charleston wasn't so bad either,"

another remarked.

"Personally, I like the little Spanish dancer back in Cadiz," the third said. "Man, did she have a pair of tits on her!"

"Well, I don't know why all the women are chasing after him," a fourth complained in a whining voice. "Why do they think he's so special anyway? He's no different from us. After all, we're all built the same."

The first sailor laughed, saying, "Hell, man, it's not what you've got, it's how you use it. Now the cap'n, he knows how to use it. Besides, have you looked in the mirror at that face of yours lately?"

The sailor decided to ignore the insult, probably because the man who made it was twice as big as he. "I still don't see what makes him so special."

"Look, you stupid ass," the first sailor said gruffly, "there are just some men who are natural-born lovers. The cap'n is one of 'em. It's a flair, he has, like some men are good thieves and some men are good gamblers. Now, somehow a woman can sense when a man's got that knack. Don't ask me how. Maybe they smell it. But that's the reason they're chasing after him and not you and me."

"Do you think the cap'n will ever get married?" the second sailor asked.

"Hell, no!" the third answered. "Why should he? Not when he can have any or as many women as he wants."

"I don't know," the first sailor answered in a surprisingly subdued voice. "But I can tell you one thing. If the cap'n ever does take a wife, she won't be one of them silly women that's always chasing after him. No, he'll find himself a special woman—a real special woman. You mark my words."

That night, as Leigh lay in her hammock, she kept sneaking glances at Matt, who sat at his desk doing his evening paperwork. Grudgingly, she admitted that he was a handsome man, but she had known many handsome men, and they had never made her so acutely aware that they were male and she was female. Was what the sailor said that afternoon true? Was the captain an exceptionally good lover and women sensed it? Was that the mysterious magnetism that drew her to him and made her so tense when she was around him? She had to admit he had certainly played havoc with her senses the night he had kissed her.

Cautiously, very cautiously, she sniffed the air. All she could smell was the smoke from Matt's pipe. Feeling relieved, she rolled to her side. No, she thought, you're just tense because you're afraid he'll discover your true identity. You couldn't possibly be attracted to him, and certainly not that way.

The next day, the weather turned foul. As Cookie and Leigh prepared the midday meal, the storm worsened. In the shelter of the galley, they could hear the ominous roll of thunder, and the wailing of the wind.

The crew came in to eat, dripping water off their slickers and making big puddles on the floor. They ate hurriedly and were strangely subdued. Leigh felt their silence was as ominous as the noise of the storm raging outside.

A head appeared in the doorway. The sailor called out, "Hey, Cookie? You dousing your fire?"

"You know damned well I don't douse this fire unless the cap'n orders it!" Cookie snapped. "You mind your business and I'll mind mine!"

Leigh was shocked. She had never known the fire in the galley to be put out, banked perhaps, but never fully extinguished. "Would ye really put out the fire?" she asked.

"Aye, lad, if the storm gets bad enough," Cookie replied in a solemn voice. "And the lamps, too. Fire's a bigger danger to us than that storm out there."

Leigh glanced up at the lantern above them. It was swaying from side to side in a wide arc. She swallowed hard.

Just as the last cabinet was being bolted, Sean ran into the galley. Leigh hardly recognized her uncle with his hair plastered down to his head and hanging in wet strands across his face. Rivulets of water ran down his beard and onto his slicker, joining other rivulets to puddle on the floor. His breath was labored; his eyes glittered strangely.

"Cap'n says to douse the fire, Cookie. Lamps, too," he said between gasps.

"Aye, I expected it," Cookie answered.

Sean looked down at his niece, saying, "I'm to take ye to the cap'n's cabin, lad. Ye'll be safest there."

As they stepped on the deck, Leigh's eyes widened with horror. She had never been one of those squeamish women who were afraid of storms, but she had never seen a storm like this. Thunder rolled and clapped as jagged streaks of blue-white lightning briefly illuminated the dark sky, leaving in their wake the strong, penetrating odor of ozone. Mountainous waves slapped at the ship, washing over her deck and trying to drag fallen sailors back with them as they returned to the sea. The ship pitched and rolled, the masts groaning, as the howling, shrieking wind sent the rigging quivering like scores of plucked guitar strings.

Noticing for the first time, Leigh called out over the noise of the storm, "What happened to the sails?"

"Ye don't try to ride out a storm like this one with full sails, lass," Sean yelled back. "Ye keep her close reefed, unless ye're tired of livin'. Here, lass, grab

69

hold of one of these ropes strung across the deck. We're going against the wind and ye'll have to pull yerself across. And whatever ye do, lass, don't let go of that rope. I'll be right behind ye."

Leigh turned into the wind, and if it had not been for her uncle's big solid body behind her, she would have been blown away.

"Bend forward and keep yer head down," Sean instructed.

Leigh grabbed the slippery rope and bent into the wind, pulling herself forward. Now she knew the purpose of the ropes that crisscrossed the deck. Without them, it would be impossible to stand or walk. Slowly, they made their way across the deck, inch by inch, the wind tearing at her baggy clothing as if to rip it from her body, and then lashing in her face and blinding her, the howling, cracking, screeching of the storm assaulting her ears.

Twice, she slipped on the slick, tossing deck. Each time, it was difficult to pull herself back up, all the forces of nature seeming determined to beat her back down. And once, a huge wave crashed over the deck, the icy cold water swirling around her legs and hips, trying to pull her from the rope she clung to with a strength born of sheer terror.

When they had almost reached the other side, the deck tilted at a steep angle as the ship climbed a mountainous wave, higher and higher, shuddering at the crest, and then plunged into the depths of the trough, leaving Leigh's stomach in her throat. The *Avenger* crashed into the bottom of the trough, her timbers groaning in agony, and Leigh was thrown violently backward, her shoulders were jerked painfully as she clung to the slippery rope.

By the time they reached the captain's cabin, Leigh's nerves were totally shattered. She stood in the small cabin shaking uncontrollably and choking back sobs.

"Here, lass, get yerself out of those wet clothes, before I be tyin' ye down to the bunk."

"Tie me to the bunk?" Leigh screeched.

"Aye, 'tis the safest place fer ye. Otherwise, ye'll be tossed about this room like a scrap of paper in a windstorm."

"But if we sink and I'm tied down to the bunk, I'll drown!"

"Nay, lass. I'll not be tyin' yer hands and feet. I'll be tyin' the blankets around the bunk over ye. Ye'll be able to get out if ye have to. And besides, lass, we're not goin' to sink. The *Avenger* is built sound. She might get tore up a bit, but she won't break up."

After her uncle had tied her down and left, Leigh lay in the tossing bunk, thinking that Sean was wrong. They would all die out here in the middle of the ocean in this violent storm.

She lay in terror throughout the long, dark night, the cabin tossing, rolling, and pitching, the timbers of the *Avenger* groaning in agony, the wind howling in her ears as the storm outside vented its fury. A small tear trickled down her cheek. Now, I'll never know what my father looks like, she thought.

Dawn came in a gray pall. Angry black clouds scuttled across the sky. Lightning still flashed, and the wind still blew hard, but the worst of the storm had passed, and every man on deck knew it. As exhausted as the crew was, their spirits lifted. Weary smiles replaced the grim looks on their faces. They had ridden out the storm; not one man had been swept overboard.

Matt had been at the wheel since the beginning of the storm. At the height of it, he and one of his mates had been lashed to the wheel, and it had taken all of both men's strength to hold it steady. Now that the wind was finally subsiding, he relinquished the wheel to one of his steersmen and walked wearily across the deck to assess the damage.

Matt's twenty-four-hour ordeal at the wheel had totally exhausted him; his reflexes were below par. So when a sudden, freakish gust of wind rocked the ship and he heard the crack of wood, he didn't react fast enough. He heard, "Look out, Cap'n!" and then he was slammed to the deck.

Lying face down on the deck, Matt shoved at the heavy, limp body lying over him. "Goddammit, get off me, you big ape!"

He finally managed to push the limp body away and, sitting up, looked down into the dazed eyes of Sean O'Neal. A small puddle of blood formed beneath his shaggy head. Matt gently turned the Irishman's head and saw the gaping hole in the back of the man's skull. Bile rose in his throat.

Then Kelly loomed above them, saying, "I saw what happened, Matt. That last gust of wind tore a yard from the mainmast. O'Neal saw it fallin', but apparently you didn't. Anyway, he threw himself over you."

"Get the surgeon up here!" Matt commanded one of the sailors standing nearby watching.

"Aye, but I don't think it will do much good," Kelly muttered. "No man can live with a hole like that in his skull."

"Cap'n? Is that ye?" a weak voice asked.

Both Matt and Kelly looked down at Sean in astonishment. It seemed unbelievable that any man with a hole the size of a man's fist in his head could possibly be conscious.

Matt leaned forward, saying, "Aye, O'Neal, it's me."

"Where are ye, Cap'n? I can't see ye," Sean whispered.

Matt leaned closer. "Right here, O'Neal. I'm right here."

Sean's hand reached up and weakly searched until it found the front of Matt's shirt. With surprising strength, he clasped the shirt in his hand and pulled Matt closer, saying in a weak, but perfectly clear voice, "Cap'n, take care of Leigh for me, will ye?"

Matt swallowed hard before he answered, "Aye, I'll take care of the lad."

"Promise me," Sean gasped.

Matt nodded his head, saying, "Aye, I promise."

Sean's breathing was irregular now, pitiful weak rasps. His color was deathly pale. "Cap'n—take Leigh to . . . to . . ."

The hand grasping Matt's shirt relaxed and then dropped limply away. The Irishman's head rolled to the side. Kelly leaned forward and placed his hand over Sean's heart. After a minute, he silently withdrew it.

"Dead?" Matt barely whispered.

"Aye, Cap'n."

Matt was no stranger to sudden death. Sudden, lethal accidents were a part of a sailor's life, and a privateer risked his life every time he took a prize. But knowing that the man lying on the deck could have been—no, should have been him—unnerved him. He looked up at Kelly and said, "You're sure he deliberately threw himself over me? He didn't just get caught by the yard himself and fall over me?"

"Nay, Matt, I saw it all myself," Kelly answered softly. "O'Neal could have easily jumped out of the way. He deliberately threw himself over you. He saved your life."

"But why?" Matt asked in an agonized voice.

"I'm afraid only God and O'Neal know the answer to that," Kelly answered quietly.

Matt rose, walked to the rail, and looked out at the gray angry sea, still thrashing in the death throes of the storm. For a long time, he stood there, silent and brooding.

Finally, he muttered, "And how in the hell am I going to tell the lad?"

Chapter 5

After the storm had passed, the *Avenger* lay rocking under gray leaden skies and a fine drizzle. Her sails hung in tattered and torn pieces, fluttering in the now gentle breeze. The rigging was twisted and tangled, and spars dangled from her masts at crazy angles. Pieces of rigging, sails, wood, halyards, and other debris littered her deck. The proud ship had taken a terrible battering.

But the *Avenger*'s masts still stood, sound and solid, and surprisingly there was no damage discovered below deck. So despite the beating the ship had taken, the crew was able to make repairs at sea. In a flurry of frenzied activity, the deck was cleared and the tangled rigging and shrouds torn down. The yards were straightened and secured. The ripped canvas was torn away, and new sails were brought from below and hung. Finally, she was re-rigged. Three days later, the *Avenger* was as seaworthy as she had been the day she sailed out of Charleston's harbor a month before.

Matt gave Leigh no time to brood over her uncle's untimely death. Sean's canvas-shrouded body had hardly been lowered to the deep gray sea when Matt took Leigh to his cabin and revealed his promise to her uncle, a promise that he took seriously. Matt had committed himself to Leigh's care and safekeeping and had decided that the lad would take the place of the younger brother he had lost, with all the same privileges and advantages.

Leigh sat, listening mutely, while Matt explained his plans for her.

"You'll go back to New Orleans with the first prize we send in. As I said before, I have relatives there, an uncle who owns a plantation just outside of the city and another who owns an import business." He laughed, saying, "And a whole parcel of cousins. I'll send a letter with you, and one of the crew that goes along with the prize can see you safely to their doorstep. When you get a little older, if you still want to be a sailor, you can come back to sea. But I don't plan on you being just an ordinary sailor, Leigh. You'll be trained for a captaincy. Someday, you will have your own ship, just like me."

Had Leigh really been what Matt thought she was, she would have probably been thrilled with the generous offer. But Leigh wasn't a male, and the opportunity being offered her couldn't apply. Besides, she had her own plans for her future, for she had only one objective in life, to find her father. It was more than just a dream; it was her reason for living. She knew that, without her uncle's help, it would be difficult, but she was more determined than ever. She decided that she would go to New Orleans as Matt wished. As soon as she could slip away from his relatives, she would take the money her mother left her and buy passage on a neutral ship going to England. Then she would go to London, for she knew that an English lord was a member of Parliament. That's where she would begin her search.

Matt sat, watching Leigh standing before him. He

76

was disappointed, even a little irritated, at the lad's lack of enthusiasm. After all, it wasn't every day that the son of a common seaman was offered the golden opportunity to become a captain. "Well, don't you have anything to say?"

Leigh roused herself from her thoughts. She knew what reaction was expected of her. She smiled and lied glibly, "Oh, aye, sir. 'Tis a grand plan."

But in the days that followed, Leigh regretted her words. She fervently wished that she had been brave enough to refuse Matt's generous offer. Because he planned for the lad to be trained for a captaincy, Matt took Leigh's free time in the afternoons away from her. Now this time was spent exclusively in his company as he taught her about sailing ships and navigation. Even her evenings were spent working by his side, for having discovered she could read and write, Matt put her to work transcribing his notes to his prize log.

Where Leigh had been uncomfortable in the captain's company before, now she was miserable. There was no escaping his overpowering male presence. She was acutely aware of every accidental brush of their bodies, brushes that always left her skin tingling, aware of the heat that radiated from him, of his scent, a mixture of salt air, tobacco smoke, and some strange masculine smell that sent her senses spinning.

The last came as a shock to Leigh. My God, she thought, what that sailor said about him was true. He did have a strange magnetism—and she could smell it!

The next day, Leigh was glad when the captain announced gun practice, for this meant a reprieve from his company. As soon as she saw the crew throwing the barrels they used as targets overboard, she beat a hasty retreat to the cabin.

Even in the small cabin, she could still hear the noises, just as clearly as if she were standing on deck. The rumble of the gun carriages, the roar of the cannons, the squealing of the tackles assaulted her ears. She could hear the mumbling and cursing of the men and their excited yells as they hit their target. She wasn't even safe from the horrible powder smoke, as it seemed to permeate the small cabin, stinging her eyes and nostrils.

Leigh remembered what those cannons were meant to be aimed at, innocent merchantmen, and she was again filled with outrage. By the time Matt entered the cabin later, she was in a foul mood. She glared up at him from where she sat on the floor, polishing his boots.

Matt walked across the cabin, saying, "I wondered where you had disappeared to this afternoon."

"I stayed inside!" Leigh snapped. "Nay, I don't like gun practice."

Matt frowned. "Oh? And why not?" he demanded.

"I don't like all them noises," Leigh replied tightly. "All that boomin' and screechin'. 'Tis a waste of gunpowder."

Matt laughed. The gun practice had gone well, and he was in too good a mood to let the lad's surly attitude disturb him. "No, lad, it's not a waste of gunpowder. If the British navy did more practicing of their own, they wouldn't find themselves outgunned every time they engaged one of our ships."

Leigh's look was one of open disbelief.

"It's true," Matt said. "I've talked to several of our naval captains. They all said the same thing. The British gunners are lousy shots, and the reasons they're lousy is that their captains don't make them practice enough. That's why practically everytime we've engaged them, our navy has been victorious.

We don't outgun them, we outshoot them. No, gun practice is not a waste of gunpowder."

Matt turned and walked to his bunk. He sat and pulled off his boots, saying, "But enough of that. I've decided I've a mind for a bath tonight. That gunnery practice is hot, sweaty business."

Leigh knew the sailor's method of bathing consisted of standing naked on the deck while a fellow crewman doused him with a couple of buckets of sea water. Thus far, she had always managed to slip below deck before she was embarrassed by having to witness these baths. In fact, judging from the yelps and yells coming from the deck, that's what the crew was doing right now. So if the captain wanted a bath, why didn't he go on deck with the rest of the crew, she wondered.

Matt read Leigh's mind and said, "No, lad, I'm not talking about being sloshed with a couple of buckets of sea water. I'm talking about a real bath, in a tub, with hot water I can soak in and ease my aching muscles."

Leigh stared at him as if he had lost his mind.

Matt laughed, saying, "So you don't know about my bathtub, then?"

"Nay, Cap'n," Leigh muttered.

"I'm surprised you haven't noticed it. It's in the cabinet we keep the cleaning supplies in. Now, be a good lad and bring it in here for me. Then you can get a couple of buckets of water from the barrico and have Cookie heat them for me."

Leigh found the big brass tub and had a devil of a time getting the heavy, awkward thing down the narrow passage. She shoved, pulled, and tugged at it, muttering curses at the captain and the tub. When she finally reached the cabin door, she was drenched with sweat and panting from her exertions. She kicked the door open, shot Matt a murderous look,

79

and dragged the tub into the cabin.

"I was wondering what was taking you so long," Matt commented.

At that minute, Leigh longed for a cannon of her own. She knew just exactly whom she would aim it at. " 'Tis heavy," she snapped.

Matt looked at the tub and then at her. "Aye, well, I guess it was a chore at that. I forgot what a puny, little lad you are."

Leigh glared at him, clenching her teeth.

"Well, just don't stand there! At this rate, I'll never get a bath. Get some buckets of water and take them over to Cookie to heat up."

Leigh stomped out of the room, mumbling a whole new set of curses, and it took three trips before she had enough water to fill the tub.

As she started to pour in the last bucket of cold water, Matt said, "No, lad, if you put too much cold water in, the water won't be warm enough. Now add those buckets of hot water."

Leigh set the bucket of cold water aside and picked up the one with hot water. Matt tested the water with his finger and said, "Add about half of that other bucket of hot water. Then I think it will be just right."

Leigh stood up from pouring the hot water in the tub and turned to face Matt. She gasped, finding herself staring at his broad, bronzed chest with its mat of fine, golden hair. She watched, pinned to the spot, as his large hands unbuckled his belt. Seeing him unbuttoning his breeches finally galvanized her. She whirled and made a beeline for the door.

"Where in the hell do you think you're going?" Matt called to her back.

Leigh froze, then stammered, "Out, Cap'n. So—so ye can be havin' yer privacy."

"Privacy?" Matt asked in an astonished voice.

"Hell, I'm not worried about privacy. I was planning on you washing my back for me."

Wash his back, Leigh thought in total horror. He expects me to stay in the cabin while he sits in the tub—stark naked?

"What in the hell's wrong with you, anyway?" Matt grumbled. "Now shut the damned door. There's a draft in here."

Numbly Leigh closed the door. Then, carefully averting her eyes, she walked to her sea chest and sat, staring at the deck in front of her. She heard the splash as Matt sat in the tub and then a deep, satisfied sigh.

"Ah, lad, there's nothing like a tub of warm water to relax you, is there?"

Leigh ventured a quick glance. All she could see was the back of Matt's golden head and his broad shoulders over the high edge of the tub. She relaxed and leaned her head against the wall, enjoying a minute of respite.

For a while, Matt just relaxed in the tub, letting the warm water ease his aching muscles. Then he said, "Hand me that bar of soap off the wash cabinet, will you, lad?"

Leigh jerked up, having almost dozed off. Reluctantly, she walked to the wash cabinet and picked up the soap. Keeping her eyes on the floor, she handed it to Matt, but the second his hand touched hers, she jerked away, and the soap fell to the deck.

"Dammit! What in the hell's wrong with you tonight?" Matt growled. "You're as jumpy as a cat."

"Sorry, Cap'n," Leigh mumbled, scurrying to pick up the bar of soap from the deck. When she rose, she found herself looking straight down at him. A wave of relief washed over her. All she could see was the upper part of his chest and two knees poking out of the water. As a matter of fact, she thought the captain looked ridiculous sitting there with his big body crammed into the little tub. She couldn't suppress her giggle.

Matt glared up at her. "What's so damned funny?"

"Ye, sir," Leigh answered, still giggling. "Ye're so squeezed into the wee tub, ye've got yer knees knockin' yer chin."

Matt looked down at himself. What the lad said was true. He grinned, saying, "Aye, that's true. If the tub had been one inch smaller, I wouldn't have made it." He handed the soap back to her, saying, "Now be a good lad and wash my back for me, will you?"

Leigh froze. It was one thing to see Matt's naked chest and shoulders. That didn't shock her. She was used to seeing the crew stripped to the waist. But touch a man's naked skin? Particularly this man's?

"Come on, lad," Matt coaxed. "You can see I can't possibly reach it in this small tub. You'd be doing me a favor."

Leigh knew there was no way she could get out of it. What reason could she possibly give if she out-and-out refused? She nodded, accepted the soap, and stepped to the back of the tub.

Matt leaned forward in the tub so she could reach his back better, and Leigh gulped. The new position offered her an excellent view of his broad back. She stared at those muscles, remembering only too well what they had felt like that night.

"Come on, lad," Matt prodded. "This water isn't going to stay warm forever."

Gathering her courage, Leigh dipped the soap in the water and then rubbed it across Matt's back. Much to her surprise, the touch of Matt's bare skin wasn't the least repulsive. The skin was firm, yet smooth, and the muscles rippling beneath her hands

82

gave her that same strange thrill she had felt before.

"Ah, lad, that feels good," Matt mumbled. "But rub a little harder, will you? You're too gentle."

Leigh was more than happy to rub harder. Maybe that way, she wouldn't feel so peculiar herself. She bent into it, scrubbing with a vengeance, but Matt only flexed his muscles more in response, making her all the more aware of those powerful muscles. When Matt began to moan, almost as if in ecstasy, it was too much for Leigh. She stepped back, almost stumbling on her weak knees, saying, "There, now, Cap'n."

Matt laughed and said, "Well, I guess nothing that feels that good could last forever, eh, lad?"

Remembering her own warm feelings, Leigh flushed.

"Hand me the soap, will you?" Matt said. "I guess if I'm going to finish this bath before the water gets cold, I'd better hurry."

Leigh handed him the soap, careful to avoid contact with his fingers. Then she walked back to her sea chest and sat down weakly. Why did touching him make her always feel so strange, she puzzled. Touching his bare skin hadn't been the least repulsive, as she had expected. In fact, the feel of his naked skin had given her a pleasant, warm feeling.

As Matt scrubbed himself and splashed in the tub, Leigh's mind took a different turn. Oh, how I wish I could have a real bath, she thought longingly. For her bathing had consisted of quick sponge baths from a bucket of sea water when she was sure the captain wouldn't return to the cabin unexpectedly. The only time she had been drenched all over since she came on board was the day she had gotten soaking wet during the storm.

Matt's voice broke into her thoughts. "How about

83

pouring the rest of that hot water over me, lad?"

Sighing in disgust, Leigh rose and walked to the tub. Matt sat in the water, his hair, shoulders, and chest covered with soapsuds. He grinned up at her.

It was that grin that did it. To Leigh, he just looked too damned pleased with himself. Suddenly, the memory of tugging and pulling the tub into the cabin and lugging the water to fill it flashed through her mind. And all that work was done so he could have the luxury of soaking in it, washing all of the dirt and grime from his body, while she, the slave, was still filthy. Rage rose in her.

Without even considering what the repercussions might be, she bent and picked up the bucket of cold water instead of the remaining hot water. She held it high over Matt's head, a malicious gleam in her eyes and said, "Ready, Cap'n?"

"Aye, lad, give it to me," Matt replied, totally unsuspecting.

With a gleeful grin, Leigh tossed the whole bucket of cold water over him. Matt yelped and came out of the tub in a flash.

Too late, Leigh realized the rashness of her action. Matt stood before her, his magnificent male body totally exposed to her eyes. And she couldn't take her eyes off him. Why, he's beautiful, like a Greek god, she thought in a lightning flash. Then her eyes drifted downward and froze, staring in dumbfounded shock. None of the little boys she had seen had ever looked like that!

Matt's black eyes were flashing dangerously. He was on the verge of venting his anger when he noticed the shocked look on the lad's face. He glanced down at himself, acutely aware of what the boy was staring at. Seeing nothing unusual, he snapped, "What in the hell's wrong with you?"

Roused from her shock, Leigh ducked her head and mumbled, "Sorry, Cap'n. I must have picked up the wrong bucket."

Matt hadn't meant the bucket of water. He was much more disturbed by the boy's gawking at his manhood than the cold water. It unnerved him. Quickly, he grabbed a towel and dried himself off. Yanking on his breeches, he thought, hell, the way the lad gaped you would think he had never seen a naked man before. Then suddenly it dawned on Matt that maybe the lad had never seen a naked full-grown man before. He didn't know how he could have missed it, particularly on board ship, but still . . . He gave Leigh a penetrating look and said, "Have you ever seen a naked man before, lad?"

Leigh was horrified. She blushed and ducked her head even lower. "Nay, Cap'n," she managed to mutter.

Matt laughed and said, "Well, I guess you were a little surprised, huh, lad? After all, there is quite a bit of difference down there between you and me."

Leigh flushed even redder, thinking, Oh yes, Captain, there certainly is a big difference, a very big difference.

Matt mistook Leigh's flush for shame and said, "Aye. I think I know what's bothering you, lad. You're worried about being so small. Well, don't worry about that. In a few years, you'll start growing down there, and by the time you are a full-grown man, you'll be as big as I am."

After Matt had left, Leigh still felt weak-kneed from the encounter. She decided to wait until morning to put the heavy tub away.

But later as she lay in her hammock, she wished she had put the tub up after all, for every time she looked at it, the memory of Matt, towering over her in his magnificent nakedness, came back to her. She could see the water coursing down his long, muscular body, the damp golden hairs sprinkled over it glittering in the lamplight. He had looked like a bronzed god, sprinkled with gold dust and crowned with a golden crown, rising from the sea.

Disgusted with herself, she turned to face the wall, but the minute she shut her eyes the vision reappeared to taunt her, the vision, followed by that same warm, weak feeling she had felt before. She tossed and turned, but the vision tormented her, seemingly burned in her memory, permanently etched in her mind. Now she had not only the memory of the feelings Matt had aroused in her at the hotel, but this vision of his naked male beauty to further taunt her.

Later, when Lucifer jumped up on the hammock to join her, Leigh buried her face in his soft fur and whispered, "Oh, Lucifer, everything they said about him is true — and more. 'Tis a devil, he is, and he's put an evil spell on me."

One evening when they were working on the prize log, Leigh asked. "Where did you put the copy of the ship's manifest on prize number thirty? I can't find it anywhere here."

Matt leafed through the pile of papers and then handed one to her. He stood back, frowning down at the top of her head as she bent to copy the manifest.

On several occasions, Matt had noticed inconsistencies in the lad's speech. Sometimes, his speech was so grammatically correct, it was almost cultured, and then, at other times, his Irish brogue was so thick Matt could barely understand him. And there had been other things that Matt had noticed that had left him perplexed. The lad's voice for one thing. Sometimes it was deep, and then sometimes a clear, lilting soprano. True, Matt had gone through that stage as an adolescent, when his voice would change octaves in mid-sentence. It had embarrassed him acutely. But the lad didn't even seem to be aware of it, and for some reason, the changes in the lad's voice didn't have that peculiar cracking quality that Matt had noticed in himself and other male adolescents.

Matt continued to scrutinize Leigh as she copied the notes. As he did so, his uneasy feeling grew. The lad's movements were smooth, well-coordinated, not at all gawky or awkward as one would expect of a lad his age. In fact, all of the lad's movements were graceful, his walk, his hands, the arch of his neck.

Matt scowled down at Leigh's face. The sun had tanned it to a golden honey color. Thick, incredibly long lashes lay like fans across rosy cheeks. He studied the delicate bone structure, the small tilted nose, the soft, sensuous mouth, the pointed chin with its tiny dimple. He's just too damned pretty, Matt concluded.

That's what had reminded him of *her*, Matt realized. It wasn't the lad's innocence, but his beauty and grace. He was just too damned effeminate all the way around. A horrible thought came to Matt's mind. God almighty, don't tell me he's going to grow up to be one of them, he thought with disgust.

At that minute, Leigh looked up and said, "Somethin' wrong, Cap'n?"

Matt looked down at the boy and immediately felt ashamed of his thoughts. Why, he's just a frail little lad, brought up in the sole company of a lone widow. Having never had a father to emulate, naturally his mannerisms would be effeminate. And as for his looks, well, no one could hold that against him. Matt had known several men whose looks bordered on being downright beautiful, and yet they had normal, even lusty, male appetites. No, all the lad needed was the influence of a strong male.

Having buried his suspicions, Matt laughed and said, "Nay, lad. I was just thinking you've been spending too much time in this cabin. Tomorrow, we'll start teaching you some of the manly arts."

Leigh watched in astonishment as the captain walked out of the cabin. Good heavens, what had brought that on, she thought. And dear God, what did he consider "manly arts"?

It turned out that Matt's idea of learning the manly arts was learning the use of a pistol and cutlass. Leigh barely tolerated the first. She hated the acrid smell of the gunpowder, the terrible noise the pistol made, and the jarring of her shoulder as the gun slammed back in recoil.

Matt stood back and watched Leigh, puzzled that the boy seemed so disinterested. Why, most boys would be excited at the prospect of learning to shoot. When it became obvious that Leigh would never have any aptitude for guns, Matt said in a disgusted voice, "Never mind, lad. Obviously, pistols aren't your choice of weapons. Perhaps you'll do better with a cutlass."

He handed a cutlass to Leigh, and as she accepted it with reluctance, he snapped. "God almighty, lad! Don't hold it like that. You're not going to hoe cotton with it, you know!"

Thoroughly disgusted, Leigh threw the cutlass to the deck with a loud clatter. Her eyes blazed. "Nay! I'll not be learnin' any of yer killin' ways!"

"Killing ways? What in the hell are you talking about?" Matt demanded.

"Ye'll not be makin' a pirate out of me!"

"Pirate?" Matt asked in an astonished voice.

"Aye, 'tis a pirate ye are, stealin' merchant ships and all! I'll be havin' no part of it!" she cried, her chin thrust out stubbornly.

Matt laughed, saying, "No, lad, I'm not a pirate. I'm a privateer. I have a commission from Congress—"

"Aye!" Leigh interrupted. "I know all about that. Me uncle explained it to me. 'Tis piracy, I say!"

Matt was furious. "I'm not a pirate, goddammit! I'm a privateer! They're not the same thing!"

Leigh was beginning to regret her rash words. At that minute, with his black eyes flashing and his fists clenched, Matt looked very dangerous. In fact, the captain looked as though he could kill her. She decided it was time to back off. "Aye, well, call it what ye like. But I'll not be any privateer. 'Tis a merchant cap'n, I'll be, an' I won't be needin' to know about pistols an' cutlasses."

Matt stood glaring down at Leigh, then threw his own cutlass to the deck and paced angrily. The damned little fool! Where in hell had he gotten all of those stupid notions about pirates and killing? Why, he sounded like a woman! That's it, Matt thought. He got those crazy ideas from his mother. Hell, it ought to be against the law for a woman to raise a boy by herself. Well, thank God, the lad wasn't a coward. That much he knew for sure. There was certainly nothing cowardly about the way he had stood up to him. Matt grinned. Stubborn, little imp! Standing there with his chin stuck out, eyes flashing, hands balled into fists as if he was going to take a swing at him any minute. Oh yes, the lad wanted to hit him. Had his mother taught him fighting was wrong also? Probably.

Matt turned back to Leigh, saying, "All right, lad, you don't want to learn how to use pistols and

89

cutlasses. But what about your fists? What if one of your crew decided to take a swing at you? Are you just going to stand there and let him beat you to a bloody pulp?"

Leigh was taken aback by the question. "Nay, Cap'n."

"Right, lad. Because a captain that can't take care of himself, can't command his men's respect. And without that respect, he won't be a captain long."

Leigh looked at the captain warily. She didn't like the way the conversation was going.

"Do you know how to fight, lad?"

"Nay," Leigh answered sullenly.

"Put your fists up, lad. Come on, see if you can hit me," Matt taunted, pointing to his chin.

Suddenly, Leigh was interested, very interested. How many times had she longed to do just that? Oh, how she would love to lay one on that arrogant chin! She balled her fists and raised them. Eyes bright with excitement, she crouched, waiting.

Matt laughed and said, "I knew it! I've never seen an Irishman yet that wasn't a natural-born fighter."

Matt cuffed her lightly on the chin. Leigh blinked in surprise. She hadn't even seen his hand; it was so lightning fast.

Matt chuckled at her surprised look. "Never let yourself be distracted by talk, lad. Keep your mind on what you're doing."

For several minutes, Leigh let Matt instruct her, putting up with his light cuffs and punches, knowing that he wouldn't really hurt her, thinking her a poor, little, defenseless lad. After a few minutes, she realized, with dismay, that the opening she had been waiting for wasn't going to come. Matt was much too accomplished. Every swing she made at him was easily blocked. This could go on forever, she thought with despair.

Then suddenly, she stopped and pointed to the deck, saying, "What's that ye dropped, Cap'n?"

Matt looked down at the deck, leaving himself wide open. Leigh balled up both fists together and, throwing her whole weight into it, caught his chin in a swift, vicious uppercut.

The blow wasn't enough to floor Matt but caught him totally unaware, and he staggered backward. The circle of sailors that had gathered to watch the boxing lesson howled with approval.

"He's an Irishman, all right, Cap'n," one sailor said, laughing with glee. "He knows all their dirty fightin' tricks."

Matt stood, rubbing his chin in astonishment. The lad carried quite a wallop there, he thought. Then he laughed and replied, "Aye, you've got to watch the sneaky little bastards."

Leigh stood in the circle of laughing men, grinning from ear to ear. She hadn't felt this good in ages!

The next afternoon, a British brig was sighted. Leigh stood on the quarter-deck with Matt and Kelly, her eyes glued to the lookout.

"She's carryin' guns, Cap'n," the lookout called down. "Thirty-two of 'em!"

A low murmur ran through the crowd of sailors. Leigh knew what they were thinking. This was no merchantman.

"The stripes?" Matt yelled back. "What stripes is she carrying?"

"Stripes?" Leigh asked in confusion.

"Aye, lad," Kelly answered, "British warships have two yellow stripes on their sides. American warships only have one white stripe."

"No stripes!" the lookout called back.

"Then she's a British privateer," Matt mumbled.

"Aye, and spoilin' for a fight," Kelly answered. "She's headin' right for us."

For the first time, Leigh glanced out to sea. She gasped, surprised to see the British ship so close. And she was heading right for them. She looked over at Matt.

His black eyes glittered strangely as a slow smile played at his lips. "Aye, she's looking for a fight, all right, and I'd hate to disappoint her." He turned to the crew and said, "What do you say, men? There'll be no prize in it. We'll both be fighting for keeps. Do we fight — or run?"

The crew had been without excitement for too long. Their cry was a unanimous "Fight!"

But the crew knew that the final decision to fight or run came from the captain. They all stood with their eyes glued to him, their faces taut with expectation.

Matt grinned and shouted, "Why in the hell are you just standing there? Man your guns!"

The crew let out a deafening "hooray" and scattered in all directions.

Matt turned, saw Leigh, and scowled. "Get to the cabin, lad, and stay there!" he ordered.

"Aye, Cap'n," Leigh cried, then ran off toward the cabin.

But as she ran across the deck, zigzagging and ducking to keep from colliding with the crewmen rushing to their stations, her mind was racing too. This wasn't going to be any simple taking of a prize. That was no defenseless merchantman out there. This was going to be a fight between two privateers, two equally matched ships. This was going to be a real sea battle, probably her only opportunity to see an authentic battle at sea.

So when she reached the bulkhead to the passage that led to the cabin, instead of going into it, she ducked behind some barrels on the deck by the bulkhead. Crouching behind the barrels, she cautiously peeked out and quickly judged her position. Yes, she thought, from here she would be able to see everything, and yet no one could see her.

No one on deck had noticed Leigh's deception. They were all intent on the battle ahead. Shirts were stripped and thrown to the deck, and rags were tied around the crew's foreheads. The gun ports slammed open as the big carronades were rolled forward, their carriage wheels creaking and rumbling in protest.

"I want the weather gauge, Mr. Kelly!" Matt roared above the noises.

"Aye, sir!"

Leigh glanced out over the rails. The two ships were closer now, angling out, running parallel to one another.

"Fighting sails!"

Leigh watched in astonishment as all of the sails, except the topsails and jibs, were reefed. She had always thought ships fought with full sail. Wasn't that how the artists pictured them?

"Grape and round shot!"

The gun crews scurried to load the big guns. When this was finished, they all turned, their bodies tense with expectation, their excited eyes glued to the captain, waiting breathlessly for the order to fire.

The two ships were running side by side now, so close it seemed their yards were almost touching. Leigh could clearly see the British crew running over the deck and manning their own guns. The tension was unbearable. Why doesn't the captain give the order to fire, she thought.

"Fire broadside as they bear!"

Every cannon in the port battery roared, spitting fire and smoke, and then slammed back against the restraining tackles. The crews frantically sponged and reloaded, and then strained to push the big cannons back in place. The slow matches were placed over the vents and the cannons thundered again, over and over and over.

If Leigh had thought the noises of gun practice was bad, it was nothing compared with this. The noise was deafening with the roaring of the cannons of both ships, the rumbling of the gun carriages, the screeching of the pulleys, the yelling and cursing of the crew, the splashing of the water as the cannon balls missed their mark, the whizzing of the musket balls, followed by the smacking noise as they hit the wooden deck or sides.

The last had come as a shock to Leigh. The first time a musket ball had flown by her and lodged in the wall behind her, she had stared at it dumbly. Where had that come from? Then, glancing up at the yards of the British privateer, she saw the sailors crouching there, firing their muskets down at them. One quick glance up at the *Avenger*'s yards assured her their crew was doing the same.

The smoke was so thick now she could barely see. The irritating smoke stung her nostrils and eyes, making them water. The heat from the cannons was almost unbearable.

"Reduce charges! Reduce charges!" Matt's booming voice rang out over the din.

And still the cannons fired, volley after volley. How much longer can it go on, Leigh wondered, her stomach a tight knot from fear. She glanced up at the British ship's yards and masts and, through a brief clearing in the smoke, saw that several yards hung limply, their sails tattered and ripped, fluttering helplessly in the breeze. Her rigging was torn and dangling. She glanced up at the *Avenger*'s masts and saw no damage had been done. With sudden dawning, Leigh realized what Matt had said was true. The British gunners were inferior, most of their cannon shots flying harmlessly through the *Avenger*'s rigging and splashing into the sea beyond them. And they even have more cannons than we do, she thought with disdain.

A loud cracking noise caught Leigh's attention, and she turned to see the British ship's mainmast and yards falling, pitching to one side. The ship rolled, ducking her gun ports below the surface of the water and tilting the deck. Had it not been for her yards and rigging tangling in the *Avenger*'s, she would have toppled completely to her side.

Now the *Avenger*'s crew were gathering in the waist of the ship, cannons forgotten, cutlasses and boarding pikes in their hands. Leigh heard the clang of the grappling hooks and staggered from the impact as the two ships bumped sides. Then the *Avenger*'s crew swarmed over the rails to the deck of the British ship. But to Leigh's dismay, just as many British sailors were boarding the *Avenger*.

Now, the furious hand-to-hand combat began on both decks as new sounds of battle filled the air: scuffling of feet on deck, clanging and clattering as cutlasses met, yells, curses, grunts, and crude taunts mingling with the cries of the wounded and moans of the dying. Leigh's eyes frantically searched the decks of both ships for the captain or Kelly, but with the smoke still rolling about and the melee, it was impossible to identify anyone, much less tell which side was winning.

She gasped as two sailors suddenly appeared beside her and quickly ducked behind the protection of the barrels. Crouched into a tight ball, her heart pounding in her ears, she heard the shuffling of their feet, the swish and clatter of their cutlasses, and the labored breathing of both men. One of the men bumped into the barrels, causing them to threaten to topple over her. Leigh waited in frozen horror as they tilted precariously above her. Then she heard a grunt, the thud as something hit the deck and, a minute later, the sound of feet running away from her.

It was at this minute that fate stepped in. The cat, Lucifer, had been sunning himself on a coil of ropes when the battle began, not far from where Leigh was hiding. Long accustomed to the noise of the cannons, he had not been the least disturbed. On the contrary, he had watched the battle with the detached air of a casual, if not bored, observer. After all, it was none of his concern what these foolish creatures called humans did. But when strange men started running over the *Avenger*'s deck, he considered it a violation of his territory and high time to let these trespassers know just who owned this ship. He rose, stretched, and jumped off the rope to the deck. Black tail straight up like a flag, he walked arrogantly across the deck, eyeing the intruders with disdain.

A British sailor ran across the deck and almost stumbled over the cat. "Why, you little Yankee bastard!" the sailor cursed and raised his cutlass to cut Lucifer down.

At this minute, Leigh peeked over the barrels, saw what was about to happen, and reacted on sheer instinct. She screeched, "No!," grabbed the cutlass of the man who lay dead by the barrels, and charged at the British sailor, swinging and hacking with the cutlass with all the strength and fury her small body possessed.

In a blind rage, she attacked the British sailor, not even aware of what she was doing. The first realization came a few minutes later when she felt a stinging pain in her left shoulder as she stumbled backward from the impact. She fell to the deck. Then, total blackness.

By this time the battle was almost over. The British sailors were swarming back to their own deck, and a few minutes later the British colors fluttered down.

Matt and Kelly, both heaving from their exertions, their faces blackened from the smoke, their cutlasses hanging limply from their hands, looked at one another and grinned.

Kelly glanced over at the British ship and shook his head, saying, "I'm afraid you're right, Cap'n. There'll be no takin' a prize. She's sinkin'."

Matt looked at the sinking ship. A wave of sadness swept over him. He hated to see anything as beautiful as a ship destroyed. "Aye, I'm afraid we'll have to scuttle her."

"Well, whatever we do, we'd better do it quick. She's sinkin' pretty fast."

"Aye," Matt said, "and if we don't get her mast untangled from our rigging, she'll take us with her." He turned and shouted to the crew, "Get up there and cut that rigging loose from her mast and yards."

A score or more of sailors scampered up the *Avenger*'s rigging and then hacked with their cutlasses at the ropes tangled around the British ship's broken mast and yards.

"And the British crew?" Kelly asked.

"Put them in their longboats," Matt answered. "There're plenty of islands around here, and I'll be damned if I'll feed them. They wanted this fight."

"Cap'n! Cap'n!"

Matt whirled to face the man running across the deck and calling to him. "What's wrong, man?"

"I think you'd better come quick, Cap'n!" the man panted.

97

Matt's heart leaped to his throat. "Have we taken a ball below the water line?"

"No, Cap'n." The sailor shook his head in confusion. "I mean, I don't know about that."

"Then what's wrong?" Matt asked.

" 'Tis the lad, Cap'n," the sailor replied.

"What about the lad?"

The sailor hesitated. He knew the captain would be furious when he learned that the lad hadn't gone to the cabin, as he had been ordered. Would that fury spill over on him, he wondered.

"Goddammit, man, spit it out!" Matt snapped.

The sailor blanched and shuffled his feet nervously. Then, he stammered, "Well, you see—you see, it was like this. Right in the middle of the fightin' your cat comes walkin' across the deck. Then this big limey stumbles over him, curses him, and starts to take a swipe at him with his cutlass."

"My cat? I thought you said it was the lad?"

" 'Tis the lad, Cap'n," the sailor said in an exasperated voice. "You see, just then, out of nowhere, the lad comes flyin' out at the limey." A look of disbelief came over the sailor's face as he shook his head and continued, "I tell you, Cap'n, I ain't never seen anythin' like it. That lad looked like the devil himself, swingin' and hackin' with that cutlass."

"The lad had a cutlass?" Matt asked in astonished disbelief.

"Aye, that he did. And I'm tellin' you, he had that limey backin' away mighty fast too! That is, until the lad sliced his leg. Must have made the limey mad, 'cause then he stopped backin' away and started fightin' back." The sailor paused, a thoughtful look on his face. "Aye, must have made him mad."

"Dammit, man! What happened then?" Matt roared.

The sailor looked up as if surprised the captain would ask such a silly question. "Why, then I killed the blasted limey, Cap'n."

"And the lad? What about the lad?"

The sailor winced and then answered nervously, "Well, Cap'n, I'm afraid I didn't get there quick enough. Mind you, I was all the way across the deck when I saw it happenin'. I ran as fast as I could!"

Matt's face was deathly pale. He could hardly force the words from his lips. "The lad's dead?"

"Nay, Cap'n. At least, I don't think so. But he was wounded. Had blood all over the front of him. I sent for the ship's surgeon and then ran here to tell you."

Matt stood in stunned silence. Another lad's death to haunt me, he thought. First my brother's and now Leigh's.

Kelly looked at his captain and friend with compassionate eyes. He knew what Matt was thinking. He clamped his hand on his shoulder and said, "It may not be as bad as you're thinkin', Matt. Go see about the lad. I can take care of things here."

Matt nodded and, as if in a trance, walked across the deck. The sailor who had brought the news to him ran before him, calling, "This way, Cap'n."

When Matt arrived at the spot where Leigh lay, a circle of curious crewmen had already formed. Off to one side, Cookie sat crying openly, big tears streaming down his grizzly old face. Seeing the old man crying sent Matt's slowly rising hopes plunging back downward. It was all he could do to shove a man aside and step into the circle.

The ship's surgeon was already there, kneeling and leaning over Leigh's body. The doctor was a massive man, so all Matt could see of Leigh was the lad's legs and his deathly pale face. The doctor's huge back obstructed the rest of his view.

Matt bent forward and said, "Is he dead?"

The doctor glanced over his shoulder and then back down to his patient. "Nay, Cap'n, he's not dead. But he's got a wound in his shoulder."

A huge wave of relief washed over Matt. He took a deep breath, not realizing he had been holding it. The lad wasn't dead. Then maybe there was hope after all. Color flooded back into his face.

Cookie shoved his way into the circle, asking anxiously, "He ain't dead? Did I hear him say he ain't dead?"

"Goddammit! He ain't dead!" the doctor roared, still leaning over Leigh. "Stop asking stupid questions, Cookie, and get down here and hold this pressure bandage for me. If I don't get this bleeding stopped pretty soon, he will be dead," he threatened.

Cookie knelt at Leigh's head and bent forward to push on the bandage on her shoulder.

"Is that why the lad's unconscious? Because he's lost so much blood?" Matt asked.

"I don't know why he's unconscious!" the doctor snapped, then said more calmly, "I'm sorry, Cap'n, but I haven't had a chance to examine him yet. It could be just this wound, or he might have others. If I could just get this goddamned shirt off him. Hell, he could have a dozen wounds under there for all I know."

From where Matt stood, he could tell the doctor was fumbling with the lad's buttons, but he still couldn't see because of the surgeon's broad back.

He waited with indrawn breath as the doctor pulled the shirt back. He saw the man freeze, as if shocked by what he saw. A quick glance at Cookie's wide-eyed look confirmed the doctor's shock. Matt's heart fell to his feet. "More wounds?" he asked in a choking voice.

For a minute, Matt thought the doctor wasn't going to answer. Then he said softly, "Nay, Cap'n. No more wounds. The one on the shoulder is the only one." The doctor hesitated, then added, "But I think there's something you ought to know, Cap'n."

"What?" Matt asked, puzzled by the man's strange behavior.

The doctor sat back on his heels, and for the first time, Matt got a clear view of Leigh's whole body. The blood-stained shirt lay opened, baring the wound on her left shoulder and her entire chest. But it wasn't the wound that Matt's eyes were locked on. He stared in stunned disbelief at Leigh's beautiful, rose-tipped breasts.

Chapter 6

Leigh struggled to open her eyes. They felt so heavy. Finally, with supreme effort, they fluttered open. For a minute her vision blurred and then finally cleared. Leigh stared at the ceiling in confusion. There was something wrong with it. No, it wasn't the ceiling. It was the way she was lying, she realized. She was lying on something soft and flat, not in her hammock. My God, she was lying in Captain Blake's bunk! But why? She started to raise herself on her elbows and gasped as a sharp searing pain tore through her shoulder. Her head whirled. Limply she fell back to the pillow.

"I wouldn't try that again if I were you. You've a wound in your shoulder and a good-sized goose egg on the back of your head."

The captain's voice, Leigh realized. But why did he sound so angry? She frowned in puzzlement and then remembered what had happened: the sea battle, her attack on the British sailor, his cutlass stabbing her shoulder. She wondered briefly at her own audacity in attacking an armed man, one who by his trade alone was certainly proficient with a cutlass. But this wasn't the time to be contemplating that. The captain was angry with her, and justifiably so. She was supposed to have been in the cabin and not on the deck.

"I be rememberin' now," she said. " 'Tis sorry, I am—"

"You can cut out the act, miss. I know what you are," Matt said coldly.

Miss, Leigh thought. Had he called her "miss"? Oh, dear God! Her hand flew to her head. The stocking cap was gone. With sickening realization, she trailed her hand down the length of her hair. She glanced down and saw the shirt she was wearing. It wasn't hers. In fact, it looked suspiciously like one of the captain's. She closed her eyes, feeling even sicker.

"I see you understand," Matt remarked dryly.

Leigh nodded and then sat up abruptly, saying, "I can explain . . ." The room reeled as Leigh fought off the wave of dizziness. Two strong hands laid her back down against the pillow.

Matt's voice was terse. "I don't think you're in any condition to discuss anything right now. But I'm warning you, miss. Tomorrow morning, I'm going to ask some questions, and you damned well better have the right answers." With that, Matt turned and slammed out of the cabin.

Oh God, Leigh thought, now what do I do? Then the dizziness engulfed her, and she plunged back into the dark abyss.

When she awakened the next morning, the dizziness was gone, and her mind was perfectly clear. For a long time, she lay pondering her problem. Then she crawled slowly from the bunk, her intense thirst taking precedence over all. Weakly, she walked to the desk and poured a cup of water. As she walked back to the bunk, she became aware of a draft on her legs.

She looked down to discover they were bare, the shirt hanging just above the knees. What happened to her breeches? Then she realized she was totally naked beneath the shirt. The next question was even more distressing. Who had undressed her? The captain? No, she told herself firmly. The doctor. It had to be the doctor.

At that minute, the cabin door opened and Matt entered. He stopped, surprised to see her up. Then his black eyes scanned her slowly, up and down.

Leigh was acutely aware of her bare legs and her disheveled hair hanging around her shoulders and down her back. The captain's penetrating look made her feel as if she were totally exposed, stripped before those dark eyes. With renewed determination, she lifted her chin proudly and walked to the bunk. She sat down and flipped the covers quickly over her legs.

For a long minute, the two stared at each other in silence, the tension thick and heavy around them.

Matt finally broke the silence, saying, "Well, miss, I see you're up. I trust you're feeling better this morning?"

Matt's sarcastic tone infuriated Leigh. Her temper rose, and she fought a hard battle to push it back down. She thought her best weapon was to act every inch the lady. If she let him rile her, he would humiliate her yet again. She answered icily, "Yes, Captain, thank you. I'm feeling much better this morning."

A golden eyebrow arched in surprise. "Ah, and what has happened to the charming Irish brogue?"

"That was just part of my disguise, Captain Blake. I assure you, I can speak English as well as you," she replied coldly.

Damn the little bitch, Matt thought. He struggled to control his anger. It was quite a struggle, for he was furious. The whole crew was laughing at him for letting O'Neal and the girl put one over on him. Of course, they completely forgot that they had been fooled by the disguise, too. But what the crew thought was so hilarious was that the captain, whom they considered very knowledgable about women, had been sleeping in the same cabin with her for almost six weeks and hadn't discovered her true identity. Dammit, it was humiliating.

Oh yes, Matt thought, it all fit in now, her aversion to weapons, the slips in her speech, her effeminate mannerisms. Of course, she was effeminate. She was a woman. And a damned beautiful one, too, he admitted. When he had walked into the cabin a minute ago and found her standing there with that mass of burnished hair around her shoulders, her shapely legs bared to his view, and those proud breasts poking at his shirt—oh, yes, he well remembered what those looked like—he had been stunned. How in hell could he have been so stupid, so blind? True, she had hidden her hair and feminine curves but how could he have ever thought that any lad could have a face like that or skin so soft and creamy? At that minute, Matt didn't know who he was the most angry with, this woman and O'Neal for deceiving him, the crew for laughing at him, or himself for being so blind.

Well, dammit, he would make her pay for humiliating him. He was captain of this ship. His word was law. By God, he would make her regret her deception!

Leigh watched the captain warily as these thoughts ran through his mind. What was he thinking? Plan-

106

ning her punishment? Would she be thrown back in the brig or, God forbid, put out to sea in an open boat? Surely, he wouldn't do that? But one look at his angry face convinced her he was capable of anything. The longer he stood with those hot black eyes boring into her, the more unnerved she became. Oh, I wish he would say something, she thought. Anything!

Leigh got her wish. Matt leaned forward menacingly over the bunk, his face just inches from hers, and said, "There's just one thing I want to know. How in hell did you talk a level-headed man like O'Neal into bringing his doxy with him on this ship?"

"Doxy?" Leigh gasped in surprise, then blanched. Oh, my God, she thought. He had recognized her after all.

Matt's control broke. He yelled, "Yes, his doxy, his mistress, his woman, his whore! Call yourself any goddamn thing you want to! All I want to know is how you managed to corrupt a good man like O'Neal? How did you get him so addled that he'd bring a woman aboard this ship, knowing full well I could strip every inch off his hide or—yes, dammit, hang him for it!"

Leigh was too shocked to respond. He had not only recognized her, but he thought she was her uncle's doxy.

Matt looked her over, his black eyes coldly appraising her face, then her curves, hidden only by the thin shirt. "Oh, you're pretty enough," he said with a sneer. "But I've certainly seen more beautiful whores than you. Is it that you're so accomplished in your trade, so knowing and skilled at pleasuring a man, that O'Neal would risk his neck for it?"

Leigh had heard enough insults. Despite her promise to herself to hold her temper and stay composed, she flew from the bunk and shrieked, "How dare you call me such vile names! And how dare you insult my Uncle Sean!"

"Your Uncle Sean?" Matt yelled back. "My God, is that what you called your lover? Even considering your profession, don't you think that's a little gross?"

Leigh was speechless with fury. She balled her fist and swung. Matt caught her flying wrist and twisted it cruelly behind her back, pulling the whole length of her hard against his body, saying, "Oh, no, little lady. I've been on the receiving end of that before!"

Leigh glared up at him, her breasts heaving in anger. Matt was very aware of those soft breasts crushed against his chest, her bare legs pressed tightly against his. He looked down at her flashing eyes and her full seductive mouth and had the sudden urge to kiss her. Realizing the direction his body was leading him, he threw her away as if she were a hot poker, saying, "And don't be thinking of playing any of your cute little tricks on me. I'm not the fool that O'Neal was."

Leigh staggered back from Matt's push and caught herself on the desk, flinching from the pain in her shoulder. She raised herself to her full height and stood before him, a small bundle of defiance. "Do you always manhandle women, Captain Blake? First you practically attack me in that hotel hallway and now—"

Matt's golden head shot up. "What did you say?" he interjected.

"I said you had no right to pounce on me at the hotel as you did, even if you did think I was that— that Monique! And neither of you had any right to accuse me of being a whore, just because I happened to be standing in the hallway."

Matt was stunned speechless. My God, she was "her," his mystery woman! She was here, on his ship, no elusive specter, but honest-to-God flesh and blood. And she was just as beautiful as he had known she would be. A feeling of happiness surged through him. And then he remembered how she had come to be on his ship. O'Neal had brought her on board.

His dark eyes narrowed. Could she possibly be telling the truth, he wondered. Was she O'Neal's niece? No, that didn't make any sense. A man might bring his whore on board ship to ease his hunger on the long voyage, but not his niece, an innocent, young lady. For what purpose would he do that? No, it was just as Monique had said. She was a common streetwalker, wandering the hotel in search of a man, and the man she had found that night had been O'Neal. And Sean, loath to leave her behind, had brought her along. At the thought of O'Neal making love to her, another emotion surfaced, one fairly new to Matt, one he had felt only since that night he had held her in his arms—jealousy.

"Personally, I don't care what you think of me," Leigh continued. "But I won't tolerate you saying such vile things about my Uncle Sean."

Matt was already angry that she, a common whore, could arouse jealousy in him, but that she thought him gullible enough to swallow her lies infuriated him. What did she think he was? A complete fool?

"Do you actually expect me to believe that?" Matt asked angrily. "You expect me to believe that O'Neal brought his own niece aboard a privateer, with two hundred women-hungry men on board? That he would expose his own flesh and blood, a young innocent girl, to that?" Matt shook his head, saying, "No, as low as my opinion of O'Neal is right now, I don't think he was that stupid."

"But that's just it!" Leigh cried. "He didn't want to do it. He knew it was dangerous, but I forced him."

Matt looked at the small female standing before him. The idea of anyone so small forcing a man the size of O'Neal was ridiculous. He scoffed, saying, "Forced him? That's a little hard to believe."

"I don't mean physical force, Captain," Leigh snapped. "It's quite obvious I would be incapable of that. I mean—I mean I blackmailed him."

Blackmailed? Oh, yes, Matt thought, that fits. It's just the kind of thing he would expect from a woman of her sort. But what had O'Neal done that he could be blackmailed? Had he committed some crime? Murder? Robbery? He had known O'Neal for years. He would stake his life that the man hadn't had any criminal tendencies. "Just what were you blackmailing him for?"

Leigh frowned, saying, "I shouldn't have used that word. It's misleading. You see, I played on his guilt."

"Guilt? About what?"

"My mother made him promise her on her death-bed that he would take me with him when he sailed. She was dying, and my poor uncle didn't have the heart to refuse her. I think he was counting on my being more reasonable. He tried to talk me out of it, believe me, Captain, but I held him to his promise. You see, he took the promise very seriously. To him, it was a solemn oath, and the only one who could release him from it was me. But I wouldn't. I played on his guilt to force him to bring me along."

"But why in God's name would your mother want a young woman to go to sea? She must have been out of her head, delirious at the end. Surely, your uncle wouldn't take her seriously?"

"No, Captain, my mother wasn't delirious. Her mind was perfectly clear to the very end. She knew what she was doing. You see, sailing with my uncle on your privateer was the only way to get me out of the country."

Matt's look turned suspicious, and Leigh laughed, saying, "No, Captain, I'm not wanted for any heinous crimes. You see, my mother wanted my uncle to take me to my father in England. Since no merchant ships were leaving Boston because of the blockade, she made my uncle promise to take me with him when he sailed."

"But —"

"Please, Captain," Leigh interrupted. "If you'll just let me finish, I'm sure I can answer all your questions."

Matt fought back his frustration. He nodded curtly.

"Uncle Sean only planned on my being on board your ship until you took your first prize. He knew that you would have discovered me by then and would insist that I go back with the first ship you sent to port. Then naturally, he would accompany me to see me settled. We planned on taking a merchant ship from France to England. He was quite upset when he discovered you didn't plan to take your prizes to France, but to New Orleans instead." She smiled, pleased with herself, and finished, "So you see, it's all quite simple."

Matt thought that he had never heard such a ridiculous story in his whole life. And to think people accused sailors of telling tall tales. My God, it must have taken her all night to dream this one up. But the young lady's story had one big flaw in it. He smiled smugly and said, "A very interesting story, young lady. But you forgot something."

"What?" Leigh asked in surprise.

"Sean O'Neal's sister was a widow. Her husband died years ago. How could O'Neal be taking his niece to a man that doesn't exist, a father that's been dead for years?"

Leigh felt sick. She hated to tell the arrogant captain of her illegitimacy. He was just the type of man to throw something like that in her face. She flushed and dropped her eyes.

Seeing her flush, Matt smiled in self-satisfaction. Now I've got her, he thought. Let's see her squirm her way out of this one. "Well?" he taunted.

I don't care, Leigh thought. I don't care what he or anyone else thinks of me. My mother and father loved one another, and I won't be shamed. Particularly, not by a damned pirate!

She raised her head proudly and looked him straight in the eye. "That's what I thought too, Captain. Only when my mother was dying, was I told the truth. My father is in England and is, in all probability, still living. The story about my father dying at sea before I was born is just that, a story." She took a deep breath, then said, "My mother was never married."

Matt stared at her in disgust, not by what she had divulged, but because he thought her the most audacious liar he had ever heard.

Leigh was fighting back tears. She couldn't stand his looking at her like that, as if she was the lowest thing on earth. "Must you stare so, Captain? Surely, I'm not the first bastard you've seen."

Matt was taken aback by the bitterness and hurt in Leigh's voice. For a minute, he wavered. Could she possibly be telling the truth? Or was she just a damned good actress? He said, "You said O'Neal was taking you to your father in England? Is he expecting you?"

Again Leigh flushed. "No, he doesn't know I exist."

An eyebrow rose. "Oh, a little surprise, huh?"

There was nothing Leigh could say. She clung stubbornly to her resolve not to let him shame her. She glared at him.

"And where in England is this father of yours?"

"I—I don't know. My uncle never mentioned our destination. We were just going to England."

"And you weren't curious enough to ask?" Matt asked in disbelief.

"No," Leigh lied, "I wasn't."

"Well, I trust you at least know his name," Matt said sarcastically.

The color drained from Leigh's face. Her lips trembled. "No, I don't. My uncle refused to tell me anything about him, even his name. And my mother only referred to him as 'his lordship.' "

Matt threw back his golden head and laughed. Then, he said "Oh God, when you weave a tale, you really believe in gilding it, don't you? You can't be just the by-blow of an ordinary man. Oh no, you make yourself the bastard of a nobleman. A lord, no less!"

Leigh was furious. She stomped her foot and said. "It's true! My mother was in his service before she came to America. And I have proof!"

Matt frowned. "Proof? What proof?"

Leigh ran to her sea chest, threw back the lid, and found the ring. Showing it to him, she said, "My father's ring. He gave it to my mother before she left England."

Matt started to take the ring from her, but she jerked her hand back, saying, "No! Don't touch it! It's mine!"

He was stunned momentarily by her ferocity. Finally, he said, "How can I see it with you holding it like that?"

Carefully, Leigh held the ring out with her thumb and forefinger so he could see the crest. Matt looked down at the heavy ring and frowned. It did look like a nobleman's signet ring, crest and all. Matt had seen plenty of those in England. But he also knew a nobleman didn't give away his signet ring. It was a family heirloom, passed down from father to son, as hereditary as the title that went with it. And he certainly wouldn't give it to a servant wench in gratitude for services rendered.

He looked Leigh straight in the eye and said, "Your mother may have been in the service of a lord at one time, but the lord didn't give your mother that ring. More than likely, it was stolen."

Leigh's face turned deathly pale. "No, she didn't steal it. He gave it to her."

Matt stood staring down at her. The more he thought about her story, the more he disbelieved it. Even if she was a nobleman's by-blow, what purpose would O'Neal have in taking her to her father? Certainly, O'Neal wasn't naive enough to think the man would acknowledge her, particularly at this late date. From the noblemen Matt had known, they would laugh in his face. No, Matt decided, O'Neal may have been a fool for a pretty face, but he wasn't that stupid.

He turned and said coldly, "Nice try, miss. But I simply don't believe you."

"But the ring!"

"Ah, yes, the ring," Matt said in a cutting voice. "A handsome payment for your services, no doubt. But then, being stolen, the man who gave it to you didn't really feel any great loss, did he?"

Leigh sank wearily to the bunk, totally defeated. She would never convince him. He had his mind made up and that was that. But now what? In a small voice, she asked, "What are you going to do to me?"

Matt looked down at the beautiful young woman sitting on the bunk. She looked so small and defenseless. Suddenly, he felt like a heel. What in hell's wrong with you, he asked himself. She's nothing but a conniving little whore, a stowaway who deceived and humiliated you. Why are you feeling sorry for her?

Totally frustrated, he turned and walked to the door. Just before he stepped out, he said in a harsh voice, "We'll discuss your punishment later."

Matt stormed across the deck. As he stepped on the quarter-deck, he was stunned by the murderous look his first mate shot him. Then Kelly turned his back on him, gazing determinedly out to sea.

"Is something bothering you, Mr. Kelly?" Matt asked in a terse voice.

"Aye, that it is," Kelly replied tightly.

"And might I ask what?" Matt snapped.

Kelly whirled and glared at him. "Aye, that you can, Cap'n. 'Tis about the lass."

"What about her?"

"You're wrong what you're thinkin' about her and O'Neal, Cap'n."

"And just how do you know what I'm thinking?" Matt asked sarcastically.

"Because I heard you, that's how!"

"Heard me?" Matt asked in surprise.

"Aye. Me and every other man on this ship. My

115

God, Cap'n, you were bellowin' like a wounded bull."

"Bellowing like a bull?" Matt yelled.

Kelly winced, then looked around the deck apprehensively. "Aye, Cap'n. And you're doin' it again!"

Matt glanced around the deck. The crew's eyes were glued on them, their looks curious. He gave the men a look that sent them scurrying, but he knew their ears were straining for every word he and Kelly were saying. He nodded curtly to the farthermost end of the quarter-deck, saying, "Mr. Kelly?"

Kelly nodded and followed him. For a minute, both men stood looking out over the ocean, seething in silence. Finally, Matt said in an icy voice, "Since when does the first mate tell the captain how to run his ship?"

"Goddammit, Matt, get off it!" Kelly said in an exasperated voice. "I've known you since you were a pup. You've been like a son to me. But I've never known you to be so blind."

Matt struggled to hold his temper. "And may I ask why you're so sure you're right and I'm wrong?"

"Because I know Sean O'Neal, that's why! Known him almost as long as I've known you. He wouldn't bring a woman like that aboard ship. It would be as unnatural for him to do as for a fish to climb a tree. He just wouldn't do it, and I know it."

"And yet, he brought a woman on board. You can't deny that!"

Matt retorted.

"Aye, but not that kind of woman."

"And since when are you such an authority on women?"

"I ain't the authority you are, that's true!" Kelly snapped. "But I damned sure know a whore when I see one! They've a look in their eyes. And one look in

116

that little lass's eyes can tell you she's as innocent as the day she was born."

Matt wavered at Kelly's last words. Then he remembered the way Leigh had seductively pressed her soft curves against him that night and hardened his resolve. "Innocent?" he scoffed. "Have you forgotten the way she deceived us?"

"That's not the kind of innocence I'm talkin' about and you damned well know it!"

"Then you really believe she's O'Neal's niece?"

"Aye, I do."

"And you believe the rest of that wild tale?" Matt asked in disbelief.

"I didn't hear anything but you calling her vile names and her screaming she's O'Neal's niece. The rest of what she told you isn't any of my business. That's between you and her. I only know she ain't no whore, and I don't like you treatin' her like one."

Matt glared at his first mate, and Kelly glared back in open defiance. Finally, Kelly said stiffly, "Now that I've said my piece, I'll be about my business." He turned and walked a few steps, then hesitated.

"Is there something else, Mr. Kelly?" Matt snapped.

He turned. "Aye, Cap'n, there is one more thing. Can I tell Cookie to take the lass somethin' to eat?"

Matt threw his hands up in disgust. "Dammit, I'm not a fiend. I don't intend to starve the girl to death!"

"Aye, Cap'n." Kelly replied. He whirled and walked angrily away.

Matt spent the rest of the day pacing the deck and wrestling with himself. By the time he walked back to his cabin that night, he had admitted to himself that he had been wrong in his appraisal of Leigh's character, but not because of what Kelly had said or even his

117

own experience with her at the hotel. It had been the recall of the night he had bathed that had convinced him. He remembered that she hadn't wanted to stay in the cabin, but he had insisted, and then the shocked look on her face when she had seen him naked. No, that hadn't been any act. Only a total innocent could have looked that stunned. And then, the things he had said about naked men. No wonder she had been so embarrassed and couldn't look him in the eye. A feeling of shame washed over him. Quickly, he came to his own defense. Well, he thought, she shouldn't have deceived him!

While Matt had convinced himself of Leigh's virtue, he was still enraged at her deception. By successfully passing herself off as a boy, she had humiliated him in front of his crew and, in Matt's eyes, cost him the loss of their respect. And a captain who didn't have his crew's respect was in a dangerous position. The fact that she was the very woman he had been desiring and losing sleep over, while she slept so peacefully not six feet away from him, only made him feel more a fool and fired his anger. He was a proud man, too proud, and being made a fool of didn't set easily with him. So even though he had admitted that he had been wrong to accuse her of being a prostitute, he was determined he wouldn't apologize. That would be her punishment for deceiving him.

As for the rest of Leigh's story, Matt didn't know what to think. If she was capable of deceiving him, wasn't she capable of lying, too? But why name herself a bastard if it wasn't true? If she was lying, she could have easily made something else up, something less damning to herself. And the ring? Had it been stolen? He still seriously doubted a nobleman would give his ring away. A pretty bauble, jewels perhaps,

118

but not his family ring. And would O'Neal really take his niece, a girl he obviously cared for deeply, to a man who didn't know she existed and probably cared less? Round and round, Matt had gone, until in frustration he finally pushed the whole puzzle to the back of his mind.

When he stepped into the cabin, Leigh was asleep. He lit the lamp and looked down on her. As usual, Lucifer lay beside her. The cat's yellow eyes watched Matt intently, his black tail swishing in short warning strokes.

Matt frowned and whispered, "Don't worry, boy. I'm not going to try and move you. I'm not about to make that mistake again."

His attention returned to Leigh. The shirt gaped open at the neck, and he could see the bandage on her shoulder. Again, he frowned. He had completely forgotten about her wound this morning. It must have been hurting, but not once did she whimper, not even when he was manhandling her. A new pang of guilt rose. Again, he defended himself. Well dammit, she shouldn't have tried to hit him. Then he grinned, rubbing his chin in remembrance. And she did carry a good wallop.

He turned and walked to Leigh's hammock. As he hung it, he thought, Dammit, it's going to be a pain in the ass sleeping in my clothes. But there's really no place else to put the girl. Of course, I could double up with Kelly. Lying in the hammock and staring up at the ceiling, he decided, I'll be damned if I'll relinquish my cabin, like she's some honored guest. I didn't invite her aboard. She'll just have to put up with me. That, too, will be part of her punishment.

Being exhausted from his emotional turmoil, Matt didn't hear the disturbance in the forecastle that night. For the argument that had begun that morning between him and Leigh was continued that night by the crew. Half of the crew sided with Matt and thought Leigh had been O'Neal's doxy. The other half of the sailors took Leigh's side, that she was O'Neal's niece.

"Why, she ain't nothin' but a slut," one big raw-boned sailor said.

"Watch who you're callin' a slut!" another hardened seaman warned.

The first sailor stuck his face into the second's and snarled, "You think you're big enough to stop me?"

"You're damned right I do! Sean O'Neal was my friend and you're not goin' to be callin' his niece dirty names!"

Almost simultaneously, other heated arguments began, and inevitably fists flew. When the furious fracas was over, the battered but victorious side returned to their hammocks wearing wide satisfied grins. The other half of the crew sulked back or, in some cases, were dragged back to their hammocks to lie the rest of the night groaning or muttering sullenly to themselves.

When Matt walked across the deck the next morning and saw the battered faces, limps, and black eyes of the crew, he was bewildered. An occasional fight between two men was to be expected on a ship. A few days in the brig usually cooled them off. But dammit, from what he could see, every crewman had gotten into this fight, and he could hardly throw the whole bunch in the brig.

When he stepped on the quarter-deck where First Mate Kelly stood, he said, "What in hell happened to the crew? They look like they've been on shore leave."

Kelly stood, staring out at the ocean, his hands

locked behind his back, rocking back and forth on his heels. "Aye, sir, 'twas a bit of a disturbance in the forecastle last night."

Matt glared at the man, who was obviously determined not to look him in the eye. "And why wasn't I informed, Mr. Kelly?"

"Ah, Cap'n, 'twas no need. 'Twas over almost before it began."

Matt was more than a little irritated. It was the first mate's job to keep him informed about anything and everything on his ship, and Kelly had never been derelict in his duty before. Was he still angry with him about their disagreement over the girl yesterday? But the first mate didn't look angry. In fact, he had a smug look on his face. A suspicion took hold in Matt's mind. "May I ask what the disagreement was about?"

Kelly continued to rock back and forth on his heels, his eyes glued to the ocean. "Aye, Cap'n, 'twas about the lass."

"The lass?" Matt snapped.

"Aye, Cap'n. You see, sir, the crew decided to continue the little argument you and the lass had yesterday mornin'," Kelly replied, then continued his silent rocking back and forth.

"And?" Matt asked impatiently.

"Well, sir, half of the crew took your side, and the other half took the lass's side." He shrugged his shoulders, as if dismissing the subject.

Matt glared at his first mate, who continued to stare obstinately out to sea. Then he paced the deck in agitation, thinking, I won't ask. Dammit, I won't give him the satisfaction of asking. But his curiosity got the better of him. He whirled and said in an icy, sarcastic voice, "And would you by any chance know

121

the outcome of that disagreement, Mr. Kelly?"

Kelly turned, a bewildered look on his face. "I beg your pardon, Cap'n?"

"Goddammit! I asked you if you know which side won the fight?" Matt roared.

Kelly's stare was directed over Matt's shoulder now. "Oh, aye, Cap'n, I believe I do." His eyes briefly flicked to Matt's, then away again. " 'Twas the lass's side."

If he so much as smirks, I'll slug him, Matt thought. He glared at the first mate, but Kelly held his mouth firm and continued to stare past him. Matt turned and, as he stepped to the main deck, heard a soft chuckle. He whirled, but Kelly's face was the picture of innocence.

Matt walked angrily across the deck to his cabin. God almighty, was there no end to the problems the girl was creating? It was bad enough that she had humiliated him in front of his crew and that he and his first mate, his best friend no less, were at each other's throats, but now the crew was fighting among themselves because of her. Hell, he was losing control of the whole damn ship. And all because of one small female.

He stormed into the cabin. Leigh was standing in one corner putting up her hammock.

"And what in the hell do you think you're doing?" he barked.

Leigh whirled. She glanced at the furious look on the captain's face; her own face blanched. "I'm— I'm—why, I'm putting up my hammock. I'm sure you want your bunk back."

"Dammit, I'm captain of this ship! You'll sleep where I tell you to sleep. From now on, you'll sleep in my bunk!"

122

Leigh's look was one of total horror. Then she lifted her head proudly, saying, "No, Captain. I don't care what you think of me. I won't do that. You can throw me in the brig, or beat me—but I won't do that!"

For a minute, Matt was bewildered, wondering at her outrage. Then it dawned on him what she was thinking. She thought he meant sleep with him. Matt's eyes swept over her. The thought was tempting, very tempting. He regretted she wasn't O'Neal's doxy. Then he would have no compunction in forcing her to do just that. But she wasn't a whore, so he had better get his mind off that direction.

He tore his eyes away from her and strode to his desk, saying in as cold a voice as he could manage, "I'm not suggesting that, young lady. I'm rather particular about whom I sleep with. I'll sleep in the hammock."

Relief swept over Leigh, then rage as she thought, so he still thinks I'm a whore, a whore not good enough to sleep with him. And him, a pirate no less! Well, since he's damned me in his mind already, I might as well act the part. Recklessly, she said, "Thank you, Captain. I must admit I'm relieved. You see, I'm rather particular about my sleeping partners, myself."

Matt whirled, a surprised look on his face. Had Monique's estimation of her been right after all? His dark eyes slowly undressed her. Despite herself, Leigh trembled under that hot, bold look. Matt saw her tremble and thought in frustration, No, dammit, she's just getting even with me for my insult. He turned away and walked to his chair, an amused smile on his lips, thinking, She's just like a kitten spitting out at me. A harmless, little kitten.

Matt sprawled in his chair, his long legs stretched out before him, his black eyes watching her intently. Leigh lifted her head arrogantly and walked to the bunk, feeling weak after the close call. She shouldn't have baited him like that, she thought. For a minute, she was afraid she had outdone herself. She would have to watch her temper. This wasn't any little boy she was playing games with. This was a man, a very dangerous and, undoubtedly, lusty one.

She sat on the edge of the bunk. Even though she was relieved, his insult still stung. Her female pride was sorely injured. Soothing it, Leigh thought, Why, there are plenty of men that think I'm attractive. I've seen their looks of admiration and, yes, open desire. I know I'm not beautiful, but I had plenty of suitors before I left Boston. And yet, this arrogant captain, this pirate, finds me lacking. Then she remembered what she looked like. No wonder, she thought with self-disgust. With my hair all tangled and my sun-burned face, I must look a mess.

Leigh had no idea just how beautiful and desirable she did look, and had she looked up at that minute, she would have seen the blatant look of admiration in Matt's face. His eyes flicked from her hair, to her face, to her sensuous mouth, down to her breasts—lingering in remembrance—and, finally, down to her legs. There his eyes stayed glued, for when Leigh had sat on the bunk the shirt had hiked up high on her thighs.

For the life of him, Matt couldn't take his eyes off Leigh's smooth, well-shaped legs. He felt the heat rise in him, the familiar stirring in his loins. God almighty, if I don't do something fast, I'm going to embarrass myself, he thought. In desperation, he yelled, "For Christ's sake, if you're not going to lie down in the bunk, put some clothes on!"

Leigh was startled by his yell and looked down at herself, horrified at the sight of her naked legs. Quickly, she scampered to her sea chest to get her breeches.

Oh God, Matt thought in self-disgust, I've got to stop this bellowing. First, I'm yelling she'll sleep in my bunk, and now, I'm yelling for her to put some clothes on. I can well imagine what the crew is thinking now. And Kelly? Hell, he'll probably take a swing at me when I step back on deck.

After Leigh had pulled on her breeches, she turned and, gathering her courage, said, "Have you decided what my punishment is to be, Captain?"

Matt scowled, thinking, Hell, if I so much as lift a finger to her, the crew will probably mutiny. If I survive the beating Kelly would probably give me, that is. He sighed in exasperation, saying, "I don't whip women."

"Then the brig?" Leigh whispered, shuddering in remembrance.

Matt felt another pang of guilt. "No, not the brig."

Leigh looked up, eyes wide with apprehension. "Then what?"

Dammit, Matt thought, why does she have to have such beautiful eyes? Smoky gray, sultry, seductive. No woman with eyes like that had the right to look so innocent. But she did look innocent. Innocent, small, and defenseless. Even if he didn't have the crew and his first mate hanging over his head, he wouldn't have the heart to punish her. He even felt sorry for O'Neal. He imagined, if the girl had a mind to, she could be very winning and convincing. But the last thing he wanted to let her know was how she was affecting him. He knew women. Show them one bit of weak-

125

ness, and they would pounce like a cat. The next thing a man knew, he was being led around with a ring through his nose.

He rose, walked to the door, and said coldly, "I've decided to let the port authorities decide your punishment."

Leigh was stunned. The port authorities? And what would they do? Throw her in prison? Hang her? Her face turned deathly pale.

Let her stew for a while, Matt thought. After all, she deserves some sort of punishment. Later, I'll tell her the truth.

He opened the cabin door, then turned, saying, "By the way, what's your name?"

"Why, Leigh."

"No, I mean your real name."

"But that is my real name."

Matt frowned. "I've never heard of Leigh being used for a female. It's a man's name."

Leigh was taken aback. She had never thought of her name. It was simply her name, the one she had known all her life. And no one else had ever remarked about it being strange. Damn him, every time she turned around, he was calling her a liar. She glared at him saying, "I don't care if you believe me or not. My name is Leigh." She stuck her chin out stubbornly. "Leigh O'Neal."

And she's still sticking to her story about being a bastard, too, Matt thought. Well, I'm not getting into that argument again. He shrugged and said, "Suit yourself. If that's what you want to call yourself, it's fine with me."

Leigh gave him a murderous look as he walked out the door.

For the second day in a row, Matt paced the deck

thinking. He had problems, and again they all centered around Leigh. His first problem was obvious. He had a woman on his ship, an awkward and potentially dangerous situation, particularly since Leigh was so beautiful. Dammit, why couldn't she have been fat, ugly, and cross-eyed? But he knew if the men got desperate enough, even that wouldn't deter them. His most immediate problem was keeping Leigh away from the crew and protecting her.

Of course, Matt had no way of knowing the crew had already solved this problem for him. The half of the crew that had sided with Leigh wouldn't have dreamed of touching her in lust, for their respect for her had reached the point of veneration. To them, Leigh was practically a saint, and even to think about her lustfully would damn them to hell. The other half of the crew, the half that had sided with Matt, had already decided the captain had claimed Leigh as his woman. And none of them was brave enough, or foolish enough, to try to infringe on his territory. So unbeknown to Matt, Leigh was perfectly safe from the crew.

Matt's second problem was more overwhelming, for keeping Leigh away from the crew and getting her off the ship wouldn't solve that one. He hadn't forgotten his promise to O'Neal to take care of her. And the big Irishman had been very precise in his wording. He hadn't said the lad, but Leigh — clearly Leigh. Oh, he knew what he was doing, Matt thought irritably. Dammit, he thought, if I could get my hands on Sean O'Neal right now, I would throttle him for putting me in this position.

Promising to take care of the lad was one thing, but how did he go about taking care of a young woman? If he sent her to one of his uncles in New Orleans,

127

would their wives accept her? As a servant perhaps, but they would never allow her to live in their house as an equal. His uncles' wives were Creole, and in Matt's opinion, the Creole society was even more snobbish than the English ton. Besides, the Creoles were strongly prejudiced, not just against the Irish, but against anyone who wasn't French. They barely accepted him with his quarter-French blood. Yes, they would take Leigh in, but only as a servant.

He considered this possibility. He didn't like the idea of placing Leigh in servitude, but for a temporary solution, it might do. At least until this war was over. Then he could take her back to his family in Charleston. He knew that his mother would welcome the orphaned girl with open arms. In the meanwhile, in his uncle's home, she would be sheltered and safe.

Suddenly, he remembered his male cousins. Like hell, she would be safe! A beautiful young woman around his randy male Creole cousins? He would be damned if he would leave her there!

His mind turned to other possibilities. The Ursuline nuns had a convent on Chartres Street in New Orleans. He knew that they took in orphans because he had donated money himself on several occasions. Would they consider taking in a young woman if he paid them room and board? Leigh would certainly be safe there. But he couldn't see a girl as spirited and stubborn as Leigh in a convent. And he didn't want to see that spirit broken, as he felt sure the nuns would feel obligated to do. He pictured some of the meek, mild-mannered, simpering young women he had known. They disgusted him. No, he couldn't stand to think of Leigh like that.

What if he set her up in a nice little business of her own, Matt thought. A shop of some kind. Hadn't

O'Neal said her mother was a seamstress? He frowned. But what kind of life would that be? Straining her eyes in some dark little room, sewing dresses for other women to wear to parties and balls. And besides, she would have no one to protect her from the world outside, the men that would undoubtedly flock to her door like so many wolves.

Matt shook his head in frustration. What in hell was he going to do with her?

Chapter 7

Three days later, when Matt returned to the cabin, Leigh was dressed in her boy's disguise, her baggy pants, boots, and another ridiculously big, floppy shirt. He watched as she fished her stocking cap out of the sea chest and then sat on the bunk to braid her hair.

He scowled, saying, "And just what do you think you're doing?"

Leigh answered icily, "Why, I'm going to earn my keep, Captain. Since my shoulder is almost healed, I see no reason why I shouldn't resume my duties. I'm going to the galley to help Cookie prepare the noon meal."

"No, you're not!" Matt said in a hard voice. "I'll tell you what your duties are. And helping Cookie in the galley is no longer one of them."

Leigh was stunned, but quickly recovered. "Then just what are my duties?" she snapped.

Matt floundered. "Well—straighten up the cabin

every day and—help me with my prize log every evening."

"That's all?"

Matt nodded.

"And what about the rest of the time?"

He shrugged.

"Then the rest of the time is my own free time?"

"I guess you can say that."

Leigh picked up her cap and headed for the door. Matt grabbed her arm, saying, "Where do you think you're going?"

Leigh turned and said, "To the galley."

"I just told you you're not to go to the galley. I don't want you in the galley."

"No, Captain, you didn't say that. You said helping in the galley was no longer one of my duties, that once I had finished cleaning the cabin in the morning, my time was my own. Well, this is my free time, and I'm volunteering it, and my services, to Cookie in the galley."

"Why?" Matt asked in a dumbfounded voice.

"Why? I'll tell you why! Because preparing and serving that meal is too much for one man, particularly an old man like Cookie. Do you have any idea of how much work that is? Why, Cookie works harder than any ten sailors on this ship! That's why I'm going to help him."

Matt was astonished. He had no idea how much work the old man did. He had assumed that if it was too much, Cookie would complain. But that wasn't his problem right now. He caught Leigh's arm as she opened the door and jerked her back into the cabin. "You're not going to the galley!"

"But why?" Leigh cried.

"Because you're not to leave this cabin."

132

Leigh's face drained of color. "Then I'm a prisoner?"

"No, you're not a prisoner," Matt said in exasperation. "This is not a punishment."

Leigh was stunned. Stay in this small cabin all day and night? With nothing to do? Why, she would go insane! "I'll go stir crazy if you lock me in here."

"I'm not locking you in!" Matt snapped. "I told you, you're not a prisoner. You can go on deck for a couple of hours a day, but only if I or Mr. Kelly accompany you."

"But if you're not punishing me, why are you doing this?" Leigh demanded.

Matt threw his hands up in disgust. "Dammit, woman, are you dense? To protect you from the crew!"

Leigh thought that was the most ridiculous thing she had ever heard. She knew none of the crew would hurt her. They were her friends. Besides, she was never alone with any of them, except Cookie, and he certainly wasn't any danger to her. She laughed harshly, saying, "Oh, come, Captain. Don't you think you're being a little melodramatic? What could possibly happen to me?"

Matt's dark eyes swept over her, his voice was dangerously low. "This is what could happen." Before Leigh could protest, he pulled her roughly into his arms, his mouth crashing down on hers. He had intended the kiss to be punishing, brutal enough to frighten her so she would obey him and stay in the cabin, but taking Leigh into his arms was his undoing. The feel of her soft feminine curves pressed tightly against the hard length of his body and the taste of her honeyed lips made Matt completely forget his intention. His lips softened; the kiss became coaxing, wooing, searching, as his big hands

133

roamed over her hips and back, stroking and caressing her.

Leigh melted under his warm, persuasive kiss, engulfed in a warm, heady sensation, her senses swimming. Her hands trailed up his muscular arms and across his broad shoulders to tangle in the golden hair at the back of his head, as she pressed her body even closer to that heat that threatened to consume her.

Matt's kiss deepened as he hungrily feasted on the sweetness of Leigh's mouth. He cupped her buttocks in his big hands, arching her hips to that hot, throbbing part of him that ached for release. But somewhere in the back of his mind, a tiny voice struggled through the haze of his rapidly rising passion. You've got to stop, he thought. Now, before it's too late. Before there's no turning back.

He tore his lips from hers and pushed her away, and Leigh staggered backward, bewildered and still reeling dizzily. Matt stood, his breathing labored, watching her with hot eyes, every fiber of his body wanting to reach for her again.

"That's why," he managed to say in a hoarse voice. Then he turned and bolted from the cabin.

Both Leigh and Matt were shaken by the encounter. Leigh had convinced herself that her puzzling surrender to Matt that night in the hotel had been due to being taken completely by surprise. But when it happened the second time he had kissed her, she was totally unnerved. She had seemed to melt, totally yielding, a boneless, spineless creature with no will of her own. The realization that she would have surrendered all had he continued, didn't just frighten her. It terrified her.

And Matt had been forced to admit that he still wanted Leigh, despite his anger at her for making a fool of him. But what had shocked him was the intensity of his hunger, a hunger he couldn't satisfy at will, not now when he knew that Leigh was no cheap whore to be taken for a quick tumble and then forgotten.

During the next few days, the tension between them was thick, the small cabin filled with electricity. They both kept their distance, each casting wary glances. An accidental touch sent them both jerking back as if burned. They were overly polite, both careful to keep their tempers in check, each fearing the loss of control of one emotion would trigger passions of a more intimate nature.

To widen the distance between them, Matt spent as little time in the cabin as possible. Instead of accompanying Leigh on her daily strolls on the deck, he assigned the duty to First Mate Kelly. Then he stood back in the shadows, watching them as they walked and talked, his eyes feasting hungrily on Leigh.

Finally, on the fourth day, a diversion occurred that enabled Matt to release at least a portion of his pent-up tension. Two British merchantmen had been sighted and were heading straight for them.

The crew stood on the deck of the *Avenger*, their eyes glued on the two ships that were sailing closer and closer, totally unaware of their danger.

"Run up our colors," Matt called.

The Stars and Stripes rose proudly on the flagstaff of the *Avenger* and snapped in the brisk breeze.

"Run out and load!"

The gun ports crashed open as the big carronades were rolled forward.

Too late, the British merchantmen realized their mistake. Both ships veered sharply to port, running yard to yard for their lives. But the *Avenger* was too swift, swooping down on them like a hawk on its prey.

"Put a warning shot over their bows," Matt called.

One cannon roared, and the shot flew past the bows of the two ships to splash harmlessly in the water beyond them. An answering shot was fired from the first merchantman. The ball splashed in the ocean a few feet from the *Avenger*, short of its mark.

"That goddamned fool!" Matt cursed, then called, "Put a shot into that first ship's bowsprit! Take some of her rigging if you can."

Again, a cannon on the *Avenger* fired. The bowsprit on the merchantman cracked as blocks and tackles fell. A moment later, the flag on the offending ship fluttered down, followed shortly by the flag of the second merchantman.

Leigh had been watching from the companionway. It was no contest at all, she thought. Two shots and the merchantmen cowered like whipped puppies. It certainly wasn't what she had pictured, no rampant destruction, no bloody gore. But still, it was stealing private property—and wrong!

Matt glanced up at that minute and saw Leigh. She shot him a look of pure disgust, then turned, and disappeared into the shadows of the companionway.

He frowned, then thought, To hell with her! Turning, he said to Kelly, "Get a boarding boat on that second ship."

"Aye, Cap'n."

Matt watched as the grappling hooks were thrown to the closer merchantman and then jumped gracefully to its deck. The captain of the British ship was waiting for him, his face suffused with blood.

"Captain Matthew Blake, of the American privateer, the *Avenger*," Matt snapped his introduction at the British captain.

"This is an outrage!" the merchant captain raged.

"It's bloody piracy. Why, you bastard, I'll see you hung for this!"

Matt held out his hand, saying in a hard voice that brooked no argument, "Your manifest, Captain."

One look at the steely look in Matt's eyes reduced the captain's objections to impotent sputtering. He fumbled in his pocket and handed the ship's manifest to Matt.

"Thank you, Captain," Matt said, his smile mocking. He turned, then whirled back, catching the captain off guard. His eyes glittered dangerously. "Firing that shot at me was a fool's stunt, Captain. You're damned lucky I didn't blow you clean out of the water!"

The captain's face blanched. Matt gave him a disgusted look, turned to one of his crew, and said, "Lock him and the rest of the crew in the hold."

"Aye, Cap'n." Grinning, the sailor pushed the outraged British captain before him, saying, "Get along with ye!"

Matt vaulted back over the rail to the *Avenger*, where Kelly waited. When he stood beside him, Kelly asked, "Will you be sendin' the lass back with the prizes, Cap'n?"

Matt frowned. He knew the best thing for all concerned, Leigh, him, and the crew, was to get her off the *Avenger*. But he still hadn't decided where to send her in New Orleans. More important, he didn't like the idea of putting her on board one of the prizes with six of his crew. Oh, he could handpick them, choose six of his most trustworthy men, but considering how Leigh had affected him, he seriously doubted if any man could be immune to her charms. He shuddered to think what might happen to her.

He glared at Kelly and snapped, "Are you crazy! Put an innocent young woman aboard with a bunch of women-hungry sailors!"

Kelly's bushy eyebrows rose in surprise. So the captain had changed his opinion about the lass after all. Now she's innocent. He gave Matt an oblique, penetrating look. Matt wanted her for himself, he realized. That explained why he had been pacing like a caged tiger this past week. Kelly frowned. He could suggest putting the lass on board with some of her supporters. Kelly knew that they wouldn't harm the lass. But he had noticed the way the lass looked at Matt when the captain's back was turned. No, the attraction wasn't all one-sided. Kelly was fond of the lass and thought if any woman could bring his arrogant, young friend to his knees, this lass could. It was high time Matt settled down to one woman. He pondered a minute, then decided. "Aye, sir. I think you're right."

Matt turned and walked across the deck to his cabin, throwing over his shoulder, "Bring the manifest on that second ship as soon as you can. I want to get them copied and send the prizes on their way as quickly as possible."

"Aye, I'll go over and bring it back, myself," Kelly replied.

When Matt entered the cabin, Leigh was busy stuffing her belongings into her sea bag. "What do you think you're doing?" he asked.

Leigh shot him a heated look, saying, "I should think that would be obvious, Captain. I'm packing. You said I'd leave with the first prize you sent in."

"Well, you can just unpack. You're not going!" Matt snapped.

"Not going? Why?"

"Because there's too much danger of the prizes being recaptured by the British," Matt lied smoothly. "These waters are well patrolled. If we're closer to

138

New Orleans when we take the next prize, you'll go on that."

Leigh sat back on her sea chest, stunned. She had prepared herself to accept whatever punishment the port authorities in New Orleans decided to give her. Now, she wasn't going. At first, she was relieved by the reprieve, but then she wondered if it wouldn't have been easier to get it over with. Now she had more time to worry about it.

Matt sat at his desk and started copying the manifest, ignoring Leigh. He was almost through when Kelly walked into the cabin and handed him the second manifest, saying, "Sorry it took so long, Cap'n, but the captain on that second ship was a stubborn old cuss and wouldn't tell us where he had hidden it. We had to search for it."

Matt reached for the document without looking up.

Kelly winked at Leigh, then said, "Ah, Cap'n, I took the liberty of bringin' these back for the lass. I found them in the captain's trunk when I was lookin' for the manifest."

Matt looked up. Kelly held several women's garments in his hands, a pair of sandals dangled from one finger.

Kelly grinned and leaned forward, whispering so Leigh couldn't hear, "The old geezer claimed he was takin' them back to his daughters as souvenirs, but I'd guess they were left behind by his Spanish doxy."

Matt looked more closely at the garments. Yes, they did look like the blouses and skirts worn by the Spanish peasant women. He wondered what Leigh would look like in honest-to-God women's clothing. Christ, he was tired of seeing her in those baggy pants and that floppy shirt. He nodded, saying, "Toss them on the bunk."

Matt picked up and copied the second manifest. Then he handed both documents to Kelly, saying, "Have you got the prize crews picked?"

"Aye, they're on board and ready to leave as soon as I hand them these manifests."

"Good. Tell them I wish them luck and I'll see them in New Orleans in a couple of months."

"Aye, Cap'n." Kelly turned and walked to the door. Then he turned back and said to Leigh, "Ah, lass, I almost forgot." He fumbled in his shirt pocket, pulled out a small package, and handed it to her. Grinning, he said, "Compliments of the British captain, lass."

Leigh stared down at the package, saying, "What is it?"

" 'Tis scented soap, lass," Kelly replied, then walked out of the cabin.

Leigh stared at the package, thinking, Why it's stolen property! Revolted, she tossed it aside.

Matt finished his notes and sat back. Seeing Leigh sitting on her sea chest, he frowned, then said, "Aren't you even curious about your new clothes?"

Leigh looked disgustedly at the garments on the bed, then snapped, "They're not *my* clothes. They're pirate's loot!"

Matt sighed deeply, and said in an exasperated voice, "I'm not a pirate. I'm a privateer."

"Pirate and privateer are the same to me. They're stolen property, and I won't wear them!" she retorted hotly, her eyes flashing.

Matt's own temper rose. He leaned across the desk, his eyes spitting black sparks, saying, "Oh, yes, you will wear them. I'm tired of seeing you in those breeches. They're disgusting!"

Leigh wavered. The breeches were a disgraceful thing for a woman to be wearing. Terribly unladylike. She glanced at the clothes on the bunk. How she would love to wear skirts again. These damned breeches chafed her legs something awful. But still . . . She raised her chin and said, "I won't wear those clothes."

Matt rose and walked toward her, his black eyes boring into her, his mouth set in a tight, firm line. Leigh longed to cower back, but she held her ground stubbornly.

He stopped and glared down at her, saying, "Either you'll put on those clothes yourself or, so help me God, Leigh, I'll strip those damned boy's clothes from you and dress you myself!"

One look at Matt's determined look, and Leigh knew he would do just that. She would have to back down, but, God, it galled her. If only she could extract something from him in exchange, something that would make her yielding not look so much like a defeat. A small glimmer lit her eyes. "All right, Captain, I'll wear the clothes," she said, then added, "on one condition."

Matt eyed her suspiciously. "What condition?"

"That you let me borrow your bathtub."

Matt's golden eyebrows rose in surprise. Then a slow smile spread over his handsome face. "Agreed," he said, turning to leave the cabin.

It took Leigh a minute to recover from Matt's smile, that same devastating smile that always left her weak-kneed. Finally, she turned and headed for the door, excited at the prospect of a real bath. Before she could open it, the door banged open, and Matt entered, carrying the tub. Leigh watched him, resenting the ease with which he carried it and the fact that he had brought it to her. Now, he was making it look as though he was doing her a favor. "I could have gotten it myself," she snapped.

"It's too heavy for you," Matt said, setting the tub

down with a grunt.

Leigh couldn't believe her ears. Oh, yes, it was fine for *her* to push, shove, and tug on that damned tub when it was for *him* to bathe in. Now, suddenly, it's too heavy, as if she had shrunk in the meantime. She glared at him.

Matt guessed her thoughts and had the grace to look a little sheepish. Then he walked to the door, saying, "I'll tell Cookie to heat some water for you." He turned and grinned. "But I'd better warn you. Prepare yourself for a lecture from him on the evils of bathing."

Despite Leigh's frustration at Matt turning what she had hoped to be a compromise into a favor, she enjoyed her bath immensely. For a long while, she just lay in the hot water, relaxing. Eventually, she picked up the strong lye soap and looked at it with disgust. Her eyes drifted to the package of scented soap, her look hungry. There was no use in letting it go to waste, she rationalized. After all, wasting was as big a sin as stealing. She stepped from the bathtub and padded across the cabin. One sniff of the sweet smelling soap broke down what little reluctance she had left. Smiling, she carried the bar back to the tub with her.

She scrubbed herself until her skin was red and shining. Then she washed her long hair, not once, but twice, until it was squeaky clean. She lay back in the cold water, thinking. I don't care if it is salt water. Just getting all that dirt and soap residue off me is a blessed relief.

After she had dried herself off and wrapped herself in a towel, she examined the clothing on the bunk critically. There were three white, scooped-necked blouses, all embroidered at the neck, and three full skirts. They were worn, the colors of the skirts faded, but they were clean. She picked up one blouse and a green skirt and put them on. She looked down at herself in dismay. The clothing swallowed her, the blouse hung halfway down her arms and the skirt hung on her hips and dragged on the floor.

Leigh wasn't the daughter of a seamstress for nothing. She quickly cut the excess material from the skirt and hemmed it. Then she took in the seams at the waistband and put several large tucks in the neckline of the blouse. Slipping the clothes on, Leigh surveyed her work. Not bad, she thought. She walked around the room, almost dancing, relishing the feel of the skirt swaying against her legs. It feels so wonderful, she thought, so free, so good not to have those rough breeches rubbing against my thighs.

She sat down on the bunk and brushed her hair until it shone and crackled with electricity. As she started to braid it, she hesitated. She had never worn braids before she had disguised herself as a boy. She spied the remnant of green material on the floor and smiled. She picked it up, tore it into a ribbon and tied her hair at the nape of her neck.

She glanced at the sandals. They were obviously too big for her. She looked at her heavy boots, her nose wrinkling with distaste. No, I'll go barefooted before I'll wear them again, she vowed.

She looked with disgust at the dirty boy's clothes she had taken off. I'll throw them away, she thought. Her brow furrowed. No, she decided, that would be wasteful. Besides, she could use the shirt for her nightgown. No sense in wrinkling her new clothes by sleeping in them.

When Matt walked in that evening and saw Leigh, his breath caught in his throat. Trying to keep from devouring her with his eyes, he said cautiously, "I must say that's quite an improvement."

Leigh preened under his frankly admiring look. Oddly, all animosity against the captain had disappeared, as if it, along with the dirt, had been washed away with the bath. For the first time in weeks, she felt human, feminine, wonderful. She smiled, her eyes twinkling, and said, "Thank you, Captain. I admit I feel much better."

Matt was vastly relieved. Thank God, she wasn't still angry with him. He had walked into the cabin not knowing what to expect. In fact, he had anticipated finding Leigh still dressed in her filthy boy's clothes. She was undoubtedly the most unpredictable and stubborn woman he had ever met.

He sat on the bunk, feeling more relaxed than he had felt in days. "I was wondering how you'd feel about working on the prize log tonight."

Leigh frowned. She had planned to alter the rest of her new clothing tonight. But she was feeling too good to be disagreeable. Besides, they hadn't worked on the ledger for a long time, not since the day of the sea battle and her injury. She smiled and said, "All right."

As they worked, Matt realized that he had made a mistake. He couldn't keep his eyes off Leigh or his mind on his work. Every time she walked from the desk to the bunk to pick up the papers Matt was sorting, he was acutely conscious of the graceful sway of her hips. The lamplight brought out the reddish highlights of her newly washed hair, and Matt longed to run his fingers through that glorious mass of curls. And when Leigh leaned over the ledger to write, the low-necked blouse gaped open, and he sat with his eyes glued to the sight of the soft swell of her full breasts, remembering how they had looked naked.

He felt the heat rise in him and, fearing his body would betray him, quickly made an excuse to go back on deck. There, he paced restlessly, agitated at his own lack of control.

He didn't go back to the cabin until late, when he was sure the lamp would be out and Leigh asleep. He hung the hammock, cursing himself for a coward and a fool, and then lay staring up at the ceiling in the darkness. Visions of Leigh as she had looked that evening tormented him. He remembered the feel of her soft body in his arms both times he had kissed her and the sweet taste of her mouth. Feeling his manhood straining impatiently at his breeches and, knowing that release for that discomfort lay only a few feet away from him, he groaned in frustration, rolled from the hammock, and crept from the cabin. That night, Matt slept on a pile of canvas in a secluded spot on deck.

The next day was unseasonably warm. By afternoon, not a breath of air stirred. Matt watched the sky apprehensively. Just as the sun was setting, a wind came up, and a line of dark, angry thunderheads appeared on the horizon. Matt considered outrunning the storm, then decided it would be a wasted effort, as the storm was approaching rapidly. He ordered the sails reefed and waited.

Lightning cracked, thunder rolled, and the rain came in torrents, but there was surprisingly little wind in the storm. Matt was grateful for the lack of wind. This was the first rain they had had since the terrible storm a month before, and their freshwater supply was getting dangerously low. He ordered the empty water barrels brought on deck and the sails reset to funnel the rain into the barrels in order to catch every possible drop of the precious liquid.

By midnight, the squall line had passed, and only an occasional flash of lightning remained. Matt headed for his cabin to put on dry clothing and then

145

find someplace to sleep below deck. The cabin was pitch dark as Matt slipped off his wet boots and clothes and slipped into a dry pair of breeches. He grabbed a shirt and walked to the door.

A small whimper alerted him. It came from the direction of his bunk. "Is that you, Leigh?" he whispered.

Silence. Then another strange, choked sound reached his ears. He peered into the darkened corner, but could see nothing. Something was wrong, he knew. He quickly lit the lamp and turned to the bunk.

Leigh was crouched in the corner of the bunk, trembling violently, her eyes wide and staring into space. A streak of lightning flashed, and she cowered even lower, a pitiful whimper escaping her throat.

She is afraid of the storm, Matt realized. Then he remembered that she had been alone in this small cabin during the last storm. She must have been terrified. And then, they had told her about her uncle's death. Why, no wonder she is so afraid, he thought with pity.

He sat on the bunk, saying softly, "It's all right, Leigh. The storm has passed. It's over." Gently, he tried to pull her from the corner. "Come on, Leigh. It's all over. Come here."

Like a frightened little animal, she crawled to him. Matt pulled her onto his lap, soothing her with gentle hands, saying, "It's all over, Leigh. I wouldn't be here in the cabin if there was any danger. It was just a little squall."

Matt sat holding the frightened girl for a long while, talking to her in a soothing voice, his hands stroking her head and arms. Leigh huddled like a child into the warmth and security of his arms. Finally, her trembling subsided, and the pitiful, little whimpers ceased. Matt felt her body relaxing, and then she was so still he thought she had gone to sleep in his arms.

"Leigh," he whispered, "are you awake?"

She nodded against his chest.

"Are you feeling better?"

Another nod.

"You're not afraid any more?"

"No," she answered in a small voice.

Before, Matt had felt only compassion for Leigh, but now his body was responding to the feel of her softness against him. The last thing he wanted to do was betray her trust. Gently, he shoved her off his lap and laid her back down on the bunk, saying, "Now try to get some sleep. There's nothing to be afraid of."

Matt started to leave, but Leigh caught his arm. "Don't go," she murmured.

So she knew he hadn't slept in the cabin last night, Matt thought. He smiled, saying, "No, I won't leave the cabin. I'll be right there in my hammock all night if you should need me."

Again, he started to rise, but Leigh's hand tightened on his arm. "No, don't go!" she cried.

Matt looked down at her, not sure he knew what she meant. Her eyes were imploring. "Stay here . . . please," she whispered.

"You're still afraid?"

She bit her lip and nodded.

Matt hesitated. She looked so beautiful—and so damned desirable. Cursing his baser nature, he lay down beside her, but didn't make any attempt to take her back in his arms. He lay rigidly, staring at the ceiling, clenching his teeth.

After a few minutes, Matt realized that there was no way he could lie passively beside her. He was too aware of her heat, her thigh pressing against his, the sweet tempting scent of her. His blood was pounding in his ears, his heart racing, his loins aching.

He started to rise, but Leigh cried, "No, don't leave!"

He turned on his side and looked down into her stricken face, saying in an agonized voice, "You don't understand, Leigh. I can't lie here beside you. I want you—too much . . . I just can't."

She said nothing, just stared at him, her eyes pleading.

A groan escaped Matt's throat as his head descended. He kissed her brow, her eyelids, her temples, the small dimple in her chin. He buried his head in her neck, savoring the smell of her hair, muttering, "Oh, Leigh. Sweet, sweet Leigh."

Leigh made no effort to resist. She was already drowning in that warm vortex. Instinctively, she lifted her arms to him.

He nuzzled her throat and kissed the pulse beat below her ear, then the one at the base of her throat, his lips lingering. Then he lifted his head and gazed into her smoky-gray eyes, his own dark ones smoldering with desire. He buried his hands in her hair, holding her head while he nibbled at her lips, teasing, softly playing, until Leigh was trembling for want of that warm, mobile mouth on hers. Finally, he kissed her, deeply, masterfully, passionately, his tongue hungry for the taste of her mouth.

Matt's hands slid down to caress her shoulders and back. With trembling fingers, he unbuttoned her shirt. One hand cupped her soft breast, his fingers teasing the rosy nipple to hardness. His mouth left hers, and he bent his head to kiss those soft mounds, his lips closing over one sensitive peak, rolling it around his tongue. Leigh moaned with pleasure, tangling her hands in his golden hair to pull his head even closer.

148

Leigh was whirling from the new and exciting sensations Matt was arousing in her. When his hard, naked body pressed against hers, her blood turned molten, pounding in her ears. It seemed as if every inch of her were on fire as his knowing hands fondled and caressed and then stroked the delicate skin on the inside of her thighs, higher and higher. She gasped, shocked at being touched so intimately. "No!" Her hand flew down to stay his, but already his fingers were working their magic, stroking, teasing, delicately exploring the secrets of her womanhood. Her hand fell limply to her side as wave after wave of new sensations washed over her.

Leigh was only vaguely aware when Matt moved over her, his knee gently nudging her thighs apart. And then, she felt something hot and throbbing against her soft womanhood.

Trembling with effort to control his own raging passions, Matt approached slowly, cautiously, until he felt the resistance of her maidenhood. Then, with one powerful thrust, he parted that thin veil and buried himself deep inside her warmth.

Leigh felt as if she had been impaled with a hot poker. A searing pain tore through her loins. She arched away in shock, crying out, "No! Stop!"

Matt groaned, then whispered, "Sssh, Leigh."

"Stop it! You're hurting me!" Leigh sobbed, twisting to get out from under him.

"Lie still," he rasped. "You're only making it hurt more."

But Leigh was past the point of reasoning. She sobbed, pushing at his chest, pounding on his shoulders. "Stop it! Stop!"

Matt could no more stop at that point than he could stop a fall in mid-descent. Leigh's thrashing and twisting were rapidly pushing him to the brink.

He decided the most merciful thing to do was to end it quickly. Grabbing her hips and holding them tightly, he moved against her and, after several deep, powerful thrusts, found his release, shuddering in its intensity and collapsing weakly over her.

Leigh was trembling beneath him, sobbing incoherently. He raised himself on his elbows and whispered, "Sssh, sweet, it's over." Tenderly, he kissed away her tears and then her lips. Then he lifted himself up and out of her and rolled to his side, comforting her and whispering endearments while she sobbed herself to sleep in his arms.

When Leigh awakened the next morning, she was alone in the cabin. She pushed back the sheet, sat up, and looked about her groggily. She glanced down at herself. Why, she was naked! Then, seeing the blood smears on her thighs, everything came rushing back. "Oh God," she murmured.

She remembered the storm, her terror, Matt comforting her, and then . . . He hurt me, she thought. I told him no. I told him to stop. Yes, he is a pirate, a thief, and now he has robbed me of my maidenhood. Bastard! Rapist!

In Leigh's mind, she refused to accept her part in the intimate encounter. She forgot how she had clung to Matt, pressed herself against his naked body, her moans of pleasure and all of the new wonderful sensations he had brought her. All she chose to remember was the end—and her pain. A little voice within her objected, saying, No, it wasn't like that. But Leigh repulsed the thought, pushed it back. No, it was all his fault!

She rose from the bed and washed herself, scrubbing furiously at the bloodstains, still raging. I hate him! When he comes to apologize, I'll spit in his face. Apologize? Will he apologize? No, of course not. He thought me a whore, didn't he? But still, he had no right to force me.

She dressed and paced the small cabin angrily, still ranting and raving, planning her revenge. The minute he walks in, I'll scratch and claw and kick and bite. I'll teach him! He'll be sorry. He'll be very sorry! But much to Leigh's frustration, Matt never came to the cabin that day.

That evening, when Kelly came to escort her on deck, she went eagerly. Now is my chance for revenge, she thought. She would denounce him before the whole crew. But when she got on deck, Matt was nowhere to be seen. She looked around her angrily and saw the crew's curious looks. Suddenly, she realized she could never denounce the captain publicly. It would be too embarrassing. Besides, if they thought her a whore too, they might not believe her or, worse yet, laugh in her face. She couldn't stand the thought of yet another humiliation.

She returned to the cabin early, feeling defeated before she had even begun. Finally, exhaustion forced her to the bunk. She lay there, still raging in her mind. Tonight. Of course. He will come sneaking back tonight. But I will be waiting for him. Oh yes, Captain Matthew Blake, you are in for a big surprise if you try to force me again! You black-hearted pirate! But Leigh's wait was in vain. She finally fell asleep at dawn, totally exhausted.

She awakened that afternoon. Most of her rage had been drained from her, but she still felt frustrated at not being able to get her revenge and, perversely, piqued that Matt hadn't come to her in the night. To Leigh, it was an insult to her womanly charms, yet another humiliation. And to think that I thought he was attracted to me, she thought bitterly. Why, I was nothing but an object for his lust! And now, he is no longer interested.

Later that afternoon, when Leigh went on deck with Kelly, she glanced about furtively for Matt. Again, the captain was nowhere to be seen. Maybe he is ashamed of himself after all, she thought. Then she heard voices above her and looked up. Two men were high in the rigging of the mainmast, setting sail. One was Matt.

He was barefooted and bare-chested, the wind whipping his golden hair about his tanned face. With breathtaking grace, he swung from one rigging to the next, the muscles in his back rippling in the bright sunshine. Leigh flushed, suddenly remembering the feel of those muscles under her hands when he made love to her.

He stopped on a main yard and glanced down. Spying Leigh, he stood looking down at her. Leigh staggered under that bold, hot look, feeling as if he had reached out and touched her. That same weak, warm feeling rushed over her. Yes, he was a devil, all right, she thought. He didn't even have to touch her, and she was powerless. The realization made her feel even weaker. She clutched the rail for support, looking quickly away.

Kelly glanced at her at that minute. "What's wrong, lass? You're as pale as a ghost. Are you ailing?"

"No, no," Leigh muttered. Then, smiling weakly, she said, "I just didn't get much sleep last night. I think I'll go back to the cabin and rest."

"Aye, lass," Kelly said, watching her with concern as she walked across the deck.

Leigh was sleeping when Matt entered the cabin that night. She didn't hear him when he lit the lamp and stood looking down at her, his eyes bold and admiring. Nor did she awaken when he undressed, blew out the lamp, and crawled into the bunk.

It wasn't until she felt his naked thigh against hers that she awakened. With sudden, shocking clarity, she realized she had been caught. She lurched away, crying, "No! Get out!"

"Leigh, don't be frightened. It's just me," Matt whispered.

He reached for her, but Leigh backed farther into the corner, until she felt the wall at her back. "Stay away from me, you—you rapist!"

"Rapist?" Matt asked in an astonished voice. "What in the hell are you talking about?" he hissed.

"As if you don't know," Leigh replied bitterly. "I told you no. I told you to stop." A little sob tore from her throat. "You hurt me!"

Matt winced, then said softly, "I know I did, Leigh, and I'm sorry. Believe me, I took no pleasure in that. But you were a virgin, and a woman always experiences some discomfort the first time. Why do you think I've avoided you all this time? I knew you were probably still sore, and I didn't trust myself around you. I didn't want to hurt you again. But I promise you, it won't hurt this time."

"This time?" Leigh cried, flattening herself against the wall. "No, not again. You'll never force me again!"

"Dammit, Leigh," Matt said angrily, "stop playing games. I didn't force you! You and I both know that!"

"But—"

Matt ignored her objection, saying, "I'm not talking about the end. I've already told you that couldn't be helped. I'm talking about before that. You can't deny you enjoyed it, Leigh. You were clutching me, moaning, begging me not to stop."

That niggardly, little voice inside her head said, See, I told you so. Leigh shook her head, whispering,

"I don't remember."

"Don't remember?" Matt asked in disbelief. His dark eyes narrowed. "Well, then, let me refresh your memory."

With lightning speed, he reached out and pulled her down beside him, pinning her with his big body. Leigh twisted and thrashed under him, but the more she struggled, the more aware she became of his body, his broad bare chest, the muscular naked thigh thrown across her legs, his heady scent that made her senses reel.

"Why are you trembling, Leigh?" Matt whispered, his hot breath fanning her neck. "Are you afraid? . . . Or are you remembering?"

Tears of frustration burned Leigh's eyes. She choked back a sob.

"Remember?" His hands trailed down the length of her body, a long, tantalizing caress. His lips nibbled at her throat and earlobe, then played at the corners of her mouth. Then he was kissing her, softly at first, then with deep, demanding, possessive kisses that left her breathless and gasping for air.

His head descended, leaving a fiery trail of kisses down her throat and over her shoulders to her naked breasts. Leigh's eyes flew open in shock. When had he unbuttoned her shirt?

"Remember this?" Matt taunted softly as his lips and tongue teased one rosy tip, then the other. Waves of delicious pleasure washed over her. Yes, she thought, he is a devil. He knows he has me in his spell, and he's throwing it in my face.

Undeterred, Matt continued his sensuous assault, his hands and lips and tongue doing wonderful, exciting things to her. And when his hand slid between her thighs, she eagerly arched to meet it.

Matt smiled knowingly and whispered in her ear,

"Tell me you don't like what I'm doing, Leigh. Tell me to stop and I will. Just say the word, sweet. Say 'stop.' "

But Leigh couldn't speak; she could hardly breathe with Matt's skillful fingers playing at her, teasing her, caressing her. She moaned.

This time when Matt moved over her, Leigh knew what to expect. She felt the brush of his long, throbbing manhood against her thigh and then that moist, hot tip against her softness. She held her breath, waiting for the pain. But Matt didn't plunge into her as she had expected. He knelt, poised over her, teasing and slowly circling at the gateway to her womanhood, exciting her in the same way his fingers had done earlier. Then he bent, kissing her with such intensity and fire that all thought deserted her. And as she was spinning dizzily, his hands slid down and cupped her buttocks, lifting her as he slid into her with one smooth motion.

His movements were slow, masterful, exquisitely sensuous, touching and awakening nerve endings Leigh never dreamed existed. Then his movements quickened, deeper, bold, powerful strokes that lifted her to spiraling, breathtaking heights, higher and higher, until she felt herself splintering, shattering as she plunged over the brink before drifting back down on a soft warm cloud.

When reality returned, Leigh sobbed softly, not from pain, but from a mixture of emotions: awe at what she had experienced, fright at its intensity, and shame for what she had done. Again, Matt kissed her tears away, rolled to his side, and pulled her into his arms. And Leigh snuggled to him for comfort, completely forgetting that he was the man she had raged at and damned for the past two days. She lay curled against his big warm body, passively allowing his

155

gentle hands and lips to soothe her. Not until his hand cupped her breast, gently massaging, did she realize that Matt's intended method of comforting her was to be a repetition of what had just occurred. It was already too late to object.

Chapter 8

The small cabin was flooded with bright sunshine when Leigh awakened the next morning. She stretched lazily, totally unaware of the contented smile on her face, and rolled to her side. For a brief minute, she luxuriated in Matt's lingering scent on the sheet beside her. Then the memories of the previous night came flooding back to her.

She lay back, her thoughts racing through her head. *He admitted that he knew I was a virgin that first time. Not only did he not apologize or act the least bit ashamed, he had the audacity to force me again.* Come now, Leigh, the irritating little voice inside her head said firmly. At least be honest with yourself. He didn't force you. And have you forgotten how you acted? A little wanton, don't you think? Leigh remembered all too well and blushed in shame.

Suddenly, the door opened, and Matt strolled in. Leigh was so surprised by his unexpected appearance that she sat up and gasped, "What are you doing here?"

His dark eyes swept over her appreciatively. He smiled, saying, "This is my cabin, remember?" He sat on the edge of the bunk and leaned forward to kiss her. Leigh jerked her head away. "What? No good-morning kiss, sweet? Is that any way to greet your lover?" he chided softly.

Leigh's head snapped around, her look outraged. "I'm not your—"

Matt cut off her words with a kiss, a very thorough kiss. Then he laid her back against the pillows, saying huskily, "As much as I'd like to crawl back in there with you, sweet, I'm afraid I can't. It's almost time for my watch." His eyes drifted down and lingered. "So be a good girl and cover up. I can't talk to you with that lovely view distracting me."

Leigh glanced down and realized that her breasts were bared. Blushing furiously, she snatched the covers up, holding them tightly under her chin, her eyes shooting daggers at him.

Matt chuckled and rose from the bunk. He walked to his desk, saying, "I've come to tell you my plans for us."

Us? What was he talking about, she thought, eyeing him warily.

Matt sat on the edge of the desk and swung one leg casually, his arms crossed over his broad chest. "You know, ever since I discovered your true identity, I've been trying to figure how I was going to take care of you."

"Take care of me?" Leigh snapped impatiently. "What are you talking about?"

"Why, the promise I made your uncle before he died. Don't tell me you've forgotten that, too?"

"No, but—"

Matt brushed aside her objection, saying, "What a fool I was, when the solution to the whole problem was so obvious. You're a beautiful, exciting," he leaned forward to emphasize his next words, "and a

158

passionate young woman. A woman any man would be proud to have as his mistress."

Mistress? Leigh was so shocked she was speechless. She gaped in astonishment.

"I have a nice town house in New Orleans," Matt continued. "You can stay there while I'm at sea. I'll hire you a few house servants, buy you a team of horses and carriage, if you like."

So, he hadn't planned to turn her over to the port authorities after all. That had been an empty threat all along. No, he had his own dark plans for her. Well, she would be damned if she would be his mistress!

Outraged, she jumped from the bed, wrapping the sheet haphazardly around her, and shrieked, "Why, you conceited ape! What in God's name makes you think I'd be your mistress? You? A bloody pirate?"

"Privateer, dammit!" Matt yelled. He stood, reached out, and jerked her to him. "And I don't remember your objecting to me last night. Or are you going to deny it? Again?"

"Last night? What has that got to do with it?"

Matt grinned. "*That*, my sweet, has a lot to do with a man's choosing his mistress. Surely, you're not that naive. Besides, I promised your uncle I'd take care of you."

"Forget what you promised my uncle! Did it ever occur to you that I might have some plans of my own for my life?"

Matt frowned and then said sarcastically, "Oh? And just what grand plans do you have, Leigh? Marriage to some poor fool, who'll keep you barefoot and pregnant, working yourself to the bone, so that by the time you're thirty you'll be an old woman?"

"No! I'm going to England to find my father."

159

"That again!" Matt spat in disgust.

Leigh's eyes flashed dangerously. "I don't care what you believe. I do have a father in England! And I'm going to find him!" She lifted her head proudly, saying in an icy voice, "So, you see, Captain Blake, you don't have to worry about taking care of me. I have a father who will do that."

She gave a haughty toss of her head and whirled away from him. When Matt failed to respond, she looked back over her shoulder to see his rapt expression. Glancing down, she realized, with profound embarrassment, what he was staring at. Her whole backside was exposed to his view.

Blushing hotly, she turned and rearranged the sheet hastily, conscious of Matt's hot eyes on her. She glared at him, snapping, "Did you hear me, Captain? I said, I'm going to England to find my father!"

It took a minute for Matt to recover from the distraction. "And may I ask just how you're going to manage all this?"

"I'm going to take the money my mother left me and buy passage to England. Then—"

"Oh? What money?" Matt interjected.

Leigh was stunned. Was he going to steal her money, too? Her instincts about him had been right all along. He was a thief. "The money my uncle gave to you to hold for him. It's mine! It came from my mother to buy our passage to England!"

Matt shrugged. "Oh, that money. And then?"

"Why—why find my father." Leigh stammered. He hadn't denied the money. Did that mean he would give it to her when they reached port after all?

"How?"

Leigh was still distracted. "What?"

"I said how are you going to find this man? You

160

don't even know his name."

"But I have his ring. I'll find him."

Crazy little fool, chasing dreams, Matt thought. "What are you going to do if you don't find him?"

"I'll find him!" Leigh insisted.

He hated to do it, but someone had to force her to face reality. "All right, Leigh. Suppose you do find him. Suppose you even convince him you're his daughter. So what? Do you actually think he's going to welcome you with open arms? Acknowledge you? Are you weaving fairy tales, Leigh? Imagining he'll take you into his grand house, dress you in beautiful clothes, introduce you to London's elite society, perhaps arrange a distinguished marriage for you to some other nobleman?"

Matt's caustic words were like a slap in the face to Leigh. Tears stung her eyes. Would her father deny her? Then she remembered what her mother had told her. Her mother wouldn't lie to her. "What do you know? You don't know my father!"

"No, I don't," Matt replied calmly. "But I've met a few noblemen in my life, and I can tell you that the majority of them have the morals of a tomcat. They bed a wench and forget her the minute they're crawling out of her bed. My God, Leigh, if a man can't even remember the woman, how can you expect him to acknowledge her child?"

"It wasn't like that. My father loved my mother."

Pity for Leigh tempered Matt's words. "Perhaps, your mother really believed that. Women always make more of an affair than there is to it. They want to believe the man loves them. Or perhaps, your father told her he loved her. But, Leigh, men often say things they don't mean in the heat of their passion."

161

Was it true? Had her father's vow of love come in the heat of his passion? Perhaps he had even lied to her mother to get her to go to bed with him. For the first time, she had doubts.

"Don't you see how foolish it would be to go looking for your father? Even if you found him, there's a good possibility he won't acknowledge you. Then you'll be left in a strange country with no friends or relatives, and probably no money. What would you do then? Become a servant yourself and become prey to men like that? Or find a job in one of those workhouses?"

"And I suppose you think what you're offering me is better?" Leigh asked bitterly.

"Yes, I do," Matt replied smoothly. "As my mistress, you'll be under my protection. You'll have a comfortable home, beautiful clothes, servants of your own." He grinned. "And of course, you'll have my charming company."

Company, ha! Leigh thought. Your lust, you mean! She glared at him.

"Come on, Leigh, be reasonable. You'll be well taken care of. I'm not exactly a poor man, you know, and I can be generous."

Why, I would be nothing but a pet, she thought in horror. A pampered pet in a gilded cage. There for him to play with when the notion struck him.

Matt continued. "When I'm in port, I'll take you to dinner parties and balls—"

"You'd take your mistress to dinner parties and balls?" Leigh blurted in a shocked voice.

Matt laughed, saying, "New Orleans isn't Boston, Leigh. Until a few years ago, it was inhabited almost exclusively by Creoles, people of French or Spanish origin. They've a continental attitude about such

162

things. Mistresses are an accepted fact of life. I'd wager that almost every one of them has a mistress or has had at some time or another. There are certain parties, balls, and social occasions where it's perfectly acceptable for a man to bring his mistress."

Yes, Leigh thought with disgust, I can just see it. The mistresses, the pampered trained pets, waiting in one room, while the men have their after-dinner port in the library, discussing whose pet can do the most tricks. It's the most revolting thing I've ever heard of! She turned and spat, "I don't give a damn what they do in New Orleans. I said 'no'! I won't be your mistress!"

No? Matt was astonished at her refusal. He knew a score or more women who would jump at the chance to be his mistress. And this stubborn little chit was telling him 'no'? Why, the little fool! What does she know of the real world out there? Doesn't she realize how hard it is for the Irish? The best she could hope for was marriage to some poor bloke or to be a rich man's mistress. And if she's going to be any man's mistress, she might as well be his. At least he would do right by her when it was all over.

He gave her a hard look, saying in a determined voice, "I'm afraid it's too late to say 'no.' I've already decided. You will be my mistress."

Leigh's eyes widened. "You'd force me?"

Matt's eye glimmered with amusement. "I think we've already been through that. No, my sweet, I may have to be a bit persuasive, a little coaxing perhaps, but I won't have to force you."

Oh, that devil! Leigh thought. How I hate him! Throwing my weakness in my face again! "You can't do that! You can't force me to be your mistress."

Matt's black eyes narrowed. "Can't I? Who's going

163

to stop me? I'm captain of this ship. My word is law here. So what are you going to do about it? Run away? Have you forgotten we're in the middle of the ocean?" He laughed. "It will be a long swim, sweet."

"When we get to New Orleans, I'll go to the authorities. I'll —"

"By the time we reach New Orleans, you'll be accustomed to the idea," Matt interrupted with supreme confidence. He turned and walked to the door, saying, "Now I've got to get on deck. I've more important things to do than stand around arguing with you over something that's already been decided."

Leigh stood open-mouthed as Matt closed the door behind him. That arrogant bastard! Did he actually think he could ride roughshod over her? Why, she . . . she'd . . .

Leigh sat weakly on the bunk as the full impact of her position hit home. She'd what? My God, what he said was true. She couldn't run away, and there was no one to help her. None of the crew would dare defy him in her name. He was law on this ship. God, law, supreme master, everything! Besides, who would help her? Kelly maybe? As first mate, he had some authority. No, Matt would tolerate no interference in this matter. Of that, she was sure. If Kelly did object, there's no telling what Matt might do to him. The captain was a hard, dangerous man. And if her friend, Kelly, was hurt because of her, she would never forgive herself. She dressed and paced the room, racking her brain.

If Leigh had known Kelly's reaction to Matt making her his mistress, she would have been even more shocked. For at that very minute, Matt was telling the first mate of his plans for Leigh, and Kelly was delighted. He had wanted Matt to settle down to one woman, and he heartily approved of Leigh as his choice. That Matt was taking her for his mistress, instead of his wife, didn't disturb Kelly in the least. Kelly, himself, had kept a mistress for over twenty years, a woman he loved deeply and was as faithful and devoted to as the best of husbands. It had simply never occurred to Kelly to marry her. She had never asked him.

When Lucifer entered the cabin that afternoon, Leigh was still pacing the floor. She turned and looked down at the cat, snapping, "And where have you been all this time? Some friend you are, deserting me when I needed you!"

The cat eyed her warily, then jumped to the top of Matt's sea chest, his favorite roosting spot. From there, he lay and watched Leigh curiously, his yellow eyes following her as she paced and ranted.

By the time night came, Leigh had concluded that if anyone was going to thwart Matt's plans, it was going to have to be her. Smiling smugly, she hung her old hammock in the corner of the cabin and then lay down in it. Now, let's just see how he manages it in this, she thought.

When Matt entered the cabin that night, it was dark. He stripped and walked to the bunk, then stared down at it dumbly when he saw it was empty. Muttering curses, he turned and spied the hammock hanging in the corner of the room. In three swift strides, he reached it, swooped Leigh up in his arms, and then tossed her, none too lightly, on the bunk.

True to his prediction that morning, it only took a bit of persuading. With his skill and expertise in love-making, Matt could be very persuasive. Under his fiery kisses and determined sensual assault, Leigh was soon soft and pliable in his arms.

When the impassioned love-making was over and reality returned, Matt lay back smiling in self-satisfaction. Leigh rolled away from him, horrified at her own body's treacherous betrayal.

"Oh, no, you don't, sweet," Matt said, pulling her back into his arms and firmly placing her head on his shoulder. "This is where you belong. If I want you again later, I don't want to spend half the night searching the cabin for you."

Then he chuckled softly, kissed her forehead, and fell asleep. Leigh was left to spend the rest of the night locked in Matt's strong arms, alternately cursing him and then herself for her own weakness.

The next day, Leigh decided to take a different approach. Matt said she was a passionate woman. What if she showed no passion at all? Would he still want her then? What if, instead of fighting him, she lay completely passive and unresponsive? Surely, a man wouldn't want to make love to a limp dishrag.

And just how are you going to manage that, the obnoxious little voice in the back of her head asked. Have you forgotten that all he has to do is touch you and you are so much putty in his hands?

Leigh pondered the problem. Somewhere she had read the Hindus in India could will themselves to feel no pain, thereby allowing them to sleep on a bed of nails or walk over hot coals. If they could do it, why not she? She would force herself to concentrate on something else, divorce her mind from her body. If she couldn't feel what Matt was doing to her, then she couldn't possibly respond.

That night, when Matt entered the cabin, Leigh was in the bunk. He looked down at her warily. It wasn't like Leigh to give in so easily. He stripped and lay down beside her, fully expecting her to come at

166

him with swinging arms and flashing claws. When she lay passively beside him, his suspicions grew. Cautiously, he bent and kissed her. It was like kissing a cold statue. He grinned, thinking, so that's what the little minx is up to. Well, we'll just see about that!

Leigh did amazingly well at blocking out the sensations Matt was arousing, especially when considering Matt's equal determination to thwart her plan. The feel of his warm tongue lazily circling the outline of her ear, then probing it, almost undid her. But Leigh forced herself to lie rigid, staring at the ceiling, summoning all her will to ignore what he was doing to her. It was inevitable, however, that Matt, with his considerable expertise, would eventually break down Leigh's defenses. She was just on the verge of losing control when Matt rolled from her and said in an angry, exasperated voice, "All right, Leigh, if that's the way you want it."

But, much to Leigh's surprise and dismay, Matt didn't leave the bunk. Instead, he pushed her thighs apart roughly, mounted her and, without any preliminaries, plunged into her, slamming against her, pounding at her with cold deliberation. And just when Leigh was beginning to climb that summit, Matt tensed, shuddered, and collapsed over her, leaving Leigh hanging in midair.

Matt rolled from her and out of the bunk. As he jerked on his breeches, he said in a cold voice, "You can have it that way, or the other. It's your decision. Personally, it makes no difference to me—as long as I get my pleasure."

Then he turned and walked from the cabin, leaving Leigh to toss and turn, mutter and curse, with unfulfilled desire the rest of the night.

Had she known it, Leigh would have probably

167

taken some solace in knowing that Matt was not as unaffected by the episode as he appeared to be. He paced the deck, just as angry and frustrated as Leigh, for although he had obtained physical relief, he had not received the satisfaction from it that he had the last few times he had made love to her. Why do you bother, he asked himself angrily. If she doesn't want to be your mistress, then the hell with her! But Matt knew he still wanted her, now more than ever. For some strange reason, she satisfied him in a way that transcended the physical. Making love to her left him with a contentment he had never known with any other woman.

He stood at the rail and stared out into the dark night, pondering this oddity. Why should Leigh bring him such total satisfaction? He knew women who were skilled and accomplished courtesans, women who knew every erotic, sensuous trick of the trade to pleasure a man. Yet they had never left him feeling the way she did. Why her, of all women? Well, he would be damned if he would give her up. He would keep at her until he eventually wore down her resistance. But dammit, he hoped she didn't pull that stunt again.

Leigh didn't. One night of suffering that kind of agony was enough for her. She set her busy little mind to planning new tactics. She decided to play the role of a shrew, thinking that no man would want to put up with that, regardless of how much he enjoyed the woman in bed. The minute Matt entered the cabin, she complained about any and every thing. She ranted. She raved. She called him vile names, some shocking enough to raise Matt's eyebrows in surprise.

For the most part, Matt ignored her. If anything, he was amused by her antics, knowing full well what she was doing. Only when she started throwing things at him, did Matt decide that a more positive action was in order. His solution to that provocation was to sweep her up in his arms, carry her to the bunk, and make torrid love to her.

By the end of the week, Leigh realized that the only thing she was accomplishing by her resistance was exhausting herself. Shockingly, her own body betrayed her at every turn. She was forced to admit to herself that she desired Matt as much as he did her, that he wielded a weapon against her for which she had no defense — her own passion. But as much as she enjoyed his sensuous, exciting love-making, she couldn't let herself accept the degrading position of being his mistress, his plaything from now on. Her pride simply would not allow it. Yet, as long as she was trapped on the small ship with him, it was useless to fight him — and her own body's demands. She finally decided to pretend acquiescence to Matt's demand that she be his mistress and save her energies for blocking his arrogant plans for her future when they reached New Orleans. She vowed that, then, she would regain control of her treacherous body, and her life.

From then on, when Matt made love to her, Leigh still resisted, a mere token resistance, as they both knew. In fact, Matt was so accustomed to it that he considered it part of their foreplay. Then, after Matt had carried her to unbelievable heights of ecstasy and she had drifted back down to reality, she would lie in his arms, smiling smugly and planning how to foil his plans for her.

As the *Avenger* beat farther south, the weather

grew warm and balmy. Leigh spent more time on deck, soaking in the sun, and letting the soft breeze play through her hair. She could hardly believe Boston was still suffering the throes of winter, while she was basking in the sunshine and, if she had admitted it, basking in the warm, appreciative glances Matt sent her way.

They swept through the Caribbean by the West Indies, taking three more prizes. Each time, they were lone British merchantmen plying the island trade, ships that had made the mistake of thinking that they didn't need the protection of a convoy, since they weren't traveling across the wide Atlantic to England. All three British captains had been shocked to find an American privateer stalking what they considered their waters.

Two days later, off the coast of Jamaica, they sighted a large convoy beating its way to the Atlantic. As usual, excitement ran high on the deck of the *Avenger*.

Leigh stood on tiptoe, straining her eyes at the horizon, trying to see the convoy. "I can't see a thing," she complained petulantly.

Matt chuckled and handed her the spyglass, taking the opportunity to put his arms around her to show her how to hold it. "Now look, sweet," he whispered in her ear after he had given it a quick kiss.

Leigh blushed, embarrassed that he should show such intimacies before the crew. Steeling herself against the feel of his powerful arms around her, she peered into the spyglass. Her eyes widened with wonder, for the whole ocean seemed to be covered with ships. Why, there must be hundreds of them, she thought.

"Move the glass to the right, sweet, and you'll see

170

one of the frigates that's running escort," Matt said.

Leigh did as Matt directed, and sure enough, there she was, the big warship. She swept the spyglass down the long broadside of the ship, seeing the gaping gun ports. Even from here, they looked intimidating. She imagined the ugly gray noses of the cannons poking through them, belching fire and smoke. She shivered, then handed the spyglass back to Matt, saying, "I don't understand. If we can see them, why can't they see us?"

"They probably could if they were watching for us," Matt replied. "But strangely enough, we've never been discovered until we were swooping down on them."

"But why?" Leigh asked. "I should think they would be watching for privateers."

Kelly, standing next to them, answered, "Ah, lass, I have my own opinions about that. 'Tis the British navy's arrogance that does them in. They think no mere privateer would dare attack a convoy under their protection." He laughed. "Aye, time and time again, our privateers sneak prizes from right under their noses, and still they haven't learned."

"But if they do sight us, will they give chase?" she asked apprehensively.

"No," Matt answered. "An escort ship is not supposed to leave the convoy unless one of the ships has been captured. Their primary purpose is to protect the convoy, not chase down privateers. Even if they did see us, they'd only tighten up the convoy and add more protection to the side the strange ship was sighted on."

Kelly was peering through the spyglass now. "I'd say from the way they're runnin', we haven't been seen. They're sailin' pretty loose. Which ones were you thinkin' of, Cap'n?"

"See those three laggers bunched up at the left? We'll keep an eye on them."

"Three?" Leigh asked in an astonished voice. "You'd try to capture three ships at one time, with the British naval escort right there?"

Matt shrugged. "Why take one if you can capture two? Why two if you can take three?"

Leigh could only stare at him in disbelief.

For three days, the *Avenger* tailed the convoy. By the end of the third day, Leigh felt she couldn't endure the tension any longer. Her nerves felt as if they had been tied in knots. She turned to Kelly, saying in an impatient voice, "What is Matt waiting for?"

Kelly chuckled. He knew what was bothering the girl. The waitin' was always the worst. "Ah, lass, 'tis not wise to pounce too quick. Do you remember me tellin' you with a convoy this large, the best the escort could do is patrol?"

Leigh nodded.

"Well, lass, this convoy is fresh out of Jamaica. The captains of those escort ships have been takin' their duties very seriously. But patrollin' is borin' business, lass, beatin' up the line, then back again, over and over. I suppose the sheer monotony of it lures the captains into a false sense of security. At any rate, if you watch them long enough, eventually a definite pattern of patrollin' will emerge. When that happens, you can predict almost to the minute when that escort ship is goin' to turn and beat her way up the line and what time to expect her back. That way, we know just exactly how much time we've got to make our move in and get back out."

Two mornings later, when Leigh stepped on deck,

the tension was palpable. All eyes were glued on the captain, who stood looking through the spyglass in the direction of the convoy.

As Leigh reached Matt's side, she heard him say, "There she goes, beating her way back up the line."

"Aye," Kelly responded. "And she won't be back for two hours." He glanced up at the sails, saying, "Wind's right, Cap'n."

Leigh glanced up, surprised to see only half of the *Avenger*'s sails set. Apparently, the wind was so brisk, they were sailing at half sail in order to hang back out of the convoy's sight.

Matt snapped the spyglass shut and stared at the horizon. Everyone on deck stood holding his breath. Leigh could hear her heart thudding in her ears; the palms of her hands turned clammy. Why doesn't he say something, her mind screamed silently.

Matt turned from the rail, saying, "Let's go get them, Mr. Kelly."

Kelly's face broke into a wide grin, his eyes sparkling with excitement. "Aye, Cap'n!" He turned and bellowed, "Set all sail!"

An ear-splitting "hooray" came from the crew as they scurried to raise the remaining sail. The wind caught in the canvas with a snap, and the *Avenger* leaped forward, skimming over the waves, the rigging humming. Within minutes, the convoy was in sight, and Leigh could see the three stragglers. She looked about apprehensively for the big frigate, but it was nowhere in sight.

"Man all guns!" Matt called out.

The crew scrambled to obey his order.

"We'll take them from the starboard side, Mr. Kelly," Matt said.

"Aye, Cap'n," Kelly replied, then called out "Roll

173

out the starboard guns and load!"

The gun ports slammed open. The gun crews bent, pushing the heavy gun carriages forward until the gray noses of the big carronades protruded from the gun ports. Then they hurried to load the big guns.

By now the *Avenger* was running parallel to the three merchantmen, slowly pulling ahead of them.

"Hoist the colors!" Matt yelled. The Stars and Stripes rose proudly over the *Avenger*, the flag snapping in the wind.

"Starboard your helm!" Matt called. The *Avenger* veered to starboard, angling down on the three ships to cut them off from the rest of the convoy.

Leigh could imagine the merchantmen's shocked reaction to the sudden appearance of an American privateer. From where she stood, she could see the crews of the three ships scurrying over the decks and up the rigging in a frantic, but futile, effort to pull away.

"Let's give them a good scare, Mr. Kelly. None of this single shot over the bow. We don't have time to play games today," Matt said in a hard voice.

"Aye, Cap'n," Kelly replied, grinning his approval. He turned, yelling, "Give them a broadside across their bows!"

All the cannons of the starboard battery fired simultaneously, with a deafening roar, spitting fire and smoke, and fourteen missiles flew through the air to splash in the water before the merchantmen's bows. As the smoke cleared, Leigh could see the crews on the merchantmen reefing the sails as their flags fluttered down in surrender.

Matt lost no time in getting the prize crews on the three ships. Almost before the smoke had cleared, the longboats were in the water and on their way, the sailors of the *Avenger* straining at the oars, knowing that their battle was now against time. In the meantime, the *Avenger* rocked in the water, her broadside facing the three ships, cannons still run out and menacing.

On the decks of the merchantmen, the captains were led away to be locked below with their crews. The first two captains were silent, their faces ashen with shock. The third captain was led away red-faced, cursing and raging, not about the attack by a privateer, but rather about the ineffectiveness and stupidity of the British navy that was supposed to be protecting him.

As soon as the prize crews signaled all was secure, the four ships sailed away, the *Avenger* bringing up the rear. Matt and Kelly watched the horizon anxiously for the frigate's return, but they were well away by the time the big warship sailed back down the line.

As soon as the crew of the *Avenger* knew they were clear, another "hooray" rang from the decks.

"I'd like to see that frigate's captain's face when he gets back and finds three of his ships missin'," one crusty old sailor said.

"Aye," another replied, laughing. " 'Twill be like an old mother hen returnin' to her nest to find three of her eggs snatched away."

Despite her disapproval of privateering, Leigh couldn't help but smile. Well, she thought, it serves the British captain right for being so cocky.

When Matt entered the cabin that afternoon, he was in an expansive mood. The taking of the three merchantmen had gone smoother than any other capture from a convoy they had done. He grinned down at Leigh, sitting on the bunk and sewing a button on one of his shirts. "Ah, sweet, I've decided

175

to give us a treat this afternoon."

Give us a treat? Leigh glanced up suspiciously at him, but the hot look in Matt's eyes that usually preceded his love making was absent. Instead, his black eyes were twinkling merrily. She relaxed, saying, "And what might that be?"

"A bath, sweet. Now, wouldn't that be nice?"

It sounded wonderful to Leigh. She dropped the shirt, a dreamy look on her face.

Matt chuckled, saying, "I thought you'd like that. I've already told Cookie to start heating the water. But I told him to have his assistant bring it to the cabin. That way, we won't have to listen to his lecture on the evils of bathing." He turned, saying, "I'll get the tub."

Leigh smiled, remembering the day Cookie had told her about his new assistant. "It was the strangest thing, lass," he had said. "A couple of days after you were injured, this big swabbie shows up, tellin' me the cap'n says he was to be my new assistant from now on. I tell you, lass, it floored me. I mean, out of the clear blue sky!" He had shaken his head as if still dumbfounded, then continued, "Well, I tell you, between me and you, I was glad to see him. But he ain't near as good as you, lass, not near as fast, and always complainin' about how much work it is and how he wishes he could get back on deck duty."

Matt came back into the cabin, carrying the tub and interrupting Leigh's thoughts. She looked up at him and reluctantly admitted that he wasn't all bad.

Matt set the tub down with a thud and said in a teasing voice, "Are you going to sit there and let me do all the work? Come on, sweet, grab a couple of buckets and help me bring in the water. After all, this bath is for both of us." He turned and walked from the cabin.

Both of us? Leigh shot the tub a quick suspicious look. Then she laughed with relief. No, it would be impossible. Matt could barely fit in the tub himself, much less both of them. She pushed herself from the bunk and hurried to help him.

By the time they returned, the buckets of hot water were waiting for them. Matt poured the water into the tub and then stood back, making a mocking bow, saying, "Ladies first."

Leigh dimpled, made a quick curtsy, and said, "Thank you, kind sir." She looked down to unbutton her blouse, then realizing Matt was still standing there, looked up and said irritably, "Well, aren't you going to leave?"

Matt grinned. "Why should I, sweet? I've seen you naked before."

Leigh blushed and ducked her head. Oh, he just had to remind her, did he? It was true, he had seen her totally naked before. But that was in the subdued light of the lamp. It was broad daylight now. She couldn't possible strip naked in this glaring light, totally revealing herself as she had never been exposed to his eyes before. No, not even for a promise of a bath.

Matt was watching her, thinking, She's such an innocent yet, despite all the times I have made love to her. Still so shy and modest. He felt strangely touched and said, "Never mind, sweet. I'll go over to the galley and heat up some more water. You go ahead."

Leigh sighed in relief as he closed the door behind him. Quickly, she undressed and climbed into the tub. Then she lay back, relaxing, letting the hot water soothe her. Without realizing it, she dozed off.

She was awakened abruptly as Matt, carrying two

buckets of hot water, kicked the cabin door shut behind him. She sat huddled in the tub, her arms protectively over her breasts, as she watched him set the buckets down with a thud. Then her eyes widened as he flashed her a grin, strode to the bunk, and sat down. When he yanked off one boot, then the other, she realized with dismay that he had no intention of leaving a second time. She had had her chance and whiled the time away.

Matt leaned back, his shoulders resting on the wall behind the bunk, his long legs crossed before him, saying, "Don't let me disturb you."

Leigh glared at him. Then, glancing down, she realized that the only thing he could possibly see from where he sat was her bare shoulders. The tub was so short that even she had to sit with her knees drawn up. Well, I'll be damned if I will let him ruin my bath, she thought. She picked up the soap and began soaping herself, but when she got to her back, she couldn't reach it in the cramped tub. Oh, I wish I had someone to wash it for me, she thought.

A little glimmer lit her eyes at the thought. She looked down to reassure herself, thinking, Yes, if I lean forward and keep my knees up, he won't be able to see a thing.

She glanced at Matt. He sat with one long leg casually drawn up, his arm resting on his knee, watching her intently. She hesitated briefly, then smiled sweetly, saying, "I believe you owe me a favor, Captain."

Matt's golden eyebrows rose. "Oh? How's that?"

"If I remember correctly, I washed your back for you once. Turnabout is only fair."

Matt grinned, pushed himself away from the bunk, and walked toward her. Leigh smiled smugly and leaned forward, handing him the soap over her shoulder. But the minute Matt started soaping her back, Leigh realized her mistake. She had completely forgotten how Matt's touch affected her until she felt his hands on her skin. She gritted her teeth, steeling herself. But when Matt's hands slipped forward around her, fondling and massaging her breasts, she gasped and jerked away. "Stop that!"

"Why, sweet, I'm only washing you," Matt said in a sickeningly innocent voice.

Leigh shoved his hands away, and Matt chuckled, beginning to wash her back again.

"No, that's enough!" Leigh snapped.

Matt shrugged, tossed the soap down, and said, "Whatever you say."

She looked up and saw Matt standing over her with a bucket of water poised. He grinned and said, "Remember, sweet, turnabout is only fair."

Leigh clenched her teeth and braced herself for what she knew was coming. But as the cold water rushed over her shoulders and back, she shrieked despite herself.

Matt threw his golden head back and roared. Then he reached down and, wrapping his hands around her waist, picked her up and swung her to the floor, saying, "That's enough for you. Now it's my turn."

Leigh stood, still stunned from the cold water, gasping as the water rolled off her and puddled at her feet. She shot Matt an angry look and then watched, her heart thudding in her chest as his amused look turned warm, then rapt as his eyes swept over her.

Blushing furiously under that hot, intense gaze, she reached to cover herself, but Matt caught her arms, holding them tightly to her sides, saying, "No!"

Leigh was forced to stand before him while his eyes

devoured her. Finally, he said with a husky timbre, "You're so beautiful, Leigh. So damned beautiful."

He bent his head and slowly licked a drop of water from one nipple, sending shivers down Leigh's spine. Then he was nuzzling her breasts and kissing them, licking the rivulets of water away, nibbling and teasing one peak, then the other. He dropped to his knees before her, kissing and nipping along her rib cage and abdomen as his hands caressed and stroked her back and hips. He lingered at her navel, slowly circling it with his tongue, exploring, then licking away the drop of water that hid in its recess.

Leigh was past the point of objecting. Her heart was racing, her blood like liquid fire in her veins, the cabin spinning crazily around her. She closed her eyes against the dizziness and then opened them to see Matt's golden head slipping lower.

"No!" she gasped, reaching to pull his head back up. But Matt cupped her buttocks, arching her to him, as he buried his searing mouth in the curls between her thighs.

"Matt, stop!" Leigh cried, pulling at his hair.

Matt only tightened the vise about her hips, holding her still, while his lips and tongue tasted her hungrily, feasting on her honeyed sweetness. Leigh was trembling all over, shock wave after shock wave of exquisite pleasure running through her, as Matt's flickering, teasing tongue searched and explored her innermost secrets. A throaty moan escaped her lips and her knees buckled from weakness. Matt scooped her up in his arms and carried her to the bunk.

"Your bath," Leigh muttered weakly.

"Later," he answered in a hoarse voice, laying her down, his lips covering hers in a passionate, searing kiss.

Later, much later, Leigh lay on the bunk watching Matt through lowered eyelashes as he bathed. She held her breath as he rose and reached for a towel. Yes, it's true, she thought in awe. He does look like a beautiful golden god. Her eyes watched hungrily as he toweled himself, drifting over his broad chest with its golden mat of curls, down the hard planes of his taut abdomen and slim flanks to his powerful legs.

Matt threw the towel aside and stood up, looking toward her. Leigh's eyes locked on the golden triangle of hair between his thighs. Her heart raced and her breath quickened as she watched in a mixture of excitement and fascination as his masculinity stirred, then hardened and rose, growing until it stood immense and bold before her. She had the most irresistible urge to reach out and touch that proud, throbbing testimony of his desire. She could hardly wait until he got back to the bunk.

Chapter 9

Matt escorted his three new prizes into the Gulf of Mexico and, once in those comparatively safe waters, sent them on their way to New Orleans. He turned the *Avenger* back to the Atlantic, passing through the Florida Strait and heading once again to the waters around the Bahamas. He hoped to sight another convoy, this time perhaps coming from England. Several days later, two ships were sighted.

"One's a sloop, the other's a brig," the lookout cried. "They've both got damage to their spars."

Matt and Kelly exchanged quick surprised looks. "Colors?" Matt called.

"The sloop is flying our colors, sir. No colors on the brig, but her lines look British. Looks like a prize to me."

"An American privateer with her prize?" Matt muttered, half to himself.

"Cap'n!" the lookout cried in an excited voice. "Unless my eyes are playing tricks on me, that sloop is carrying a white stripe!"

Kelly was peering through the spyglass at the two ships in the distance. "He's right, Cap'n. She's got our navy's stripe on her, all right. But I didn't know

183

the navy had any sloops."

Matt's brow wrinkled. "Now that you mention it, I did hear some talk in Charleston. Something about the navy commissioning Doughty to design some heavy sloops, ships that would be superior to the British brigs, yet faster . . . Yes, I remember now. There were three of them, the *Frolic*, the *Wasp*, and the *Peacock*. But it seems the navy's had a bit of bad luck with them."

"How's that?" Kelly asked.

"Well," Matt answered, "the *Frolic* was captured by a British brig in the Florida Strait its first trip out. The *Wasp* sailed to the English Channel and made an impressive record for herself, taking several prizes, capturing one brig and sinking another. Then she just disappeared, lost at sea."

"So you think this might be the third, the *Peacock*?" Kelly asked.

"Either that, or some damn privateer is painting white stripes on his ship," Matt answered. "Hoist our colors, and let's go take a closer look."

The *Avenger* sailed toward the two ships, and as they got closer, it became apparent the brig *was* a prize and badly damaged. She was barely limping along.

"The sloop's signalin' us, Cap'n," Kelly said.

"Can you read them?" Matt asked.

"Aye. The captain's askin' permission to come on board."

"Signal him back and tell him we'd be honored," Matt replied. "Then reef the sails."

Leigh appeared on deck that minute and asked, "What's going on?"

"We're going to have a visitor, sweet," Matt answered. He pointed to the sloop that was almost upon them. "The captain of one of our warships."

The sloop sidled neatly up to the *Avenger*. The grappling hooks were thrown, and a minute later the captain of the sloop jumped to the *Avenger*'s deck.

Leigh was surprised to see the captain was a young man, probably a few years older than Matt. She admired his dark-blue uniform, thinking that he looked very dashing in it. She glanced at Matt's plain white shirt and dark breeches and wondered what he would look like in that uniform. Devastating, came the answer. Yes, with his golden good looks, he would be absolutely, totally devastating, she admitted silently.

The sloop's captain smiled and extended his hand to Matt, saying, "Captain Lewis Warrington of the United States Navy."

Matt clasped the man's hand firmly and shook it warmly. "Captain Matthew Blake of the privateer, the *Avenger*."

Warrington's eyebrows rose. "The *Avenger*, you say? Well, Captain Blake, you've set quite an impressive record for yourself."

Matt nodded in acknowledgment of the man's compliment, then turned to look at the British brig limping past them. The ship was yawing badly. "It looks like your prize took a good beating."

"Yes, she did," Warrington replied. "She's got damage both above and below deck. It's been all we can do to keep her afloat."

"Where did you pick her up?" Matt asked.

"I ran into a small convoy outside Havana," Warrington answered. "The *Épervier*"—he motioned to the British warship—"was running escort and turned to fight. It was a fool thing to do. Her captain should have kept her with her convoy. She was carrying a hundred thousand dollars in gold and silver. Private money, not government."

Matt was impressed. He whistled, saying, "A hundred thousand dollars in gold and silver? Her captain was a fool to risk that."

"Yes," Warrington answered, "but I guess he figured he wasn't really taking any risk." He grinned, his eyes twinkling. "You see, he thought he could beat us."

Matt grinned back, saying, "Did he put up a good fight?"

"No, not really. His first broadside damaged my spars, but after that he hardly hit me. Seems his carronades were defective."

"And he hadn't remedied it?" Matt asked in an astonished voice.

"He claims he didn't know it," Warrington scoffed. "Which just goes to show he hadn't carried out his gunnery practice as he should have."

Matt nodded in agreement, then said, "Will you join me in my cabin for a drink, Captain Warrington? I have some excellent bourbon on board, and I'd like to toast your victory."

"Thank you, Captain Blake, but I'm afraid I'd better keep moving. As I said, we've had a time keeping that prize afloat. I wanted to ask you if you know anything about the present status of the blockade, which ports might be the least heavily patrolled?"

Matt shook his head, saying, "I'm afraid I can't help you there, Captain. We sailed out of Charleston back in January. We've been at sea ever since."

"Then you've been at sea longer than us," Warrington replied, frowning. "We ran the blockade out of New York in March."

Matt looked at the damaged brig. He would have suggested taking the prize to New Orleans, except he knew the ship would never make it that far. In fact, the way she was taking on water, he wondered if Warrington could get her to any port.

Warrington laughed and said, "I know what you're thinking, Captain Blake. I should have scuttled her. But the *Peacock* is my first command, and the *Épervier* is my first prize. I'd like to get her to port if I can."

Matt nodded his understanding. Having to sink any prize was defeating. But the first? That would be even worse. He said, "Savannah is the closest port. Do you think you can make it?"

Warrington grinned. "I'm sure as hell going to try!"

During the entire conversation, Warrington had been sneaking curious glances at Leigh, who stood a few feet away observing them. I've heard some pretty wild tales about these privateers of ours, he thought, but never have I heard of one taking his woman to sea with him. But then, if I had a woman who looked like that, I'd be reluctant to leave her behind, too, he admitted to himself.

Matt had been aware of the naval captain's admiring glances. He walked to Leigh and put his arm around her shoulders possessively, saying, "Captain Warrington, may I introduce Miss Leigh O'Neal?"

So, Warrington thought, his mistress and not his wife. He smiled his most charming smile and said, "My pleasure."

Leigh dimpled prettily and replied, "I'm pleased to meet you, Captain Warrington."

"Cap'n Warrington! Cap'n Warrington!" the lookout from the *Peacock* called. "Three sails astern!"

Warrington whirled and looked up, calling back, "The frigates again?"

"Aye, sir, it looks like 'em!" the lookout yelled.

Warrington turned and said to Matt, "Damn! I thought I had left them behind. They've been on my tail off and on ever since the day after the battle. I'm sorry, Captain, but I'd better get going."

"Good luck, Captain," Mack said, clapping Warrington on the shoulder as he turned.

"Thanks. I'm going to need it," Warrington called back over his shoulder as he vaulted the rail to the *Peacock*'s deck.

Matt turned back, saying, "We'd better get out of here ourselves." He called to the crew, "Hoist full sail."

Both the *Avenger* and the *Peacock* sailed away from the approaching British warships. Soon, the *Avenger* was well away, but the *Peacock*, held back by the crippled brig, lagged behind. Matt, Leigh, and Kelly stood watching as the frigates slowly gained on the *Peacock* and her prize.

Kelly shook her head, saying in a grim voice, "Warrington is never goin' to make it—not draggin' that crippled prize with him. He should have scuttled her."

Matt frowned. He admired Captain Warrington's determination and sympathized with his reluctance to scuttle his first prize. And from what Matt could observe, the captain was a damned good sailor, doing better at moving the damaged ship along than most would. Still, it wasn't going to be good enough. He looked at the frigates, his eyes narrowing, saying, "No. But if he had a little more time, he might make it."

Kelly looked at Matt suspiciously. "What are you thinkin', Cap'n?"

"I'm wondering if we could lure those frigates away from the chase for a few hours," Matt replied.

"That wouldn't work, Cap'n," Kelly replied. "They don't want us. They want that one hundred thousand dollars back."

Matt answered, "Have you ever seen a dog who could resist the urge to scratch a flea?" He grinned. "Particularly if that flea bites him."

"Come on, Matt, spit it out!" Kelly snapped. "What kinda crazy scheme are you hatchin' up now?"

"I'm wondering if they could resist chasing us if we fired on them."

"Fired on them?" Kelly said in a shocked voice.

"Yes," Matt replied in an infuriatingly calm voice. "Make a quick sweep, fire a volley or two, and then run. Don't get close enough for them to hit us, or us to hit them for that matter. Just close enough to insult them, dare them to give chase."

"You're crazy!" Kelly retorted. "The most they'd probably do is send one frigate after us. Then the other two would keep chasin' Warrington. What good would that do? Those frigates are carryin' fifty guns or more each. Why risk our necks for nothin'?"

"It would distract them for a while," Matt answered. "In the first place, they wouldn't know if we are really going to attack or not. They couldn't afford to ignore us. They'd have to take time to prepare for battle. If we can hold them off for an hour, maybe Warrington can shake them under cover of darkness."

"I don't know, Cap'n," Kelly said in a disgruntled voice, "it still sounds crazy to me. Besides, have you forgotten the lass? What if one of those frigates caught us?"

Matt frowned, looking down at Leigh. He sighed, saying, "You're right, Kelly. I can't take that chance."

"No!" Leigh objected. "You've got to try it! Those are Americans out there. If you don't, some will die, no telling how many. And the rest will go to prison. No, I won't have that on my conscience. I couldn't live with it. Besides, didn't you say no British ship could outsail the *Avenger*?"

189

Matt and Kelly both stared at her, dumbfounded.

"If you don't try to help Captain Warrington, I'll never forgive you as long as I live! Why—why, I'd be ashamed of you. Both of you!"

Both men were frowning, still hesitant.

"All right then, don't do it!" Leigh snapped. "But don't you dare try to put the blame on me. You're nothing but cowardly pirates who prey on innocent, helpless merchantmen!"

It was the first time Leigh had accused Kelly of being a pirate, and his feelings were gravely injured. "Nay, lass, we're not pirates we're—" Leigh gave him a murderous look, and Kelly stopped in mid-sentence, shocked by its vehemence.

Matt threw his head back and laughed. "All right, sweet, you've made your point. It seems if we're going to live with you, we're going to have to do what you want. Right, Kelly?"

Kelly scowled and turned, saying in a sullen voice, "I still say it's a crazy plan."

Matt turned the *Avenger* around and headed straight for the three frigates, putting the *Avenger* between the *Peacock* and its prize and the three British warships. As the *Avenger* swept down on the frigates, the warships slowed, as if stunned, and then swung their hulls to put the *Avenger* on their broadsides, their sails reefed to fighting sails. Just before the *Avenger* reached gun range, she veered sharply and fired a full broadside. The shots were short, just as Matt had planned. On sheer reaction, the warships answered fire, their judgment of gun range distorted by the totally audacious attack, for who would have thought a lone privateer would be reckless enough to attack three frigates?

As the British balls splashed harmlessly into the water far to the port side of them, Matt turned to

Kelly and grinned smugly.

"You're just damned lucky they're carryin' carronades like us, instead of long guns. Otherwise, we'd be blown clean to hell by now!" the first mate snapped.

The *Avenger* swept past the three frigates at full sail, and before one of the heavier, less maneuverable warships could turn to follow, Matt swung her back sharply to make another sweep.

"You're a fool!" Kelly grumbled. "They won't fall for the same trick a second time."

Matt laughed, saying, "Ah, but how can they be sure it was a trick? Maybe they'll figure I misjudged my gun range that first sweep. We'll come in closer this time, then veer at the last minute."

The second sweep was much closer, the balls from the British frigates falling mere feet from the starboard side of the *Avenger*. Kelly's face turned ashen. He said in a weak voice, "No more, Matt. That last sweep was too close for comfort."

"I'm afraid it will have to be our last," Matt replied. "Look."

Kelly glanced back behind them. One of the frigates had set full sail, pulled away from the other, and was following. Now, the chase began.

Leigh glanced off to the side, wondering what had happened to Warrington and his prize. Much to her surprise and pleasure, the two ships had disappeared over the horizon.

"Well, I'll be damned," Kelly muttered in a disbelieving voice. "Would you look at that?"

Matt and Leigh turned back to look at the frigates. One ship's spar dangled at a precarious angle, its rigging dangling and its sails torn and tattered. Already, the British crew was scrambling up the rigging to repair the damage.

Matt's eyes widened with surprise. "I must have misjudged my gun range on that last sweep. We were closer than I thought."

"Goddammit, Matt!" Kelly said angrily. "You'd better thank God those British gunners are lousy shots!"

It took the *Avenger* two hours to shake the trailing frigate, using every inch of canvas. It was a hectic, nerve-shattering two hours. When the warship's sails disappeared over the horizon, an audible sigh of relief could be heard from the crew.

Matt turned to the crew, crying out, "Good work, men! I think we just may have given Warrington the edge he needed to escape, and to show my appreciation, you'll each find an extra twenty dollars in your next prize money. And a hundred goes to the gun crew that put the ball in that frigate's spar!"

The crew went wild, from the release of tension, the knowledge that they had helped their fellow Americans escape, and the anticipation of more money to spend on their next shore leave. They yelled, slapped each other on the back, and hugged one another. Two danced a merry little jig, grinning like monkeys.

Leigh was caught up in the excitement. She turned to Matt and cried, "Oh, Matt, that was wonderful!" She threw herself in his arms and hugged him tightly.

The minute she looked up, she knew she had made a mistake. Matt's smile had faded, his look intense, his eyes growing warmer by the second. "Come on," he said in a husky voice, dragging her across the deck to the cabin.

Leigh was horrified. Why, one look at Matt's face, and everyone on deck would know his intention. She glanced around in acute embarrassment at the crew, most of who were completely ignoring them. "No!"

she cried softly.

Matt whirled, saying, "If you don't hurry, I'll throw you over my shoulder and carry you."

Leigh knew Matt would have no compunctions about fulfilling his threat, and to be carried away like a sack of potatoes would be even more humiliating. Reluctantly, trying to look as ladylike as possible under the circumstances, she allowed Matt to hurry her away.

One sailor, seeing Leigh and Matt's quick exit, turned and lewdly winked at another, saying, "Aye, we get twenty bucks, but look what the cap'n gets. Lucky bastard!"

Matt was so excited, he didn't even wait until they were in the cabin. Once in the companionway, he pulled her into his arms, kissing her passionately, his hands fumbling impatiently at her clothing. Another step, another hot, fierce kiss, and other pieces of clothing fell to the floor.

He opened the cabin door, pushed her in, and kicked the door shut behind him, pulling her impatiently to the floor. There, he took her with an urgency and savagery that frightened, thrilled, and excited Leigh beyond her wildest dreams.

They lay on the hard wooden deck, their breathing coming in rasps, their bodies perspiring, still entwined. Matt kissed her lips, her eyes, her ears, and nuzzled her neck and breasts. Then he picked her up and carried her to the bunk, where he made slow, leisurely, exquisitely tender love to her.

Some days later, when they were in the cabin and Leigh was petting Lucifer, she asked, "How long have you had Lucifer?"

"I found him one night about ten years ago on a wharf in Cadiz," Matt answered. "He was just a kitten. His eyes weren't even open yet. I guess he got separated from his mother. Anyway, there he was, half-starved, mewing pitifully and stumbling around in the dark. He almost wandered off the wharf into the water before I caught him. We were fixing to sail at the time, so I just took him with me."

"And he's been with you all these years? He doesn't even try to leave the ship when you dock?"

"Oh, he leaves the ship at every port," Matt answered, then grinned. "For a little courting, you know. But he always seems to know when we're about to set sail. Instinct, I guess. Anyway, he's never missed a sailing, which is more than I can say for some of my crew."

"Why did you name him Lucifer, of all names?"

"I didn't name him. For a long time, I just called him 'kitty.' The crew named him. Called him a little devil because he was so unfriendly and skittish. The next thing I knew, everyone was calling him Lucifer."

Leigh looked down at the cat, stretched out in her lap, saying, "It seems strange that he's content to stay on a ship. You'd think he'd prefer land."

"Why?" Matt asked. "He has a comfortable home at sea, a lady friend in every port, and his independence. What more could he ask for?"

What more indeed, Leigh thought with a twinge of bitterness. Just like his master, undoubtedly. A home at sea, independence, and a woman in every port. And if Matt had his way, she would be just one of many, his New Orleans mistress. And the others? She remembered the two women in Charleston. Obviously, they hadn't been forced into their position, not from the way they were throwing themselves at him. And they had both been very beautiful women.

Leigh felt a sudden stab of raw jealousy and was shocked by its intensity. What's wrong with you, she asked herself angrily. Why should you care how many

194

mistresses he has or how beautiful they are? You're not like them. If they're willing to accept the degrading position as his mistress, a position made only more ignominious by the fact that they shared him, like so many cake crumbs, then let them! Just because they let their passion rule their senses is no reason you should. No, you have more important things to do with your life than be at the beck and call of some arrogant, overbearing man who has no consideration for your future plans, a man who treats you like a child with no mind or will of your own. To hell with Captain Matthew Blake and his damned mistresses!

Several days later when they were standing on deck, Leigh asked Matt about his younger brother.

He turned from the rail, a frown on his face. "Who told you about him?"

"Uncle Sean," Leigh replied.

She saw the stark look of pain cross his eyes before he turned away, saying, "That was a long time ago."

Leigh's heart filled with compassion. "Matt," she said softly, "you shouldn't blame yourself. You tried to stop them from taking him."

Matt glanced back at her, his eyes flashing. "Not hard enough, I didn't!" As he stared off into the horizon, his face took on a haunted look. He said in a hushed voice, "My God, I can still see him. He was only twelve, but tall and sturdy for his age, a good-looking lad. He had a keen mind and salt water in his veins. With his intelligence, spirit, and natural sailor instincts, he would have made a damned fine captain." His voice became anguished. "If only I hadn't stopped, never let them on board in the first place, kept on going, it wouldn't have happened. And he'd be alive today."

Leigh laid her hand on Matt's arm, wanting to comfort him, saying, "Matt, you couldn't have stopped them from boarding. You were unarmed. And you had no way of knowing they'd take your brother, just a boy. Besides, what makes you so sure he's dead?"

"My God, Leigh!" Matt cried, turned to face her. "Do you have any idea what kind of life those sailors on British warships live? It's hell! Only the toughest can survive more than a few years, and Mark was just a boy. They flog them for the smallest infringement, the slightest show of spirit. And if they aren't killed, they're whipped to idiocy or left permanently crippled." He sighed, turned, and leaned heavily on the rail, saying in a hoarse whisper, "No, he's dead. I know he is."

After a minute, he whirled suddenly, his look furious. "But I swear to God, I'll get that Benjamin Coke if it's the last thing I do! Somewhere, somehow, he's going to pay!"

"Benjamin Coke?"

"The captain of the warship that took Mark. I went to London afterward, looking for him. But he had sailed for India. But I'll catch up with him someday, and when I do . . . I'll kill him!"

The last was said in a deadly earnest voice. Leigh shivered, knowing that Matt would do just that, search the ends of the earth for the man responsible and avenge his brother's death. But killing the captain wouldn't bring Matt's brother back. It would only get Matt in trouble. He would be hunted down as a murderer. Fearing for his life, she cried, "Matt, you can't do that!"

Matt's black eyes glittered dangerously. His voice was hard, unrelenting. "Don't ever tell me what I can't do." His eyes bored into hers. "And don't ever mention my brother to me again." He turned and walked away, his back rigid.

That night, Matt didn't make love to Leigh. He lay in the bunk, staring at the ceiling. Leigh lay beside him, wishing she had not said anything, knowing that she had opened up old, painful wounds. Only when his breathing had become deep and regular and she knew she was asleep, did she raise up on one elbow and look down at him. For the first time, she noticed the scar on his chest, just inches above his heart. She reached out and gently touched the small puckered mass, knowing that it was the scar of the bullet wound that had almost cost him his life. Without thinking, she bent and kissed it tenderly, whispering, "But you did try to save him, Matt. You did, and you should stop tormenting yourself."

A few days later, Matt announced they were going to stop by an island to pick up fresh water.

"An island?" Leigh cried in an excited voice. "Will there be a town? People?"

"No, I'm afraid not," Matt answered. "Like many small islands scattered around the Caribbean, it's uninhabited. But there is a small pool of fresh water on it and we can fill our barrels."

She was disappointed that there would be no town. She was hungry for the sight of civilization, any civilization, even if only grass huts and natives.

After Matt had left, she began to imagine what the island would look like. She envisioned a gently rising stretch of beach, with golden sand and swaying palm trees. In the interior of the island, surrounded by thick, lush vegetation and a profusion of exotic blooms, would be the pool, wide, deep, with sparkling clear water. Fresh water, not salt water. And she would bathe in it. Yes, after Matt had filled all the empty water barrels and everyone had returned to the beach, she would sink down in it and wash off every particle of gritty salt on her body. It would be heavenly, marvelous.

When she asked Matt if she could go along, he frowned and said, "Are you sure you want to?"

Her face took on a dreamy look. "Oh, yes, I want to."

The *Avenger* was forced to anchor a good way from the island. Matt explained that many of the Caribbean islands were surrounded by coral reefs that could rip the bottom of a ship, and it was too risky to get too close. The only thing Leigh could see from the *Avenger* was a speck of land in the distance.

Looking down the Jacob's ladder to the bobbing longboat below, Leigh almost changed her mind about going. Only the thought of a bath in fresh water gave her the courage to step over the rail and climb down the swaying rope ladder. Halfway down, she glanced down at the boat rocking below her. Suddenly, everything whirled as a violent wave of dizziness swept over her. Terrified, she clung to the rope, the wind whipping her hair and skirts around her, her heart racing in her chest. Oh God, she thought, I can't do it.

Leigh couldn't move. Her hands seemed to be glued to the rope, her legs frozen as if they were two blocks of ice. She couldn't move down—or up.

"Come on, Leigh, it's just a few more feet. You're almost to the bottom," Matt coaxed her from the longboat.

Leigh shook her head, muttering, "No, I can't."

A sudden gust of wind shook the ladder and billowed Leigh's skirt. "What a beautiful view," Matt said, his eyes on her legs.

My God, can they see up my skirt, she thought in horror. In a flash, she scrambled down the ladder and felt Matt's strong hands catch her waist and swing her into the boat.

She turned to him, pushing his hands away, glaring at him. Matt laughed, saying, "Don't worry, sweet. We couldn't see anything but a pair of pretty ankles."

"But you—you made it sound like—like . . ." Leigh sputtered.

Matt shrugged, then grinned, saying, "How else was I going to get you off that ladder? Now, be a good girl and sit down so we can get started."

Leigh plopped down on one of the wooden seats, acutely conscious of the men's amused looks and a muffled chuckle or two. But the more she thought of it, the more she realized that if Matt hadn't done something drastic, she would still be hanging onto that rope for dear life. She remembered one of her teachers at the academy saying that a lady would rather die than lose her modesty. At the time, Leigh had thought the statement ridiculous. But faced with the choice of having her bare bottom leered at by the men below, or the possibility of falling into the ocean and drowning, she had certainly made a quick enough decision, even to the extent of throwing all caution to the wind. She smiled, thinking ruefully, No wonder men accuse women of being strange creatures.

Leigh watched as they rowed closer to the island, barely able to contain her excitement. Then, as it came into view, she stared in disbelief, thinking, Where are the palm trees? The island was bare, one rolling sand dune after another, the only vegetation an occasional clump of scrubby grass. She felt sick with disappointment. And the pool? Surely, it would have trees around it. Even an oasis in the middle of the desert had date palms, didn't it? Maybe, all the trees were beyond the sand dunes where she couldn't see them.

Leigh held on tightly as the breakers caught the

small boat and sped it toward the beach. She saw a cluster of rocks protruding from the water before them and, fearing that the boat would be dashed against them and splintered into pieces, held her breath. Only when they had rushed past the rocks did Leigh realize that she had been digging her finger-nails into the wooden seat. She looked down in dismay at the ugly splinter in the end of her finger.

The boat shuddered as it hit solid ground. Two sailors jumped out, splashing in the water, and pulled the boat up on the sand. Matt vaulted over the side and, lifting up his arms, swung Leigh to the beach.

As soon as Matt put her down, Leigh turned and took a few steps. She stumbled, feeling suddenly dizzy and nauseated. Matt steadied her with his hand, saying, "Easy, sweet."

"What's wrong with me?" she asked in a weak voice.

"Nothing," Matt answered. "You've just got to get your land legs back. Your body has become accustomed to the roll of the ship. Now, it has to adjust to the feel of something solid under your feet. Just give yourself a few minutes, and then don't move too suddenly."

By the time the empty water barrels were unloaded from the longboats, Leigh had regained her land legs. She followed the line of men carrying the barrels over the sand dunes, which turned out to be higher than she had thought. She sank almost to her ankles in the soft warm sand, and toward the top of the dune, she sank even deeper, so that the mere act of walking became a struggle. By the time she had reached the top of the third dune, she was exhausted. She plopped down, gasping for breath, perspiration trickling down her face and the valley between her breasts.

"How much farther is it?" she asked in a petulant

voice.

"Just over the next dune," Matt answered. He frowned, then said, "I guess I should have warned you about these sand dunes. Do you want to go back to the beach? It's cooler there."

"No, I've come this far, I'll manage the rest of the way," Leigh answered irritably.

Matt helped Leigh climb the last dune, higher and steeper than the others. When they reached the top, she could have cried from disappointment. From where they stood, she could see the entire island. It was nothing but sand dunes, not a tree in sight.

"Where are all the palm trees?" she asked in a bitter voice. "I thought the Caribbean islands were supposed to be beautiful, with lush tropical vegetation and exotic blooms?"

Matt laughed, saying, "Many of them are, Leigh. Virtual islands of paradise. But not the really small islands like this one. During a hurricane, when the sea is running high, islands like this are totally submerged."

"Hurricanes?" Leigh asked.

"Tropical storms."

"You mean like the bad storm we went through?"

"No, much worse," Matt replied. "The winds in a hurricane are unbelievably high and have a peculiarity unlike any other storm at sea. The wind comes at you from one direction and then, after the eye, or center of the storm, passes, from the opposite direction. This is where the worst of the wind occurs, right after the eye has passed. Hurricanes are seasonal storms, occurring in the summer and autumn months, from June to October, but usually in the warmer latitudes. There have been accounts of entire Spanish armadas being caught in one of these storms and sunk, every last ship broken up and going to the bottom. That's why the Caribbean and Gulf of Mexico are swarming with treasure hunters, men searching for sunken treasure that went down with the Spanish galleons."

Leigh looked around at the small island. "And you say an island like this one can be completely submerged?"

"Yes. The storm generates huge waves, sometimes fifty to a hundred feet in height. A wave that big can completely sweep over a small island such as this one, twisting and uprooting trees, carrying away any houses that might be there, drowning every living thing on it."

Leigh shivered, despite the heat.

When they finally reached the pool, Leigh could only look at it with disgust. It couldn't have been over four feet in diameter. The only vegetation growing around it was the same spindly tufts of grass she had seen before, here and there in the dunes. True, the grass was lush and dark green around the pool, but it was far from what she had expected. And judging from the number of barrels Matt and the crew had carried across the dunes, by the time they were filled, there wouldn't be enough water left to keep a sand flea alive. Her dream of a bath in fresh water was shattered.

Kneeling by the pool, Matt cupped one hand and scooped a handful of water up, tasting it cautiously. He looked up and grinned, saying, "Still fresh."

Murmurs of relief were voiced by the crew. Then they were kept busy dipping the barrels into the pool and hammering the lids down tightly. While one group filled the barrels, another rolled them off toward the beach and the waiting longboats.

Matt motioned Leigh to one of the full barrels, saying, "Come try this, sweet. It's been a long time since you've tasted water like this."

Leigh walked to the barrel, dipped her cupped hand in, and drank. Her eyes widened with delight. She had become so accustomed to drinking the brackish water on the ship that she had forgotten what fresh water tasted like. "It's heavenly, pure nectar of the gods," she said, laughing, and taking another handful, then another.

By the time they had finished filling the barrels, the hot sun was beating down on them, the heat made even more unbearable by the glaring white sand that reflected it and sent up shimmers of heat waves. The men were drenched in perspiration and covered with a light coating of sand that the steady wind blew with determination. Leigh sat to one side, feeling miserable. She felt hot, sticky, and gritty from the sand that seemed to cling everywhere on her body, even in her ears, nostrils, and eyelashes.

When the last barrel was filled, she looked down at the pool. Only an inch or two of water remained. "How long will it take to refill?" she asked, clinging to one last hope. If Matt said only a couple of hours, maybe she could talk him into waiting and still have her bath.

Matt shrugged, saying, "Probably weeks. It's just a small spring."

Again, Leigh's dream was dashed. Disgusted, she turned and started for the beach, but after she had walked a couple of yards, she realized that the sand, which had been comfortably warm a few hours ago, was scorching hot now. She stood, hopping from one foot to the other.

"What's wrong?" Matt asked.

Leigh glared at his boots and spat, "The sand. It's hot!"

Matt glanced down at her bare feet, and then he

scooped her up in his arms.

Embarrassed at being carried in Matt's arms before the crew, she cried, "No, put me down! I'll walk."

Matt only tightened his grip, saying, "And have me waiting hand and foot on you the next few days because your feet are burned? Not on your life!"

Laughing, he sauntered off toward the beach, and Leigh was amazed at the ease with which he carried her over the steep dunes. Doesn't anything ever get him down, she thought irritably.

As he swung her back into the longboat, he said in a joking voice, "Sometimes, sweet, you're more trouble than you're worth."

Leigh glared at him. She was in no mood for his teasing. She was hot, sticky, and gritty from the sand and, undoubtedly, sun-burned, judging from the way her face and arms stung. "Thank you, Captain," she snapped.

Matt grinned and whispered so the crew couldn't hear, "Oh, you're quite welcome. Besides, sweet, I fully intend to claim my reward later."

Leigh's eyes bored holes into his back as he walked back up the beach to help with the water barrels.

The trip back to the *Avenger* took longer than the trip in. The boats were heavy with the added weight of the filled water barrels, and the crew was rowing against the breakers, which seemed determined to throw them back on the beach. The men would row furiously to climb up one wave, and then the boat would dip into a deep trough, then up again, and down, over and over. By the time they had passed the breaker line, nausea and a splitting headache had been added to Leigh's miseries.

As she climbed back up the swaying Jacob's ladder she thought bitterly, Well, so much for the beautiful Caribbean islands.

Several days later, the *Avenger* took two more prizes. To show her disapproval, Leigh stayed in the cabin.

When Matt walked into the cabin later, he frowned and said, "I suppose you're going to accuse me of piracy again."

Leigh shot him a disgusted look.

Matt threw up his hands in exasperation, saying, "I'll be damned if I can figure your logic!"

"My logic?" Leigh retorted. "What about yours? Just how do you think you're getting even with the British navy by preying on British merchantmen? No, you're only doing it for the spoils, and I consider that piracy."

"I don't want revenge on just the British navy. Leigh. I want revenge on the British merchants, the government, the people themselves."

Leigh was shocked at the extent of his hatred. "But why?"

"Because the merchants, government, and people have given the British navy its power," Matt replied in a calm voice. "They knew what was going on, the harassment of our trade, the confiscation of our ships, the impressment of our sailors. The merchants didn't care. The more ships of ours forced from the sea, the more trade for them. The people didn't care. Everytime the British navy impressed one of our seamen to fill their navy's insatiable need for men, that was just one less Englishman the press gangs took. And as long as the merchants and people turned their backs to the disgrace, the government hesitated to chastise the high and mighty Admiralty. So in my opinion, they're all guilty."

"But just how is taking merchantmen going to solve anything?" Leigh snapped.

"Simple," Matt replied. "Hit them where they're the

most vulnerable, where you can cause them the most pain — in their pocketbooks. If we take enough prizes, the merchants are going to feel the pinch first. Even if they have been lucky enough not to lose any ships themselves, the insurance rates will get so high they won't be able to afford overseas trade. And when that trade stops, the British people are going to feel it. For the rich, there won't be the luxuries they're accustomed to having. For the poor working man, there won't be any raw materials to run the factories, and he'll be out of work. Then the merchants and the people are going to remember who got them into this war — the British navy with its high-handed methods. Then there'll be a howl so loud not even the government will be able to ignore it. They'll have to buck up and put the Admiralty in its proper place. Then, and only then, will the oceans be safe for all men, not just Americans, to trade freely."

"And in the meanwhile, you conveniently get rich, stealing merchantmen," Leigh said sarcastically.

Matt shrugged his broad shoulders. "I can't deny I've done well. But when I stop to consider the two ships the British confiscated from me before the war and the profits I've lost from not being able to trade freely all these years, I find it difficult to feel sorry for them. Those merchantmen know they're gambling every time they take to the seas. If I happen to be the winner of that particular game, that's their tough luck. Men who can't afford it, shouldn't gamble."

Leigh was still doubtful. Regardless of the reasons Matt had given her, she still thought it a roundabout way of getting revenge. And she doubted seriously that the American privateers could hamper the British trade to such an extent that it would actually hurt the entire country's economy. No, she thought, they're just excuses to ease his conscience.

Later, Leigh stood on the deck, awed by the beauty of the night. A full moon shone, throwing a wide silver path across the dancing water, which sparkled like millions of brilliant diamonds. She glanced up at the heavens, filled with twinkling stars, and felt the soft, warm breeze caressing her face and lightly ruffling her hair. She took a deep breath, reveling in the clean, salty smell. On a night like this, she could easily see how a man could get the sea in his blood. She had never seen a more beautiful sight, so beautiful it left her feeling intoxicated.

Matt stepped up behind her, slipping his hands around her waist and pulling her back against him. His warm breath fanned her ear as he whispered, "Beautiful, isn't it? Almost as beautiful as you, kitten."

The spell was broken. Leigh hated Matt's new endearment for her—kitten. Every time he called her that name she cringed. It reminded her too vividly of what he considered her, a pet to amuse himself with. She whirled in his arms and spat, "Don't call me that!"

Matt's eyebrows rose in surprise. "What? Kitten?"

"Yes, kitten! I hate it. I'm not an animal!"

Matt laughed softly and pulled her back into his embrace. "Ah, sweet, but you are just like a kitten. Everytime I come near you, you spit at me and flash your claws. Until I pet you, that is. Then you turn soft and cuddly, rubbing yourself against me, arching your back to my stroke, begging me for more."

Leigh flushed hotly at Matt's words, filled with sexual innuendos. Furious, she pushed away from him and walked angrily across the deck to the cabin. How dare he throw her passion in her face! And how dare he compare her to an animal!

Matt caught up with her in the companionway and,

in one swift movement, swept her up in his arms. She squealed in outrage, pounding at his chest, hissing, "Put me down, you beast!"

Matt laughed and tossed her over his shoulder. Leigh dangled over Matt's back, her long hair trailing behind. She struggled, trying to kick, but Matt held her legs in a firm grip. She pounded at his back, cursing him. Matt totally ignored her.

After Matt had kicked the cabin door shut, Leigh shrieked, "Put me down!"

"Not yet, sweet," Matt said softly.

She gasped. One of Matt's big hands had stolen under her skirt and was fondling her between her legs, moving slowly, insidiously higher and higher. "No, stop that!" Leigh cried.

She struggled, but Matt held her in a firm grasp. The only thing she could do was twist her hips from side to side, which only intensified those warm tingling feelings Matt's knowing, teasing fingers were stimulating. She was trembling all over, the warm waves beginning to engulf her. My God, she thought, he's going to take me to the brink right here, with me slung over his shoulder like a limp carpet. "Please, Matt," she moaned.

"I thought you'd never ask," Matt mumbled in a husky voice.

He walked to the bunk and flung her on it. His body covered hers quickly, his mouth coming down and kissing her deeply, hungrily, urgently, leaving her senses whirling. His lips left hers to nip and play across her chin to her ear, licking and probing, down her throat, supping at the pulse that hammered there. Then, they were both naked, and Leigh snuggled against him, drawn to his heat in that same mysterious way a moth seeks a lamp.

Matt's lips and tongue and hands seemed to be

everywhere at once, stroking, teasing, caressing, nuzzling, nipping, lingering over those areas that raised her to feverish heights, below her ears, her breasts, the insides of her thighs. Unbearably excited, Leigh clutched at him, her own hands exploring boldly down the rippling muscles of his back, over his taut flanks to the area between his legs. She touched him tentatively at first, and then, fascinated by the feel of him, hot, throbbing, and growing even larger in her hand, she stroked and fondled him.

"Oh God, Leigh," Matt groaned. His hand closing over hers, he whispered urgently, "Yes, kitten, like that. "Oh God, yes . . ."

For the first time, Leigh experienced the euphoria of knowing her power over him. That knowledge, plus his groans of pleasure, excited her even more. Suddenly, she was aching for him, feeling a fire in her loins that only he could satisfy. She wanted him inside her. She begged, "Matt . . . please . . . take me. Now!"

Matt moved over her, and Leigh arched her back to meet him hungrily as he plunged into her. Her legs wrapped around his hips to bring him even deeper. She thrilled at the feel of him inside her, hot, pulsating, filling every inch of her, and then moving slowly, powerfully, skillfully seeking and finding those hidden sensitive areas that sent Leigh moaning with shock after shock of delicious agony. Then the pace quickened, driving them both up to that lofty crest, trembling in anticipation at the zenith, and then plunging over in an explosion of brilliant colors and flashing lights, their cries of ecstasy mingling. And when it was over and Matt rolled to his side, Leigh snuggled up to him, cuddling, her hand playing absently with the damp golden mat of curls on his chest. She sighed deeply, a little animal moan of pure contentment. Her eyes flew open in shock. My God! Was that me that just purred, she thought in horror.

As if guessing her thoughts, Matt bent and kissed her tenderly. Chuckling softly, he whispered, "Sleep tight, kitten."

Matt paced the deck slowly, thinking that the last six weeks had been the happiest he had ever known. He was at sea, the prizes were coming in at a steady rate, and he had Leigh. He smiled, thinking of her. Oh, true, she was still reluctant or, at least, she pretended to be. But slowly and surely, her resistance was melting. And Matt was surprised at how much he still wanted her, for instead of diminishing, as he would have expected, his desire for her had intensified. And even stronger yet, he found himself seeking her company, even when he didn't want to make love to her. She had a quick intelligence and the Irish warm sense of humor, providing she wasn't angry with him for something at the time. He grinned, remembering her hot Irish temper. Yes, living with Leigh would never be dull.

He stopped and leaned against the rail, looking out over the water. They had been at sea for almost four months now. He had managed to restock his water supply from the rains and at the island, but his food supply was getting low. He would have to make for port soon. Besides, he was anxious to reach New Orleans. He wanted to show Leigh off to his cousins and friends. They would be green with envy. None of them had a mistress who even began to compare with Leigh's beauty or spirit. And he wanted to show her New Orleans, feeling sure that she, like him, would be fascinated with the exciting city. He regretted that he couldn't take her to Europe. He would love to show her Lisbon, Madrid, and Paris. Well, after this war was over, he would take her. Maybe, he would take her to Italy and Greece too, providing those damned Barbary pirates were behaving themselves at the time. But why just take her for a visit, he asked himself. No, he would take her with him when he sailed, he decided. He would show her the wonders of the world, and what he hadn't seen himself, they would discover together.

He turned and walked back to the cabin, smiling broadly, intent on telling Leigh that they were heading for New Orleans. As he passed the crew, the men exchanged knowing glances. They had noticed the change in the captain over the past few weeks. He had always been fair, but he was a hard taskmaster, pushing himself and his men in his obsession to get revenge on the British navy. The last few weeks, however, he had laughed openly with the crew, smiled more, and even cracked jokes. Yes, he was a new man, much happier and much more relaxed, and the crew knew that the reason was the lass. They heartily approved of her, one and all. They admired her courage and spirit and felt that any woman who could make a hard man like the captain that contented and happy had to be the special one for him.

Chapter 10

Leigh paced the quarter-deck impatiently, occasionally stopping to give the limp sails a disgusted look. Of all the times for the wind to fail, why did it have to be when they had almost reached the Mississippi delta? They had remained here for over three hours, not moving an inch. She looked over the waters of the Gulf of Mexico. It was as smooth as glass. Not a ripple could be seen.

"Cat's-paw, astern," the lookout cried.

Leigh whirled and saw the slight roughening of the surface of the water that signaled the advance of a breeze. She held her breath and watched anxiously as the sails filled and finally snapped in the wind. They were on their way, she thought, feeling euphoric as the *Avenger* shot forward. Today, they would reach New Orleans. Yes, and Captain Matthew Blake was going to be in for a rude awakening. She could hardly wait to demand her money and present her threat to go to the authorities if he refused. How shocked he would be, the smug, domineering bastard. Try and make a pet out of her!

The object of Leigh's scorn walked up and stood beside her, looking out over the fore quarter-deck.

She looked at him from under lowered lashes. Yes, he was a handsome devil. And there was a certain aura about him. He absolutely reeked of masculinity. Feeling his magnetism, Leigh stepped away warily, still shocked by the outrageous way he affected her. Just seeing him, being near him, sent a flush over her body and her heart racing. No one had ever warned her that women could have the same base nature as men. Was this a deliberate oversight, or was there something wrong with her? Was she perhaps a wanton, after all, one of *those* women?

The thought disturbed her more than the presence of the man standing next to her. She stepped to the rail, peering into the horizon, determined to distract her mind from the virile captain and his disturbing effect on her. Her eyes narrowed, seeing a wide, dark patch of water that contrasted drastically against the blue-green waters of the gulf on both sides of it.

She pointed to it, saying "Is that darker area deeper water?"

Matt smiled and answered, "No, kitten, that's the Mississippi River."

Leigh looked about them. She couldn't see any land. "The Mississippi River?" she asked in disbelief. "But we're still in the gulf!"

"The current of the Mississippi is so strong it flows miles out to sea," Matt explained. "That darkened area is the mud and silt the river has swept downstream with her. If you were to taste that water, it would be fresh, yet the water on each side of it would have a decidedly salty taste."

"Then we're almost to New Orleans?" Leigh asked in an excited voice.

"No, sweet," Matt answered, smiling in amusement at her almost childish excitement. "We're almost to the mouth of the river. New Orleans is still another hundred and ten miles up the Mississippi. We won't get there until tomorrow."

Tomorrow. Another day still. Leigh's spirits fell, disappointment written all over her face.

Hoping to distract her from her disappointment, Matt pointed to a line of small, narrow islands that followed the coastline, saying, "Look over there, Leigh."

Leigh glanced to where he was pointing. Then, as they sailed closer, her eyes widened, seeing that the twisted oaks on the islands were covered with hundreds of birds of every color, looking like rainbows in the trees. For a minute, she stared in awed disbelief, then asked, "Where did they all come from?"

"They're migratory birds, on their way back from wintering in South America. Those islands, or *cheniers* as they're called, are the first land they sight after their long flight across the Gulf of Mexico. Being exhausted, the birds stop there to rest up before they continue north. At this time of the year, the trees are always covered with them. They're a beautiful sight, aren't they?"

Leigh could only nod in agreement, her eyes still locked on the arresting sight.

A while later, they entered the delta of the river, and Matt pointed to a larger island some distance off to the left, saying, "That's Grand Terre Island. Jean Lafitte has his headquarters there."

"Jean Lafitte? Who's he?"

Matt smiled. "Ah, kitten, you can't go to New Orleans and not know about Jean Lafitte. His name is a household word. Even a child knows who Jean Lafitte is."

Leigh bristled. "Are you inferring my education is lacking?"

Matt chuckled, saying, "No, sweet, but in New

215

Orleans Lafitte is notorious, his exploits a frequent subject of conversation."

"Well, are you going to tell me who he is or not?" Leigh said impatiently.

"Who he is depends upon whom you talk to in New Orleans. He has a letter of marque from some small country that's been at perpetual war with Spain." He grinned. "And like me, he's been accused of piracy by some people."

"Then he's a pirate?"

Matt shrugged, saying, "As I said, that depends upon whom you're talking to. The Americans consider him a pirate. The Creoles did, too, until a few years ago, but now he's their hero."

"Why the change of heart?"

"Because Lafitte and the American governor, Claiborne, have had a running battle going for years. The governor keeps trying to capture Lafitte, but he continues to elude him. This tickles the Creoles to death, since Lafitte is French and they have no love for Americans. So as of late, he's become their hero."

"And I suppose you think he's a hero, too, being a pirate yourself," Leigh said sarcastically.

Matt chuckled, then said, "To tell you the truth, I've never met the man, and I'm loath to have an opinion about anyone on rumor alone, good or bad. Actually, very few people know Lafitte personally. He's a man shrouded in mystery. There's a lot of speculation about who he really is, where he came from, why he's chosen this means to make his living, why he has such a strong hatred for the Spanish. If the rumor that he has a personal vendetta against the Spanish because they murdered his wife and children is true, then I suppose we are brothers at heart. I understand how something like that can affect a man. But I must admit, I have wondered about his letter of marque."

"Why?"

"Well, my letter of marque clearly states that all prizes must be appraised and sold by an admiralty court. I don't have the authority to sell any of it myself. Yet, Lafitte sells the merchandise from the ships he captures himself. Periodically, he has a big auction on Grand Terre, and everyone from New Orleans and the surrounding territory comes to it, Americans as well as Creoles." He smiled, saying ruefully, "It seems the Americans may consider him a pirate, but they have no compunction about buying stolen goods from him. Another strange thing is that Lafitte runs a whole fleet of ships. Now my letter of marque is written for the *Avenger*. My ship is commissioned, not me."

"So you think he is a pirate?"

"Frankly, I don't know what to think. Perhaps his letter of marque is written differently from mine and gives him permission to sell his prizes and run more than one ship." Matt looked off, silent for a minute, then shrugged, saying, "I don't know if Lafitte is friend or foe. I suppose only time will tell."

For a few minutes, they stood in silence, Leigh pondering over what Matt had said. Then she asked, "Just who are these Creoles you keep talking about?"

"A Creole is any person of European descent born in the West Indies or Spanish America, or any person descended from the original French settlers in Louisiana. In New Orleans, there are both French and Spanish Creoles, since Louisiana has been both a French and a Spanish colony. But most are French, since they were the original settlers and have been in Louisiana longer. For years, the French and Spanish Creoles never mingled, each maintaining rigid, separate social circles, even entire communities. But the last few years, they've united against a common enemy, the American."

"But New Orleans is American now," Leigh objected. "That makes them Americans, too."

Matt shook his head, saying, "Not in the Creole's mind, he isn't. He still considers himself European, whether French or Spanish. The Creoles have never forgiven Napoleon for selling Louisiana to the United States. Some even go as far as swearing the whole transaction was illegal. No, to the Creoles, French and Spanish alike, the American is the interloper, and they resent his presence in what they consider their territory."

"Well, they'll get used to the idea," Leigh remarked.

Matt looked thoughtful, saying, "Eventually, perhaps. But it's going to take some time. Many of the French and Spanish are descendants of minor aristocracy. They're class-conscious people, highly polished and well educated. They take life at a leisurely pace. They consider the Americans raw, coarse, and ill-mannered, too bold, too aggressive, too industrious. The American manner grates on their nerves, irritates them. And the Americans resent the Creoles' snobbish, superior attitude."

"Didn't you say you had two uncles in New Orleans? They're Americans. How do they get along with the Creoles?"

"No, they're not Americans, at least, not by birth," Matt answered. "You see, my father and uncles were all born on the island of Martinique in the West Indies, which makes them Creoles. My eldest uncle stayed on the island, but the four younger brothers all migrated as young men, my father and one uncle to Charleston, and my other two uncles to New Orleans. The French Creoles in Louisiana accepted my uncles, but only because they were half-French and born on

French territory. The both married Creole women, although I suspect my aunts' families still frown on the unions, preferring pure French bloodlines."

"And you? Are you accepted by the Creoles?"

Matt laughed, saying, "Barely. But not because of my uncles and their Creole wives. I'm accepted only because the Creoles in New Orleans wouldn't dare refuse the grandson of their illustrious marquise into their social circle."

"Your grandmother is a marquise?" Leigh asked in surprise.

Matt laughed again, saying, "Actually, no. She's the daughter, not the wife, of a marquis. But that's a technicality the Creoles choose to ignore. You see, the Creoles are snobbish, very impressed with nobility. Now, a marquis is second in rank only to a duc, much higher than the minor nobility from whom the Creoles have descended. That, plus the fact that my grandmother was once a lady-in-waiting to the queen of France, has earned her a rather lofty position in Louisiana's Creole society." Matt chuckled, saying, "It's really rather ridiculous. The Creoles cling to every word she says. I honestly believe she could tell them to stand on their heads and they'd do it."

Leigh laughed and turned her attention back to the river. The water had turned to a muddy yellow, and now she could see the broad coastal plain with its marshes of brackish water. On both sides of them, stretching to the horizon, the landscape was covered with reeds and cattails, a virtual sea of endless grass, broken only by an occasional small island. All about them were splashes of vivid color where spring wildflowers bloomed in profusion.

"The Louisianans call this the trembling prairie," Matt remarked.

Leigh looked about her, thinking that the name was

very appropriate. The grass waved and undulated in the strong gulf breeze, never still, always moving.

As they sailed upriver, Leigh was amazed at the enormous number of waterfowl, not only the sea gulls following them and cawing down at them, but thousands of birds of innumerable species that inhabited the marshes. In fifteen minutes, she counted fifty pelicans, big, white birds with large yellow bills and pouches, some standing in the marshes and dipping their heads into the water as they fished, others coasting through the air, then suddenly swooping down to the water, ducking their heads, and then sweeping back up into the sky, the tail of a fish flopping in their bills.

Leigh was distressed when they reefed the sails and dropped anchor for the night. Matt explained, with the possibility of hitting a log floating down the river or grounding the ship on a partially submerged sandbar, sailing the Mississippi at night was much too risky.

She was up early the next morning, but when she stepped on deck, she was disappointed yet again. An oppressive blanket of greenish fog covered the river, so thick that she couldn't even see the river banks. It was past mid-morning before the sun finally burned the fog off and they were able to proceed.

At a sharp bend in the river, they passed Fort St. Phillip and Fort Bourbon, both old French fortifications that had guarded New Orleans, ninety miles upstream, for years. Matt told Leigh that the forts had been used to protect the city from pirates and were still in use, now manned by Americans to protect the United States' vulnerable back door from the new enemy, the British.

As they sailed up the Mississippi closer to New Orleans, cypress swamps appeared on both sides of the river. Leigh stared in fascination at the huge cypress trees, with their reddish bark, grotesquely twisted roots, and delicate, fernlike leaves. She looked curiously at the clumps of pink that were scattered over the swamp. "What's that pink over there?" she asked Matt.

"Swamp roses," he answered. "I wish you could see them up close. Each flower is extremely delicate, and yet they're amazingly hardy. In spite of the wet, salty conditions, they manage to flourish and blossom."

Finally, the swamps gave way, and ground appeared, still very low, but dry. Here massive oak trees grew, draped with Spanish moss that waved in the gentle breeze like long, gray beards. Low palmetto palms and wild ferns studded the ground beneath them. Then huge sugar plantations appeared, and the land was covered as far as the eye could see with newly sprouted cane, cane that would grow as tall as a man.

As they sailed up the river, they passed several ships traveling downriver. Leigh paid special attention to their colors. Two flew American flags, but one carried the French tricolor and one a flag that Matt identified as Swedish. Leigh was relieved, convinced that she would have no trouble finding a ship traveling to England.

It was afternoon before she saw the wharves built on the levees and the ships massed around them. The port was crowded with all kinds of sailing ships: brigs, brigantines, luggers, schooners, cutters, and other smaller coastal vessels. And intermingled with these were the barges and flat-decked riverboats.

"Is this it? Is this New Orleans?" Leigh asked in an excited voice.

"Yes, sweet, this is it," Matt answered in an amused voice.

Leigh could hardly contain herself while Matt had a last conference with Kelly and the crew. Not until the gangplank was lowered and the crew began drifting down it, calling and waving to her as they left, did the full impact of her leaving strike her. For the first time, she realized she would never see these men or this ship again. A strange nostalgia filled her.

By the time Cookie and Kelly came on deck to tell her good-bye, she was depressed and teary-eyed. At the sight of her two friends, her composure broke and she threw herself in first one, then the other's arms, hugging them tightly and choking back tears. "Good-bye. Thank you for everything. I'll never forget you."

By the time it was over, Cookie stood, his weathered face wet with tears, sniffling. Kelly stood, shuffling his feet awkwardly, strangely misty-eyed, a pained look on his face.

"Come on, Leigh," Matt said irritably. "This isn't really good-bye. You'll be seeing these two old buzzards from time to time."

But Leigh knew she would never see her friends again. She forced back her tears and smiled bravely, saying, "Of course, how silly of me."

Matt took her arm and led her to the gangplank. Leigh stopped abruptly, seeing Lucifer sitting by the gangplank, his yellow eyes watching her intently. With a little sob, she fell to her knees, scooping the cat up and burying her face in his soft body. Huge tears ran down her cheeks and onto the cat's fur as she whispered, "Good-bye, Lucifer. Now, you be a good boy, hear?"

Lucifer tolerated her mauling patiently, but as soon as Leigh set him down, he began to bathe himself, apparently disgusted at the display and his coat being wetted by Leigh's salty tears. And then, as if to forgive her, he rose and rubbed himself against her skirt, purring loudly.

Leigh would have picked him up again, but Matt impatiently caught her arm and pulled her down the gangplank, mumbling in disgust, "For God's sake, this could go on all day. It's not the end of the world, you know."

Before Leigh knew it, Matt had firmly set her in an open carriage and himself beside her. As he reached for the reins, Leigh looked back over her shoulder at the *Avenger*. The last thing she saw was Lucifer strolling arrogantly down the gangplank, his tail held up proudly, his nose in the air, looking first one way, then the other with disdain.

As they drove over the levee and onto the streets that bordered the port, Leigh's distress at leaving her friends was forgotten as she was enveloped in the exciting sights and sounds of New Orleans. The streets around the harbor were crowded with lumbering drays, hauling crates of all sizes and kegs of molasses from the surrounding warehouses. Carriages weaved in and out of the slowly moving wagons, many of the carriages driven by slaves dressed in fancy, sometimes gaudy, livery. The occupants of these carriages were the affluent, the women dressed in beautiful muslin dresses of every shade of the rainbow and holding frilly parasols over their shoulders, the men dressed in cutaway frock coats, colorful cravats, ruffled shirts, knee breeches, and high, polished boots.

The streets were surrounded by tin-roofed buildings that were hardly more than shanties: shipping offices, sailmaker and caulker shops, noisy taverns, dingy hotels, stores that sold sailors' trinkets, and brothels, where the ladies of the night leaned from their windows, many in a shocking state of undress, and called to the men below.

The sidewalk, or *banquettes* as Matt called them, were swarming with people, many rushing about intent on their business, others strolling leisurely. Sailors in their baggy pants and striped shirts mingled with the loud-talking, swaggering river boatmen and with frontiersmen in their buckskins and coonskin hats, all heavily bearded, most carrying their long muskets with them. Mixed in with these were barefoot slaves in their coarse homespun shirts and breeches, an occasional Indian with a colorful blanket draped over his shoulder, and Creole gentlemen with their fine clothing and silk top hats, many sporting mustaches and neatly trimmed goatees. And intermingling with this strange mixture of men, were gaudily dressed, heavily rouged whores plying their trade, hawkers crying their wares, and street urchins darting to and fro and looking for victims, people whose pockets could be easily picked.

Leigh's eyes were wide with wonder, her ears filled with a mixture of strange languages: French, Spanish, and gumbo—a peculiar French dialect spoken by the slaves who served French masters. Never had she seen or heard anything like it.

Matt smiled as he watched Leigh craning her head this way and that, her eyes filled with excitement. He was getting almost as much pleasure watching her as she was from the new sights.

When they drove into an open square a few minutes later, Matt said, "This is the French Market."

Leigh looked about her in amazement. The *banquettes* and the square itself were crowded with open stalls. As Matt drove slowly through it, Leigh's eyes darted from one stall to another, greedily trying to absorb all the new sights. There were vegetable and fruit stalls, some loaded with produce she had heard of, but never seen, and some she had never even known existed: yams, tomatoes and mustard greens, melons and citrus fruits and strawberries, bananas from Central America, and coconuts and pineapples from the South Pacific. Several stalls on the *banquettes* were butcher shops, where the meat was cut to the customer's specifications. Next to each sat a crate of cackling chickens or quacking ducks.

Matt stopped next to one stall, saying, "This is something you won't see in any other city in America. The French Creoles prefer their coffee laced with chicory, a roasted root that gives it a rather bitter taste."

Leigh watched as the merchant scooped up the fresh roasted coffee beans from one barrel and then picked up a small piece of root from another. He tossed them into a grinder. The heavenly aroma of freshly ground coffee wafted through the air.

A little farther down the *banquette* was a small bakery. The tantalizing smell of freshly baked bread filled the air. Leigh's stomach grumbled loudly in response. Matt chuckled, stopped the carriage, and jumped down. In a few minutes, he returned, carrying two rolls, one of which he handed to Leigh.

"What is it?" Leigh asked as she bit into the delicious crescent-shaped roll.

"It's a croissant," Matt replied. "A sort of breakfast roll."

Leigh nibbled on her croissant hungrily as they drove around the marketplace, passing another stall where red and yellow peppers, garlic bulbs, fresh herbs, and ground spices were sold, and then a seafood stall displaying fresh fish, shrimp, crayfish, crabs, and oysters still in their grayish shells.

Leigh wrinkled her nose at the offensive odor coming from the fish stall and stared at one particularly horrible looking fish in revulsion. The fish was huge and black, with what looked like big black whiskers near its mouth. She pointed at it, saying with disgust, "What kind of fish is that?"

Matt chuckled, saying, "It's a catfish. They come from the river."

"People actually eat them?" Leigh asked in disbelief.

"Catfish is delicious, Leigh. Besides, it's also cheap. Seafood is the main ingredient in much of Louisiana cuisine since it's so abundant."

As they drove from the French Market onto the streets of the city itself, Matt said. "This is the Vieux Carré, the old French Quarter. This is the original spot picked by Bienville, the first French colonizer, back in 1718. At that time the city was named Nouvelle Orleans, after the Duc d'Orleans. It's built on a high spot by the river, the old camping grounds of the Houma Indians."

Leigh looked around her, again having never seen anything like it. The stucco houses sat side by side, painted in pastels of pink, yellow, green, and blue, their exteriors decorated with lacy grillwork and their balconies filled with pots of brightly blooming begonias, petunias, and geraniums. In fact, Leigh had never seen so many flowers. Climbing roses and vines of honeysuckle, jasmine, and wisteria grew up the walls of the houses and cascaded over the balconies in splashes of reds, pinks, yellows, oranges, whites, and lavenders. Even the trees were blooming, the huge, creamy magnolia blossoms adding their heavy scent to the sweet aroma that filled the air. No, Leigh thought, gazing about her in wonder, Boston was never like this. Compared to New Orleans, it seemed dull and dreary.

Matt stopped the carriage in front of one of the houses, saying, "This is my town house."

Leigh looked at the building in confusion. To her, it looked like a shop of some sort. In fact, a small business sign, written in French, hung across the front door, and people were coming from the building carrying small packages. She glanced up at the other two stories, saying, "You live over a shop?"

Matt chuckled at her dismayed look and said, "Yes. The lower floor of these town houses is not used as living space because of the danger of floods. The front is usually rented out to small businesses, and in back, you'll find the stables, kitchens, and laundry. The real living area is on the second floor, while the third floor is usually the servants' quarters."

Matt jumped down from the carriage and helped Leigh down. He grabbed Leigh's sea bag from the back of the carriage, flung it over his shoulder, and, taking her arm, led her to a wrought-iron gate at one side of the town house and opened it.

They walked down a dim corridor between the buildings. Leigh gasped in delight. A beautiful, cobblestone courtyard greeted her, its center dominated by a huge oak tree draped with Spanish moss. Leigh gazed around her in surprise, for the house was built around this sun-dappled courtyard with its lush green foliage. Her eyes flew over the colorful rosebushes, banana trees, azaleas, gardenias, then up the walls of the house where climbing roses and jasmine vied for space. Her eyes flew back to the ground, and, seeing a shrub she had noticed throughout their drive through the city, she asked, "What's that shrub with the long narrow leaves and pink blooms?"

"That's oleander," Matt replied. "The blooms are beautiful, but the leaves are deadly. Very toxic."

Leigh heard a tinkling sound and moved toward it. In one corner of the courtyard was a small fountain, the water trickling down its three tiers to a small pool and glistening in the sunlight. She gazed down at the water lilies in the pool and then blinked, hardly believing her eyes. Small golden fish darted here and there beneath the water's surface.

Matt smiled at her look of surprise, saying, "I don't suppose you've ever seen goldfish before. They're a tropical fish. Most are gold, but some are silver and gold."

Leigh sat on the side of the fountain for a few minutes, watching the goldfish with rapt fascination. The fish gazed back, apparently just as curious about her. One particularly brave little fish cautiously investigated her hand as she trailed it in the cool water.

Then she gazed about the courtyard again, drinking in its beauty. "I've never seen anything so lovely."

"The courtyards in New Orleans are more than ornamental," Matt informed her. "They act as a funnel to draw the air in. In another month, you'll see why. New Orleans can be stiflingly hot in the summer." He took her arm, saying, "Now come and see the house."

Matt led her up a curved marble stairway and opened the door at the top. They stepped into a wide foyer with a high ceiling from which a crystal chandelier hung. To one side, another marble staircase spiraled up to the third floor. Leigh peeked into the room at one side, seeing the long row of French doors at one end and the beautiful, pink marble fireplace at the other.

Matt took her arm and led her in, saying, "This is the petit salon. Beyond those doors is the grand salon. If you open the doors to combine both rooms, you have a room big enough for a small ballroom."

Leigh looked around the beautifully furnished room. There wasn't a speck of dust to be seen. Her eyes rested on a vase filled with fresh roses. "Someone lives here while you're gone?"

"I have a caretaker. He lives in a small apartment down by the stables." He frowned, looking about the room, mumbling, "Where are the dust covers?" His look turned angry. "That son-of-a-bitch! If he's been living in this house while I've been gone, I'll throttle him!" He dropped Leigh's sea bag to the floor and rushed from the room, bellowing, "Benson! Where are you?"

A few minutes later, Matt returned to the foyer where Leigh stood. Scowling, he said, "I can't find that bastard anywhere, but when I do—"

"*Sacre-bleu!* Matthew? Is that you?" a soft, feminine voice called from above them.

Chapter 11

Leigh glanced up the circular stairway from where the woman's voice had come. Seeing no one, she looked back at Matt. He stood with a surprised, dumbfounded look on his face.

Who was this woman in his town house, Leigh wondered. His old New Orleans mistress? From the look on Matt's face, he obviously hadn't expected to find her here. Had he told her to vacate the house before his return? And now, what would he do with two mistresses in his house? Awkward, to say the least. Leigh suppressed a giggle. Oh, this should be interesting, she thought, smiling smugly and stepping back into the shadows of the foyer. Let's see how the clever captain gets himself out of this one.

"*Mon dieu!* It *is* you, *mon* handsome *capitaine*," the woman said, sweeping down the stairs.

Leigh saw a blur of black as the woman threw herself into Matt's arms and he whirled her around. As he set her back down, grinning with pleasure, Leigh stared in surprise, for instead of being a voluptuous, beautiful, young woman as she had expected, the woman was exquisitely tiny and gray-haired.

"Grandmère!" Matt exclaimed. "What are you doing here? I thought you were in Martinique."

Grandmother? Leigh thought. This was Matt's French grandmother? The one that was a marquise? Or rather, the daughter of a marquis.

"*Non, non!*" the little old lady replied, throwing her small hands up in disgust. "Since the *stupide Anglais* have captured Martinique it is so—so . . . so dull!"

Matt chuckled, saying, "So you don't approve of the English on your beloved island?"

Grandmère's black eyes flashed. "*Non!* And now that the fool, Napoleon, has been beaten, they threaten to keep the island. Ridiculous! Martinique has always been French, and it always will be!"

Matt's grandmother turned slightly, and Leigh had a better view of her while she talked. Although her hair was gray, there was certainly nothing old about her actions. The little old lady vibrated with vitality, her features were animated, her black eyes sparkled with a youthfulness that belied her wrinkled face. Matt's eyes, Leigh realized.

Grandmère continued, "So I decided to visit with my sons in America until this foolishness in Martinique is settled. I would have gone to visit your *père* and *oncle* in Charleston, but the blockade prevented that. Those *stupide Anglais* again! So I came to visit your *oncles* in New Orleans instead."

"But Grandmère," Matt said, "what are you doing here then? Why aren't you at Uncle Paul's or Uncle Marcel's home?

"*Non, non*, Matthew!" Grandmère's eyes twinkled

mischievously. "Have you forgotten what silly wives they have? So frivolous. So snobbish. *Mon dieu!* I could not stand it!" She shrugged her elegant shoulders, saying, "For a short visit, perhaps, but not as a steady diet. So, since your town house was vacant, I decided to stay here instead."

"And my uncles allowed this?" Matt asked in disbelief. "They allowed you to stay here by yourself?"

Grandmère bristled. "*Mon dieu!* I am not a child. And I am not so old that I cannot look after myself. Have you forgotten I maintain my own household in Martinique? And I am not alone. I have my own servants with me." She smiled slyly, saying, "Besides, your *oncles* do not know I am in New Orleans yet."

"Don't know?" Mat gasped.

"*Non!*" She gave him an impish grin and said. "Once I have set up housekeeping here, they could hardly stop me. *Tu comprends?*"

Matt grinned and shook his head, thinking, Sneaky little minx, isn't she?

"You don't mind my using your town house, do you, Matthew? I mean, since you are gone most of the time anyway."

Matt frowned. Ordinarily, he wouldn't mind his grandmother using his town house, but he had planned on setting Leigh up here, and he could hardly have his grandmother and his mistress in the same residence. No, that arrangement would set even New Orleans back on its ear. Unable to find a graceful way out of his predicament, he stammered, "No—no, of course not, Grandmère."

While Matt had been trying to figure a way out of the awkward position he suddenly found himself confronted with, Grandmère's sharp eyes had caught

233

sight of Leigh. She peered into the shadows of the foyer, saying, *"Sacre-blue!* What have we here?"

Realizing she had been caught, there was nothing for Leigh to do but step forward.

Grandmère gave Leigh a quick, appraising look and then glared at her grandson, saying, "Shame on you, Matthew! I should think *mon petit fils* would have better manners than this. Why have you not introduced me to your lovely *amie?"*

Lovely? Leigh thought, feeling sick with humiliation. She was acutely aware of the finely dressed, exquisite lady standing before her and her own ragged appearance. Why, with my worn-out clothing, my loose, stringy hair, and my bare, dirty feet, I must look like a street urchin, she thought with self-disgust. She fervently wished the ground would open up and swallow her.

Matt colored under his grandmother's criticism. Then he frowned, saying, "My apology, Grandmère. Please allow me to introduce Miss Leigh O'Neal."

Leigh smiled nervously and bobbed a quick curtsy. "How do you do, your . . ." She frowned, then blurted, "Your highness."

Grandmère drew back, a surprised look on her face. "Your highness?"

Leigh flushed, saying, "I'm sorry. I'm afraid I don't know how to address a marquise."

"Marquise? *Mon dieu!* Has my grandson been filling you with a lot of nonsense about my being a marquise? *Non, non, ma petite."* Her dark eyes twinkled. "It's bad enough that these silly New Orleans Creoles believe such foolishness. But you, *ma amie? Non,* I can tell you're much too intelligent to believe that rubbish."

"Then—then, what shall I call you?" Leigh stammered.

"Why, Grandmère, of course. That's what all of my younger *amis* call me." She turned, dismissing the subject, and looked at her grandson, her delicate eyebrows raised quizzically.

Seeing her look, Matt groaned silently, thinking, Oh God, now I've got to explain Leigh and what she's doing here. For lack of a handy lie, he blurted the truth, or at least part of the truth. "Leigh is the niece of one of my sailors, Grandmère. Or rather, he *was* one of my sailors. You see, he was killed aboard ship during a storm. A spar fell, and he threw himself over me and saved my life. Before he died, I promised him I'd take care of his niece. Her mother had died just a few months earlier."

Grandmère looked at Leigh with compassion. "*Mon dieu*, the poor *petite* has no one?"

"No," Matt answered firmly, shooting Leigh a warning look.

Leigh ignored his look and stepped forward, saying hotly, "That's not true! I have a father in England. My uncle was taking me to him when he was killed."

Matt threw up his hands in disgust, saying, "You're not going to start that foolishness again, are you?"

"It's not foolishness!" Leigh spat back.

"To hell it isn't!" Matt roared.

Grandmère had been watching the heated argument in amazement. But it was beginning to look as though the argument was going to get more physical. She interrupted them, saying, "*Non, non*, children! Calm yourselves!" She looked at the two young people glaring at each other and then turned to her grandson, saying, "Does she have a father in England?"

Matt sighed in exasperation, saying, "Who knows?

She claims her mother didn't tell her about him until she was dying. Until then, she had always thought her father had died at sea before she was born."

Grandmère turned to Leigh. "Is this true, *petite*?"

"Yes," Leigh answered. "My mother told me about him right before she died." She took a deep breath and raised her chin proudly, a defiant look in her eyes. "I never knew I was illegitimate until then. She made my uncle promise to take me to him."

If Leigh had thought her illegitimacy would shock grandmère, she was mistaken. Having been a lady-in-waiting at the licentious French court and having led a full, robust life, there was very little that shocked the old lady. Without so much as a quirk of an eyebrow, she turned to Matt, saying, "And what did this uncle tell you about her *père*?"

"Nothing!" Matt snorted. "He never said a damned thing about her having a living father, much less his being a lord," he added sarcastically. "He asked me for my promise to take care of her and I gave it to him."

"Lord? Your father is an English lord?" Grandmère asked Leigh.

"Yes, he is!" Leigh said stubbornly. "And I can prove it. I have his ring, the ring he gave my mother before she sailed from England."

"That's a lot of bilge water!" Matt spat. "I told you that ring was probably stolen. Nobles don't give their signet rings to servant wenches."

Leigh fought back the tears stinging her eyes. She stamped her foot angrily and yelled, "I don't give a damn what you think! All I want is my money, you — you pirate!"

"Money? What money?" Grandmère asked, confused.

"The money my uncle gave him for safekeeping," Leigh answered, shooting Matt an accusing glare. "It's mine! My mother gave it to my uncle to pay for our passage to England."

"And is this what you plan to do with it? Go to England and find your father?" Grandmère asked.

Matt scoffed, saying, "Find her father? How in the hell is she going to do that? She doesn't even know his name, or where he lives, much less if he'll acknowledge her."

"That's not your problem, Captain!" Leigh shot back. "Just give me my money and I'll leave!"

Grandmère thought things were getting out of hand again. Besides, she needed time to think all of this through. She said in a soothing voice, "Come, come, let's all go into the salon and having something to calm our nerves."

She turned regally and walked out of the foyer before either Matt or Leigh could object, forcing them to follow her.

Once in the salon, Grandmère sat sedately in a chair, every inch the aristocrat. Leigh flounced down in a chair opposite her, while Matt walked angrily to the liquor cabinet to pour drinks.

"I'll have sherry, Matthew, Grandmère said. She turned to Leigh, saying, "What about you, *petite*?"

"Nothing, thank you," Leigh replied tightly.

Grandmère suppressed a chuckle. What a *magnifique*, stubborn little one, she thought. *"Non,"* she said softly. "Have a sherry, *petite*. It will help you relax."

Matt handed a small glass of sherry to each woman. The older woman accepted hers gracefully. Leigh, however, took the glass reluctantly and shot Matt a sullen look.

Matt glared back at her, then turned and walked back to the liquor cabinet. He poured himself a stiff drink and downed it quickly. Damned the little bitch, he thought, furious. Not only had she embarrassed him in front of his grandmother by making him lose his temper, but she was still thinking about that father of hers. And all this time, he thought that he had talked her out of that foolishness. He wouldn't be surprised if she had deliberately waited until they reached New Orleans to spring that little bit of deception on him. Yes, she had deliberately lulled him into thinking she was agreeable to being his mistress. He should have known better than to trust a woman, especially her. Well, he would be damned if he would give her that money. She wasn't going to get away from him that easily.

While Matt had been thinking these dark thoughts, Grandmère had been thinking her own. She was willing to accept Leigh's illegitimacy with a grain of salt and didn't for one minute doubt that she might be the daughter of an English lord. She knew all about noblemen and their by-blows, but she had to agree with her grandson about the girl going to England to find her father. Even if she knew his name and where to find him, it would be foolish. Noblemen hardly ever recognized their bastards born to women of noble birth, much less to servant women.

But Leigh's birth and foolish plans was not what was teasing Grandmère's curiosity. Despite Matt's explanation that he was looking after the girl because of a promise made to her uncle, Grandmère sensed that there was much more to their relationship than that, for she was no fool. If he simply felt responsible for her, he wouldn't have brought her to his own home. No, by bringing her here, he had all but declared her as his mistress. And if she was his mistress, that meant he wanted her very badly, for Grandmère knew Matt had never had a mistress before, many affairs, yes, but never one he cared for enough to make his mistress. And Grandmère had a spy system that would have made Napoleon green with envy. There was nothing, absolutely nothing, that she didn't know about her considerable family or, for that matter, most of the French Creoles on Martinique and in New Orleans.

She appraised Leigh from under lowered lashes while she sipped her sherry. She could understand why her grandson was attracted to the girl. Even in her ragged clothing and under all that dirt and horrible tan, Leigh was a rare beauty. And the girl certainly wasn't mealy-mouthed or meek. Grandmère detested that kind of woman. They disgusted her. No, from the way Leigh had stood up to Matt, she had spirit. Grandmère chuckled to herself. *Mon dieu*, the sparks had certainly flown between those two for a few minutes there.

Grandmère continued to study Leigh discreetly, noting her intelligent gray eyes, her graceful movements, the determined set of her chin and shoulders, the proud tilt of her head, her mobile mouth. Grandmère was an astute judge of character. She had learned years ago that more could be learned by observing a person when they didn't know they were being watched than by anything they might otherwise say or do. Grandmère decided that she liked what she saw. The glimmer of a sneaky plan sparked in her crafty mind. *Oui*, she thought, this girl would do nicely.

Having finished the appraisal to her satisfaction, Grandmère reached across and patted Leigh's knee, saying softly, "Drink your sherry, *petite*. It will make you feel better."

Leigh had been silently railing at Matt, again calling him every ugly name she knew. When Grandmère touched her and spoke gently to her, Leigh suddenly felt ashamed of herself. Goodness, she thought, what must Grandmère think of her, screeching like a common fishwife? It certainly wasn't this sweet old lady's fault. And it's a wonder she and Matt hadn't caused Grandmère to have a heart attack with all their yelling at each other. She smiled weakly at the old woman and hesitantly took a sip of her drink. Having never drunk any spirits before, she had been prepared for a fiery and bitter taste. But surprisingly, the sherry tasted mellow and warmed her stomach, relaxing the hard knot that had formed there. She sat back and sipped again at her drink.

Grandmère's attention turned to Matt, who was pacing the floor in agitation, nursing his third drink. She knew her handsome grandson was upset about more than just the argument. She had never seen Matt lose control. He was always maddeningly calm and cool. The fact that he had reacted so violently told her volumes. Obviously, he didn't want to let the girl go. Just how badly was he smitten? How far would he go to hold her?

Grandmère's look turned speculative. For years, she had been anxiously waiting for this favored grandson to marry. She was eighty, now, and beginning to worry. Why did men always have this insane, obstinate obsession with what they referred to as giving up their freedom? Giving one's heart and loving someone didn't rob one of anything. *Mon dieu*, how ridiculous! If anything, that giving enhanced the giver and strengthened the depths of his

240

character.

Ah, there was nothing to do but take things into her own hands, Grandmère decided. These two must marry, but she would have to be careful about how she arranged it. It wouldn't do for her grandson to get suspicious. If he ever suspected what she was doing, he would balk. Stubborn fool that he was!

Grandmère sighed and said, "*Mon dieu*, Matthew! Will you sit down? All that pacing is exhausting me."

Matt shot Leigh a hot look, then flopped into an overstuffed chair, his long legs stretched out before him.

Grandmère smiled sweetly at him, saying, "You are very lucky I was here when you arrived, Matthew."

Matt's eyebrows rose. Lucky? He had been thinking just the opposite. As much as he loved his grandmother, she had certainly messed up his plans for making Leigh his mistress. Well, by God, he wasn't about to give Leigh up. He would just find another house for her. By hook or by crook, he would keep her. She had become a fever in his blood, and he wasn't going to let her go until that fever had been quenched. "Oh?" he replied dryly. "In what way?"

"*Ma foi!* That should be obvious," Grandmère answered innocently. "With me to act as chaperone, you'll be able to house your ward in your own home."

Matt shot up in his chair. "My ward?"

"*Oui*. Did you not say you promised her uncle you'd look after her? That makes you her guardian and her your ward."

Leigh's look was horrified. "No! That's impossible! I have a living father. How can he"—she shot Matt a heated look—"be my guardian?"

Grandmère looked at Leigh, her expression one of studied compassion, and said softly, "*Non, ma petite.*

241

Since your parents weren't married, your father isn't your legal father. When your mother died, your uncle, as your only living relative, became your guardian. And when he died, he turned that responsibility over to Matthew." She patted Leigh's hand, saying in a soothing voice, "Don't you worry about a thing, *ma petite*. I assure you my grandson takes his obligations very seriously."

"But he can't be my guardian," Leigh objected. "There was no will."

"Non," Grandmère answered smoothly, "but a will isn't necessary, *petite*. If there were witnesses present, my grandson's word is as binding as his signature. Tomorrow, he will go to the magistrate with the witnesses and get the papers drawn up."

Leigh smiled smugly. "But he can't be my guardian. I'm over eighteen."

Grandmère's eyebrows rose. Ah, she would have to watch herself with this one. She was as sharp as a tack. "How old are you, *petite*?"

"I'm nineteen," Leigh replied.

"Ah, what a shame," Grandmère said in a sympathetic voice. "But I'm afraid my grandson is still your legal guardian. In Louisiana, the legal age for a woman is twenty-one." Grandmère had no idea what the legal age in Louisiana was, nor could she have cared less. She wasn't about to have something as insignificant as legality ruin her plans. Typically, if something got in her way, she simply brushed it aside.

Leigh sat back, too shocked to speak.

Matt grinned with smug satisfaction, thinking, If Leigh was his ward, he had control of her money. She would have to forget that ridiculous plan of going to England to find her father. Then he frowned, thinking, But if she's my ward, how can she be my mistress? There was a lot of his grandmother in Matt. Like her, if anything didn't suit his purpose, he simply tossed it aside, Well, no one will have to know what goes on in the privacy of my own home, he thought. As soon as Grandmère's visit was over, he would find a companion who would mind her own business and make Leigh his mistress again.

Grandmère knew what Matt was thinking. That didn't suit her plans at all. She smiled sweetly at Leigh, saying, "Don't you worry, *ma petite*. I'll stay here until you are of age and make sure my grandson turns your money over to you. Then, if you still want to, you can go to England to find your father."

"You'll stay here for two years?" Matt blurted.

"*Oui*, Matthew. *Mon dieu*, what's wrong with you? This lovely girl is your ward. We must protect her reputation at all costs!"

Leigh blushed hotly at the mention of her reputation, thinking that Matt had already ruined that. She could hardly tell the old lady that her grandson had forced her to be his mistress. She would be so shocked, she would probably have a stroke. No, she would have to keep silent about that, if only in consideration for Grandmère.

Grandmère's sharp eyes hadn't missed Leigh's blush. So, she thought, he has already claimed her. The rogue! Now she was even more determined to pursue her plans. She glanced at her scowling grandson. He looks like a little boy who has had his favorite toy taken away, she thought. Well, he can have her back—but on my terms.

Grandmère rose, saying in a firm voice, "And now I think it's time I showed your lovely ward her room." To Leigh she said, "Come, *ma petite*, you look tired. Sea travel is so exhausting, *oui*? Maybe you will have

243

time for a nap before dinner."

Grandmère left her grandson stewing while she led Leigh away.

Leigh followed Grandmère down the long hallway, turning several times before they walked into a large bedroom. Stepping into it, she gasped with delight. The room was decorated tastefully in muted greens and blues. A large four-poster bed dominated the room. A comfortable chaise longue was by the French doors that opened onto the balcony overlooking the courtyard. A large dressing table, with a massive mirror over it, lined almost one entire wall.

"Do you like it, *petite*?"

"It's lovely," Leigh answered in all honesty.

Grandmère glanced at Leigh's dirty, ragged clothing and said, "I'll have a bath sent up to you. And then, if you wish, you can take a nap before dinner."

The bath sounded wonderful to Leigh, but the nap was definitely out. No, with all these new developments, she needed time to think, not sleep. "Thank you, Grandmère. The bath sounds wonderful. But I think I need more than just a nap. I really am exhausted. If you don't mind, I think I'll just go to bed and sleep straight through till morning."

Grandmère looked at Leigh thoughtfully. The girl did look drawn and pale beneath that tan. "*Oui*, I understand. But you mustn't go without something to eat until morning. I'll have a light snack sent up with your bath."

"Thank you," Leigh replied.

Grandmère walked to the door, then turned, saying, "I hope you are feeling better in the morning."

"I'm sure I will," Leigh answered, wondering how she was going to get out of this mess.

Grandmère closed the door behind her and sought

out her maid. Leaving word for her to attend to Leigh's needs, she walked quickly back to the salon where Matt waited. She could hardly wait to put the rest of her plan into action.

She walked into the salon, saying, "*Oui*, Matthew, she is lovely. A rare jewel. A treasure."

Matt glared at her, but Grandmère ignored his scowl, saying, "But really, Matthew, those filthy clothes she's wearing!" She wrinkled her aristocratic nose with distaste. "*Affreux!* You can't have your ward looking like that."

"Well, you can't blame me for that!" Matt snapped. "If it weren't for me, she'd have arrived here in a pair of men's breeches and a floppy shirt."

"Men's breeches?" Grandmère gasped, truly shocked for the first time in many a year.

"Yes, dammit! That's what she had on when we discovered her. She was a stowaway, you know."

"A stowaway?"

"Yes," Matt said in a disgusted voice. "Her uncle sneaked her on board to get her through the blockade. He planned on taking her to France, and then to England. Hell, she ran around in that damned boy's disguise for a month after he was killed, before we discovered she was really a female."

Grandmère's eyebrows rose another notch. "And how did you discover that?"

"When she was injured, fighting a British sailor."

"*Mon dieu!* She fought a British sailor?"

"Sit down, Grandmère," Matt said with an exasperated sigh. "I'll tell you the whole story. If you're going to take on Leigh, you'd better know what you're getting yourself into."

Matt told his grandmother the whole story, carefully deleting his taking Leigh for his mistress, of course. She had already guessed that part, but she was fascinated with the tale. What a clever girl, she thought. So spirited. So brave. Her appreciation of Leigh rose to new heights and, with it, her determination to have her as her grandson's wife. She smiled, saying calmly, "We'll just have to get her some new clothes first thing tomorrow."

"You mean you're still willing to take her on?" Matt asked in disbelief. "Knowing her deceit and obstinacy? She's incorrigible!"

Grandmère chuckled to herself. She knew why her grandson was so outraged. The girl had bested him, and his male pride was injured. She looked at him with a perfectly straight face, saying, "*Oui*, Matthew, but she is still your responsibility." She sighed deeply. "*Oui*, I'm afraid it's our Christian duty."

Matt glanced at his grandmother suspiciously. She had never been an overly pious woman. This sudden sanctimonious attitude didn't suit her at all.

Grandmère continued, "You do not mind my buying her a few clothes?"

Matt didn't mind at all. In fact, that was one of the first things he had planned to do when they reached New Orleans. Leigh was a beautiful woman. He was anxious to see her dressed in equally beautiful clothing. "Of course not!" he snapped.

Grandmère smiled sweetly and threw in her trump card. "And as soon as she had been properly attired, I shall introduce her into Creole society."

Matt stared at her in disbelief, then laughed harshly, saying, "You can't be serious. Haven't you forgotten something? She's an American. You know how these Creoles feel about Americans."

"*Oui*." Grandmère shrugged her shoulders. "But they'll accept her. Particularly, when I tell them she's

246

the daughter of a lord. You know how impression-able they are."

"You expect them to believe that?" Matt exclaimed. "That she's the daughter of an English lord? With a last name like O'Neal?"

"Sacre-bleu! Of course, I won't tell them she's the daughter of an English lord. *Non*, Leigh will be the daughter of an Irish lord."

"Irish lord?" Matt asked in astonishment.

"For your information, Matthew, O'Neal is a noble Irish name. When I served at court, we had an Irish lord by the name of O'Neal visit, and the king and queen received him themselves. *Non*. These silly Creoles won't care if she's Irish or English. Just as long as she has noble blood in her, *n'est ce pas*?"

"Haven't you forgotten something?" Matt said in an exasperated voice. "Leigh was a stowaway on my ship. She was a lone woman on a ship for almost four months with over two hundred men. How do you think your snobbish Creoles are going to feel about that? When they hear that, they won't touch her with a ten-foot pole."

"But they won't know that," Grandmère replied in a cool voice.

"Won't know it? Hell, every man on my ship knew about Leigh. I'm sure the story has spread all over the port by now."

"Mon dieu! Your crew and my Creoles don't mix. And to squelch any rumors they might hear, I shall tell them the *petite* has been living with me on Martinique for the past year and arrived in New Orleans with me."

"Arrived with you?"

"Oui. I told you, your *oncles* do not know I am in New Orleans yet. And I brought my own servants

247

with me. The *petite* could have easily been overlooked in my large entourage when we docked. Besides, the Creoles will believe anything I tell them." Her black eyes sparkled with amusement. "They wouldn't dare question me. Their own marquise?"

Matt sighed in exasperation and ran his fingers through his thick golden hair. Of course, the damned Creoles would believe Grandmère. Hell, she could tell them Leigh was a saint, newly arrived from heaven in a gilded carriage, and the stupid fools would believe her. And she *would* tell them that story about Leigh. His grandmother had absolutely no compunction at all about lying if it suited her purpose. He, himself, had heard her tell the most outrageous fibs. But Grandmère made an art out of lying. She told her fabrications with such flair and boldness that no one, not only the Creoles, ever doubted her for a minute. Grandmère's habit of rearranging the facts to suit her purpose had always amused Matt—up till now.

He said in a disgusted voice, "Grandmère, don't you think you should mend your ways? Lying? Particularly at your age!"

"*Mon dieu!* You're calling your own grandmère a liar?" she asked in outrage.

"Yes, dammit! You and I both know it. And I don't want Leigh having any part of it."

"But, Matthew," Grandmère said in a hurt tone of voice, "I'm only doing it for you. After all, we have to introduce the *petite* into society if you are going to fulfill your obligation as her guardian. How else would you arrange a proper marriage for her?"

Matt shot to his feet, bellowing, "Marriage! What in the hell are you talking about?"

"Calm yourself, Matthew!" Grandmère said in a firm voice. "As the girl's guardian, it's your responsi-

248

bility to contract a suitable marriage for her, one to her best advantage. And the New Orleans Creoles certainly have enough eligible bachelors, many independently wealthy men. With her beauty we should have several offers in no time at all."

"She's too damned young to get married."

"*Non, non*. The Creole girls are married by the time they're sixteen. Or at least betrothed. In a few years, the girl will be a *vieille fille*, a spinster."

"I won't have it, Grandmère," Matt said in a hard voice. "I'll not have Leigh placed on the marriage market and paraded around in front of a bunch of randy Creoles!"

Grandmère jumped to her feet. "*Sacre-bleu!* What in the world is wrong with you, Matthew? We are not going to force the girl. She can make her own choice. Even her own father would make every effort to see her safely married. I can't understand your objection."

Matt could hardly admit to his grandmother what his real objection was. How could he tell her he didn't want to see Leigh married because he wanted her himself—as his mistress. He glared at the old woman.

Grandmère ignored him and paced the room, pretending to be thinking. Then she turned, saying, "I think I know the perfect match for her—René."

"René? That rake!" Matt yelled.

"*Mon dieu!* Calm yourself! I will not have you calling *mon petit fils*, and your cousin, such a name. *Affreux!* I am ashamed of you."

"Grandmère, you know as well as I do that René is the biggest womanizer in New Orleans."

Grandmère shrugged. "Honoré then. He's such a sweet boy."

"Baby, you mean! At least you could pick a real

man."

"*Oui*, Honoré is a shy boy," Grandmère answered thoughtfully. "But then there's your other cousins. Aumont, Jean, Philippe. And that handsome Diego de Leon. He's Spanish, of course. But he does own his own plantation."

"My God, Grandmère! Everyone of them would try to sneak Leigh off into the bushes the first chance he got."

Grandmère whirled, saying in a stern voice, "*Non!* There will be no seductions! I, myself, shall watch over the *petite*. I'll be as strict as a Spanish duenna. I'll not take my eyes off her for one second. The man who wants her for his own will have to do the honorable thing and marry her."

Matt looked at the steely gleam in his grandmother's eyes and frowned. Had Leigh told her of his seduction? No, Leigh wouldn't do that, if for no other reason than to save herself from embarrassment. But Matt had the distinct impression his grandmother's words had not been an announcement, but rather a warning. His frustration rose to the breaking point, for Matt was a man accustomed to getting what he wanted, and on his own terms.

He glared at his grandmother, saying hotly, "All right, dammit! Do what you want with the girl!" He turned and walked angrily to the door, shouting over his shoulder, "And don't wait dinner for me! I won't be back tonight!"

Grandmère could hardly contain herself until Matt left the room. She clapped her hands like a happy child and chuckled gleefully, thinking, This is working out even better than I thought. I've hardly begun, and already he is blind with jealousy.

Matt stormed through the courtyard and out to the

250

carriage. There was no doubt in his mind now that Grandmère had issued him an ultimatum. If he wanted Leigh himself, he would have to marry her. And give up his freedom? No, by damn! No woman had brought him to his knees. To hell with her! There were plenty of women even more beautiful than Leigh. And he knew just where to find them. He climbed into his carriage and drove off, heading for the most exclusive bordello in New Orleans.

Chapter 12

Leigh was still pacing the bedroom in agitation long after she had finished her bath and eaten the small snack Grandmère had sent to her, her thoughts racing through her head.

Dammit, if only she had her money. Now she was trapped here just as she had been trapped on the *Avenger*, but this time not by the broad expanse of sea, but by something as ridiculous as her age. And now, she not only had Matt fouling her plans to search for her father, she had his grandmother to contend with, too. Oh, she knew the sweet old lady was only doing what she thought was best for her. At least, her intentions, unlike her grandson's, were honorable. But she couldn't stay here, remaining in a vacuum, for two years. It was unthinkable. She was anxious to find her father and sick and tired of people interfering in her life! None of it would have happened if her Uncle Sean hadn't asked Matt to take care of her.

She looked toward the heavens and muttered,

"Damn you, Uncle Sean! Just look at the mess you got me into! And I told you not to give my money to that pirate!"

She had to have money. How else could she buy passage to England? Her eyes flew across the room and landed on a pair of silver candlesticks on the mantel over the fireplace. She imagined that they would bring a good price at a pawnshop. Should she? It would serve Matt right for being so overbearing in insisting upon taking care of her. And besides, he had her money. But, no, she couldn't steal. Just because he was a thief, was no reason for her to sink to such depths, no matter how desperate she was.

A knock at the door startled her. "*Mademoiselle* O'Neal?" a feminine voice called softly.

That was Marie's voice, Grandmère's maid, Leigh realized. But she was supposed to be in bed and asleep by this time.

Leigh rushed to the bed, yanked the covers back, and crawled in. Holding the bedcovers tightly up over her shoulders so the maid couldn't see she was still wearing the wrapper Marie had loaned her, she called, "Come in, Marie."

The door opened and the maid stepped into the room, saying, "Pardon, *mademoiselle*, but I believe this belongs to you." She held out Leigh's sea bag.

Leigh pretended to rub the sleep from her eyes and muttered, "Oh, yes. I must have left it downstairs. Just put it there on that chair. I'll see to it in the morning."

After the maid had left, Leigh sat up and stared at the sea bag, a sudden glimmer coming to her eyes. That's it, she thought. That's how I can get to England. I'll disguise myself again and hire out as a cabin boy. And then, I can use the money I earn to tide me over until I find my father. Why, I even have experience, but I won't tell the captain I served on the *Avenger*. No, I'll make up some other ship.

The covers went flying as Leigh tore from the bed and rushed to her sea bag. Within minutes, she was dressed in her old floppy shirt, baggy pants, and sea boots. As she braided her hair, doubts entered her mind. What if you're discovered, that familiar little voice in her head asked. I won't be, Leigh assured herself. If it hadn't been for that silly fight with the British sailor aboard the *Avenger*, they never would have discovered my true identity.

She slung her sea bag over her shoulder, walked to the French door, and peeked over the gallery to the courtyard, thinking that she was glad Matt had gone for the night. Even from her room, she had heard him yelling he wouldn't be back tonight. It would be just like him to catch her sneaking out, but this way, they wouldn't miss her until morning. By that time, if she found a ship that sailed tonight, she would be long gone. Oh, she would just love to see the look on Matt's smug face when he found her missing. Try and make a pet out of her! Oh, no, that was the last time he interfered in her life!

Seeing no one in the courtyard below, Leigh cautiously crept down the gallery and then the stairs to the ground level. She darted across the courtyard and through the gate, then swaggered down the street, ignoring the curious glances sent her way by the Creoles out for an evening stroll.

By the time she reached the French Market, it was growing dark and she became confused in the maze of stalls, stalls that were now closed and boarded up tightly. She gazed about the deserted square. She had passed several streets, but couldn't remember which one she and Matt had taken when they had driven from the harbor to the city. Then, spying a street at the end, she headed for it.

After making a few more turns, Leigh realized she was lost. How could she have possibly missed the harbor? She knew it was somewhere in this direction.

She looked around her, swallowing nervously. It obviously wasn't the best of neighborhoods. Squatted all along the street were saloons, barrelhouses, nickel-and-dime hotels, gambling joints, and sleazy brothels, the weather-beaten buildings looking all the more sinister in the dim lamplights that dotted the narrow street. A stench filled the air, the smell of damp, rotting wood and scummy mud puddles mixed with sour whiskey, stale tobacco smoke, unwashed bodies, vomit, and the musky odor of sex. From inside the buildings, the sound of tinny piano music, rolling dice, boisterous male laughter, loud, foul-mouthed curses, and shrill women's laughter drifted out into the damp air. Men swarmed over the streets, like bees to honey. Sailors, buckskin-clad frontiersmen, and river boatmen staggered drunkenly from one saloon to the next, brushing shoulders with sleekly dressed, crafty-eyed gamblers and sly pickpockets. And in almost every window and every doorway, a whore stood, some with breasts brazenly exposed, calling their specialties to the men.

Leigh blushed furiously at the harlots' vulgar language, then almost jumped out of her skin as a woman's shrill scream for help rent the air. She looked about her wildly, but apparently, no one else had even noticed. She wondered at the others' indifference. Had they not heard the cry above the din of the other noises, or had they heard and deliberately ignored it, too intent on their own pleasures to be bothered?

The sound of a low moan drew her attention. She turned and peered down the darkened alley behind her, barely able to see a man lying face down in a mud puddle. A split second later, another man darted from the alley and flew by her, stuffing a handful of silver dollars into his pocket, the other hand holding a blood-stained knife. Leigh's knees buckled; she staggered back into the shadows of the building next to her, her heart racing in fear. My God, this place is dangerous, she thought in horror.

She turned to beat a hasty retreat and then froze, her eyes wide with shock. A woman was dancing in the street, if that's what one could call her wild gyrations, and except for a very brief apron tied around her waist, she was totally naked. Drawn by the spectacle, a circle of men crowded around her, laughing lewdly and making crude comments. Despite herself, Leigh couldn't help but stare in a mixture of disgust and fascination, the sight made even more obscene by the fact that the woman was grossly obese, her huge breasts bobbing like melons and her fat buttocks quivering like two massive blobs of jelly.

Her eyes still glued to the outrageous dancer, Leigh stepped forward, then bumped into a burly sailor going in the opposite direction.

"Here, now, mate, watch where you're goin'," the sailor said in a gruff voice, pushing Leigh backward so roughly she dropped her sea bag.

Leigh looked up at the glaring giant, his face covered with a black, bristly beard, and then at his three companions, sneering at her and swaying slightly. The smell of whiskey coming from their breaths was overpowering.

" 'Cuse me," she mumbled and bent to pick up her sea bag.

"My, ain't he polite?" one of the sailors asked sarcastically.

Leigh ventured a quick glance at the man. One side of his face was horribly scarred, giving him a sinister, evil appearance. Fear crawled up her spine. She grabbed her sea bag and scrambled around the line of sailors blocking her way.

The giant caught her arm and swung her around, asking in a belligerent voice, "What's your hurry, mate?"

Leigh jerked her arm away, crying, "Let me go!"

A third, weasel-faced sailor said, "I'll lay you odds he's rolled some drunk in one of these alleys, and that's why he's in such a hurry to get away."

"That's not true!" Leigh denied.

The fourth sailor, short but powerfully muscled, looked over his shoulder into the alley behind him. There was something about his long, hairy arms and stocky body that reminded Leigh of an ape. "Hey, that's true! There's some bloke lying on the ground back there."

The giant glared down at Leigh, his black eyes narrowing beneath his bushy eyebrows.

"I didn't do that!" Leigh cried. "Someone else did."

The weasel-faced man stepped forward, saying, "Hey, mate, we ain't gonna tell nobody. Not if you hand over what you took off him, that is," he added in a threatening voice.

"Yeah," the scarred sailor said, "hand it over and we'll let you go."

Leigh dropped her sea bag and jerked her arm free from the giant's grasp. Before he could react, she ducked around him and started to dart away.

"Catch him!" weasel-face cried.

The apelike sailor reached out his long, hairy arm and caught Leigh's shoulder, dragging her back. She struggled furiously, and in the scuffle, her stocking cap was knocked off, and her long braid came tumbling down. The sailor's eyes widened in surprise.

"Well, would you look at that! He's a girl!" weasel-face said in an astonished voice.

The giant caught Leigh's arm and swung her around to face the lamplight. "Aye, and a right pretty one, too."

Before Leigh realized what he intended, he caught the neckline of her shirt in his other big hand and ripped it open, the buttons popping and flying everywhere. Leigh looked down at her bared breasts in horror.

"Man, would you look at them tits? I ain't never seen such lovelies," the ape-man said in a hoarse voice, his eyes glittering with lust.

Leigh jerked her arm from the giant's hamlike fist and pulled the gaping shirt closed over her breasts, her heart racing in fear. "Stay away from me," she hissed, stepping back, her eyes darting wildly from one man to the other.

The giant towered over her, his dark eyes boring into hers, asking in a suspicious voice, "Who're you runnin' from in that disguise? The police? You running from something, girl? Did you rob someone, or kill someone?"

"Who cares why she's runnin'?" Weasel-face said in a whining voice. "She's the best-lookin' thing I've ever seen an' I got an itch that needs scratchin'."

The scarred sailor leered down at Leigh. "I could stand a taste of that, myself."

Leigh looked at the ugly, twisted face. A line of saliva dribbled down his chin. She shivered in both revulsion and fear.

"Yeah, Cap'n. What you say we take this little piece upstairs to our room and have a little fun?" the apelike sailor chimed in.

Captain, Leigh thought in surprise. She glanced

quickly up at the giant, looming over her. He's a captain? Surely, he wouldn't stand by and watch his crew rape her. But one look into the giant's lust-filled eyes and Leigh knew he would not only do just that, but was anticipating taking part in the gang rape himself.

Terror, like none she had ever known, seized her. She whirled to flee and then, when the giant caught her arm again in a bone-crushing grip, screamed at the top of her lungs, "Help! Someone help me!"

"Shut up, you little bitch!" the apelike sailor spat, cuffing her jaw before he caught her other arm.

Leigh's senses spun; she saw stars. She struggled for consciousness, knowing that if she lost it, she was as good as dead. As the two sailors dragged her to a doorway, she screamed again, "Help! Please!"

Matt drove his carriage through the darkened streets, a furious look on his face.

He had gone to the most exclusive brothel in New Orleans and picked out the most beautiful courtesan there, but when they had gone up to her room, to his total horror, he had discovered that he couldn't become aroused. Oh, he couldn't fault the woman. She had tried every trick she knew. But despite everything, he had remained as limp as a dishrag. It had been the most humiliating experience in his life.

Furious with himself, he had dressed, slammed the money down on the courtesan's dresser, and stormed out of the house. Now, as he drove through the cool night air, he was still seething, his angry thoughts on Leigh.

Damn the deceiving little bitch! What had she done to him? Put some crazy hex on him? Christ! She made a fool of him at every turn. First, humiliating him in front of his crew, and then, embarrassing him in front of his grandmother. And now, she had unmanned him!

Oh yes, he knew it was her fault that he hadn't been able to respond. He hadn't wanted the prostitute; he had wanted Leigh. The little witch! She had woven her silken web around him so tightly that even his own body wouldn't obey him anymore. Damn, if he could get his hands on her right now, he would throttle her!

To make matters worse, he couldn't even go back to his own house, not without arousing Grandmère's curiosity, he thought angrily as he turned a corner sharply. He had told his grandmother that he wouldn't be back tonight, and he knew she had guessed where he had gone. Well, he would be damned if he would go sneaking back to the house like some whipped puppy. No, he would spend the night on the *Avenger*.

He turned another corner, taking a shortcut to the harbor, anxious to be back in his cabin where he could drown his anger in a bottle. As he drove down the dim, noisy thoroughfare, he looked about him warily. Gallatin Street was the roughest, toughest street in New Orleans. In a city that had more than its share of saloons, gambling joints, dives, and cribs, the worst were on this street. Here, crime and white slavery flourished. Hardly an hour went by that there wasn't a stabbing, a robbery, a killing, or a brawl. Well, just let someone try something with me, Matt thought. The way I am feeling, I would just love to bust a few faces or smash a few skulls!

A woman's scream for help tore him from his dark thoughts. Matt slowed the horse and looked about him, every muscle in his big body tense. Ahead of him, he saw four sailors struggling with someone on

261

the sidewalk. And then, as the men pulled the smaller form into the light of a doorway, he froze and stared in disbelief. My God! That was Leigh!

Leigh dug in her heels and jerked wildly to free her arms as the giant and ape-man pulled her through the door of a saloon, the other two sailors pushing her from behind. She looked frantically about the dimly lit, smoky room, seeing the piano player banging noisily on his piano and the sailors and river boatmen seated at the squat tables and standing at the small bar at one end. The placed reeked of whiskey and vomit.

Over the din of the piano music, coarse laughter, and loud talking, Leigh again screamed, "Help!"

To her horror, her cry was ignored. Those who heard her just laughed at her plight and sat back, enjoying the scene as if it were some show offered for their amusement, some crying encouragement to her captors—who were still struggling to subdue her—or making obscene remarks, while others leered at her exposed breasts.

"Get her up the stairs to our room!" the ape-man called to his companions.

Leigh fought with a desperation born of terror as they pulled her toward a staircase against the front wall. She jerked at her arms and twisted and kicked out. At one time, her heavy boot made contact with the ape-man's shin. He yelped in pain, then yelled at the two smaller sailors, "Goddammit! Grab hold of her legs, you stupid bastards!"

The two men caught a foot each, and the four sailors carried Leigh up the stairs, one at each limb. But Leigh was determined that she wasn't going to make it easy for them. She kicked and bucked like a wild animal, not even caring that her breasts were totally exposed as the shirt dangled from her arms.

"Godalmighty, she's a regular wildcat," weasel-face complained as he struggled to hold one of Leigh's wildly thrashing feet. And then, as he lost his grip and Leigh's heavy boot caught him in the groin, he let out a blood-curdling howl and dropped to the stairs, cupping himself with both hands and groaning in pain.

Leigh's eyes gleamed with satisfaction at her small victory. She twisted her body and craned her head, sinking her sharp teeth into the giant's wrist. He grunted in pain and jerked his hand back, freeing one of Leigh's arms. She fell to the stairs, wincing as her shoulder hit the sharp edge of one step.

The giant looked down at the bleeding wound on his wrist in disbelief, and then, glaring at Leigh, he raised his fist, bellowing, "I'll teach you to bite me, you slut!"

"I wouldn't do that if I were you," a low, steely voice warned him from the bottom of the stairs. "Not if you value your life."

Whereas Leigh's scream had drawn little attention, Matt's soft, but deadly threat caught the attention of everyone in the room. The piano player's hands stopped in midair as every eye in the room swiveled to the scene on the stairway. A sudden silence prevailed, so quiet a pin dropping could have been heard, everyone watching with hushed expectancy.

The three sailors who were hovering over Leigh's sprawled body stared down at the stranger standing at the foot of the stairs. The fourth, curled in a ball on the stairs a few feet below them, was oblivious to his surroundings, still writhing in pain. Seeing the dangerous gleam in Matt's eyes and the determined set of his mouth, the scar-faced sailor felt a shiver of fear run up his spine.

The giant narrowed his eyes, sizing up the man,

and felt a twinge of unease himself. Then, remembering there were four of them and only one of him, he snarled, saying, "Mind your own business, mate."

"But I'm afraid this *is* my business," Matt said in a low, deadly menacing voice. His dark eyes flashed with anger. "You see, that happens to be *my* woman you're manhandling."

Leigh had been immensely relieved to see Matt standing at the foot of the stairs, looking like a vengeful god. But when he called her "my woman," she flinched, thinking bitterly, There he goes again, treating me like a piece of property."

"Yeah?" the giant snorted. He glanced quickly at his companions, as if to reassure himself of their presence. "Well, if you want her, you're gonna have to come get her. Right, mates?"

The ape-man and the scar-faced sailor nodded in silent agreement, watching the stranger at the foot of the stairs with bated breaths, neither particularly liking the prospect of tangling with this man. There was something about him, a barely suppressed savagery, that their instincts warned them against. Both found themselves regretting their involvement with the girl and hoping that the stranger would back down.

But they were disappointed. Without a second's hesitation, Matt stepped forward, the look in his dark eyes absolutely murderous. Seeing that their bluff had been called and knowing that there was no way out, the sailors rushed down the stairs at Matt. Since he had been standing lower on the staircase, scarface was the first to descend. Taking a flying leap aimed at Matt's broad shoulders, he flew through the air. Matt ducked, and the skinny sailor went sailing over his head and skidded, belly first, over the floor, his head crashing into the opposite wall. There, he lay, perfectly inert.

Matt didn't notice. He was occupied with the other two sailors. As the ape-man came barreling down the stairs, Matt caught his chin with a vicious right uppercut, lifting the short man off his feet and sending him crashing over the side of the stairs, half of the railing going with him. The giant was right behind him, roaring an oath as he came at Matt with both fists flying.

Leigh watched the furious fistfight from her perch on the stairs, fearful that Matt would be massacred by the huge man. The giant was a full head taller than Matt, his shoulders massive-looking. But to Leigh's surprise and relief, Matt was holding his own, making up for the discrepancy in their sizes with his skill and agility. While the giant pounded at Matt, none of the blows hit a vital area, whereas Matt's punishing blows were well aimed.

Thinking that they just might get out of this dangerous situation after all, Leigh crept down the stairs and then, seeing something from the corner of her eye, froze. She watched in horror as the ape-man struggled to his feet and staggered toward Matt and the giant. Knowing that Matt couldn't possibly fight both men at once, Leigh did the only thing she could think of. She took a flying leap from the staircase and landed on the ape-man's back, wrapping her arms around his thick neck and her legs around his long arms and torso.

The apelike sailor staggered under the impact and then, realizing that his arms were pinned to his sides, bellowed in a deafening voice, "Get off my back, you bitch!"

He bucked his back several times, then jumped up and down, trying to shake Leigh loose. But she held on with a grim tenacity, riding him around the room like a wild bronco. The crowd watching the fight roared their approval, only making the ape-man angrier.

Then, like spontaneous combustion, the whole saloon was filled with fistfights as the other men, their blood lust aroused, flew at each other. The sounds of curses and grunts, smashing fists, and screams from the whores watching from the sidelines filled Leigh's ears as she spun dizzily around the room, the ape-man bucking and twisting to rid himself of her.

Finally, with one mighty heave, the ape-man broke Leigh's grip on him, and she went tumbling to the floor, landing on her bottom so hard that it knocked the breath from her.

In the meantime, Matt had managed to send the giant staggering backward with one well-aimed blow. He turned just in time to smash his fist into the ape-man's jaw before the sailor could raise his arms. For the second time, the apelike sailor went flying through the air and hit the floor. This time, he didn't get up.

Matt glanced at Leigh briefly before he was whirled around by the giant, barely having time to block the blow aimed for his jaw. As they battered at each other, Leigh crawled to the side of the saloon, fearing that she would be trampled beneath the feet of the fighting men. There, she huddled, watching the wild melee all around her.

Then she saw the weasel-faced sailor creeping down the stairs, having finally recovered from Leigh's kick. Her heart rose in her throat, her eyes glued to the wicked-looking knife he held in one hand. As he crept toward Matt's back, Leigh rose to her knees and yelled, "Matt, look out!"

But Matt didn't hear her warning over the noise.

He continued with the grim business at hand, totally unaware of the man sneaking up behind him.

Just as the weasel-faced sailor raised his arm to sink his knife into Matt's back, Leigh reached for the closest thing she could find—a big, brass spittoon next to her. She picked it up, leaped to her feet, and rushed at the sailor. Raising it high over her head, she swung the spittoon down with all her might.

From the corner of his eye, Matt caught the gleam of metal as the spittoon made an arc through the air. Thinking that it was aimed at him, he ducked and whirled around, and saw the scar-faced sailor fall to the floor as the spittoon crashed down on his head, the contents flew everywhere, and the knife skittered across the floor. Matt looked at Leigh in astonishment.

Her braid had come undone in the earlier struggle, and her hair hung about her shoulders in a tangled mass of burnished curls. Her gray eyes glittered with excitement as she smiled smugly down at the sailor sprawled at her feet, self-satisfaction written all over her face.

Why, the little minx! She's enjoying this, Matt thought. Despite his anger at her, he couldn't help but admire her spirit. A broad grin broke out on his face. Leigh grinned back, feeling immensely proud of herself.

Then Matt glanced down and saw Leigh's bared breasts. Fear for her safety rose up in him again. "For Christ's sake! Cover yourself!" he yelled.

The distraction caused by Leigh's bared breasts was almost Matt's undoing. The giant's hamlike fist came flying out and caught Matt on the chin, sending him staggering backward into the bar. Matt clung to the bar for support, shaking his head to clear it, his ears ringing from the blow. As the giant moved in for the kill, Leigh stuck her foot out and tripped him.

Off balance, the giant rushed at Matt, his swing missing Matt's head by a fraction of an inch. Matt slammed his fist into the man's belly, and the giant's breath left him in a loud swoosh as he doubled over. As he did so, Matt raised his knee and smashed it into the big man's jaw, snapping his head back and sending him flying into a table. The table broke in two, and the giant crashed to the floor, the whole room shaking from the impact of his fall.

Matt caught Leigh's hand, saying, "Come on!" Then he ducked, pulling Leigh down with him as a chair flew through the air and over their heads.

They ran for the door, Matt shoving their way through the crush of fighting men. Several times, they were forced to stop and duck, once as another chair whizzed through the air, again as a sailor flew past them. When they finally reached the door, they came to an abrupt halt. Two sailors barred it, leering at Leigh's partially exposed breasts.

Matt glanced about quickly, seeking another exit. The glint of metal on the floor caught his eye. He swooped up the knife that the weasel-faced sailor had dropped. Pushing Leigh behind him, he crouched, waving the knife menacingly, snarling at the two men, "Get back."

The sailors' eyes darted to Leigh, and then to the knife. Reluctantly, they stepped away from the doorway, their eyes glittering with anger.

Matt shoved Leigh through the door, yelling, "Run for the carriage!"

Leigh raced down the darkened sidewalk as fast as her legs could carry her. A minute later, she heard Matt running behind her. By the time she had reached the carriage, Matt had caught up with her. He picked her up and literally tossed her in, and leaped in behind her.

Leigh barely had time to sit down before Matt picked up the reins and yelled at the startled horses. Frightened by all of the sudden activity, the animals bolted forward. And not a minute too soon. The two sailors who had been running after them were already trying to climb into the carriage. One was thrown off when the carriage lurched away. The other hung on for dear life, cursing and running beside the carriage, until Matt took a corner on one wheel and the man was flung away. Unable to stop himself, the sailor ran straight into a lamppost, the impact causing the light to sputter and then go out.

Their flight was a wild ride through the darkened streets, a ride Leigh would remember for the rest of her life. Matt drove like a madman, racing the carriage down the narrow streets, totally oblivious to the people he sent scurrying to the sidewalks for safety. They took the corners on one wheel, Leigh clinging desperately to the seat and fearing that they would topple over any minute. Not until they reached the quiet streets of Vieux Carré, did Matt finally slow down and stop.

Leigh sighed in relief, then almost jumped out of her skin as Matt roared, "What in the hell were you doing down there? And why in God's name are you wearing those damned boy's clothes again?"

Leigh looked up at Matt's furious face. A lump the size of an egg formed in her throat. She swallowed hard, trying to force it down.

Matt caught her shoulders and shook her roughly, shouting, "Answer me, goddammit!"

"I—I was . . . I was trying to find the harbor. I got lost."

"The harbor? What in the hell for?"

"I—I was going to find a ship going to England

and hire out as a cabin boy," Leigh answered nervously, her heart racing in fear. Matt looked angry enough to kill her.

"Hire out as a cabin boy?" Matt asked, an incredulous expression on his face. Then his look hardened, as he spat, "You crazy, little fool! How long do you think that disguise would have fooled them? And then do you know what would have happened? The same thing that almost happened tonight! You'd be passed around to every man, raped over and over, until you were dead, or wished you were. Then, if they didn't throw you overboard for shark bait, they'd have sold you to the first white-slaver they could find when they reached port."

Leigh shuddered, fearing that what Matt had said was true. Tonight, it hadn't taken those sailors long to discover her true identity. For the first time, she realized how foolish and risky her plan had been. She had only gotten away with posing as a boy on the *Avenger* because her uncle had convinced them that she was his nephew. She had been under his protection, then under Matt's. But obviously, not every captain would offer her protection from the others. The giant certainly hadn't. And even if he had, that wouldn't have saved her from his lust. Look at the way Matt had forced her to become his mistress. Her bitterness rose up in her, stronger than ever.

Matt had been watching Leigh as these thoughts ran through her mind. He had never been so terrified in his life as when he had seen those sailors pulling her into that saloon. Just thinking about what would have happened to her if he hadn't shown up, left him weak with fear. For the first time, he noticed the swelling on her jaw. His anger at the men — and at her for placing herself into such a dangerous position — rose up in him. The crazy, little fool! And all because of her obsession to find her father. She was the most impossible woman that he had ever met!

A glimmer lit Matt's eyes. Hadn't he warned his grandmother that Leigh was incorrigible? Maybe now, after Leigh's little escapade tonight, Grandmère would believe him. Maybe she would realize that Leigh was too much for her to handle and forget those silly plans for making Leigh his ward and introducing her into Creole society. And then, after Grandmère had bowed out and gone back to Martinique, he could set Leigh up as his mistress as he had planned. He smiled smugly and popped the reins.

Leigh sat stiffly as they drove through the dark streets toward the town house. If Matt expects me to thank him for rescuing me, he has another thought coming, she thought hotly. He is no better than those sailors, forcing his will on me. If he really and truly cared for me, it might be different. But, like them, all he is interested in is satisfying his lust. And I'll be damned if I will admit running away was a foolish thing to do, either. She lifted her chin stubbornly and stared straight ahead.

Matt glanced over at Leigh and saw the defiant set of her chin. What's going on in her head now, he wondered, an uneasy feeling creeping over him. More plans for escape? Well, he would be damned! He would watch her like a hawk, and then, when he shipped out again, he would put her under guard if he had to. By God, she wasn't going to get away from him. And dammit, she needed his protection. What had almost happened tonight proved that. Why couldn't she see it?

By the time they reached the house, Matt's anger at Leigh was just as aroused as when he had left the brothel. He jumped from the carriage and jerked her out of it, pushing her before him through the courtyard and up the stairs.

Grabbing Leigh by the scruff of her neck, he dragged her into the salon, where Grandmère sat reading a book. When she saw them, the old woman's eyes widened with shock. Matt's clothes were in tatters, his knuckles raw and bleeding. One eye was darkening, and a trickle of blood ran down his chin from his split lip. And Leigh didn't look any better. Her long hair was tangled all around her shoulders, an ugly bruise marred her chin, and her floppy, dirt-smeared shirt hung open, half revealing her heaving breasts.

Grandmère shot to her feet, the book dropping to the floor, crying, "*Mon dieu*! What happened to you two?"

Matt shoved Leigh forward roughly, thundering, "I'll tell you what happened! Do you know where I found her? On Gallatin Street! Being dragged into a saloon by four sailors who planned on raping her."

On Gallatin Street, Grandmère thought in horror. *Mon dieu*, not even the police ventured onto that wild, lawless street. Her face turned deathly white. "But, *petite*, what were you doing down there?" she asked Leigh in a weak voice.

"She was trying to find the harbor," Matt answered before Leigh could open her mouth. "She planned on hiring herself out as a cabin boy to get to England. If I hadn't happened along, she'd probably be dead by now, or sold to some white-slaver."

Realizing what Matt said was probably true, the old woman sank weakly back into her chair.

"Now do you see what I mean when I told you she is incorrigible?" Matt asked, shooting Leigh a disgusted look. "She's nothing but a deceiving, conniving little chit. Just look at the way she sneaked away from you. And don't ever expect gratitude from her, either. I've never seen such an ungrateful wench. She didn't even thank me for rescuing her."

"I didn't ask you to rescue me!" Leigh cried out hotly. "I was doing fine by myself."

"Like hell you were!" Matt roared. "Oh, I admit that you'd managed to put one man temporarily out of commission, but what about the other three? If I recall correctly, one of them was about to bash your brains in when I arrived on the scene."

"Well, you didn't do so well yourself!" Leigh retorted. "If it hadn't been for me, you'd have a knife in your back right now."

"*Mon dieu*! What are you talking about?" Grandmère demanded.

"The fight!" Matt yelled. "Hell, do you think she'd stay out of it, like any sensible woman would? Oh, no! Not her! She had to get right into the middle of it, brawling like some tavern slattern, jumping on one man's back and riding him all over the room, then smashing a spittoon over another's head."

She had done all of those things, Grandmère thought, her admiration for Leigh's spirit rising to new heights. Oh, how she would have loved to have seen that fight! It must have been something. Grandmère was even more determined to have Leigh as Matt's wife. She was a woman worthy of her high-spirited, adventurous grandson. There would never be a dull minute in their marriage. But she had underestimated Leigh's determination to find her father. She would have to watch the girl more carefully.

"Calm yourselves! Both of you!" Grandmère said sternly. Then, turning her attention to Leigh, she said in a soft voice, "*Ma petite*, don't you realize you could have been killed. Promise me you won't do anything that foolish again."

Leigh squirmed under Grandmère's pleading eyes,

273

loath to lie to the woman who was obviously concerned for her welfare. She had no intention of giving up the search for her father so easily, or of waiting for two years to start it. But then, Grandmère hadn't asked her not to try to escape again, Leigh reminded herself. Oh, she knew that's what Grandmère had meant, but that wasn't what she had said. Grandmère had asked her not to try anything so foolish again. Well, she wouldn't. Her flight had been precipitate. She hadn't thought it through. She had simply reacted. No, the next time, she would plan it much more carefully.

"I won't," Leigh replied.

"*Merci le bon dieu*," Grandmère sighed.

Matt stared in disbelief at his grandmother, saying, "Surely, you don't believe her?"

"Of course I believe her!" Grandmère snapped. "She promised me, didn't she?"

Leigh felt a twinge of guilt and dropped her head, unable to look Grandmère in the eye.

"Then you're still going through with those ridiculous plans for her?" Matt asked his grandmother, glaring at her. "Introduce Leigh into Creole society and place her on the marriage market?"

Leigh's head snapped up at Matt's words. Was that what Grandmère planned? Find her a husband? Of course, Leigh thought bitterly. The old woman didn't want to sit around for two years, waiting for Leigh to come of age. What better way to relieve herself of the responsibility of Leigh than by placing that responsibility on someone else? But Grandmère was in for a big disappointment. Leigh wasn't interested in marriage right now. All she wanted was to find her father.

Grandmère flinched at Matt's words. He made it sound so crude, as if she were placing Leigh on the block to be sold to the highest bidder. "*Mon dieu,*

Matthew! Have you forgotten your promise to her uncle so soon?" She turned to Leigh, saying, "Forgive my grandson's crudity, *petite*. He makes it sound as if I were going to force you into something. On the contrary, I only want to give you the opportunity to meet some young gentleman who would be worthy of you. Naturally, I feel it's my responsibility to do so. But if you don't find any of them to your liking, I'd understand. In no way do I wish to pressure you."

Once again, Grandmère was foiling Matt's plans for making Leigh his mistress. His anger at his grandmother rose. Desperate to discredit Leigh in Grandmère's eyes, he yelled, "I can't believe you're serious. My God, Grandmère, look at her! Do you actually believe you can pawn that—that wild hoyden off on your snobbish Creole gentlemen, men who demand that their wives be every inch a lady?"

"*Ma foi*, Matthew!" Grandmère cried, her dark eyes flashing angrily. "I'm ashamed of you. How dare you insult Leigh in such a manner!"

Matt instantly regretted his rash, insensitive words. He hadn't meant to hurt Leigh, only to discourage Grandmère. He glanced at Leigh warily.

So, Leigh thought bitterly, Matt thought her good enough to be his mistress, his whore, but not good enough to be a gentleman's wife. Why, she could be just as much a lady as any other respectable woman, not that he had ever given her the opportunity to behave like one. And obviously, Matt didn't think she could attract a gentleman with honorable intentions. Her anger rose. Well, she would show him! She would have those men eating out of her hand in no time at all!

Leigh turned to Grandmère and smiled sweetly. "There's no reason for you to apologize for Matt, Grandmère. I realize he's still angry with me for what

I did this evening," she said graciously. She shot Matt a hot, oblique look, saying, "And I'd love to meet some of your nice, young gentlemen."

From the corner of her eye, Leigh saw Matt's look of total astonishment. She smiled smugly.

Chapter 13

Leigh stretched lazily in the big four-poster and sighed. The bed felt good, soft and roomy, its sheets smelling of fresh air and sunshine. Smiling, she rose and pushed the filmy mosquito netting away. Then, she padded to the French doors and opened them. A soft breeze entered the room, billowing the thin nightgown that Grandmère had loaned her and ruffling her hair.

She stepped onto the small balcony and looked over the lacy railing to the courtyard below. The lush foliage was still wet with dew, the beads of moisture sparkling like diamonds in the early morning sunlight. The sweet smell of jasmine and roses filled the air. Birds sang their greeting to the sun and darted from tree to tree.

Leigh's eyes caught a beautiful red robin in flight and followed his path to a bird nest under the eaves of the tiled roof above her. A frantic chirping came from the nest as three baby birds in it bobbed their heads; their little yellow beaks opened greedily. The robin was joined by his duller red mate, and then both birds fluttered away to search for more food to satisfy the voracious appetites of their young family.

She glanced down at the courtyard, her eyes as hungry for its sights as the baby birds were for their breakfast. She hadn't realized how much she had missed the trees, grass, and flowers during her months at sea. Strange how we take such things for granted, she thought. It seems we can't fully appreciate these gifts of God until they've been denied us.

Her eyes drifted across to the French doors on the balcony opposite her. She wondered which Matt's bedroom was. The doors were all closed and the curtains still tightly drawn, so it was impossible to tell.

Her thoughts wandered. Several times, she had awakened in the night and, half-asleep, rolled to nestle against Matt's warm, muscular body. Not finding it, she had felt a sudden stab of loneliness. The realization that she actually missed his presence in her bed disturbed her. Oh God, she thought, had her body become addicted to him? Yes, he was a devil, casting his dark spell over her even in his absence.

Then, she remembered Matt's insults the night before, and her anger rose. He had called her a strumpet, an ungrateful wench, a wild hoyden, and inferred that she wasn't lady enough for any respectable man to want for a wife. His insults had hurt her pride deeply. Well, she would show him, she thought, furious. Yes, for the time being, she would play along with Grandmère's plan to introduce her into New Orleans' elite, Creole society, just long enough to set Captain Matthew Blake back on his ear.

For that reason, Leigh submitted to the messy facials, which Grandmère insisted would bleach her tanned face to the creamy, ivory complexion that the Creole so prized, facials that ranged from smelly mud packs to a sticky concoction made of buttermilk and cucumbers. Then she was forced to endure the hot oil treatments for her hair. When the ordeal was finally over, Leigh couldn't see that her face was any paler, but admitted that her hair, dried out by the sun and salt air, did look better, the mahogany tresses lustrous and shining with red highlights.

While Leigh barely tolerated the facials and oil treatments, she was more than willing to cooperate when Grandmère announced that Leigh was to be outfitted with a new wardrobe—at Matt's expense. Leigh thought it fitting justice that the captain should have to pay for his arrogance in insisting upon taking care of her. But then, when the *couturière* arrived that afternoon, followed by an army of assistants, and Grandmère made her selections, Leigh began to get nervous. As the bed was piled higher and higher with nightgowns, chemises, bolts of material with their matching trims, hats, shoes, gloves, and parasols, Leigh thought, My God, Matt will have a fit when he sees the bill.

Leigh almost fainted when Grandmère asked to see the sketchings of the ballgowns, saying, "We'll need several, but I want a very special gown for her coming-out ball in two weeks."

After the dressmaker left, Leigh was kept busy putting her new clothes away. As she reached for one of the ready-made dresses that Grandmère had selected to tide her over until her new clothes could be made, Grandmère said, "*Non, petite*. I'm anxious to see how that one looks on you. Try it on for me, please."

Dutifully, Leigh slipped on the violet-sprigged white muslin. The dress was fashioned in the current mode—short puffed sleeves, low necked and empire waisted. As she looked down to tie the violet ribbon below her breasts, Leigh was shocked to see the amount of cleavage showing. She stepped before the mirror and gasped. The dress clung to her curves seductively, the material so thin she could almost see the outline of her nipples.

She turned to Grandmère, saying, "Don't you think it's too sheer? Why, you can almost see through it."

Grandmère chuckled, secretly pleased with Leigh's modesty. "*Non, ma petite, non*. That is the style now. Everyone is wearing it. At least, we don't dampen our muslins here in Louisiana as they do in France."

"Dampen them?" Leigh frowned. "You mean wet them?"

"*Oui*."

"But why?"

"To make them even more transparent and clinging."

"Why, that's terrible!"

"*Non, ma petite*, it's *stupide*," Grandmère answered calmly. "They think it makes them more seductive, but it's too blatant, too obvious. To be truly seductive, a dress must maintain a certain mystery, expose only enough to tease and tantalize, a subtle hint of what's beneath, *n'est ce pas*?"

To Leigh's dismay, Grandmère insisted that she wear the dress to dinner that night. When she stepped into the dining room, Matt was standing there. His dark, bold eyes swept over her, leaving Leigh feeling breathless and weak-kneed. She realized what Grandmère had said about partially revealing clothing was true. Even when she had stood before him totally naked, Matt's look had not been that ravenous.

When Leigh had told Grandmère she would be happy to meet some of the young Creole gentlemen, Matt had been astonished. For all of her deceiving ways, he could have sworn that Leigh wasn't one of those husband-hunting women, that she was only interested in finding her father, particularly after her little escapade that night. The more he had thought of it, the more convinced Matt had become that Leigh was only pretending to go along with Grandmère's plans to lure the old woman into a false sense of security, and that all the while she was secretly planning her escape. Matt had set a guard on the house, with instructions to come to him if Leigh left the premises unaccompanied by Grandmère. But now, seeing how beautiful she looked when properly attired, Matt was assailed with doubts. He could only hope that his suspicions were true. Undoubtedly, as beautiful and desirable as she was, Leigh would have no trouble finding a husband among the Creoles if she set her mind to it.

Matt and Leigh were both tense that evening at dinner, Matt fighting to maintain his air of indifference and to keep his eyes from devouring Leigh, and Leigh nursing her anger at him. Only Grandmère made the meal bearable by relating stories of the time she had spent in the French court. As soon as the meal was over, Leigh excused herself, saying she was tired and wanted to retire early.

After Leigh had left the room, Grandmère turned to Matt, saying, "I've invited your *oncles* and their wives to dinner tomorrow evening. Will you be here?"

"No, I won't be here!" Matt snapped. "You know I don't approve of your deceitful plans for Leigh."

"Deceitful?" Grandmère asked, raising her aristocratic eyebrows.

Matt's black eyes flashed dangerously. "Yes, deceitful! Passing her off to your snobbish Creoles as some nobleman's daughter. It's disgusting!" Then, before Grandmère could say anything else, Matt threw his napkin down on the table, rose, and stormed from the room.

Grandmère wasn't in the least daunted by Matt's angry words. In fact, she was relieved that Matt wouldn't be present when she introduced Leigh to her sons and their wives. She didn't trust him not to interfere. As angry as he was at her, she wouldn't put it past him to call her a liar in front of them, and then, she would have to reveal the truth. And that would never do. If her daughters-in-law knew that Leigh was illegitimate, they would never accept the girl, even if she did have noble blood.

Grandmère was waiting in the salon the next evening when her sons and their wives arrived. After the greetings had taken place, her son Paul said in a stern voice, which irritated Grandmère no end, "Mére, why are you staying here at Matt's? You know you're perfectly welcome to stay at my or Marcel's home."

Grandmère fought her irritation down and smiled sweetly, saying, "*Oui*, Paul, I know. Both your wives are such charming hostesses." The daughters-in-law both preened under Grandmère's praise. "But I didn't want to impose, since I have Matthew's ward with me, and we plan an extended visit."

"Matthew's ward?" Grandmère's other son, Marcel, asked. "I didn't know Matt had a ward."

"*Oui*," Grandmère replied. "She's been in Martinique with me for over a year now. Such a lovely girl. I've brought her to New Orleans for her coming-out." She looked pointedly at her daughters-in-law, smiled another sweet smile, and said, "The Louisiana Creoles are so much more sophisticated and charming than the Creoles in Martinique, *n'est ce pas*?"

The daughters-in-law beamed, nodding their heads in agreement.

"But where did this girl come from, Mère?" Marcel asked.

Grandmère's face took on a pained expression as she answered, "*Mon dieu*, it is such a sad story. Her father was an Irish lord. He got involved in one of those rebellions against the English that the Irish are always having. It turned out to be a disaster. *Affreux!*

He was killed in the rebellion and all his lands and money confiscated. It was such a shock to the poor girl. So traumatic! To this day, if anyone mentions her father, or Ireland, she goes into hysterics."

"How dreadful," the daughters-in-law chorused.

"Oui," Grandmère answered, dabbing at an imaginary tear. "She was left stripped of her heritage, penniless, and all alone."

"And you say our nephew, Matt, is her guardian? How did that happen?" Paul asked, a suspicious gleam in his eye.

"Why, the lord appointed him in his will, of course," Grandmère lied smoothly. "He and Matt had been friends for years, and apparently the lord was afraid the rebellion would end badly. He specified in his will that he wanted his only daughter removed from Ireland. *Mon dieu!* I suppose he was afraid of repercussions against her."

Paul frowned. The whole story sounded a little strange to him, and he knew his mother frequently wove tales. On the other hand, he really knew very little about his nephew, except that he was a sea captain, traveling all over the world, and was now a privateer. Matt was a close-mouthed young man, somewhat of a mystery to him and his brother. Perhaps, the young man did associate with such illustrious people.

Grandmère continued with her story. "After the girl's father was killed, Matthew enrolled her in an exclusive finishing school in Boston. And then, when she graduated, he brought her to me in Martinique."

"But why you? Why didn't he take her to his family in Charleston?" Marcel asked, his suspicions also aroused.

"Mon dieu," Grandmère answered, "you don't know what a considerate young man your nephew is.

283

He thought I might be lonely in that big, old house by myself and would enjoy her company. Matt was right. You have no idea how much I've enjoyed Leigh. She's such a lovely girl." The last was said with complete honesty, for Grandmère had become quite fond of Leigh over the past few days.

"And you've brought her here to find a husband?" one of the daughters-in-law asked.

"*Oui*, as much as I hate to give her up. But she's nineteen now, and it's time for her to be settled."

"Nineteen? So old?" one of the daughters-in-law blurted.

"*Oui*," Grandmère replied, and then, with a shameful look, added "I'm afraid I've been very selfish. I hate to lose her."

The daughters-in-law exchanged skeptical looks, both thinking that the girl must be fat, ugly, cross-eyed, and knock-kneed not to have been married by now. Grandmère probably hadn't been able to pawn her off on anyone in Martinique and was now trying her luck in New Orleans. But still, she was a nobleman's daughter. That should count for something.

"Veronique," Grandmère addressed one of her daughters-in-law, "I was wondering if I could ask a favor of you. You have such a beautiful home, with such a magnificent ballroom. I was hoping you might let me have the girl's coming-out ball at Twelve Oaks. Of course, Matt would pay for everything, but these town houses are really too small for a large ball."

"You mean you aren't going to present her at the French Opera House, according to Creole custom?" Veronique asked in a disapproving voice.

Grandmère frowned. She really didn't want to fool with the opera house. Then she would have to wait yet another week or two to have the ball, and she was anxious to put her plan into action. No, not until

284

Matt saw all of the Creoles vying for Leigh's hand would he finally come to heel, the obstinate fool.

"No," Grandmère answered, "I don't think that would be appropriate under the circumstances. You see, Leigh isn't Creole. She's Irish. Therefore, she should be presented according to her people's customs, with a coming-out ball, *n'cest ce pas*?"

The daughters-in-law glanced at each other doubtfully, then shrugged. If Grandmère said it was appropriate, then it must be. After all, she should know. She was a marquise.

"*Oui*, Grandmère," Veronique said, "I would be honored to have Leigh's coming-out ball at Twelve Oaks."

"*Merci*, Veronique," Grandmère replied. "And now, I think it is time to introduce you to Leigh."

Grandmère walked from the salon and, a few minutes later, returned with Leigh in tow. As they walked into the room, Grandmère smiled in self-satisfaction at the stunned looks on her daughters-in-law's faces. She knew what they had been thinking—the little bitches! A quick glance at her son's reaction to the vision of loveliness she had just presented confirmed her suspicions. Yes, judging from their warm, appreciative looks, they still had some juice left in them. They were just like their sons, rogues, only older.

Leigh smiled nervously, remembering what Matt had told her about the Creole's dislike of Americans. But as the evening progressed, she decided that he must have been mistaken. The Creoles were charming, accepting her warmly, almost as if she were a member of the family. The two women fawned over Grandmère, almost embarrassingly so, and Leigh sensed their hostility to each other. But Grandmère's sons were delightful.

From under lowered eyelashes, Leigh studied the two older men. They were both handsome men, very distinguished-looking, with those silver wings across their temples. What puzzled her, however, was that they looked absolutely nothing like Matt. Matt was tall, broad-shouldered and golden-headed, but these men were dark, shorter, and more slimly built. In fact, the only familial resemblance she could see was their hot, dark eyes. Leigh was left to conclude that Matt must look like his mother.

By the time the congenial evening was over, the two daughters-in-law were very impressed with Leigh, and each was secretly plotting her son's marriage to her. As for Grandmère's sons, they were infatuated, both secretly regretting that they were not thirty years younger and single.

As their carriage drove away that night, Grandmère smiled complacently. The groundwork had been nicely set. Within days, all of New Orleans and much of the surrounding territory would know of Leigh and her story. Her daughters-in-law would see to that. And Leigh would never know the falsehoods she had told about her. Grandmère was positive that none of the Creoles would mention Ireland or her noble Irish father to the girl. The last thing in the world the Creoles would want was a hysterical woman on their hands. And she wouldn't be the least bit surprised if she didn't get a call from her Creole grandsons the next day.

True to her suspicion, Grandmère's grandsons did come to call the next day. Aumont, Jean, and Honoré arrived in the morning. René and Philippe arrived two hours later, as they had farther to travel, having come from the plantation, Twelve Oaks, outside New Orleans.

Grandmère sat in the salon surrounded by the

young men, thinking proudly what a handsome, charming group of men they were. Of course, she knew they had not really come to see her. If so, they would have paid their respects and been gone long ago. No, they had come to see the beauty their parents had told them about.

Grandmère sat, silently chuckling to herself at the sly, anxious glances her grandsons sent toward the doorway. Deliberately, she delayed bringing Leigh in to introduce her, thinking that the anticipation would only whet their appetites. And when she finally led Leigh into the room, the men were so stunned a pin dropping could have been heard.

The young Creoles quickly regained their composure and were soon vying for Leigh's attention, smiling at her charmingly, complimenting her lavishly, their eyes devouring her when they thought Grandmère wasn't looking. Of course, Grandmère saw the looks. Her sharp eyes missed nothing. Let them look, she thought. The hungrier, the better. But there would be no touching. This one belonged to her golden grandson. She felt a little pang of remorse for having to use these grandsons to bring another to heel. *Mon dieu*, why did Matthew have to be so obstinate?

She glanced about the room and saw Honoré. The young man sat outside the circle surrounding Leigh, sending shy, admiring glances in her direction. Grandmère smiled sadly. Unlike his brothers and cousins, who were bold and aggressive, polished and charming, Honoré was extremely shy and awkward. There was a special spot in Grandmère's heart for this sensitive young man. Why couldn't he have more self-confidence, she thought. He was just as handsome as her other grandsons, and certainly more warm-hearted.

Strangely, Leigh was more aware of Honoré than

the other dashing young men. His soulful look reminded her of a little lost puppy. It tore at her heart. For that reason, Honoré received more than his share of her warm smiles, a fact that irritated and puzzled his brothers and cousins, for Honoré had never been any competition in the past.

As the afternoon wore on, Leigh began to get a little bored with all of the lavish compliments and the rather mundane conversation. She glanced up and saw Matt standing in the doorway, a scowl on his handsome face. Remembering her vow to prove to him that respectable gentlemen could find her attractive, she turned to the young man sitting beside her, who happened to be René, and gave him an absolutely dazzling smile.

Thinking that he had been singled out and that Leigh was particularly attracted to him, René's heart raced and his dark eyes glittered with excitement. *Mon dieu,* he could hardly wait to get this beauty alone. With his skill, he had no doubts that he would be able to seduce her. His heart raced at the thought.

When Matt had walked by the salon and had seen his cousins circled around Leigh, he had come to an abrupt halt, once again assailed by doubts. And then, when Leigh turned to René and gave him a smile like none she had ever given Matt, jealousy and anger welled up in him. Anger won out. She is just like all women, he thought, anxious to trap some poor man and put a ring through his nose. Well, if marriage was what she wanted, she could have it. But not to him, by God! No, no woman would lead him around by the nose. Furious, he whirled around and stormed away.

Seeing the hot look in René's eyes, Leigh was pleased with how successful she had been. She stole a quick glance at the doorway to see what Matt's reaction had been. But to her keen disappointment, the only thing she saw was his broad back as he walked away. He doesn't even care, Leigh thought. Sudden tears loomed in her eyes. Furious with herself, she blinked them away and forced herself to turn her attention back to the young Creoles surrounding her.

Grandmère's Creole grandsons came to call often during the next week. If Leigh knew Matt was about, she was particularly charming to the young men. But to her dismay, Matt never stayed around long enough for Leigh to prove he was wrong in his estimation of her. After a curt greeting to his cousins, Matt always left, leaving Leigh frustrated and appalled at his rudeness. The young Creoles couldn't have cared less. They hadn't come to see their surly American cousin. They had come to see his beautiful ward.

Watching from the sidelines, Grandmère was amused. An expert on human nature, she knew that Matt had wounded Leigh's female pride with his unthinking insults. She knew that Leigh was trying to show him up. That was fine with Grandmère. It only made Leigh more cooperative with her plans. Yes, unknowingly, Leigh was helping Grandmère bring Matt to his knees, and unwittingly, Matt had helped bring about his own downfall.

For the better part, Grandmère kept her promise to herself: her Creole grandsons could look, but not touch. She watched Leigh with the ferocity of a lioness guarding her cub. By the end of the week, the young men were grumbling in frustration to themselves.

One afternoon, when Grandmère was napping, Leigh heard the knocker on the front door. Still unaccustomed to having servants about, Leigh automatically walked to the door and opened it.

René was taken aback when Leigh opened the door. Then, glancing around him quickly and seeing that no one was about, he quickly recovered from his surprise, thinking smugly, This was the opportunity he had been waiting for.

"Come in, René," Leigh said, stepping back.

René stepped into the foyer, saying, "It's a beautiful day, and I thought you might enjoy a ride through the city. I'd love to show you the sights."

Seeing New Orleans sounded wonderful to Leigh. Matt had promised to show it to her, but that promise had been made before Grandmère had foiled his plans to make Leigh his mistress and Matt had become angry with her. Except for that short drive through the city the day they had arrived, she had seen nothing of the exciting city, with its foreign air, other than that horrible neighborhood she had stumbled into the night she had run away. And that, she preferred to forget. Her eyes sparkled with excitement. "That sounds wonderful. I'll send Marie to wake up Grandmère from her nap.'

"Non!" René blurted. The last person he wanted tagging along was Grandmère. Not for what he had in mind.

Leigh was stunned by René's almost violent reaction. She looked at him quizzically.

Gaining control of himself, René said smoothly, *"Non*, Leigh, don't wake Grandmère. She needs her rest, particularly at her age. Besides, there's no need for her to accompany us. I'm family. A chaperone isn't necessary."

Leigh wondered. Then she remembered that René knew the accepted customs of New Orleans better than she, and she did want to see the city badly.

Seeing her hesitate, René said, "Come, Leigh, it's perfectly acceptable for me to accompany you alone.

After all, what could possibly happen in broad daylight, sitting in an open carriage where everyone can see us?"

That's true, Leigh thought. She whirled around, calling over her shoulder, "Let me get my parasol and I'll be right with you."

René drove Leigh through the city, pointing out the landmarks: St. Louis Cathedral, the Cabilto, the French Opera House, Exchange Alley, where the fencing masters lived. As they drove through the streets of the old French Quarter, Leigh looked around her, drinking in the sights hungrily.

René turned down another street, saying, "You haven't seen New Orleans until you've seen Dueling Oaks."

Leigh glanced around her warily. They were leaving the city behind and traveling into the countryside. "Is it far?" she asked.

"*Non*, not far," René lied adroitly, hiding a smug smile.

As they drove further into the countryside, Leigh's apprehension grew. All signs of civilization had disappeared, and on both sides of the shell road, huge oak trees stood, their Spanish moss fluttering in the gentle gulf breeze. Then, hearing the sound of a rapidly approaching carriage behind them, Leigh turned in her seat and saw Matt racing his carriage at breakneck speed toward them.

René saw, too, and muttered an oath, then whipped his horses to a faster speed. Leigh clung to the seat for dear life as they sped down the narrow road, the trees flying by them in a blur, the sound of the horses' pounding hooves in her ears.

Finally, Matt pulled up beside them, and through the cloud of choking dust around them, Leigh saw the furious look on his face. "Pull over!" Matt called.

"The hell I will!" René shouted back, whipping his horses even harder.

"Goddammit, pull over, or I'll force you off the road!" Matt yelled. To prove that he meant what he said, Matt moved his carriage closer. The shrill sound of grinding metal filled the air as the hubs of the front wheels on the two carriages met and sent sparks flying.

René paled at the sound. He glanced across at his cousin and saw the murderous gleam in Matt's eyes. He's a lunatic, René thought, pulling back on the reins.

When both carriages had finally come to a stop, Matt vaulted from his and quickly walked to René's carriage, his dark eyes boring into Leigh. Despite the heat of the day, Leigh shivered.

"Get out, Leigh," Matt demanded.

René rose and glared down at his cousin. "Wait a minute, Matt. You have no right to interfere."

Matt's dark eyes swiveled to the young Creole, spitting sparks. "The hell I don't! Leigh is my ward. That means I'm her legal guardian. It's my responsibility to protect her from rakes like you!"

René stiffened. His black eyes glittered angrily. "I beg your pardon," he said stiffly. "I was simply taking Leigh for a tour of the city."

"The city!" Matt roared. He motioned at the thick woods around them. "This is the city?"

"He was taking me to see Dueling Oaks," Leigh explained.

"Oh, sure, he was," Matt said sarcastically. "First, a little stroll through the trees—and then, a quick roll in the grass!"

Leigh glanced at René, wondering if that was what he had planned. Seeing the slow flush creeping up his face, she knew he had planned a seduction. But strangely, she was more angry with Matt than René. She resented Matt's interference. As always, he didn't give a damn about her. He was just being overbearing, sticking his nose into her business—again! And that remark about protecting her from rakes. That was a laugh! After the way he had forced her to be his mistress, he was a fine one to accuse another man. The hypocrite!

Leigh turned to René, deliberately placing her back to Matt, "Will you please take me home now, René."

Before René could answer, Matt spat out an expletive, reached into the carriage, and swooped Leigh up in his arms. In three swift strides, he reached his carriage and tossed Leigh in so roughly she bit her tongue.

René sprang from his carriage and whirled Matt around to face him. "How dare you treat her like that! Like a piece of baggage! I demand you apologize to the lady!"

"Lady?" Matt scoffed. He looked at Leigh, his eyes glittering with anger. "This lady happens to be my—"

Leigh stiffened and held her breath, terrified that Matt would say "mistress." And if he did, she would die of humiliation.

Matt saw Leigh's face pale. He had been about to say "mistress," thinking that once René knew he had already claimed her, his cousin wouldn't want her anymore. At least, not as a wife. He knew Creoles demanded virginity from the women they married. But Matt found he couldn't do it to Leigh. Cursing himself, he turned back to René, saying, "—my ward. I can treat her any way I like."

Leigh's head snapped up at Matt's words. So, she thought, he still considers me as property. First, his mistress, and now, his ward. Not a person. Just someone to dictate to and push around.

"I don't care if she is your ward!" René retorted hotly. "I won't stand by and watch you mistreat her!"

Matt's dark eyes narrowed. "Oh? And what do you intend to do about it? Challenge me to a duel?"

René met Matt's dark eyes levelly, answering, "If need be, yes."

A duel? Leigh thought in horror. My God, René would be no match for Matt, a privateer who made his living by his proficiency with cutlass and pistol. If René was killed by Matt, even if he was a rake, she would never forgive herself. Nor would Grandmère forgive her.

"No!" Leigh screamed, coming to her feet.

Matt and René turned to Leigh in surprise, both so caught up in their confrontation that they had forgotten about her. Leigh looked at René, saying, "There's no need for Matt to apologize. He *is* my guardian." She swallowed hard, barely able to force the words from her mouth, "That means he's taking the place of my father. Surely, you wouldn't challenge my father to a duel and leave me defenseless?"

René's hot Creole blood had cooled, at least enough for him to realize how close he had come to getting himself killed. Like Leigh, he knew he was no match for Matt. He decided to take the opportunity to back out gracefully. Besides, he had offered to fight in Leigh's behalf. That should soften her heart to him. She might even forgive him for his little planned seduction.

René looked up into Leigh's pleading eyes, saying, "But, *petite*, I can't stand to see anyone mistreat you. A beautiful, fragile flower like you should be treated gently, cherished like the delicate prize you are."

Both Leigh and Matt winced at René's flowery speech, but before either could say anything, René continued, "However, if you say so, Leigh, I'll withdraw my demand. I'd never want to do anything to displease you."

"Thank you, René," Leigh answered, sinking weakly back down to the carriage seat.

René gave Leigh a little bow, shot Matt a murderous glance, and turned to walk back to his carriage. Matt frowned at his retreating back, knowing that René had somehow managed to turn the tables on him, making Matt look like a bastard in Leigh's eyes. The knowledge didn't sit easily with him. Scowling, Matt whirled and vaulted into the carriage.

A minute later, they were headed back to the city. Matt glanced over at Leigh, sitting rigidly beside him and staring straight ahead. He knew that stance only too well. She was angry with him—again! Dammit, he was only trying to protect her. Why did she have to be so obstinate? And then, remembering that she was husband-hunting, he hardened his resolve.

As they drove through the streets of New Orleans, Leigh wondered how Matt had known she had gone from a ride with René. Had Grandmère awakened and found her missing? No, that couldn't be it. Grandmère had no way of knowing she had left with René. Then, it dawned on her. Matt had set a guard on her. How dare he! How dare he treat her like a prisoner! Her anger at him flared anew.

She turned to him, spitting, "How dare you spy on me!"

"What are you talking about?" Matt asked in surprise.

"You've put a guard on me, haven't you?"

So, she has guessed, Matt thought. Well, maybe it was just as well she knew. That way, if she was still plotting an escape, she would know it was useless to try and run away again. "Yes, I have," Matt admitted. "I have no intention of allowing you to run away again. Unlike Grandmère, who believes you're a woman of your word, I know better. I know just how deceiving you can be."

Matt's words cut Leigh to the quick. Obviously, he hadn't changed his low opinion of her in the least. And by becoming his ward, she hadn't gotten out from under his arrogant domination, either. Just look at the way he had come chasing after her this afternoon, as if she were some naughty child. She ought to accept the first marriage proposal she received, just to spite him. Then, he couldn't stick his nose into her business anymore.

When they pulled up before the town house, Matt jumped down from the carriage and lifted his arms to swing Leigh down. But instead of turning her loose, he held her close to his tall, muscular body, saying, "I said it once and I'll say it again. Sometimes, you're more trouble than you're worth, kitten."

Matt's taunt pushed Leigh over the brink. "I'm sorry I'm such a bother to you, Matt."

Matt was totally taken aback by Leigh's unexpected words. He stared at her, a wary look in his eyes.

Leigh smiled smugly and pushed herself away from him, saying, "But hopefully, you won't have to worry about me much longer. As soon as I can find a husband to take care of me, you'll be relieved of that responsibility."

Leigh turned and walked regally into the courtyard. Matt stared at her back, a sick feeling creeping over him.

Chapter 14

Grandmère waited until three days before Leigh's coming-out ball to tell Matt it was to be held at Twelve Oaks.

"Twelve Oaks? What in the hell are you talking about?" Matt demanded. "I thought you were having it here."

"*Non*, Matthew. A town house is much too small for a coming-out ball. We'd hardly be able to get everyone in the ballroom, much less have room for dancing."

"Then rent the ballroom at the Hotel de la Marine."

Grandmère's face turned pale. She gasped in shock, saying "*Sacre-bleu!* Rent a ballroom at a hotel for a coming-out ball? *Non, mais non!*"

"Then cancel the goddamned thing!"

"*Non*, that's impossible! The invitations have been sent, the wine and food purchased and delivered, the gowns made. Even the musicians have been hired. *Mon dieu*, Matthew, what's wrong with you? I had no idea you hated your Aunt Veronique that much."

Matt didn't hate his aunt. He thought her a vain, frivolous woman, but that was not what was bothering him. Ever since Leigh's threat to marry and relieve him of his responsibility of her, Matt had been tormented by visions of her in another man's arms. Invariably that man had been René, and Twelve Oaks, one of the largest and most beautiful plantations in

Louisiana, was René's home, his inheritance some day. Matt assumed that Leigh must be attracted to his dashing cousin if she had accepted a ride from him that day. But to throw in Twelve Oaks, too? Could any woman resist the temptation of being mistress of that beautiful plantation, a showplace that would impress anyone, much more a young girl like Leigh, who had been raised in plain, simple surroundings. Matt could almost feel Leigh slipping through his fingers.

Matt looked around him at his town house. Compared to Twelve Oaks it was small and insignificant. But it was his, not his father's, bought by his own toil. He doubted that René had ever worked a day in his life. He glanced over at his grandmother's pale, worried face. To refuse to use Twelve Oaks at this late date would only embarrass her, and she had put so much work into planning and arranging this ball. No, he couldn't do that to her. Besides, to refuse would make him look like an ass in Leigh's eyes, one more black mark against him.

"All right, Grandmère," he said in a defeated voice. "We'll use Twelve Oaks for the ball."

"*Merci*," Grandmère sighed. "You gave me quite a fright there."

The next day, Grandmère asked if they could stay over at Twelve Oaks the night of the ball.

Spend the night at René's home, Matt thought, frowning. He wouldn't put it past that rake to slip into Leigh's room. He had already tried to seduce her once. "Absolutely not!"

"But Matthew, it's such a long drive. You know how late these balls last. We'll all be tired. It would be so much simpler to stay over."

"It's a two-hour drive to New Orleans. If that's too long a drive, then cut the damned dance short. It's ridiculous to stay up half the night dancing, anyway."

Grandmère started to say something, but Matt beat her to it. "No, we will not stay overnight!"

Grandmère looked at the steely gleam in Matt's eyes and decided not to push any further. She sighed, saying, "*Oui*, Matthew, if that's what you say, then we'll return to New Orleans after the ball."

The day of the ball, Grandmère encouraged Leigh to take a nap as soon as lunch was over. After Grandmère had left to take her own nap, Leigh tossed and turned in her big bed. It was impossible to sleep. She was much too excited. She had never been to a real ball before.

She slipped from the bed and paced the room, still thinking about the ball. Her eyes settled on the beautiful ballgown that Grandmère had selected for her, hanging in the middle of the room. The gown was sheerer and much more daring than any she had ever worn. She wondered what Matt would think when he saw her in it.

Thinking of Matt was Leigh's undoing. The same longing that she always felt when she thought of the dashing, virile captain filled her. Despite her vow to free herself of her body's weakness for him, she hadn't been able to do it. She still reached for him at night and then, not finding him, lay awake for hours, aching for his kiss and his touch. Her hunger for his love-making, instead of abating as she had hoped, seemed to be growing. It was as if she no longer had any control over her body.

Well, to hell with him, she thought, half-angry at herself and half-angry at Matt. Tonight, she would show him just how desirable she could be to other men. Of course, she had no intention of accepting any marriage proposals. She had been angry at Matt when she had said that. She had to find her father first. But Matt didn't know she wasn't interested in marriage, and tonight, he wouldn't be able to leave the dance. As her guardian and, technically, the person introducing her into society, he wouldn't dare. Yes, tonight, she would have him as a captive audience. She would show him!

The preparations for the ball began that afternoon. Leigh was bathed in perfumed water and her hair shampooed. Then she sat at the dresser in her underclothes, draped with a sheet for modesty's sake, to await the arrival of the *coiffeuse*.

When the hairdresser walked in, Leigh almost fell off her stool. The hairdresser was a man! At least, she thought it was a man.

The dapper little hairdresser bowed to Grandmère, saying in a haughty voice, "Madame."

"Good day, Henri," Grandmère answered. "I'm glad you could come. I'm sure, with the ball tonight, you must be very busy."

The hairdresser's thin nose rose another inch in the air. "*Oui*, madame, but I am never too busy to serve the marquise."

Grandmère's mouth quirked with amusement. "This is *Mademoiselle* O'Neal, my grandson's ward." She motioned to the ballgown hanging in the middle of the room, saying, "And that is the gown she will wear tonight. What hairstyle do you suggest?"

The little man circled the gown slowly, eyeing it critically. Then he stared at Leigh. He stood, his chin in his hand, pondering the problem as if he were making a monumental decision. The minutes ticked by.

He picked up Leigh's heavy tresses, weighing them in his hand, cocking his head one way, then the other. He bent, staring at Leigh's face so hard, she feared she had grown a wart on her nose.

Abruptly, he turned to Grandmère, saying, "Ah,

madame, with her heart-shaped face and dimpled chin, she is perfect for the new hairstyle that goes so well with these new fashions. I shall cut her hair, then curl it in tight ringlets all over. You are familiar with the hairstyle, *oui*?"

Cut my hair, Leigh thought in horror. After I wore that damned stocking cap for months to hide my long hair, he is going to cut it now? Over my dead body! She jumped to her feet, crying, "No! You're not going to cut my hair!"

The hairdresser could not have been more shocked if the chair had talked. No one ever questioned his opinion, particularly not a young girl. He looked at Leigh with disdain, then turned to Grandmère. "Madame, I assure you the hairstyle I am referring to is the rage in France."

"I don't give a damn what they do in France! You're not cutting my hair!" Leigh screeched.

The hairdresser looked as if he might faint.

Grandmère smiled and said, "*Oui, ma petite*, I agree. Your hair is much too lovely to cut." She gave Henri a firm look, saying, "I'm afraid that won't do."

Henri looked highly insulted. He bristled, then said in a sullen voice, "*Oui*, madame, if that's what you wish." Turning to Leigh, he pushed her back down on the stool and began to pile her long hair on top of her head, saying, "Then perhaps, with curls piled on top of her head, and intermingled among the curls, seed pearls and ribbons?"

Grandmère frowned. "I was thinking of a simpler style, something simple, but elegant."

Sighing in exasperation, Henri dropped Leigh's long tresses. He stood back, looking at her intently. Suddenly, his dark eyes glittered. "I know," he said in an excited voice, "a Grecian knot!"

In a flurry of activity, he laid out his combs,

brushes, and curling irons. Then he lit the small brazier and placed the irons on it. He picked up the brush and quickly brushed Leigh's hair back from her face. Then, with a quick flip of his hand, he tied her long hair in a single knot high on the back of her head. Leigh twisted her head, seeing the long rope of curls hanging down her back. She smiled in approval.

But as Henri picked up the scissors, she drew back in alarm. "*Non, mademoiselle*," Henri said. "Please, just a bit over each temple for a small curl."

Leigh watched him warily as he snipped off some hair on one side, then the other. He picked up the curling iron, curled both wisps, and then stood back, exclaiming, "*Parfait!*"

Leigh looked in the mirror. The two curls before the ears softened the severity of the hairstyle. "That's lovely," she said.

But as Henri picked up the large curling iron and lifted it to the mass of curls hanging down Leigh's back, Grandmère frowned, saying, "What are you doing?"

"Why, straightening her hair, madame."

"Straightening it?"

"*Oui*, madame. With a Grecian knot, the hair should hang perfectly straight."

"Like a horse's tail?" Grandmère asked in horror. "*Non*, leave it alone!"

"But madame—"

"*Non!* It looks lovely that way. *Mon dieu!* I won't have you ruining her hair by straightening it!"

Henri's face flushed with anger. He turned and slammed his equipment back into his case. Then, walking to the door in a huff, he said stiffly, "Good day, madame."

After he had slammed the door behind him, Grandmère chuckled, saying, "I'm afraid that's the last we'll see of Henri."

"I'm sorry, Grandmère. But I just couldn't let him cut my hair."

"Of course not!" Grandmère agreed. She smiled, saying, "Personally, I think my maid, Marie, is just as good a hairdresser as Henri. From now on, we won't even bother with him."

After Grandmère and Marie had helped Leigh into her ballgown, Leigh stepped up to the mirror to view herself. She flushed. The sheer, dusky-blue material clung to every curve, and the silver-leafed trim around the low neckline and under her bust seemed to emphasize her high, proud breasts.

"Ah, madame, she looks absolutely beautiful," Marie whispered in an awed voice, admiring Leigh.

"*Oui*, she does," Grandmère agreed, "but the dress still needs something to touch it off. Marie, go down to the courtyard and bring me some fresh gardenias."

When Marie returned with the creamy white flowers, Grandmère said, "Tuck a few of them around that knot in her hair."

Taking one of the gardenias, Grandmère sewed it to a piece of leftover silver-leafed trim. "Hold her hair up, Marie, while I sew this band around her neck."

When she had finished, Grandmère stepped back and admired Leigh. The gardenias in her hair and the one at her throat gave the seductive gown just the touch it needed, a touch of freshness and innocence. "Ah, *petite*, you look exquisite."

When Grandmère and Leigh stepped into the saloon, Matt was waiting for them. This was the first time Leigh had seen him dressed in anything other than his white shirt and dark breeches, as Matt scorned the elaborate dress the Creole men wore. Reluctantly, Leigh admitted that he looked absolutely devastating in his dark evening wear. The coat was beautifully tailored and fit his broad shoulders like a second skin. The snowy cravat accented his deep tan and good looks. Despite her resolve to keep her body under firm control, Leigh felt that familiar tingling, that warm curl deep in her belly. It is just the excitement of the ball, she told herself.

On seeing Leigh, Matt's breath caught in his throat. He had never seen her looking so beautiful — or so desirable. Then he remembered his resolve, and his expression hardened. He forced his eyes away from the vision of loveliness and turned to Grandmère, saying, "If you want to get there early, we'd better leave."

Leigh was taken aback by Matt's abruptness. When he had first looked at her, she had thought his look admiring, almost rapt. She had expected a compliment. Tears of disappointment stung her eyes.

All day long, Matt had steeled himself for this ball, promising himself that no matter what happened, he wouldn't reveal his true feelings to anyone — and certainly not to Leigh. As they drove to Twelve Oaks, he stared out the window, his air one of cool indifference to the two women sitting in the coach with him. But, as time passed, he found his eyes repeatedly drawn to Leigh.

His eyes drifted over her shell-pink ear, down the slender column of her throat, lingered at her mouth, and then dropped hungrily to the lush swell of her creamy breasts. Feeling his own body betraying him, he looked quickly away, only to have his eyes irresistibly drawn back to her loveliness again and again. By the time the coach drove down the circular drive to Twelve Oaks, he was squirming uncomfortably in his seat and finding it difficult, if not impossible, to keep his resolve.

As they drove to the house, Leigh could see why the plantation had its name. Twelve huge oak trees lined the driveway, dripping with Spanish moss. Masses of azaleas and gardenia bushes hugged the bases of the trees. The grounds around the house were magnificent, scattered with broad-leaved magnolia trees and narrow, leathery-leaved willow oaks. Huge beds of rosebushes dotted the landscape, blooming in a riot of color. And looming above all this natural grandeur, was the huge plantation house, the lower story of brick and the upper stories of wood.

They were greeted in the foyer by Grandmère's son and daughter-in-law. After the initial greetings were over, Matt turned to his aunt and said with a forced smile, "Aunt Veronique, I want to take this opportunity to thank you for letting us use your beautiful home for my ward's coming-out ball."

Aunt Veronique was feeling a little awed herself. She had seen this striking, golden-haired man only once before, many years ago. She had forgotten how devastatingly handsome and masculine he was. And so charming, she thought, especially for an American. She flushed, not from his compliment of her home, but rather from his effect on her. "You are most welcome, Matthew," she finally managed to say in a breathless voice.

Matt glanced over his aunt's shoulder and saw Leigh looking about her in wide-eyed wonder. She gazed at the intricately carved walnut staircase with its white marble stairs and then at the huge glittering chandelier in rapt admiration. Seeing her look, Matt felt sick with despair. When his uncle suggested a drink in the library, Matt almost bolted from the foyer, unable to watch Leigh's admiration of René's home any longer.

"Would you like to see the rest of the house before the ball?" Aunt Veronique asked Leigh.

"Oh, yes," Leigh answered with a small sigh.

Leigh was stunned by the size of the house. It must have at least fifty rooms, she thought in awe. The rooms were all large and furnished with massive, carved furniture, the beds larger than any she had ever seen. When they stepped into the ballroom, Leigh's breath caught. The polished oak floor gleamed beneath six huge chandeliers on which hundreds of candles flickered. The windows and French doors lining one wall were draped with lush green velvet. Chairs and small loveseats, upholstered in rich brocades, lined the wood-paneled walls. At one end of the room, a massive marble fireplace stood, and at the opposite end, a dais, surrounded by potted palms and ferns, where the orchestra was already warming up. Leigh wondered what it would be like to live in such opulent surroundings. She decided that she would feel uncomfortable in it. She much preferred Matt's town house. Despite its luxury, this huge house lacked the warmth and charm of Matt's home.

By the time Leigh and Grandmère returned to the ballroom after freshening up, the room was filled with talking and laughing Creoles. Again, Leigh heard that strange mixture of French, Spanish, and English. She glanced about the room at the men in their evening finery and the women in their beautiful ballgowns. The gowns seemed to be of every shade in the rainbow, soft pastels in watered silk, vivid shades in rich brocade, and muted, darker shades in velvet, preferred by the older women. A tingle of excitement ran through her.

Because the ball was given in her honor, the dancing was delayed until Leigh had been introduced to all the guests. By the time the introductions were over, Leigh was so confused she doubted if she would remember anyone's name. She glanced at a group of young, pretty Creole women standing near her. She smiled warmly at them, hoping that she would make some new friends. She was hungry for female companionship of her own age.

The young women saw her smile but Leigh was stunned by their venomous looks before they turned away from her, laughing and chattering among themselves, clearly showing Leigh that her friendship was not welcome.

Suddenly, the young women stopped talking, staring wide-eyed at something across the ballroom. One pretty, young woman gasped, *"Mon dieu!* Who is he?"

Leigh turned to see who held their rapt attention and saw that Matt had just walked into the ballroom. With his height, he towered over the Creole men and looked like a tall, golden god. She glanced back at the young women, still staring in fascination. The silly fools, she thought. They look like a bunch of dead fish with their mouths gaping open like that. She felt the sharp sting of jealousy.

"He's coming this way," one of the young women said in an excited voice.

Leigh saw Matt threading his way across the ballroom toward her. Naturally, she assumed he was joining her. He was her escort, since he had brought her to the dance, and therefore, the first dance was his. At least, that's what they had taught her in the ladies' school in Boston. The first and the last dance always went to your escort for the evening.

She was stunned when Matt walked right past her, without so much as a glance in her direction. He bowed before the group of now-preening young women, smiled his devastating smile, and said in his deep, rich voice, "Good evening, *mademoiselles*. May I see your dance cards?"

Leigh felt as if she had been slapped in the face. For the second time that night, she blinked back tears. But she didn't have time to dwell on Matt's insult, for a second later, she was besieged by a bevy of eager, dashing Creoles, asking to see her dance card.

Some of the young men she already knew, Matt's cousins. When René handed her back her card, deliberately brushing his fingers against hers, he looked at her meaningfully, saying in a low voice, "I must see you alone tonight. I have something very important to discuss with you."

René was shouldered aside by the other Creoles waiting to sign her dance card. Leigh was so puzzled by René's words that she didn't pay any attention to who was signing her card. When it was finally handed back to her, she looked down to see who had signed it. Matt's name was conspicuously absent. She felt yet another pang of deep hurt. Then, seeing the reserved dance she herself had marked earlier, she glanced around the ballroom to see if she could spy the man for whom she had saved the dance. Honoré stood off to the side, looking shy and nervous, just as she had known he would.

She walked up to him and smiled, saying, "Don't you want to sign my dance card, Honoré?"

He flushed and stammered, "I — I wanted to, but — but I'm sure you don't have any dances left."

"Yes, I do. I have one dance left," Leigh answered.

"You do?" he said in a surprised voice.

"Yes. It's the sixth dance. Would you like it?"

His eyes glittered with excitement. *"Oui, oui,* I'd like it very much."

Leigh turned away, saying over her shoulder, "You won't forget?"

"Mon dieu! Non, I won't forget."

The next minute, Leigh was whisked away for the first dance. As the evening progressed, she discovered that the Creoles were exceptionally good dancers and she was enjoying herself thoroughly, laughing at the young men's witticisms or just enjoying being whirled around the room to the beautiful music.

When the sixth dance arrived, Honoré was anxiously waiting for her. Unfortunately, he was as awkward in his dancing as in everything else. He blushed, saying, "I'm afraid I'm not a very good dancer."

Leigh smiled and said, "May I be very honest with you?"

His dear eyebrows arched. "*Oui*, certainly."

Leigh groaned, "My feet are killing me. How in the world can you Creoles stand dancing all night like this?"

Honoré smiled and said, "I don't. That's why I'm such a poor dancer. Would you like to sit this one out?"

"Would you mind?"

"*Non*. In fact, I feel silly up here, stumbling all over you."

As Honoré led her off the dance floor, she whispered, "Do you know an out-of-the-way place I could slip off my shoes?"

Honoré smiled, saying, "I know the perfect spot."

He led her to a couch behind a cluster of potted palms. As they sat down, Leigh said, "This is perfect. How did you know it was here?"

A sad look crossed his handsome face. "Because this is where I usually sit to watch everyone dance."

Leigh felt a stab of compassion. But she knew it would never do to show Honoré pity. Instead, she laughed, saying, "Well, don't be surprised if you find yourself having company tonight." She slipped her shoes off under her skirt and sighed with relief. "Oh, that feels so good," she mumbled.

"What?" Honoré asked.

"I said, it feels good to get my shoes off."

Honoré's eyes widened in surprise. He had assumed when Leigh told him her feet were hurting, it was just an excuse to keep from having to dance with him. "You mean you actually took your shoes off?"

"Of course I did. I told you my feet were killing me. I'm not used to all this dancing. But don't you dare tell anyone."

Honoré's lips twitched. "*Non*, I promise I won't tell. Would you like some cold punch?"

"Not unless I can put my feet in it," Leigh replied with an impish grin.

Honoré threw his head back and laughed, a very hearty, male laugh. Leigh joined him. When they were finished laughing, Leigh said, "You know, Honoré, I think we're going to be good friends."

Honoré looked at her and said in a sincere voice, "I hope so, Leigh. I'd like that."

After Honoré had left to get some punch for them, Leigh slipped one shoe back on. But she couldn't find the other one with her foot. Sighing in disgust, she leaned over and lifted her skirt, peering under the couch for the missing shoe.

"Are you looking for this?" a deep, male voice asked.

Leigh jerked up to see a tall, swarthy-faced man standing over her, her shoe in his hand, an amused look in his dark eyes.

Leigh flushed and snatched the shoe away. As she bent to slip it on, the stranger asked, "May I help?"

"No—no—thank you," Leigh stammered, humiliated at having been caught with her shoes off.

When she looked back up, the stranger was still standing before her. She gave him a heated, go-away look.

He chuckled, saying, "I believe this is my dance, *senorita*."

His dance? The Spaniard was a ruggedly handsome man, well-built, almost as tall as Matt. Goodness, Leigh thought, how did I ever miss him?

"My name is Diego de Leon, *senorita*. If you care to check your card . . ."

Leigh was embarrassed at her own rudeness. "No, of course not," she interjected. "It's just that I don't remember seeing you sign my card."

He laughed, flashing even, white teeth. "I am not surprised, considering the mob I had to fight off to get to your card."

As they danced, Leigh found that she was very uncomfortable. Not that Diego said or did anything that was the least bit improper. To the contrary. The handsome Spaniard was charming and polite, a perfect gentleman. But Leigh sensed a virility about the man that frightened her. He is like Matt, she thought. He has a certain magnetism.

When the dance had finished, Diego said, "You look flushed, *senorita*. Let us step out on the gallery for some fresh air."

Leigh opened her mouth to object, but, to her dismay, Diego quickly whisked her through a nearby French door and out onto the gallery.

Seeing her shocked look, Diego laughed softly, saying, "Forgive me for being so rash, but I'm afraid your beauty has robbed me of my senses, and my manners. I just had to get you alone for a few minutes."

"I think I'd better go back in," Leigh said in a haughty voice.

As she turned to walk away, Diego asked, "Are you afraid of me, *senorita*?"

There was a mocking tone in Diego's voice that told Leigh the Spaniard was challenging her. The last thing that she wanted him to know was that she feared his magnetism. She turned back, saying, "No, of course not."

"Ah, good," Diego said smoothly, taking her arm and leading her to the railing.

When they stood beside it, Diego turned to her and said, "I would not want you to fear me. You see, you fascinate me, *querida*. I would like to get to know you much better. Surely, you can't fault me for that?"

Despite herself, Leigh felt drawn to this handsome Spaniard. His soft accent was lulling her, his warm appreciative gaze melting her resistance. She hardly noticed his words as he inched closer. Then his warm hand caressed her neck, lifting her chin for his kiss.

Diego was an artful seducer. His lips were soft, persuasive, as he slowly and patiently coaxed her response. Leigh felt herself melting into his embrace. But as his kisses became deeper and more amorous, she felt strangely detached, wondering where the magic had gone. It wasn't anything at all like being kissed by Matt. True, Diego's kisses were pleasant, but there was no fire, no feeling of drowning in a whirlpool of sensations, exciting her, leaving her weak-kneed, breathless, and aching for more.

As Diego drew away, Leigh was, at first, disappointed at her lack of response, and then, relieved, realizing that she had nothing to fear from this man. Despite his masculine attractiveness, he would never have the hold over her that Matt had, that strange, overpowering magnetism that robbed her of her will and senses.

"You are angry with me, *querida*?" Diego asked softly.

Leigh looked into his dark, liquid eyes, eyes that would have left any other woman swimming. She felt absolutely nothing, not even anger. She smiled, saying, "No, Diego, I'm not angry. The kiss was very pleasant."

She saw the knowing, smug look in his eyes. This, rather than his kiss, infuriated her. *The conceited bastard. He actually thinks he impressed me. The fool!*

She smiled, and then said, "But don't bother to kiss me again, Diego. It would be a waste of your time. As pleasant as the kiss was, I'm afraid I was very disappointed. You see, I had expected much better from you."

As she walked away, Diego stared at her back, stunned. Then, he threw his head back and laughed. *Dios!* What a magnificent woman she was! And what a challenge! He was even more determined to have her.

When Leigh stepped back into the ballroom a minute later, she was claimed by another of Grandmère's grandsons. The dance went on and on. Leigh danced stately minuets, lively contredanses, and courtly pavanes. She was amazed at the Creoles' endurance, as none of them seemed the least bit tired.

Throughout the dance, Leigh was aware of Matt whirling his partners about the room. It was hard not to see him with his golden head towering above the others. His partners were the young Creole women, many very beautiful, and all obviously enchanted with him. It infuriated Leigh to see them flirting with him, brushing their bodies against his. *Are you jealous,* the obnoxious little voice in her head asked, a voice that had been silent for a long time. *No, of course not,* Leigh denied angrily. *I don't care what he does, or whom he does it with!*

Then René stood before her, smiling at her, his eyes hot and possessive. "Come, *chérie,*" he said, taking her arm. "We need to talk."

Once again, Leigh found herself being rushed out onto the gallery. And then, to her further dismay,

313

René ignored her objections and pulled her down the stairs to the garden and through a maze of hedges and rosebushes.

Finally, Leigh managed to pull her arm away. She whirled on him angrily, but before she could open her mouth, René was raining passionate kisses over her mouth, her face, her throat, while his hands, which Leigh could have sworn numbered twelve, instead of the usual two, fondled her possessively. Furiously, she struggled against him.

When Leigh finally managed to wiggle out of his embrace, he caught her hands, kissing them amorously, muttering, "*Non, ma amour*, don't run away."

Then, looking deeply into her eyes, he said in a passionate voice, "I love you, *ma amour*. I adore you. I worship the ground you walk on. Please, tell me you will be my wife."

Leigh was even more surprised by his sudden proposal than his attack. Loves me, she thought in astonishment. But how could he? He doesn't even know me. She was amazed that this man, a man who barely knew her, could avow his love, while Matt, who knew her so well, so intimately, had never mentioned the word. Then she realized with disgust what René really meant was that he wanted her. To give the devil his due, Matt had never lied to her by pretending to love her. No, at least he had been honest with her about his emotions.

She jerked her hands away, saying coldly, "I'm afraid that's impossible, René. I'm not interested in marriage right now."

René's look was one of total disbelief. "Not interested?" Then he smiled smugly, saying, "Ah, *ma amour,* don't tease me."

"Tease you?" Leigh snapped irritably. "What in God's name makes you think I'm teasing? I repeat, I'm not interested in marriage."

René's look turned angry. "Stop playing games with me, *chérie*. Everyone knows marriage is every girl's dream, to have a rich husband to take care of her, protect her."

The arrogant fool, Leigh thought. Why did men assume that all women were so anxious to marry, that they had to be protected as if they were children, that the only purpose of a woman on earth was to be the wife of some overbearing male, to bear his children, to be used?

"Perhaps, I should rephrase my statement, René," Leigh said angrily. "What I really meant to say was 'I'm not interested in marriage to you!' In fact, I find you repulsive!"

With that, she turned and, picking up her skirts, rushed away, leaving René to deal with his shattered ego.

Leigh ran through the garden and hurried up the stairs to the gallery. Suddenly, she was whirled about. Gasping in surprise, she looked up to see Matt glaring down at her. "Matt! What are you doing here?"

"Keeping an eye on you, my pretty little seductress."

"Seductress?"

Matt's dark eyes flashed dangerously. "Yes, seductress! I saw you sneaking off with that Spaniard, and then with René. Quite a busy little night you've had."

Did he think that she had deliberately encouraged them? Well, let him! She would be damned if she would give him the satisfaction of explaining. She raised her head haughtily and started to step around him.

Matt caught her arm in a viselike grip, grinding out between clenched teeth, "What happened down there in the garden?"

"That's none of your business!"

Matt's eyes glittered with anger as he caught Leigh's

shoulders and pulled her forward roughly. "Answer me, dammit!"

Despite her own anger, Leigh was just a little frightened. Matt looked furious enough to kill her. "All right, if you must know, René proposed to me."

Matt felt as though he had been kicked by a mule. Then his jealousy flared, white-hot. "No! You're mine!"

"You're crazy! You don't own me. I'm not a piece of property. You have no right!"

"Oh, yes I do have the right," Matt said in a low steely voice. "You're mine, kitten. I was the first — and by God, I'll be the only man in your life!"

His mouth swooped down on hers. Leigh struggled. He slammed her into the wall behind them, pinning her with his big body as his lips ravaged hers. Leigh tried to fight it, her mind screaming "no," but again her body, denied for so long, betrayed her. She turned soft and yielding in his arms, a low moan rising in her throat.

Matt felt her response and released her arms, slipping his hand behind her back and molding her body to his. His lips left hers to rain fiery kisses over her brow, down her temple, across her chin, lingering at the sensitive spot just below her ear.

"Oh, God, kitten, I've missed you. I need you," he groaned, pressing her closer to the proof of that need, hot and throbbing against her. "I need you so badly."

He kissed her throat passionately, and Leigh arched her neck to his warm lips. His hands stroked her back and hips as his head lowered to drop soft kisses over her shoulders and the swell of her breasts, nuzzling their velvety softness.

Through a haze, Leigh heard a voice calling, "Matt? Leigh? Where are you?"

Leigh pushed weakly at Matt's shoulders, gasping,

"Matt, it's Grandmère."

He ignored her, nuzzling her neck, his hands trembling and fumbling at her bodice.

"Matt? Leigh?" The voice was louder now.

This time Matt heard it and muttered, "Dammit!"

"Matt, let me go," Leigh pleaded. "Grandmère's coming."

He kissed her fiercely, then whispered urgently against her ear, "Let me come to you tonight, Leigh. You want me as much as I want you. Don't leave me like this. Aching for you." He nibbled at her earlobe, sending shivers of delight through Leigh. "Oh, kitten, stop torturing me like this. Let me come to you tonight."

Matt wasn't the only one who felt tortured. Leigh's body screamed "yes" to his request, her mind "no." She sobbed in frustration.

"Please, kitten, when we get back to the town house, let me come to you," Matt whispered in an agonized voice.

"I've got to go," she whispered weakly.

"Please," he groaned, burying his face in her breasts.

She wiggled out of his grasp and hurried away before he could catch her again.

Grandmère saw Leigh rushing toward her. She glanced behind the girl and saw Matt standing in the shadows. A quick sweep of her eyes told her that René was nowhere in sight. She almost collapsed in relief. *Sacre-bleu*, when she had seen René rushing Leigh from the ballroom and Matt following, an absolutely murderous look on his face, she had feared the worst. She had been a fool to pit those two hotheads against each other. *Merci le bon dieu*, nothing terrible had happened.

When Leigh stood before her, Grandmère knew by

the girl's flushed face, bruised lips, and disheveled state what had happened. But she wasn't sure just which grandson to blame. Regardless, she couldn't take the girl back into the ballroom looking like that.

Standing before Grandmère, Leigh felt like a child caught with his hand in the cookie jar. She could have cried with gratitude when the gracious old lady said in a sympathetic voice, *"Mon dieu, ma petite*, you look exhausted. These balls can be so tiring. Why don't we walk up these stairs to one of the bedrooms, where we can rest for a few minutes?"

After Leigh had washed her face, straightened her mussed clothing, and composed herself, she and Grandmère returned to the ballroom. Leigh was miserable throughout the rest of the ball, still shaken by Matt's impassioned kisses and her own spontaneous response. As she danced, his plea echoed in her ears, over and over, like a litany, "Let me come to you tonight, let me come to you tonight." When the music ended and the guests began leaving, Leigh was relieved that it was finally over.

As Grandmère and she were walking out of the door, Grandmère's son said, "I don't understand why you don't just spend the night, Mère. It's a long ride back to New Orleans."

"Oui," his wife agreed. "You know you're welcome to stay here."

Grandmère smiled wearily and replied smoothly, "I know, but at my age, I find it difficult to sleep in a strange bed. I would rather just go back to New Orleans tonight. Then I can sleep all day tomorrow if I want to."

Matt was waiting for them by the coach. He looked at Leigh intently, his eyes searching, questioning. Leigh ducked her head, pretending not to notice, and scampered into the coach. She sat far to one side and stared with fixed eyes out the window.

When Matt helped Grandmère into the carriage, he said, "Why don't you sit on the other seat, Grandmère? That way, you can put your legs up and rest."

"*Oui*, I think I will," Grandmére answered in a tired voice.

Grandmère allowed Matt to help her out of her shoes and then swung her legs back on the seat, leaning her head back in one corner of the coach. Grandmère was a remarkably active woman, but she was eighty years old. Not until she lay back did she realize how exhausted she was. Within minutes, she was sound asleep.

As they drove down the moon-dappled road, Leigh kept her eyes glued to the landscape. She didn't trust herself to even look at Matt. But she was exhausted, too, and soon her eyelids were drooping, her head nodding.

When Matt saw Leigh was asleep, he smiled and gently pulled her into his arms, cradling her head on his shoulder. There, she slept like a baby until the lurching of the coach awakened her as it pulled to a stop.

She sat up, confused and still half-asleep, seeing Matt leaning across Grandmère and shaking her shoulder, saying, "We're home, Grandmère."

After Matt helped Grandmère with her shoes, he assisted her out of the carriage. The old lady hurried into the courtyard, anxious to get to her bed. When Matt and Leigh entered the courtyard and Leigh noticed Grandmère was completely out of sight, she quickened her steps.

Matt caught her arm, pulling her back, saying, "Leigh?"

Leigh knew what he was asking, what he wanted. The hard part of it was that she wanted it also. But she couldn't submit, not again. Not only would she be betraying herself, but Grandmère's trust in her too. "No!" she whispered, then turned and ran into the town house.

Matt stood for a minute, watching her disappear into the house, stunned. Then his look became angry. To hell with her, he thought, furious. He whirled and stormed back out of the courtyard.

Leigh had stopped in the salon. She looked out the French door and saw Matt walking angrily through the courtyard. He will go to one of those other women now, she thought. She leaned her head against the glass pane, a small tear trickling down her cheek.

But Matt didn't go to another woman. He had already tried that, with disastrous results. He knew now that no woman could substitute for Leigh. Instead, he headed for the waterfront, where he became reeling drunk and staggered from one tavern to another, picking fights.

When Grandmère awakened the next afternoon, a message was waiting for her. Taking the note from her maid and opening it, she recognized Matt's bold handwriting. It read: Have gone back to sea. Don't know when I'll return.

Chapter 15

Matt's abrupt departure from New Orleans stunned Grandmère. The last thing she had expected him to do was bolt. His flight threw all her plans astray and left her in an awkward position. Leigh had been officially introduced to Creole society the night before, and Grandmère knew they would be besieged with eager suitors the next day, suitors that were no longer necessary to bring Matt to heel, now that he was gone.

Matt's sudden sailing left Leigh in a perplexing situation also. When she heard the news of Matt's departure, her first thought was to flee while he was gone. But, to her dismay, she found she couldn't do it. It wasn't so much the guards that Matt had placed on the house, guards that Leigh noticed were still there, but her own conscience that held her back. She had told Grandmère that she wanted to meet some of the young Creole men and had played along with the old woman's plans for her. After all the money and time Grandmère had spent on her coming-out, to run away now would only confirm Matt's estimation of her character, that she was deceitful and ungrateful, and Leigh didn't want Grandmère to think badly of her. Leigh found herself caught in a trap of her own making.

So, when a score or more of eager, almost voracious suitors descended on the town house the next day, Leigh and Grandmère acted out their part in the charade, a game neither of them really wanted to play. Grandmère chaperoned Leigh and the young gentlemen on innumerable rides through the city, to luncheons and dinners at New Orleans' many fine restaurants, to the opera, and to several balls, sticking to the young couple like glue, her sharp eyes missing nothing. The Creoles were careful to be gentlemanly in their wooing, fearing the old lady's wrath if they should make any overt advances. Even Diego de Leon, Leigh's most persistent suitor, moved carefully, feeling that he would rather face an irate father on the dueling grounds than cross the formidable old woman with her fierce black eyes.

After a few weeks of chaperoning Leigh and her suitors, Grandmère was exhausted. After all, she was eighty years old and, despite her active life, not accustomed to so much social activity. She missed her leisure time. Besides, with Matt gone, there was no point to it. She abruptly announced that since Leigh's guardian was absent, she felt the courting was inappropriate. The Creoles would have to wait until Matt's return to press their suit. The young men backed off reluctantly. Grandmère knew it was only a reprieve, but a welcome one.

Leigh more than welcomed Grandmère's edict. Although she had enjoyed seeing all of New Orleans' exciting sights, she, too, was weary, not just of the activity, but of the company, too. Not one of the young men attracted her, despite their charm, polish, and good looks. She found herself comparing them to Matt and, to her dismay, finding them sadly lacking. She was shocked by how much she missed the rugged privateer. It was as if Matt had been the stabilizing force in her life, and without him, she was floundering, drifting aimlessly until he returned.

Herein lay another reason why Leigh had not fled in Matt's absence, probably the primary reason, a reason that Leigh firmly refused to admit even to herself. She couldn't walk out of Matt's life. She couldn't bear to never again see his handsome face and devastating smile or hear his deep, rich voice and hearty laughter or thrill to his touch and his kiss. Without him, her life would be dull, empty. When she had fled before, a part of her had secretly wanted Matt to stop her, but to leave now, would put an ocean of distance between them, and Leigh wasn't sure Matt cared enough to follow. Therefore, without admitting the true reason for her doing so, Leigh waited anxiously for Matt's return and her life to begin again.

A few days later, several of Grandmère's grandsons came calling, smiling smugly and thinking to court Leigh on the sly. Grandmère quickly set them straight. They would not take advantage of their relationship to her to woo Leigh. They would be allowed to call only once a week, for only an hour, and then, to see her, not Leigh. The young men left grumbling under their breaths.

The only exception to this rule was Honoré, not because Grandmère felt him of no danger to Leigh because he was so shy, but because she knew he was no longer a suitor. She had watched the friendship between Leigh and Honoré develop and approved heartily. Honoré's visits kept Leigh from becoming bored, but more important to Grandmère was the remarkable transformation of Honoré in Leigh's company. He walked taller, conversed more freely and with an intelligence that Grandmère had never known he possessed. She watched in amazement as the shy, awkward young Creole blossomed into a confident, self-assured man.

Sometimes when Honoré was visiting, Grandmère would join him and Leigh, and the three of them would play one of the card games that was then the rage. But most of the time, Grandmère would leave them to their own devices, and because of the heat, the two young people often retired to the courtyard where it was cooler.

On one such visit, Leigh sat by the fountain, trailing her hand in the water, trying to entice one of the goldfish to nibble on her finger. Honoré sat on the ground near her, his back propped against a tree.

"Do you have a girlfriend, Honoré?" Leigh asked casually.

Honoré looked up in surprise. "A girlfriend?"

Leigh smiled and sat down beside him, saying, "You know what I mean. Someone you're courting."

Honoré flushed. "*Non*, I'm not courting anyone."

"But isn't there any girl you particularly like? A special girl?" Leigh persisted.

Honoré glanced away in embarrassment.

"Oh, come on, Honoré," Leigh said in exasperation. "We're friends, remember? You can tell me."

Honoré said hesitantly, "Well, there is a girl . . . but she wouldn't be interested in me," he finished with a defeated voice.

"Why?" What's wrong with her?"

"Wrong with her?" Honoré repeated in confusion.

"Yes," Leigh answered firmly. "There must be something wrong with her if she's not attracted to you. You're handsome, intelligent, and the nicest person I've ever known."

Honoré blushed beet red.

"It's true, Honoré! Why, I think the girls in New Orleans must be blind."

"I'm too shy," Honoré mumbled.

"And what's wrong with being shy?" Leigh retorted. "Has it ever occurred to you that there are some women who might be terrified of an aggressive, domineering man? Why, they'd feel as though they were going to be trampled underfoot. No, Honoré, there are many women who much prefer a gentler, more sensitive man like you. One they wouldn't be afraid would eat them alive."

"Do you really think so?" Honoré asked in an amazed voice.

"I don't think it, I know it! I'm a woman too, remember?" Then she grinned impishly, saying, "Now tell me about this girl."

Honoré smiled, saying, "Well, her name is Maria Ortegon. She's one of the Spanish Creoles."

Leigh nodded eagerly, encouraging him.

"Oh, Leigh, she's so beautiful," Honoré said in a dreamy voice. "She's so tiny, so exquisite. Her eyes remind me of a doe's, so soft and warm. But . . ."

"But what?" Leigh asked impatiently.

"Well, you see, she's shy." He laughed, saying ruefully, "Would you believe it? She's even shyer than me."

"Then she'd be perfect for you, and you for her. She's probably terrified of the other young men. Have you ever seen her glancing at you?"

"Once or twice, I thought I did," Honoré admitted. "But it's impossible, Leigh. I wouldn't begin to know how to approach her. If anyone looks at her, she acts as if she wished she could disappear. The only time I ever saw her full in the face was when she was passing a cockfight in her carriage one day. I think that's when I fell in love with her. She was furious, those beautiful brown eyes of hers flashing like fireworks. I always hated cockfights myself. It makes me sick to see two creatures pitted against each other for amusement. It's cruel and senseless. I knew she felt the same way, and I loved her for it."

"Then that's it!" Leigh cried, clapping her hands.

"What?" Honoré asked in bewilderment.

"That's your key to courting her."

"What are you talking about?"

"Oh, Honoré," Leigh sighed impatiently. "Don't you see? You both love animals. You could give her a pet."

"A pet?" Honoré asked in disbelief. "She wouldn't accept a gift from a man, a complete stranger."

"For heaven's sake! It wouldn't be an out-and-out gift. Use your imagination! You could tell her it's your pet, but you can't care for it properly, since you have to go out of town for a while. Tell her you're going to have to give it away, but you want to give it to someone you know loves animals and won't mistreat it. If she really loves animals, she won't refuse you. Then everytime you see her, you can ask about the pet. It would give you something to talk about until you both got over your shyness with each other."

"Do you think it would really work?" Honoré asked in an excited voice.

"It's worth a try," Leigh responded. Her forehead wrinkled. "But what kind of a pet?"

"I know!" Honoré cried. "A bird."

"A bird?"

"Yes, they sell tame birds at the marketplace. Little yellow canaries that sing their hearts out. And parakeets, little green and blue birds that look like miniature parrots. They claim you can teach them to talk."

"But where would she keep a bird?"

"They sell the cages, too. Pretty gold and silver

ones, with tassels on the bottom. You hang them by a hook on the top."

"Oh, yes, that would be perfect! She could keep it in her own room. Then everytime it sang or she looked at it, she'd be reminded of you. Oh, Honoré, how clever you are!"

They continued to talk for a few minutes, but Honoré was clearly distracted. Finally, Leigh laughed and said, "For heaven's sake, Honoré! Why are you sitting around here and talking to me? Get down to the market and buy that bird! I'm dying of curiosity to know if our plan is going to work."

Honoré eagerly rose to his feet. Then he looked down at her, his eyes warm with appreciation. "You're wonderful, Leigh."

Leigh grinned and replied with all sincerity, "Just between us, I think you're pretty wonderful, too."

During this period, Leigh and Grandmère's relationship deepened also. Grandmère discovered in Leigh a depth that she had never known existed. She found herself enjoying the girl's intelligence and quick wit. A deep respect grew between the two women, and despite the great span in their ages, a warm, sincere friendship developed.

One particularly hot day, Grandmère unbuttoned the neck of her dress, saying, "*Mon dieu*, I have never seen it so hot this early in the summer."

Leigh noticed the gold chain hanging around her neck. "Is that a medal?"

"*Non, petite*," Grandmère answered, pulling the chain out and showing Leigh the gold ring that dangled at the end of it. "It's my wedding ring. Since my husband died, I have worn it on this chain around my neck, where it could be close to my heart."

Leigh was touched. "You must have loved him very much."

"*Oui*, I loved him with all the love and passion in my body. We were more than just husband and wife, *mon amour*. We were lovers, right up to the day he died."

Leigh blushed at her intimate revelation. Seeing her blush, Grandmère chuckled, saying, "Do I shock you, *petite*? My friends thought it shameful that I shared my husband's bed all those years. The fools! *Mon dieu*, I wanted him as much as he wanted me. To have denied my sexuality would have been to deny a part of myself. Strange, how many women deny this part of themselves. A shame, too, for they only cheat themselves in the end. *Oui*, I loved him with every fiber of my being, Matthew, *mon amour*."

"Matthew? That was your husband's name?" Leigh asked in surprise.

"*Oui*."

"Then Matt is named after his grandfather?"

"*Oui*, at my insistence." Grandmère looked thoughtful, saying, "You know, it is strange. Of all of my sons and grandsons, only Matthew inherited his grandfather's coloring. Much to my disappointment, all the others are dark-haired and dark-eyed. When I saw Matthew's golden hair, I insisted that he be named after my husband."

"So Matt looks like his grandfather?"

"*Oui*, he is the spiting image of my husband, tall, handsome, broad-shouldered, golden-headed. He even has my husband's smile and his deep dimples. My only disappointment is that Matt inherited my dark eyes. My husband's eyes were blue, as blue as the Caribbean." She glanced speculatively at Leigh's blue-gray eyes, saying, "I keep hoping that someday I will have a blond, blue-eyed great-grandchild."

This was the reason Grandmère was so anxious to see Matt married. She felt that the only hope of having a blond, blue-eyed great-grandchild lay in him, her golden grandson. And more than anything else before she died, Grandmère wanted to be assured that the living image of her beloved husband still walked the earth.

"I wondered about that," Leigh remarked. "When I saw your sons and other grandsons, I thought it strange that Matt looked nothing like them. I assumed he looked like his mother's side of the family."

"*Non*, he's the image of *mon capitaine*."

Leigh's head shot up. "Your husband was a sea captain, too?"

"*Oui*," Grandmère replied with an amused smile. "And only Matthew's father and his sons inherited my husband's love of the sea. All my other sons and grandsons are land-lovers. Only Matthew is just like *mon* handsome, *Anglais capitaine*."

"English?"

"*Oui*. My husband was the third son of an English baron. The baron disinherited him because of some indiscretion my husband committed." She chuckled. "*Mon* Matthew would never tell me what he did to get disinherited, but I suspect it involved a woman, the rogue. But he went to sea and became a pirate. I think he did it to get even with his father for disinheriting him, to embarrass him even further."

Pirate? Leigh couldn't believe her ears. Surely, she must have misunderstood. "You mean privateer?"

Grandmère chuckled. She loved the reaction she got when she told this part of her life story. Everyone always looked so shocked. "*Non, ma petite*, he was a pirate."

Leigh couldn't hide her shock, much to Grandmère's delight. She couldn't believe that this aristocratic woman, a woman who had once been a lady-in-waiting to the queen of France, a woman who was the pampered daughter of a French marquis, a woman to whom the elite Creole society of New Orleans bowed and scraped, had actually married a pirate. "How in God's name did you ever meet a pirate?" she blurted.

"Why, he captured the ship I was sailing on," Grandmère replied calmly.

"What ship?"

Grandmère smiled and said, "Patience, *ma petite*, and I shall tell you all. It's true I am the daughter of a marquis, but I was his seventh and youngest daughter, and even a marquis had trouble arranging proper marriages for that many daughters. By the time he got around to arranging my marriage, the only suitable man he could find was a lesser nobleman who was seeking to increase his dwindling fortune on a plantation in the West Indies. So the contract was signed, and I was shipped off to meet my betrothed. When we reached the Caribbean, the ship I was sailing on was captured by pirates. As *capitaine* of the pirate ship, my husband claimed me as his own personal prize."

His prize? Did Grandmère mean he forced her? Or did he marry her then, Leigh wondered.

Guessing her thoughts, Grandmère said, "*Oui*, he made me his mistress." She grinned, adding, "Much to my relief."

Leigh was so shocked she almost fell off the bench. Her look was one of utter disbelief.

Seeing her look, Grandmère said, "Stop and consider. I was a young girl, eager for life and excitement. The man I was being sent to marry was old enough to be my grandfather, fat, bald, crippled with gout and almost blind as a bat. I was not looking forward to being bedded by that. Nor was I looking forward to be isolated on a lonely plantation, far from civilization."

"Then why didn't you object to the marriage? Refuse to go?"

It was Grandmère's turn to look shocked. "*Mon dieu! Non*, that is not the way of nobility. The marriages are arranged to match bloodlines and unite fortunes, not for love. The woman has no say in the arrangements. If she finds her husband physically repulsive, she just has to live with it. So you see, when this handsome *Anglais aventurier* stepped into my life and saved me from this fate, I was relieved. I would have been crazy to prefer an old, half-crippled man to *mon capitaine*." Her look turned dreamy. "Ah, *ma petite*, you would have to have known *mon* Matthew to understand. He was so virile, so masculine, a beautiful golden god, an exciting lover." Grandmère groped for words. "There was something about him, something different, something no man I had ever met possessed . . . A strange magnetism. *Tu comprends?*"

Leigh blushed, understanding only too well what Grandmère was talking about. Just thinking about Matt made her heart quicken. And apparently, Matt had not only inherited his grandfather's golden good looks and love of the sea, but his predilection for piracy and his magnetic male virility also. Yes, she could understand why Grandmère welcomed the exciting Englishman into her life. If she had to choose between Matt and any other man, she'd . . . The thought was so disturbing Leigh refused to even finish it.

Grandmère had been watching Leigh's face closely. The young woman's facial expressions told her volumes. She had wondered what Leigh's true feelings were toward her grandson. As she had come to know the girl and love her for herself, she had felt guilty about using Leigh to attain her own selfish goals. She

331

loves my grandson, Grandmère realized with sudden clarity. Only she doesn't know it herself, yet. She is just like I was, Grandmère thought, fighting it, denying it. But she will come around. Grandmère's guilt flew out the window.

"But he did marry you?" Leigh asked.

"*Oui*," Grandmère replied, chuckling to herself. She wouldn't tell Leigh how long it had taken her to bring her handsome pirate to his knees. She had even had to run away from him before the stubborn fool had admitted he loved her. And then, as it is so often true in men who are reluctant to give their love, clinging to it with an almost fierce obsession, once he had admitted to it, he had given it totally, completely, lavishing and bathing her in its warmth. *Dieu*, what a full, wonderful life they had shared, she and her *capitaine*, her pirate, her lover, her only *amour*.

"And did he always remain a pirate?" Leigh asked, breaking into Grandmère's reminiscing.

"*Non*. After we were married he got a pardon. We settled in Martinique, where he set up a profitable shipping business in the West Indies trade."

"Have you been a widow for long?"

"*Oui*, for ten years now." Grandmère smiled, saying, "Ah, *ma petite*, I cannot complain. We had such a wonderful life together, much more than most married couples. But still, I am anxious to join him." Again, she glanced at Leigh's eyes, saying in a strange hushed voice, "But not quite yet."

A week later, Leigh, Grandmère and Honoré sat in the shade of the oak tree in the courtyard, drinking lemonade and fanning themselves. The heat was unbearable, oppressive, the humidity so high their perspiration clung to them, adding its stickiness to their misery.

Leigh glanced at the crepe myrtles, blooming in a

profusion of pinks, purples, reds, and whites. There wasn't enough breeze to even ruffle their delicate crinkly petals. "Is it always this hot in July?" she asked.

"*Oui*, New Orleans is often this hot in the summer," Honoré admitted. "But we usually have a good breeze. It's much too still. I'm afraid there may be a storm in the gulf."

"A storm?"

"*Oui, ma petite*," Grandmère answered. "A hurricane."

A hurricane? In the Gulf of Mexico? Matt was out there somewhere, Leigh thought in terror. Icy fear clutched at her heart. Where was he? In the gulf? The Caribbean? The Atlantic? Oh, God, where was he?

Unbeknownst to Leigh, Matt was at that very minute sailing up the Mississippi River to New Orleans.

Matt's sudden departure from New Orleans had been spurred by the supposition that if he could get Leigh out of his sight, he could get her out of his mind. Once a good distance was put between them, he could forget her.

But after a few days at sea, Matt realized that forgetting Leigh wasn't going to be easy. Much to his dismay, everything on the *Avenger* seemed to remind him of her. It was as if she haunted the ship. He saw her in the galley, dressed in her ridiculous boy's disguise, serving the meal. He saw her standing on deck, the wind blowing her rich mahogany tresses about her face and molding her clothes to her curvaceous body. He saw her standing in the moonlight gazing out over the seascape, looking like an ethereal goddess, bathed in silver.

It was even worse in his cabin, for that was where

333

the memories were the strongest. He looked at the desk and remembered her sitting there, chewing her lip in concentration as she wrote in his prize log. Everytime he glanced at the sea chest, where she had kept her pitifully few belongings, he could see her kneeling there, searching for something. Even the cat, Lucifer, reminded him of Leigh. He could see her sitting in the middle of his bunk, petting the lazy cat in her lap. And was it his imagination, or did Lucifer really glare at him as if he was accusing him of something?

But Matt's worst agonies were suffered in his bunk, for there the vivid memories of their lovemaking washed over him, almost drowning him. He remembered the feel of Leigh in his arms, her silky skin, her incredible softness and warmth. Even her sweet scent seemed to have permeated the wood, wafting out around him to further torment him. Matt lay, tossing and turning, muttering and cursing, his loins throbbing and aching for the relief that only Leigh could satisfy.

After a few miserable, sleepless nights, he abandoned the bunk in favor of the hammock. But even there, the memories were too strong. He took to the deck, pacing restlessly all night, cursing the day he had met her.

And to make matters even worse, it seemed to Matt the only topic the crew could talk about was Leigh. And my God, the exaggerations! Now, the tale was Leigh had attacked not just one sailor, but three, and had neatly skewered them all. And goddammit, she didn't knock him out cold, she barely tapped him.

Thank God, the crew didn't know about Leigh's little escapade the night she had tried to run away, Matt thought ruefully. If so, by the time they finished embellishing that story, they would have Leigh slaying all four of her captors, single-handedly. Despite his misery, Matt smiled, remembering how Leigh had joined in the brawl.

When the crew wasn't talking about Leigh's exploits, they were extolling her beauty. They argued over whether her hair was red with brown highlights or brown with red highlights, whether her eyes were blue with a touch of gray or gray with a touch of blue, whether the little dimple in her chin sat more to the right side or more to the left.

The crew's constant discussion about Leigh within hearing distance of the captain was no coincidence. It was deliberate on the part of the crew. They strongly disapproved of the captain leaving the spunky, beautiful girl behind without having firmly established her as his before he left New Orleans. They hadn't necessarily expected him to marry her. They were sailors themselves and felt just as strongly as Matt about giving up their independence. But they had expected him to have her firmly entrenched as his mistress. Instead, they had heard through the waterfront grapevine that the girl was being courted by a bunch of rich Creoles. The crew had been horrified. They had a proprietary air about Leigh. To them, the only man good enough for her was the captain. And certainly, no strutting foreign peacock was going to have her, not if they had anything to say about it. And so, cursing the captain for being every kind of fool, they had set about to constantly remind him of what he had so carelessly left behind.

As the weeks passed, Matt's mood got fouler and fouler. He paced the deck like a caged tiger, cursing, snarling, snapping at the crew. Behind his back, they winked knowingly and grinned.

To add to Matt's miseries, a new worry began to gnaw at him. He knew Leigh couldn't marry without

335

his permission as her guardian. Oh, she could accept a proposal, but the actual ceremony couldn't take place until he signed the marriage certificate. But that didn't rule out seduction. And by now, the courting must be going hot and heavy. A hard knot formed deep in his belly.

As if sensing his thoughts, the crew's conversations abruptly switched from Leigh to speculation about the Creole men and their notorious reputations as superior lovers and accomplished seducers. The finishing touch was when one crew member said, "I heard one of those damned Creoles was so damned good at seducin' women that there ain't a woman left in Louisiana that he ain't bedded. He was some Spaniard, named Diego somethin' or another."

The next day, under the pretext that the *Avenger* had sprung a mysterious leak, Matt turned the ship around and headed for New Orleans, without having taken a single prize. Matt was surprised at the crew's lack of disappointment at turning back.

When he mentioned this to Kelly, the first mate grinned knowingly, then answered with a perfectly straight face, "I guess they didn't have time to spend all their prize money before we sailed."

Chapter 16

Matt stood in the moon-dappled courtyard and gazed up at Leigh's bedroom. At this time of the night, the town house was dark and perfectly quiet, the only sound reaching his ears the soft chirruping of crickets. He felt a brief hesitancy at what he was about to do. Then firming his resolve, he walked into the town house.

A few minutes later, he stood outside Leigh's door. He opened it, relieved that it hadn't been locked, and stepped into the room. The French doors were wide to admit the breeze, and the room was bathed in the soft light of the full moon outside.

He stepped to the bed and gazed down at the sleeping girl. Her sheet had been kicked away because of the heat, and her gown was tangled about her hips, revealing her slim, shapely legs. Her long hair fanned about her face like a dark cloud.

For a minute, Matt stood feasting on the lovely sight. God, she is even more beautiful than I remembered, he thought as his eyes scanned her face, her slim throat, her creamy shoulders and locked on her soft breasts, the rosy nipples showing as a darkened area beneath the almost transparent material of her gown.

Feeling the heat rising, Matt quickly undressed and, parting the mosquito netting, lay down beside her. Leaning over her, he whispered, "Leigh, wake up."

Leigh moaned in her sleep and rolled away from him. Matt took her shoulder and gently rolled her back, whispering, "Wake up, Leigh. It's me, Matt."

Leigh blinked her eyes sleepily. I must be dreaming, she thought. She blinked again. No, the vision was still there. "Matt?" she mumbled drowsily.

"That's right, kitten."

Slowly, she began to wake up. Matt was back. Here in her room, in her bed. In her bed? My God, and he was naked! Leigh bolted up, hissing, "What are you doing here?"

Matt grinned, saying, "I should think that would be obvious, sweet. I'm going to make love to you."

"You're crazy! Get out of here! If Grandmére knew—"

"What are you going to do about it, kitten?" Matt taunted softly, moving his body intimately against hers. "Scream?" He kissed her neck softly, nuzzling. "Scare Grandmère to death?" He kissed her bare shoulder. "Or have her run in here and find us like this?" He lifted her hair, nipping at the nape of her neck, then kissing it.

Leigh shivered in response, then whispered, "Get out! Get out, you devil!"

Matt chuckled and pulled her down, quickly pinning her with his muscular leg. "No, sweet, not until I've made love to you."

"I'll tell Grandmère," Leigh threatened. "She'll kill you!"

"I'll deal with Grandmère in the morning," Matt replied calmly, kissing her throat, nibbling, then sucking her small earlobe.

Oh, God, no, it's happening, Leigh thought in despair, recognizing the signs of her own body's betrayal. "No, I won't let you," she sobbed.

338

"Won't you?" Matt mumbled, caressing her sides, then cupping her breasts, his hands massaging the sensitive flesh gently as his tongue flicked at the corners of her mouth.

"I don't want you," Leigh hissed, trying desperately to convince herself as well as him.

"Liar, beautiful, little liar," Matt muttered as his warm lips covered hers, nibbling, teasing, playing, his tongue enticing on her lower lip, then raking her teeth, until Leigh groaned in frustration and threw her arms around his muscular shoulders. Matt's kiss became earnest, a deep, searching kiss, and Leigh wondered briefly why only this man's kisses could make her feel so warm and wonderful. But soon Leigh's thoughts were blotted out by sheer sensation as Matt's lips, tongue, and hands skillfully played her body, working their magic on her.

Matt slipped the gown up and over Leigh's head in one swift movement. Then he gazed down at her in the moonlight, mumbling in an awed voice, "God, you're beautiful." His head lowered, his tongue tracing lazy patterns over her breasts, flicking erotically at one rosy tip, then the other. His hands stroked and caressed her thighs, slowly inching upward, until Leigh moaned, her loins aching for his touch, and then sighed in delight as his fingers deftly explored, seeking her innermost secrets, stroking her to a fevered pitch of excitement.

Matt loomed above her, a golden god bathed in silver, and Leigh accepted his hard, pulsating maleness eagerly, arching toward it, wrapping her legs around his slim hips as if she feared he would slip away at the last moment.

Matt felt Leigh's soft, moist heat enveloping him and groaned in pleasure. "Oh, God, kitten, I've missed you," he whispered in her ear before his mouth captured hers in a fiercely possessive kiss. Then he was moving, at first in slow, deep, sensuous strokes that sent shock waves up Leigh's spine and her blood coursing hotly through her veins, and then faster, driving her up the familiar ascent, spiraling up and up, until he brought them both to that mindless peak of exquisite rapture, bursting in a golden shower of sparks and whirling into space.

When their breathing had returned to normal and reason returned, Leigh blinked back tears of self-disgust and sobbed, "I hate you!"

"Do you, kitten?" Matt whispered, gently brushing back a damp tendril of hair and kissing her forehead tenderly. He smiled down at her, saying, "If this is the way you act with someone you hate, then God help me if you ever love me." He chuckled. "I don't think I could stand it."

Before Leigh could retort, he was kissing her again, hot, demanding kisses that left her breathless and clutching. She realized with shock that he was growing inside her, hardening and throbbing. He can't mean to make love to me again, she thought. So soon? But as he began his masterful movement, she realized . . . he did!

Matt left Leigh that morning, sleeping in exhaustion. He had made love to her over and over, attempting to sate his desire for her once and for all. He realized now that was impossible. He would never stop wanting her, never get enough of her. His mind was firmly made up, and he was determined to follow through with his plans. He went to his room, bathed, dressed, and then headed for Grandmère's room, his chin set stubbornly.

When he walked in, Grandmère looked up in surprise. "Matthew! When did you get back?"

"Last night."

"*Mon dieu*, why didn't you wake me?"

Matt smiled smugly and said, "You need your beauty rest."

Grandmère's quick mind had recovered from her surprise. Now that he's back, on with the plans, she thought. "*Merci, le bon dieu*, you are back. Shame on you, Matthew, leaving me in such an awkward position with all those suitors to contend with. Leigh must have had at least a dozen proposals, and you not even here to give your consent."

Matt smiled, his eyes glittering strangely. "I'm afraid marrying a Creole is out of the question now, Grandmère."

Grandmère was wary. Why was he acting so peculiarly? So smugly? He was up to something. "Oh? And may I ask why not?"

"Because I'm afraid I have a confession to make. You see, I went to Leigh's room last night and seduced her."

Grandmère stared at him. Why is he telling me this, she wondered.

Matt frowned at Grandmère's expressionless face. "Don't you see? I made love to her. I took her virginity. You know how obsessive these damned Creoles are about their wives being virgins. She can't possibly marry a Creole now."

Mon dieu! He *is* up to something! I know damned well he took the girl's virginity a long time ago. Does he think he can claim her for his mistress now? Or does he expect me to demand that he do the honorable thing and marry her? Then he can blame me for the marriage and not his own desire. Either way, *non!*

Dammit, what was wrong with her, Matt thought. Why wasn't she raising the roof, demanding that he marry Leigh. Matt glared at his grandmother. Grandmère stared back. Finally, Matt took a deep breath and said, "If it will relieve your mind, Grandmère, I intend to do the honorable thing."

"Oh? And what might that be?"

Matt exploded. "Why, marry her, of course!"

Grandmère felt like jumping up and down with joy, but she was determined that he would not be able to blame her for this marriage. She replied in an indifferent voice, "*Oui*, if you like."

Matt stared at her in disbelief. If he liked? Dammit, no! He really didn't like the idea of marriage at all, but if that was the only way to be assured Leigh was solely his, then he would do it. But hell, Grandmère could make it a little easier for him. The way things were progressing, it was going to look as though it was all his idea, and he didn't want Leigh to know that. There must be a graceful way out. Some explanation that wouldn't be so obvious.

"Well, frankly, Grandmère, I don't particularly like the idea of marriage, but I realize it's expected of me as my father's only heir." He shrugged. "So if I have to marry someday, why not Leigh? She's beautiful, intelligent, spirited. I could certainly do a lot worse. And after all, I have dishonored her. I owe her that much."

Grandmère felt sick. What was all this trash about honor? Who did he think he was fooling? *Mon dieu!* The lengths a man will go to save his damned pride! Why didn't he just admit he wanted her? She was tempted to tell him to stop worrying about Leigh's honor. With her beauty, she would have no trouble finding a husband, virgin or not. But that would only destroy her own plans. Besides, she knew Leigh was in love with her grandson. And him? How deeply did his feelings go?

She asked, "You care nothing for her?"

Matt was stunned by the question. He flushed,

saying, "She's a very desirable woman. I'd be out-and-out lying if I denied I didn't want her. After all, I'm only human."

"Do you love her?"

Love her? The question hit Matt like a slap in the face. He had been very careful not to delve too deeply into his feelings for Leigh. He wasn't about to begin to now. "No!" he denied emphatically, too emphatically.

Oui, he's just like his grandfather, Grandmère thought with disgust. Stubborn fool! "But you would take good care of her?"

"Of course, I'd take care of her! I wouldn't let anything or anyone hurt Leigh. And as my wife, she'll lack for nothing!"

Ma foi! He wants to make love to her, protect her, and take care of her, give her anything her heart desires, but he doesn't love her. The idiot! She asked, "And what does Leigh say to all this?"

Matt's look was blank.

"*Sacre-bleu!* You *did* ask her to marry you?"

Of course he hadn't asked Leigh to him. He had only planned to tell Grandmère of his seduction and then let the old woman take over from there. He had expected Grandmère to insist they marry immediately and, in her usual domineering manner, totally override both his and Leigh's objections. Not for one minute had he doubted that Grandmère could manipulate Leigh to the altar. But she had turned the tables on him, and he would be damned if he would look like a fool. "I haven't talked to her yet, but she'll agree," he answered confidently.

The arrogant bastard, Grandmère thought. She looked at him, saying, "Oh? How can you be so sure? Because you're young, handsome, rich, and charming? Ha! So are your cousins, but Leigh didn't agree

343

to marry them. Or maybe you are one of those fools
that think every woman *wants* to get married, every
woman *wants* security and a man to protect and take
care of her. *Ma foi!* Leigh is not every woman. She's
different. And I hope to God, you don't think
because you have dishonored her, she'll be thankful
that you're offering marriage and rush to the altar
like a scared rabbit. I should think you would know
Leigh better than that!"

A muscle jerked in Matt's jaw as he struggled to
hold his temper. "It may come as a surprise to you,
Grandmère, but Leigh isn't indifferent to me. I admit
that I seduced her, but I didn't force her. She was very
willing."

"So what does that prove? *Mon dieu*, you think
because she enjoys your lovemaking, she'll jump at
the chance to marry you?"

Matt had assumed just that and, truthfully, a little
of all the other things Grandmère had suggested.
After all, he wasn't considered a bad catch. He had
certainly had enough women chasing him to prove
that. His male ego was taking a good bruising under
Grandmère's caustic words. His temper and stubbornness rose to his defense. Dammit, he had never
even considered marriage to another woman. Leigh
wouldn't dare refuse!

He turned and walked to the door angrily, saying,
"She'll marry me, by God!"

"Matthew!"

Matt hesitated at the stern tone of Grandmère's
voice. He turned to face her, his lips compressed, his
jaw set obstinately.

"In the month you were gone to sea, I have come to
know Leigh very well. She is just as proud and
fiercely independent as you are. If you really want
her, don't be a fool. Ask her. Don't tell her."

Matt glared at his grandmother, then, nodding curtly, turned and stormed from the room.

"*Mon dieu*, I hope the young fool doesn't ruin everything," Grandmère muttered in disgust.

As Matt walked to Leigh's room, he considered everything Grandmère had said. It was true. Leigh was proud and independent—and very stubborn and unpredictable. But dammit, he wanted her more than ever, and he was determined to have her. He would just have to be very careful how he approached her.

When Leigh heard the knock on the door, she assumed it must be Grandmère or the maid. She answered, "Come in."

She gasped when Matt stepped into the room. "What are you doing here? If Grandmère comes in and finds—"

"Grandmère knows I'm here, Leigh," Matt interrupted. "I just came from her."

My God, had Grandmère found out about last night? Had she sent Matt to apologize? Or worse yet, to offer to do the honorable thing and marry her? How humiliating. "Did Grandmère send you?" she asked.

"No, she didn't send me. I came to ask you something."

"What?"

Matt took a deep breath and said, "I've come to ask you to be my wife."

Leigh turned deathly pale. She gasped the bedpost, whispering, "Grandmère knows about last night, doesn't she? She sent you."

For the first time, Matt was ashamed of himself and regretted having told Grandmère of his seduction. He had never stopped to consider the humiliation Leigh would feel knowing the older woman knew of their intimacies. Grandmère was right. He was a fool!

"No, Leigh, Grandmère didn't send me. This is my idea," Matt replied, feeling a sense of relief at having admitted the truth.

Leigh was stunned. Then she asked, "Why? Why are you asking me to marry you? Because of the promise you made my uncle?"

"No, Leigh, I could easily take care of you without marrying you."

"Then why? Have you forgotten that I'm deceitful? That I'm an ungrateful wench? That I'm a wild hoyden?" Leigh asked, her anger rising at the memory of Matt's hurtful accusations. "You implied I wasn't good enough to be a man's wife — just his mistress! So why are you asking me to marry you?"

Matt winced at the repetition of his cruel words, then said, "I didn't mean those things. At the time I said them, I was angry and frustrated. I wanted you, and I didn't want to give you up. Which brings me to the reason I'm asking you to marry me. I still want you. I've never lied to you about that. I realize now that I made a mistake in trying to force you to be my mistress. You're much too proud to accept that arrangement. So, now, I'm asking you to be my wife."

No mention of love, Leigh thought bitterly. Just I want you. Well, at least he's honest and not like René, lying to me about loving me. I much prefer that.

"And Leigh, if you would be honest with yourself, you'd admit you want me, too," Matt continued.

"And for that reason, I should marry you? Marry you because we're physically attracted to each other? Because we both enjoy making love?"

Matt flushed, then said, "There have been many marriages that started out with a lot less, Leigh. And don't underrate our sexual relationship. Because of your lack of experience, you don't realize how extraordinary it is. It's very rare for a man and woman to find such total physical satisfaction in one another, to be so perfectly attuned to each other's bodies, to reach such exceptional heights of ecstasy. It's true it won't make a marriage—but it won't hurt it either. And maybe, if we could stop fighting about that, we might find other things we have in common."

"Like what?" Leigh asked sarcastically.

"Well, for one thing, I think we're both adventuresome. I can't see you puttering around the house all day, day in and day out, waiting for your husband to come home every evening, any more than I can see myself trudging back and forth to an office every day. No, we're the kind of people who need excitement in our lives. I was thinking, after this war is over, I'd like you to sail with me. We could see the world. Not just Europe, but the Mediterranean, Mexico, South America, the tropical islands of the Pacific, the Orient, India. My God, Leigh, there's a whole world of new sights and sounds out there just waiting for us!"

See the world? That would be wonderful! Exciting! Then she remembered that she couldn't, that first she had to find her father. She knew that Matt couldn't understand her obsession, but she couldn't continue with her future, until she had found this missing link in her past. She turned away, mumbling, "I can't. I've got to find my father."

Despite Matt's resolve not to lose his temper, he spat, "Why? Do you think he'll arrange a better marriage for you than I'm offering? Someone richer? Someone more important? Someone more exciting? A nobleman, perhaps?"

Arrange a marriage? For the first time, Leigh considered this possibility. If her father accepted her, would he do that? What was it Grandmère had said about arranged marriages, the women had no say in it? Would her father marry her off to someone old, someone she found physically repulsive? No, if she had to marry, she would much rather marry Matt. At least she knew she wouldn't mind being bedded by him, and he was young and exciting. He also gave her credit for having some intelligence, sometimes that is. Of course, she and Matt didn't love one another, but then she wouldn't be in love with the man her father chose for her either.

As Leigh was thinking, Matt was waiting anxiously. He couldn't lose her, not now. "All right, Leigh," he said, "I'll make a deal with you. If you marry me, when the war is over, I'll take you to England and help you find your father."

Take her to England to find her father? She considered this. She had no idea how to go about looking for him, but Matt would know. He knew people in England who could help. Hadn't her uncle said he knew London like the back of his hand? Yes, if anyone could find her father, it would be Matt. She whirled and said, "Do you really mean it?"

"Yes, I promise."

"You won't go back on your promise?"

Matt smiled, saying, "If you like, I'll sign a premarital agreement to that effect. The Creoles do it all the time, except it usually involves land or property, but—"

"That won't be necessary," Leigh interjected. "I'll take your word for it."

Matt's heart was racing in his chest. "Does that mean you *will* marry me?"

Leigh smiled, wondering how she could feel so calm when she was taking such a monumental step. "Yes, Matt, I'll marry you."

Grandmère never knew what Matt said to Leigh to

convince her to marry him, but she was ecstatic over the news. And she was determined to get the young couple to the altar quickly, before either of them could change his or her mind. That very afternoon she went to the cathedral to arrange for the reading of the banns, to be read each Sunday for three consecutive weeks, and reserve the church for the Monday after the third reading. That left a little over two weeks to prepare for the wedding.

The second thing on Grandmère's agenda was to have a talk with her grandson. In a stern voice that brooked no disobedience, she told Matt there would be no more sneaking into Leigh's room at night. As his future wife, she deserved his respect.

Matt had smiled ruefully and agreed to behave himself, thinking, he had gone two months without making love to Leigh. He supposed he could manage three weeks.

Then the whole household was caught up in a whirlwind of activity as Grandmère set her mind and energies on the wedding preparations. Once again, the *couturière* and her swarm of assistants descended on the town house, this time to fit Leigh for a wedding gown and trousseau.

"But I don't need any more clothes," Leigh objected. "I just got a whole new wardrobe. Why, I haven't even worn a third of my new dresses yet."

"*Non, non, ma petite*. You'll need several more ballgowns, traveling suits for the honeymoon, and more nightwear."

"More nightgowns? For heaven's sake! I already have one for every night of the week."

"*Non, ma petite*," Grandmère said in a disapproving voice. "A new bride does not wear her plain nightgowns. You'll need new gowns and negligees."

"Negligees? What's that?"

When the *couturière* showed Leigh the new night-gowns and negligees, Leigh blushed furiously, the bevy of attendants tittering at her reaction. The sheer gowns and robes were obviously not designed to sleep in, but for seduction. She couldn't see herself prancing around in front of Matt in something like that. Why, the gowns were an open invitation. As if Matt needed any encouragement. Besides, knowing him, he would have it stripped off her in two minutes. It seemed a waste to spend money on something that was just going to lie on the floor.

The engagement ball was held two nights later and, at Matt's insistence, at the town house. Before the guests arrived, Matt took Leigh's left hand and slipped on her engagement ring, a huge fire opal, surrounded by rubies.

Leigh looked down at it, saying softly, "Oh, Matt, it's beautiful."

"Do you really like it, kitten? It's not the most expensive ring in the world, you know. I looked at diamonds, but they didn't seem to suit you. They seemed too cold. The same for emeralds. But this ring reminded me of you, the rubies of your warmth, the fire opal of the sparks in your eyes when you're angry."

Leigh was so touched by Matt's words that she didn't even mind his reference to her temper. Obviously, he had put thought, time, and consideration into buying the ring, to find something that he felt suited her temperament.

As Leigh and Matt stood in the receiving line that evening, the young Creole suitors gave Leigh one last wistful look and congratulated Matt sullenly. René's absence was conspicuous, and no one believed his mother's tale that he was out of town. When Diego de Leon came down the line, Matt stiffened. But the handsome Spaniard was every inch the gentleman, and Matt was both puzzled and delighted at Leigh's indifference to his charm. So when Honoré stepped before them a minute later, Matt was stunned by Leigh's obvious delight to see his cousin.

"Honoré! I'm so happy to see you," Leigh cried.

Honoré took Leigh's hands in his own, saying, "Leigh, you look absolutely beautiful."

Leigh? Honoré? Matt thought. What in the hell is this first name business? And what's that bastard doing holding my fiancée's hands? Matt was just beginning to step forward to assert his rights, when Leigh said, "And how is the romance coming, Honoré?"

Honoré flashed a dazzling smile, saying, "Perfect. I proposed last night, and Maria accepted. I'm going to talk to her father tomorrow night."

"So soon?" Leigh asked in surprise.

Honoré laughed. "Why waste time on a long courtship when we both know what we want? And Leigh, I've told Maria all about you. She can hardly wait to meet you."

"And I'm anxious to meet her, too."

Honoré turned to Matt, giving him a warm, sincere smile and shaking his hand firmly. "Congratulations, Matt. I was secretly rooting for you all the time."

Matt stared in disbelief at the broad back of his cousin as Honoré walked off. That self-assured man couldn't possibly be the same shy boy he had seen only two short months ago, he thought. What had caused that amazing transformation?

With the engagement ball out of the way, Grand-mère's entire energies were devoted to the wedding itself. She sat Matt and Leigh down the next day, saying, "Now, first we have to decide on the wedding party. *Petite*, I'm sure either of my sons would be

351

happy to give the bride away."

Leigh frowned, saying, "That's very nice of them, but I really had someone else in mind."

"Who?" Grandmère asked.

Leigh smiled nervously at Matt and said, "Do you think Kelly would consider it?"

Matt smiled back saying, "Kelly would be proud as a peacock, Leigh."

"Who is Kelly?" Grandmère asked.

"Kelly is my first mate and best friend. He's been like a second father to me and thinks the world of Leigh."

"Your first mate?" Grandmère asked with raised eyebrows.

"Don't worry, Grandmère," Matt said. "Kelly will be perfectly acceptable to your snobbish Creoles. He's a perfect gentleman and would have had his own captaincy years ago, except he preferred to sail with me. Only this leaves me floundering for a best man. I had planned to ask Kelly."

"*Mon dieu*, Matthew, that's no problem," Grandmère said. "Not with all of your cousins."

Matt's eyes flashed. He would be damned if he would have any of his cousins as his best man! The same men that had so furiously courted his woman? Then, he remembered Honoré at the dance the night before. He couldn't have been courting Leigh if he had just proposed to another woman. He frowned, asking, "What about Honoré?"

"He would be the perfect choice," Grandmère said. "Particularly, since he and Leigh are such good friends."

Matt's head shot up.

Grandmère chuckled, saying, "*Non, non*, Matthew. Don't look so fierce. It may surprise you, but there are some men and women who can be friends without the slightest physical attraction to one another. Not all men are rakes like you and your other cousins."

Matt flushed and Leigh choked back a laugh.

"And now, *petite*, for your bridesmaids?" Grand-mère asked.

Leigh didn't have a single female friend in New Orleans, much to her disappointment. Honoré had been her only real friend. "Do you think if Honoré agrees to be Matt's best man, his fiancée would consider being my maid of honor?"

"Fiancée? Honoré has a fiancée?" Grandmère asked in a shocked voice.

Oh no, Leigh thought, I've let the cat out of the bag. "I shouldn't have said anything, Grandmère, but I thought you knew."

"*Non, non*," Grandmère said in an excited voice. "Tell me, who is this girl?"

"Her name is Maria Ortegon."

Grandmère looked impressed. "That lovely little Spanish girl?"

"Oh, Grandmère, I could kick myself," Leigh wailed. "I shouldn't have told you. I'm sure Honoré wanted to break the news himself."

"*Oui*, he will probably tell me this afternoon when he visits. But don't worry, *ma petite*. I shall act appropriately surprised. Ah, what a perfect match those two are! And who would have ever thought Honoré would be my first Creole grandson to marry! But as for your question, yes, I think Maria will agree to be your maid of honor. But what about the other attendants?"

Leigh frowned. "Do I really have to have more? It would be different if I had more friends in New Orleans, but to have perfect strangers as your wedding attendants . . ." Leigh trailed off.

"I agree, *petite*. *Non*, one attendant apiece is all

that is really necessary. After all, you only need two witnesses. *Mon dieu*, I have been to weddings where the wedding party was larger than the guest list. Ridiculous!"

"Speaking of guests, Grandmère," Matt said in a firm voice. "If you intend to invite half of New Orleans, you had better rent the ballroom at the hotel for the reception. I absolutely will not have our wedding reception at Twelve Oaks."

The idea of renting a ballroom for social functions appalled Grandmère. She frowned, saying thoughtfully, "*Eh bien*, I will have to cut down on the guest list then."

"I think you'd better rent the ballroom, Grandmère," Leigh said. "I want to invite the crew of the *Avenger.*"

Matt looked at Leigh in surprise, Grandmère in perfect horror. "*Mon dieu, petite*, you can't do that!" the old woman cried.

Leigh raised her chin stubbornly. "And why not? Except for your family, Grandmère, I hardly know these Creoles. The crew of the *Avenger* are my friends."

"But, *petite*, you can't mix a bunch of American sailors with these hot-headed Creoles. Instead of a wedding, we'd have a brawl."

Grandmère saw the determined look in Leigh's eyes. *Mon dieu*, would the girl call the whole thing off over something like this?

"I'll vouch for the behavior of my men, Grandmère," Matt said. "I don't think they would do anything to embarrass Leigh or myself."

With Matt siding with Leigh, Grandmère had no choice but to agree. "*Oui*, Matthew, if you say so. But the question is, can I vouch for the Creoles' behavior?"

354

And how in the world am I going to get the snobbish, clannish Creoles to accept this, Grandmère wondered. Someway or another, I will have to convince them that this is very chic, this democracy. No, I have an even better idea. Since many of the Creoles think Matthew is a pirate anyway, I'll just hint that he and their hero, Jean Lafitte, are considering merging forces. Grandmère's eyes twinkled mischievously. *Sacre-bleu*, the Creoles will be talking about this wedding for years!

From then on, Leigh hardly had a spare minute to herself. Grandmère rushed her back and forth from portrait sittings, to trousseau fittings, to the printers, the florists, and the caterers to make her selections. And sandwiched between all of this were the score or more of brunches and afternoon teas, given by Grandmère's friends in Leigh's honor. During this frantic time, Matt hardly saw her and had to practically make an appointment to talk to her about their honeymoon plans.

On the day he finally cornered her, Leigh slumped into a chair in exhaustion, groaning, "Why don't we just elope?"

Matt laughed, saying, "And rob Grandmère of all her fun?"

"Fun?" Leigh snapped. "Do you have any idea how much work is involved in preparing for a wedding?"

"And Grandmère is enjoying every minute of it, Leigh. She never had any daughters of her own, you know. Do you have any idea how much pleasure she is getting out of all this?"

Leigh sighed, "I suppose she is enjoying it. But she's running circles around me. I'm exhausted, and she's still going strong. Has she always been like this?"

Matt chuckled. "Yes, as long as I've known her."

"But my God, she's eighty years old! Where does she get all that energy?"

"I don't honestly know. Sometimes, I think she's discovered the fountain of youth and is holding back on the rest of us."

Leigh smiled, saying, "She's the most remarkable person I've ever met."

"I agree, sweet, but I didn't bring you here to talk about Grandmère. I wanted to ask you what you'd like to do for our honeymoon? What I'd really like to do is take you to Europe, but with this war and blockade, that's impossible. We'll just have to postpone that trip until after the war."

Another decision, Leigh thought wearily. "I don't know, Matt. What do you think?"

"Well, I suppose we could go to Natchez."

"Where is that?"

"About one hundred fifty miles up the Mississippi."

"Is it like New Orleans?"

"If you mean does it have a foreign air like New Orleans has, the answer is no. Even though it's part of Florida now and Spanish territory, Natchez was settled by the English. It's much like our southern states, surrounded by plantations."

Leigh frowned. She loved traveling and seeing new cities, but from what Matt had said, and his disinterested tone of voice, Natchez didn't sound very exciting to her.

"Of course, if we go there," Matt continued, "there's the problem of how we would travel." A frown crossed his handsome face. "Overland is out of the question. Traveling through all that swampy terrain at this time of the year would only be courting illness. We don't want to take any chances on getting yellow fever. Besides, the roads are bad and travel is slow."

"Can't we sail the *Avenger* up to Natchez?"

"No, sailboats don't venture past New Orleans. In the first place, there's not enough wind. In the second place, sea-going vessels have a deeper draft than river boats."

Matt looked thoughtful, then said, "I've heard they have a packet running from New Orleans to Natchez now. One of those new steamboats. Personally, I've never trusted the things too much."

"Why not?"

"Because those boilers are unpredictable. More than just a few of them have been known to explode."

"Explode?" Leigh asked in horror.

Seeing the look on her face, Matt said, "Maybe I'm just being an alarmist. I'm a sailing man myself, and like all seamen, I have a natural distrust of machines. If you like, we can go down to the waterfront tomorrow. Then we can decide."

Leigh enjoyed the ride to the waterfront the next afternoon. This was the first time she had been alone with Matt since he proposed. Surprisingly, they had little to say to each other, both being content just to be together.

As they drove down the levee, they could see the steamboat rocking on the muddy waters of the Mississippi. Leigh was disappointed at the size of the steamboat. Compared to the *Avenger*, it looked like a toy boat. It seemed to be all paddle wheel and smokestack.

"I think we have a few minutes before it leaves," Matt said, scowling down at the boat. "Do you want to take a closer look?"

Just then the steamboat blew its whistle, and Leigh jumped in surprise at the sudden shrill noise. She watched the gangplank being pulled up and said, "I think it's leaving now."

The paddles started spinning slowly, throwing muddy water in the air. Even from where they sat on the levee, they could hear the loud clattering noises of the engine as the paddles moved faster and faster and see the vibrations from the engines shaking the small boat. But it wasn't until Leigh saw the red-hot cinders shooting from the smokestack and drifting down on the deck, that she firmly made up her mind. Remembering what Matt had said about explosions, she vowed that no one was going to get her on one of those dangerous things.

"Well, what do you think?" Matt asked.

"Why don't we just forget the trip to Natchez?"

"That's fine with me," Matt replied, obviously relieved. "But that still leaves us with our problem. What are we going to do for our honeymoon?"

"What do the Creoles do for their honeymoons?"

"They lock the couple up together for a week. They can't even come out for meals. They're brought to them."

"I'm serious!" Leigh snapped.

"So am I, sweet. That's what they do. They think the couple needs to be alone to get better acquainted." He grinned, his black eyes twinkled. "Now, I wouldn't mind that so much."

"You would, too! In two days, you'd be pacing like a caged animal. And so would I." She tilted her head to the side, asking curiously, "Is that all the Creoles do for their honeymoon?"

"No. Then they go visiting their relatives," Matt answered, wincing at the thought.

"Isn't there anything else we could do?"

Matt smiled, saying, "Well, I do have another idea, but I don't know if you would like it."

"What?"

At that minute, the steamboat's whistle blew again, and both Matt and Leigh cringed at the noise.

"Let's go someplace where it's quiet," Matt said, flicking the reins.

Only when they were completely away from the waterfront and into the city itself, did Matt resume their conversation. He pulled the carriage off to one side of the street under a huge spreading oak tree and turned to Leigh, saying, "As I said, you may not like this idea at all. My uncle has a small cabin down on the beach. I drove down there one day last week and looked at it. Believe me, it's nothing luxurious. In fact, it's pretty rustic. But it's well built and would protect us from the elements."

Leigh frowned.

Matt took her hands in his, saying, "Leigh, I'm going to have to go back to sea in about a month. I don't want to leave you, but it's not fair to my crew for me to loll around. They're not in the financial position I am, and if I don't go back to sea soon, they're going to be leaving me and signing up with other ships. They're too good a crew to lose."

Leigh was stunned. Going back to sea? So soon?

"So you see, kitten, we're not going to have much time together, and frankly, I don't want to share you with anyone else. I guess I'm selfish, but I want you all to myself, for a while at least. And I think we need this time together, too. Remember what I said about maybe discovering other things we might have in common?"

Leigh nodded.

"Well, we'd be alone at the little beach house, except for the caretaker, who'd fix our meals and keep the place straightened up. And from what my uncle says we won't even know he's around. We'd be able to just relax, be ourselves, do what we feel like doing when we want to do it. We won't even have to eat regular meals if we don't want to."

Leigh had to admit it did sound appealing. She was exhausted from all the running around and getting ready for the wedding. Her nerves felt as though they were coiled into a hundred springs. It would be nice to laze around and unwind. But the beach meant sand and salt water. She remembered how miserable she had been the day they stopped at the island for water. She looked at Matt, saying, "We'll go, on one condition."

"What's that?"

"That I can have a bath in fresh water every day."

Matt grinned, saying, "That's no problem."

"You're sure?" Leigh asked suspiciously.

"I'm positive," Matt assured her.

Chapter 17

The day of the wedding, the sun rose in a spectacular ball of fire, bathing the courtyard and Leigh's room in bright, golden sunlight. The birds sang unusually lustily that morning, vying in their serenading of her, as if they knew this was a special day. And Leigh was oblivious to it all.

When she awakened that morning, the full realization of what she was about to do rushed in on her. She panicked. What am I doing, she thought. I can't marry Matt. I don't love him. And he doesn't love me either. Why did I agree to this? What was I thinking of? How can I get out of it? Run? But where?

She paced the floor, her nerves growing into a tighter and tighter knot, her stomach a hard ball in her abdomen, her mind racing frantically, until, mercifully, a numbness crept over her.

She resembled a manikin while she was bathed, perfumed, and dressed in her sheer undergarments. She hardly noticed as the beautiful ivory satin and lace wedding gown was pulled over her head. She was oblivious to Grandmère fluttering about her, tugging and rearranging the folds of the gown and draping the lace mantilla over her head. She heard none of the servants' "ohs" and "ahs" of admiration as she was led down to the carriage. It wasn't until she was standing in the back of the cathedral, her hand resting on Kelly's strong arm, that reaction set in. Every muscle in her body began to tremble.

Kelly looked down at the vision of loveliness beside him and said, "Are you frightened, lass?"

Leigh bit her lip and managed a nod.

Kelly chuckled softly, saying, "Havin' afterthoughts, are you? Aye, you wouldn't be normal if you weren't. But young Matt's a good man. He'll make you a fine husband."

Leigh said nothing, but her eyes screamed her doubts. Kelly saw her look and patted her arm reassuringly, saying softly, "Do you trust me, lass?" Leigh nodded. "Then take my word for it. Everythin' will work out fine with you two. I've a good feelin' about this marriage. You and Matt were made for each other. There's only one thing I regret."

Leigh finally found her voice. "What?"

"That Matt's parents can't be here to see you now. Ah, lass, they'd be so proud of you."

The beginning strains of the wedding processional reached Leigh's ears. She froze, her eyes wide with terror.

Kelly smiled down at her and said, "Is this my brave lass from the *Avenger*? The same lass who fought a British sailor with a cutlass almost as big as she?"

"I wasn't brave. I was just foolish," Leigh whispered.

"Not to me and every other man on the *Avenger*, lass. Look in there at the crew. They're waitin' for you. You're not goin' to let them down, are you?"

Leigh looked down the aisle of the crowded church. The Creoles stood stiffly, their eyes turned reverently toward the altar. But not the crew of the *Avenger*. They all stood with their eyes glued expectantly on Leigh, grinning proudly. And for the first time, she realized they were all on *her* side of the church. No, she couldn't let them down. She smiled bravely and stepped forward.

A hush fell over the church as Kelly led Leigh down the aisle. It was as if an angel had stepped into their midst, and everyone was afraid to breathe for fear she would disappear. Matt, standing at the altar, was no less awed. To think that this ethereal vision was to be his wife. A knot formed in his throat, his heart swelled with pride.

Leigh saw Matt standing at the altar, a shaft of light beaming down on him, his golden hair shining in the sunlight and framing his handsome face, his dark eyes shimmering, his lips curved in a warm smile. Suddenly, the whole cathedral seemed filled with his presence, this man, this tall golden god. And he was waiting for her. She was filled with the wonder of it.

From that minute on, Leigh floated in a warm haze, drifting on a soft cloud. She was hardly aware as she and Matt exchanged their vows and Matt slipped on her wedding ring, the band that would bind them for life. She knelt through the long, solemn nuptial mass beside her new husband, totally mindless of the priest's intonations and Matt's warm eyes locked on her face. It wasn't until they were outside the church and Matt was kissing her warmly, that reality returned. When his lips released hers, she looked up at him and said in a dazed voice, "Is it over?"

Matt chuckled softly, saying, "Yes, sweet, it's over." He shouldered his way through the crowd of excited guests, smiling with pride and nodding his acknowledgment of their congratulations, one arm protectively about his new bride, as he led her to the carriage that would whisk them away to the reception.

After the carriage had rushed away from the church, Matt turned to Leigh and looked at her, his eyes drinking in her beauty. His voice was almost a whisper as he said, "When I saw you coming down that aisle, I thought that nothing that beautiful could possibly be real." He touched her face gently, hesitantly, as if he was afraid she would disappear.

He fumbled in the inside pocket of his cutaway coat and pulled out a long black box. "I wanted to give you this last night, but Grandmère said it would be inappropriate at the time."

Leigh accepted the box he handed her, saying, "What is it?"

He smiled, his eyes soft. "My wedding gift to my bride."

Leigh immediately felt ashamed. She had nothing for him.

"Aren't you going to open it?"

Leigh fumbled with the box until she finally opened it. She gasped when she saw the string of perfectly matched, creamy pearls. Lying on a black velvet background, they seemed to glow with a life of their own.

Matt smiled at her awed look. He lifted the pearls, saying, "Again, I rejected diamonds. These pearls reminded me of your skin, but now I can see where they can't begin to compare."

He lifted the mantilla from her head and tossed it on the seat opposite them. Then, turning her slightly, he draped the pearls around her neck and fastened the catch at the back. He sat back saying, "I hope you like them."

Leigh fingered the pearls, her touch almost loving. Tears stung her eyes. "Oh, Matt, they're beautiful."

Matt smiled and reached for the box. Showing her the earrings, he said, "These go with them."

Leigh reached for one of the delicate earrings. She tried to put it on her ear, but her hands were trembling so badly she couldn't manage it. "I can't do it. I'm too nervous."

"Here, let me," Matt said, taking the earring from her.

Leigh tilted her head to one side. Matt bent to place the earring on her small earlobe, but he couldn't resist the urge to kiss it first. Feeling Matt's warm lips against her ear, Leigh shivered with delight. Then he turned her head and did the same for the other side.

He sat back, gazing at her with warm admiration. Leigh felt herself drowning in that look. One finger hooked under her chin, raising it for his kiss. He was just lowering his head as the carriage lurched to a stop and the door was flung open. "Damn," he muttered against Leigh's lips.

Leigh couldn't help but giggle at his obvious frustration.

Matt scowled, saying, "It's not funny, kitten. I'm about to burst from wanting you. I'll be glad when all this foolishness is over, and we can be alone." Still grumbling under his breath, he climbed from the carriage and reached up to help Leigh alight.

The reception came off beautifully, much to Grandmère's relief. Matt's crew were at their best, so well behaved that Matt was astonished at their gentlemanly manners. He wondered ruefully where they had been hiding them all this time. The sailors and the Creoles mixed with surprising ease, the Creoles almost in awe of the Americans.

There was one close call, however. And as Grandmère had feared, it was a Creole that almost started a brawl. When Matt swung Leigh onto the ballroom floor for the bridal dance, holding her close and gazing into her eyes warmly, a cocky little Creole, standing behind Kelly, snickered and said to his friend standing next to him, "*Mon dieu*, what a hasty wedding! You wouldn't want to place a little bet, would you? I'll wager she's already *enceinte*."

Kelly heard the Creole's words. His face turned deep red with anger; his blood pounded in his ears. He whirled, glaring at the Creole, his fists clenched tightly, and said in a low, deadly voice, "Mister, you've got exactly two minutes to retract that statement."

The Creole looked up at Kelly in shock. Then he became aware of the other Creoles and the crew of the *Avenger* watching him with bated breath. If he refused, both groups would be at each others throats, he realized. No, he wouldn't be alone. His Creole friends would come to his defense.

He looked at Kelly's massive shoulders and the bulge of the muscular arms under the frock coat. He glanced up at the first mate's eyes, their look absolutely murderous. This man could tear him limb from limb with one hand tied behind his back! He shuddered and laughed nervously, saying, "I'm sorry, *m'sieur*. It was a bad joke."

"That won't do," Kelly said in a carefully measured voice. "Now, you've got one minute."

The Creole looked at the fierce American. His face blanched and he stammered, "I . . . I'm sorry . . . I apologize for my . . . my insult to your friends, *m'sieur*."

Kelly longed to smash his fist into the Creole's face, to beat him to a bloody pulp. But he knew if he did, it would only embarrass Matt and the lass. He struggled for control and, finally, nodded curtly. The

Creole beat a quick retreat from the ballroom, thankful for his life, while Leigh and Matt danced, totally oblivious to the whole incident.

After the wedding reception, Leigh and Matt returned to the town house. Out of respect for their privacy, Grandmère had gone to one of her sons for a few days' visit. They were met at the door by Grandmère's maid, Marie, who quickly rushed Leigh away to Matt's room.

Leigh looked around the room as Marie unbuttoned the long row of buttons down her back. It was much larger than hers, requiring two French doors for ventilation, instead of the usual one. And it was strongly masculine in its decor, a fact that only reminded Leigh that this was Matt's room, a room that she, as his wife, would now share with him.

Ever since she had entered the room, she had been tense and nervous. After Marie had helped her change into her gown and negligee, brushed her hair until it shone, and left the room, Leigh walked out onto the balcony. She had to get out of the room. It reminded her too much of what would happen there tonight, the consummation of her and Matt's marriage.

Why am I so frightened, she thought in bewilderment. Matt has made love to me before, many times. He has never hurt me. But those times had been spontaneous, and this seemed so calculated, so cold. She stood looking down at the courtyard, letting the soft breeze and night noises soothe her.

She heard the door open and Matt's footsteps behind her. She froze, her fingernails biting into the balcony railing, her heart racing in fear. Stop it, she told herself firmly. You must get control of yourself. She forced herself to let go of the rail and turn to face him.

He stood in the open French doors with two wineglasses in his hands. Leigh was relieved that he was still fully clothed, having shed only his frock coat and cravat, and loosened the top buttons of his shirt. She had half-expected to find him standing there stark naked, ready to pounce on her.

He smiled, walking toward her, saying, "I thought, after today, we deserved something to help us unwind."

He handed one glass of wine to Leigh. She accepted it gratefully and drank from it, feeling its soothing warmth in her stomach. They stood side by side at the railing, looking down at the courtyard, sipping their wine, each silent. Slowly, Leigh felt her tension begin to ease.

Matt set his empty glass on the balcony railing and turned to Leigh. "Are you nervous, kitten?" he asked softly.

Leigh looked away, stammering, "I — I know it's silly. It's — it's not my first time. I — I don't know what's wrong with me."

"Would it make you feel any better to know I'm nervous, too?"

Leigh looked at him in disbelief.

"It's true. Look at my hands."

He held out his hands and Leigh could see they were trembling. "But why should you be nervous?" she asked.

Matt took the wineglass from her and set it aside. He put his big hands on her shoulders and smiled down at her, saying softly, "Because this is a first time for me, Leigh. I've never made love to my wife before."

His wife. Suddenly, she wasn't frightened anymore. She smiled shyly at him.

His hands framed her face, but instead of kissing

her, he stood gazing into her eyes, his long fingers gently massaging the back of her head and neck. Then he bent and kissed her softly — oh, so softly — his warm lips supping at her in an agonizingly sweet kiss.

Leigh felt herself enveloped in a warm cloud. She leaned into the kiss, her arms wrapping about his broad shoulders. He bent and picked her up, carrying her into the bedroom, their lips still locked in that sweet, sweet kiss.

He laid her across the bed, himself beside her. For a long time he gazed down at her, his eyes slowly roaming over her. Then he picked up a long lock of hair and brought it to his face, rubbing his cheek with it before he kissed it. A hard lump formed in Leigh's throat at his tenderness. Strangely, she felt like crying.

He bent and covered her face with soft, butterfly kisses, then nuzzled her throat, his lips lingering at the pulse beat at its base. Leigh felt his warm fingers at the top button of the negligee as he unbuttoned it, then his lips kissing the newly exposed skin. Matt's fingers unbuttoned the next button, his warm lips following. Slowly, ever so slowly, his fingers, followed by his lips, descended, inch by inch, button by button. Leigh felt her desire rising, impatient for the next button to fall away. And just when she thought she would scream with frustration, Matt's hands and lips would descend another inch. And then Leigh realized with wonder that he wasn't just making love to her, but worshipping her. Again, the strange tears stung her eyes.

Finally, the negligee fell away, and Matt buried his face in the valley between her breasts, softly nuzzling and kissing them. Leigh sobbed with gladness, tangling her fingers in his golden hair and pulling him even closer, wishing she could totally absorb him.

Matt made slow, sweet love to Leigh that night, with a tenderness and sensitivity that amazed her. No bridegroom could have been more gentle or more considerate, treating her as if she were made of fragile glass, as he slowly — ever so slowly — coaxed her up to rapturous heights. And when it was over, and Leigh lay in his warm embrace, his hands still caressing her, Leigh realized no bride had even been made love to more beautifully. She felt pampered, cherished and — very loved.

Leigh was the first to awaken the next morning. She stretched lazily and smiled with contentment. Then she glanced at her sleeping husband. She raised herself up on one elbow, taking this opportunity to examine him closer. Her eyes drifted over the golden lock of hair against his forehead and across his face, lingering on his sensuous mouth, shivering in remembrance of the delights those lips could bring her. Her eyes dropped to his broad chest with its golden mat of hair. Not even the puckered scar above his left nipple could mar its perfection. For a long time, she watched his steady heartbeat and the rise and fall of his chest in fascination.

Then her eyes drifted downward over his taut abdomen, across the golden nest of curls between his legs, down his long, muscular legs. She smiled, thinking that even his toes were perfect. It was hard to believe that this beautiful male, this golden god, was her husband. Her heart swelled with pride.

"I hope you like what you see, kitten," Matt's voice said softly. "You're stuck with it for the rest of my life."

Leigh jerked her eyes away guiltily, averting her head.

A roughened finger hooked under her chin and raised her head, forcing her to look at his face. "No more of that," Matt said firmly. "We're married now, remember? I belong to you just as much as you belong to me. You can look or touch as much as you like."

Leigh knew what he said was true. He was her husband now. Nothing was forbidden. But still, that would take some getting used to.

Matt laughed, saying, "Well, don't leave me in suspense, sweet. Did I pass inspection?"

Leigh gathered her courage and smiled impishly. "You'll do."

A golden eyebrow rose. "I'll do? Is that all you can say? I thought wives were supposed to build up their husband's egos."

Leigh giggled. "Your ego doesn't need any building up."

"Why, you little minx!" A long arm wrapped around her waist and pulled her down beside him. Leigh snuggled even closer, enjoying the feel of his warm skin against her. For a few minutes, they dozed, then Matt asked, "Are you hungry?"

Leigh thought briefly about it, then answered sleepily, "No."

Matt rolled her to her back, looking in her face, saying in a husky voice, "Well, I am."

Leigh looked up at his eyes, growing increasingly warmer by the second. Suddenly, she realized he wasn't talking about food.

Several hours later, Leigh was awakened with a swat on her behind and a "Wake up, sleepyhead."

With a yelp of outrage, she sat up. Matt stood by the bed, fully dressed and grinning at her. She looked about the sunwashed room and frowned, saying, "What time is it?"

"Almost noon."

"Noon!" she gasped.

"Yes. It's a good thing we didn't plan on going to the beach house today." He grinned. "I hope my lazy wife isn't planning on sleeping this late every morning."

"You know perfectly well why I slept so late," Leigh retorted. "If you would stop interfering with my sleep at night, I wouldn't have to sleep all day."

Matt chuckled and turned away. He picked up a tray sitting on the dresser and set it in the middle of the bed. The aroma of freshly baked croissants teased Leigh's nostrils. Matt sat on the bed opposite her, the tray between them.

"We'll get crumbs all over the bed," Leigh objected.

Matt shrugged, picking up one of the pots and pouring from it. "We'll just brush them off."

Leigh was sitting with the sheet pulled up in front of her to hide her nakedness. She kept glancing about the rumpled sheets and off to the floor. Matt grinned, reached behind him, then handed her her negligee, saying, "Looking for this?"

Leigh snatched it and slipped it on quickly. Then sitting on her heels, she reached for a croissant and bit into it hungrily.

Matt leaned back against the bedpost, sipping his coffee and smiling in amusement. The thin negligee hid absolutely nothing, but apparently, Leigh didn't realize that. Matt sat, eating very little, enjoying the view.

Leigh pointed to the tray, saying, "Why are there two pots?"

"One has coffee, the other hot chocolate."

"Coffee? Why I haven't had any coffee since we arrived in New Orleans." She reached for the coffeepot.

Matt stopped her, saying, "Wait a minute, Leigh. You'd better try a swallow of mine first."

Leigh took Matt's cup and took a sip. She sputtered, her nose wrinkled in distaste. "My God! That's awful! What's wrong with it?"

"It's laced with chicory. Remember, I showed you the coffee stall at the marketplace?"

"But how can you stand to drink it?"

Matt shrugged, "You get used to it. But I thought you didn't like coffee."

She smiled sheepishly. "I didn't used to, but when I was on the *Avenger* and my tea supply ran out, I was forced to drink it. As you said, you get used to it. But I don't think I'll ever get used to it with chicory. I'll stick to hot chocolate."

Matt insisted upon feeding her the melon balls. Leigh played along with him for a while, then pushed back his hand, saying, "Stop it, Matt. I feel silly. Like a little bird waiting for his mother to drop a worm in his mouth."

A while later, Leigh dressed, and they sought refuge from the heat in the courtyard. Matt tossed a blanket on the ground by the fountain and lay down on it. Leigh stood by the fountain for a minute, trailing her fingers in the cool water. Then she sat down by Matt and looked about the courtyard, saying, "I love this courtyard. Are all the courtyards in New Orleans this lovely?"

Matt rolled to his side and propped his head in one hand before he answered, "Yes, most of them are. I'll have to admit the Creoles have a good idea here. Which reminds me, where do you want to live after the war? Of course, we'll be at sea most of the time, but we'll have to have a home port. We can stay here, or if you prefer, we can build a home in Charleston."

Leigh frowned. What were the homes like in Charleston? She knew the city was surrounded by plantations. "You mean like Twelve Oaks?"

Jealousy stabbed at Matt. He knew Leigh was his now, but he still disliked the idea of her admiring René's home. He hadn't really planned on building such a lavish home, but if that was what Leigh wanted. He answered tightly, "If that's what you want."

"No, Matt, I don't really want anything that big. I'd feel uncomfortable in it. I much prefer this town house to Twelve Oaks. In fact, I've fallen in love with it."

Matt was amazed. She preferred his town house to Twelve Oaks! "Then you won't mind staying here until the war is over and I return? I asked Grandmère if she would stay with you. I don't want to leave you alone."

"No, I don't mind," Leigh answered, wondering why she felt so distressed every time he mentioned leaving.

"You don't think you'll get bored?"

"No, particularly since I've met Honoré's fiancée and have a friend of my own age. She's the only friend I've made among the Creole girls. For some reason, they don't seem to like me."

Matt laughed, saying, "Kitten, it wasn't that they didn't like you. They were jealous. Now that you're no longer in competition, you'll probably make many friends."

"Jealous? Whatever for? They're lovely girls, with their dark hair and dark eyes. I can't see why they would be jealous of me."

She's not being coy; she means it, Matt thought with amazement. She honestly doesn't know how beautiful she is. He studied Leigh's face, realizing for the first time that much of Leigh's beauty lay in the fact that her face was unusual, striking. She really didn't have the classic features that everyone considered beautiful. Her nose was a little too short, her eyes a little too wide, her face heart-shaped rather than oval. And that dimple in her chin certainly didn't mark her as a classic beauty. Yet, these things he found the most intriguing about her.

Matt's close scrutiny was making Leigh nervous. She glanced about the courtyard and spied a robin. "Oh, look," she cried, pointing to the bird. "I wonder where the rest of the family is?"

"Family? What family?"

Leigh laughed and pointed to the abandoned bird nest under the eaves. "See that nest? When we came here, there were three baby robins in it. Oh Matt, I wish you could have seen it. It was amazing how well the mother and father birds cared for their babies. But the most exciting thing was the day they taught them to fly. The mother robin got on one side of the baby bird, and the father on the other. Then slowly, they nudged the little bird out of the nest." Leigh clapped her hands, her eyes twinkling with excitement. "And the next thing I knew, the baby robin was flying." She leaned forward, saying, "There was one little bird that had trouble learning. He landed on the ground. The mother bird flew down and tried to coax him up, while the father bird kept circling and scolding. At first I thought the father was angry with the baby robin, but then I saw what he was upset over. There was a big cat crouching in one corner of the courtyard, watching the baby bird. Oh, Matt, I was terrified! And then, suddenly, the baby bird flew up and away!"

Matt watched Leigh's animated face as she talked. Suddenly, something within him stirred, a strange, unidentifiable emotion. It wasn't desire. It wasn't pride. It disturbed him. He frowned.

"Why are you frowning?" Leigh questioned.

"What?" Matt asked in a distracted voice, then, "Oh, I guess was thinking about the cat."

"You shouldn't frown like that. You'll get wrinkles."

A golden eyebrow lifted. "And I suppose now that you're my wife, you think you can tell me what to do?" Matt answered in a teasing voice.

"I might try," Leigh replied saucily.

"All right, Mrs. Blake, what are you going to tell me to do next?" Matt retorted.

Mrs. Blake. Mrs. Matthew Blake. Yes, it sounded good, Leigh thought. Suddenly, she wished he would kiss her. Did she dare ask him to? She summoned her courage and said, "Kiss me."

Matt's heart was racing. Leigh had never made any overtures before. He wanted Leigh to touch him, kiss *him* for a change. He lay back on the blanket, his arms folded under his head. He smiled up at her, saying, "No. You kiss me. In marriage, everything is supposed to be equal. I'm tired of doing all the work."

"Work? You're telling me it's work to kiss me?" Leigh asked in half-outrage and half-disbelief.

Matt grinned, saying, "Come on, kitten, kiss me. I won't bite."

She hesitated.

" 'Fraidy cat," he taunted softly.

Leigh was never one to ignore a dare. Besides, she ached for the feel of his lips on hers. She leaned forward and firmly pressed her lips against Matt's for a minute. Then she sat back, saying, "How's that?"

Matt frowned and said, "Not so good."

"Not so good!"

"You kissed me like a little girl. I expect my wife to kiss better than that. Try again."

Leigh bent and kissed him the second time. This

time, she moved her lips softly over his. She sat back, feeling very proud of herself. "Well?"

Matt shrugged. "Better."

"Better? Just better?"

"That time you kissed me like a proper little lady."

"Well, how do you expect me to kiss you?"

Matt smiled, his eyes warm. "Like a woman who means it."

Well, I'll just show him, Leigh thought. She framed his face with her hands and bent her head. Recalling all of the things that Matt did when he kissed her, she imitated him. Her lips moved softly over his, then played at the corners of his mouth, teasing and supping. She nibbled at his lips, then lightly bit the full lower one. The tip of her tongue teased his lips, raked his teeth, and then entered his mouth, tentatively at first, then more boldly.

Matt groaned, his arms coming around her and crushing her to him, kissing her back, their tongues intertwining. Leigh struggled and pulled back, gasping, "That's not fair. I'm supposed to be kissing you."

Matt sat up, then stood, saying down to her, "I tell you what. We'll share the work. You kiss me and I'll kiss you."

He reached for her hand and pulled her up. "Where are we going?" Leigh asked.

"Back upstairs." He grinned, his eyes shimmering warmly, saying, "Unless you'd rather 'work' right here in the courtyard."

Chapter 18

The next day, Leigh and Matt drove to the beach house. The ride took most of the day, first by public coach to a small coastal town, and then by buggy to the beach house itself. It was almost evening when they arrived.

Leigh looked around the beach in disappointment. No palm trees here either, she thought with disgust. The beach itself was a wide expanse of white sand rising to softly rolling dunes. Just as Matt had said, the beach house was small, framed in cedar that had grayed under the hot sun and saltwater air. To the back of the house, was a small lean-to and a fenced-in area for horses. Off to one side of this was a windmill, its wooden blades whirling in the brisk breeze.

When they entered the beach house, Leigh remembered that Matt had warned her it wasn't luxurious. There were two large rooms, one a bedroom, its bed surprisingly large and comfortable, and the other a room for lounging, eating, and cooking combined. Leigh stared at the large stone fireplace. She couldn't imagine why they had built such a big fireplace just for cooking. She voiced her thoughts to Matt.

"It's not just for cooking. It's for heat also," he replied.

Leigh was acutely aware of sweat trickling down between her breasts from their hot drive down the beach. "For heat?" she asked in disbelief. "It gets that cold here at night?"

"No. My uncle comes down here in the winter months, too."

"In the winter? What does he do here in the winter?"

"As I said, Uncle Paul comes down here just to get away for a few days and relax. He enjoys being near the ocean. I guess he's got a little sea water in his veins, after all. In the summer, he fishes in the surf, and in the winter, when this beach and the marshes behind it are full of ducks and geese, he does a little hunting. But I think mostly he enjoys beachcombing, wandering up and down the beach in search of stuff that's been washed ashore."

As they toured the small cabin, Leigh watched for the bathtub. She already felt sticky and grimy and was anxious for a bath. But she didn't see a tub anywhere. She turned to Matt with an accusing look in her eyes and said, "You promised."

"Promised what?"

"You promised I could take a bath every day in fresh water. I haven't seen a tub anywhere!"

"Whoa, kitten. Don't get your Irish temper up," Matt said with a grin. "Come on, I've got something to show you."

She followed him through the back door and stepped onto a boardwalk. He led her to a very small shed beside it. He pushed aside a curtain on its door, and Leigh looked inside. It looked like a small wooden closet. But why would anyone put a closet outside, she wondered. She looked at Matt, puzzled.

He grinned, saying, "Watch what happens when I pull this cord." He reached for a heavy cord hanging in the closet. A minute later, water showered down on his arm.

Leigh looked up at the ceiling of the closet and saw the holes bored in it. She laughed, saying, "What it looks like is a small rain shower."

"Taste it," Matt said.

Leigh stuck her hand into the water and then licked her finger. "It's fresh water!" she said in amazement. "But where does the water come from?"

"I understand Honoré rigged up this contraption," Matt said. He pointed, saying, "See that windmill?"

Leigh nodded.

"Well, it pumps up fresh water from the ground and into that big wooden cistern." He pointed to what looked like a giant washtub on stilts. "Now you watch that cistern while I pull this cord."

When Matt pulled the cord, a trap door at the bottom of the cistern opened, and water rushed out from it and down a wooden trough to the top of the wooden closet. Leigh laughed with delight.

"There's another trough that goes inside, for drinking and cooking water," Matt said.

"How clever of Honoré."

Matt looked at the closet thoughtfully, then said, "Yes, I think it has possibilities."

Leigh could hardly wait to try out Honoré's invention. As soon as they had eaten the picnic lunch that they had brought with them, she took a towel and bar of soap and headed for the shower closet. When she pulled the cord and the water spilled down on her, she squealed in surprise. The water was much colder than she had expected. As she bathed, she discovered that if she stood in one corner, she could keep from getting her hair wet. But to Leigh, there was one disadvantage. She couldn't sit and soak in the water. In fact, hardly any water remained in the bottom of the closet, for it drained through holes bored in the floor almost as fast as it came in. Then, Leigh admitted that for the beach it was perfect. No one wanted to sit in a tub with its bottom full of gritty sand.

When Matt and Leigh emerged from the bedroom the next morning, Leigh saw a plate of sweet rolls and a bowl of fruit on the table. "Where did that come from?" she asked.

"That must be our breakfast the caretaker brought," Matt replied. He looked at the fireplace and saw the small fire. A coffeepot hung over it. "Good, he brought fresh coffee, too."

"I didn't see any caretaker," Leigh said.

"No, and you probably won't, from what my uncle said of him. Remember, I told you he said he slips in and out, and you hardly know he's around? That's the nice part of it. He won't be in the way."

"But where does he live? I didn't see any other beach houses."

Matt poured two cups of coffee and set them on the table. "Uncle Paul said he has a small shack back up in the dunes. He lives like a hermit."

Leigh picked up one of the rolls. It was still warm. "He must have baked these rolls himself."

"That's the second nicest part of it. Uncle Paul said he was an excellent cook. For that reason, everytime he's down here, he has the hermit cook his meals and then deliver them to him. Apparently, the old man is glad to make a little extra money, since he doesn't work."

"But how did he know we were here?"

"Uncle Paul made the arrangements with him. He told him what day we would arrive and what day we would leave. I told Uncle Paul to tell him to bring us our breakfast and evening meal and something to snack on for lunch." He pointed to a loaf of bread and a hunk of cheese on the counter. "I guess that's today's lunch."

"Then you haven't seen him?"

"Who?"

"The hermit," Leigh snapped.

"No, I've never seen him. Uncle Paul made all the arrangements. He even paid him for me. He said the old man is kind of peculiar. He doesn't like to be around people."

Leigh bit into her second roll. But how did the hermit know what time they would get up, she wondered.

After they had eaten, she and Matt walked along the beach, gazing out at the greenish-blue water of the Gulf of Mexico. Leigh wore one of her old blouses and skirts she had worn on the *Avenger*. Matt was shirtless, wearing only a pair of breeches, cut off at the knee. They were both barefooted.

After their walk, they strolled back to the soft rolling dunes and spread out a blanket. Sitting on the blanket, Leigh watched the sea gulls, some cawing down at them as if scolding them for invading their private beach. She peered up at the sky, admiring the snowy birds' gracefulness as they soared and glided effortlessly through the air. Then for a long time she watched the sandpipers and laughed at their antics. Leigh thought the little birds funny looking with their long stiltlike legs and quick abrupt movements. They seemed to always run, and like quail, they stayed in bevies. If one little sandpiper spied something in the sand a few yards away and ran to investigate it, the whole group ran with him, pecking furiously at the sand.

Leigh inched herself to the edge of the blanket. Sitting there, she wiggled her toes and buried them in the warm sand, mumbling, "That feels good."

Matt, watching her, rose and stood. "That reminds me."

Leigh looked up, stunned to see Matt stripping off his breeches. "What are you doing?" she gasped.

"I'm going to take a sunbath," Matt replied, sitting back down on the blanket. "I'm going to lie here and let my body soak up some of this good sun." He grinned across the blanket at her. "Care to join me?"

Leigh was shocked. "Strip to the skin and lie stark naked out in the wide open? I should say not! What if someone saw us?"

Matt smiled, saying patiently, "There's no one here but you and me and God. Now, I've seen you naked, and you've seen me naked, and God has seen us both naked."

He fished in his pocket and brought out a bottle of oil. Pouring some in his hand, he began to smear it on his shoulders, chest, and legs. Seeing Leigh's questioning look, he said, "It's to keep from getting burned. You're sure you won't join me?"

Leigh tossed her head indignantly, saying, "No, thank you."

Matt grinned, amused at her modesty. He handed her the bottle of oil and flopped down on his stomach, saying, "Then be a good little wife and rub some of this on my back for me."

Leigh looked down at Matt's long, naked body and frowned, wondering if this was some kind of a trick, if as soon as she got close enough, Matt would grab her and try to make love to her here in broad daylight.

Matt looked over his shoulder, saying, "Well?"

Cautiously, Leigh rubbed the oil over his shoulders and back, again marveling at the feel of his rippling

384

muscles under her hands. She looked at his tight buttocks and hesitated. Then gathering her courage, she spread oil over them and down his long legs. The texture of Matt's skin never ceased to amaze her. She had always imagined a man's skin would be rough, but Matt's was firm and smooth. She was shocked at just how much she enjoyed touching him so intimately.

When she finished, she quickly returned to her corner of the blanket, gazing pointedly out at the water to show her disapproval. The minutes ticked by. Obviously, Matt couldn't care less if she approved or not, she thought, irritated at his lack of concern. Sighing deeply, she threw her head back to face the warmth of the sun.

She had to admit the sun did feel good on her face. She glanced over at Matt. He was lying with his head pillowed on his folded arms and seemed to be asleep. Careful to make no noise to wake him, she eased her skirt up to her hips and pulled her blouse down on her shoulders. She sat back, thinking, see, you can soak up the sun and still retain your modesty. Imagine, stripping stark naked in broad daylight! It's disgraceful!

But while the sun felt good on her exposed legs and shoulders, she found she was perspiring under the bunched skirt and blouse. Again, she glanced at Matt. Why did he have to look so damned comfortable and contented? She wondered how long Matt would sleep.

She glanced up and down the beach. It was totally deserted. Blushing at her own audacity, she took off her blouse and skirt, then stretched out on her stomach.

She was just getting comfortable when she heard Matt say, "You'd better let me rub some oil on you, or you'll get burned."

Her eyes snapped open to see Matt kneeling beside her. When did he wake up? She tensed as she felt Matt rubbing oil over her shoulders and back, fearing that this would lead to something else. Surprisingly, his fingers were very businesslike. But, as he rolled her over to rub oil on her front, Leigh snatched the bottle of oil from him and sat up, snapping, "I'll do it myself."

Matt chuckled and lay back down. Leigh stretched out on her stomach beside him, watching him warily, realizing now that just because he had his eyes closed it didn't mean he was asleep. Under the warmth of the sun on her back and legs, she relaxed, thinking, this must be terribly wicked. It feels too good. Soon, she dozed.

"Better roll over, sweet," Matt drawled lazily. "That oil helps, but you don't want to expose your skin to too much sun the first day. You can still burn."

Roll over, Leigh thought in horror. And totally expose myself? No, it's bad enough having my rear exposed. Stubbornly, she stayed as she was, totally ignoring Matt as he rolled on his back.

But after a few minutes, Leigh realized her back, instead of feeling comfortably warm, was beginning to sting. She glanced over at Matt. He lay with one arm over his eyes. If he says I told you so, I'll hit him, Leigh thought as she rolled on her back. Fortunately, Matt made no comment, and Leigh never saw his lips twitching with amusement.

They lay side by side, basking in the warmth of the sun, for twenty minutes. Then Matt said, "I think we'd better go back to the cabin for a while. You're not used to this sun. Your nose is beginning to get a little pink."

Leigh scrambled into her clothes, thinking that

there was a lot more of her getting pink than her nose. Thankfully, Matt hadn't mentioned that.

As they walked back to the cabin hand in hand, Matt said, "We'll sunbathe everyday, and by the time we go back to New Orleans, we'll be as brown as a couple of Indians."

Leigh could imagine Grandmère's reaction when she saw her. More mudpacks and buttermilk with cucumbers? No, Leigh thought fiercely. I'm a married woman now, and if Matt doesn't mind my being brown, I can do what I want.

As soon as they reached the cabin, Leigh headed for the shower closet to wash off the oil and sand. The cabin may be rustic, but the shower was a decided luxury, she thought. Imagine, being able to take a bath anytime she wanted without having to lug buckets of water to fill the tub.

She lathered and rinsed quickly, being careful not to get her hair wet. She was just about to step out when the shower curtain was jerked open. Matt stood on the boardwalk, grinning at her, stark naked.

As he stepped into the shower, Leigh gasped, "What do you think you're doing?"

"I'm going to join you in your bath."

Leigh smiled smugly and said, "No, you're not. I've already finished bathing."

She started to step out, but Matt blocked her, saying, "Good. Then you can help me with my bath."

Leigh glared at him.

"Come on, Leigh. You've helped me bathe before. Remember?"

Leigh wished he hadn't reminded her of the day she had washed his back on the *Avenger*. To her dying day, she would remember him standing in the tub, tall and muscular, dusted with gold. Nor would she ever forget her reaction to the sight of his magnificent male body.

"Come on, sweet," Matt said in a coaxing voice. "Be a good little wife and help your husband."

Leigh still didn't trust him. It wasn't like Matt for them both to be totally naked and him not take advantage of the situation. She shook the soap warily, saying, "Only if you promise to behave yourself while I'm bathing you."

Matt managed to look affronted before he answered, "I promise."

After Matt had wet down his skin, he turned his back to her. Leigh lathered his long torso in a quick, no-nonsense manner. Then he turned and grinned down at her. He's daring me, she thought. Steeling herself not to blush, she quickly soaped his front, keeping her eyes averted as much as possible. Feeling proud of herself, she stood back up, saying, "There now!"

Looking down at himself, Matt said, "You missed something."

Leigh was almost afraid to look down, but when she did, she saw Matt wiggling one big toe that was bare of soap suds. "Oh, for heaven's sake!" Leigh said in disgust.

She bent and soaped the toe, and then, as she was rising, she heard Matt say, "Ready?"

She shrieked, "No, Matt! My hair!"

But it was too late. The water was pouring over her, totally drenching her. Matt laughed, then hooked one arm around her waist, pulling her to him and kissing her.

Leigh struggled as the water poured over them and Matt continued kissing her. She finally managed to tear her lips away, gasping, "Stop it! You'll drown us both."

Matt let go of the cord that controlled the shower.

Then both arms were around her, pulling her even closer. Leigh pushed the wet strands of hair out of her face and looked up at him. The teasing look was gone from his dark eyes. They were now warm with open desire.

"You promised," she reminded him.

"I promised to behave myself as long as you were bathing me. Well, I'm through with my bath now." Matt's head descended, his mouth covering hers in a warm, searching kiss, as he cupped her buttocks and pressed her against his maleness, already hardening in anticipation.

As he continued kissing and fondling her, Leigh realized he intended to make love to her in the small closet. But that would be impossible, she thought. It wasn't big enough for them both to lie down, or even sit for that matter. Between his torrid kisses, she managed to gasp, "We can't do it in here."

"You want to bet on that?" Matt asked in a husky voice. Then Leigh felt herself being lifted from the shower floor.

Later, as they were drying off on the boardwalk, Leigh looked back into the shower. She could hardly believe they had made love in that small closet. Standing up no less! Well, at least Matt was standing, she amended. It seemed her new husband was rather inventive himself.

Matt saw her look and grinned. "I told you I thought it had possibilities."

When she and Matt returned from the beach that evening, their dinner was waiting for them on the table. Leigh lifted the lid of one pot and, seeing the shrimp, oysters, and crab meat floating in a rich brown sauce, realized it was jambalaya. The other pot held fluffy white rice. The two pots and the loaf of crusty white bread beside them were still warm.

As they ate, Leigh discovered she was ravenous. Had the salt air stimulated her appetite, or was this really the most delicious food she had ever tasted? She told Matt what she was thinking.

"I don't know," he answered. "I've tasted a lot of jambalaya in my lifetime, but I've never tasted any this damned good."

The next day, Leigh discovered she had a bit of beachcomber in her. As she and Matt strolled down the beach, she was fascinated with the things that had washed up on the sand. She found several old bottles, a coconut, a piece of tattered sail, an old, half-rotted sea chest, and even a water-logged book, its paper so ink smeared it was impossible to read one word. She was amazed at the driftwood that littered the beach, some twisted in peculiar shapes, stripped of all bark, and weathered to a dull gray, and some that had apparently been on the beach so long it had petrified.

She stared at a huge tree trunk, its roots still attached and shriveled by the sun. "Where do you suppose that came from?" she asked Matt.

"It's hard to say," he answered, examining the trunk closely. "I don't recognize the bark. For all we know, it could have washed down the Mississippi from as far north as Fort Detroit. Or it might have floated here from Florida or Cuba or Mexico."

"From that far away?"

"Yes, Leigh, things can float completely around the world. The possibilities are endless. My uncle once showed me a carved wooden statuette he had found out here. He was so curious about it, he took it to a curator in Paris. The curator said it came from the island of Tahiti, far off in the Pacific Ocean."

From then on, every piece of driftwood Leigh saw, she imagined it from far-off, exotic place.

One day, Leigh found a gold coin. Not recognizing

the lettering on it, she showed it to Matt.

"It's an old Spanish coin, Leigh. You'll find them washed up on the beaches all around the Gulf of Mexico and the Caribbean. Remember my telling you about the sunken Spanish galleons?"

Leigh kept her eyes out for another Spanish coin, but that was the only one she found.

As much as Leigh enjoyed beachcombing, her favorite pastime was collecting sea shells. She would stand staring down at the tiny, fan-shaped shell in her hand, its outside creamy white, its inside colored with shades of iridescent pinks and salmons and creamy yellows, thinking that nothing in the world could be more beautiful—until she found the next one. She even thought the oyster shells pretty, despite their rough gray or black exteriors, for inside no two were alike with their iridescent grays, blues, greens, creams, and silvers. But the day she was the most excited was the day she found the large, brightly colored, spiral-shaped shell. She showed it to Matt.

"That's a conch shell, Leigh. You only find them in the tropics. Put your ear to it. They say you can hear the sound of the ocean in them."

Leigh put the shell to her ear and heard the slight roaring noise. Her eyes widened with wonder. Then she laughed and handed the shell to Matt.

He looked down at his pockets, already bulging with shells that Leigh had asked him to carry for her. "I'm afraid not, sweet. You'll have to carry that one yourself. What are you going to do with all these shells and driftwood you're collecting?"

Leigh hated the thought of leaving them behind when they went back to New Orleans. They were her own little treasures, and she hated to give them up. She looked up at him, saying, "Would you mind if I took them back to New Orleans with us? I thought I might go through them and pick out the prettiest and set them on a display shelf somewhere."

Matt was touched by the pleasure she found in such simple things. He smiled, saying, "That sounds like a wonderful idea. Then every time we look at them, we'll remember our honeymoon on the beach. But, sweet, you're going to have to control yourself. At the rate you're going, there won't be room for us in the carriage."

Matt taught Leigh how to surf-fish. He was remarkably patient with her, not even the least bit irritated when she dropped her pole and he had to swim and retrieve it for her. His reward came when she caught her first fish. He stood back watching her squealing with delight, her eyes flashing with excitement. When she held up her fish proudly, it was hard to say who was the most pleased, Leigh with her fish, or Matt with her.

Matt smiled and said, "That will be our dinner tonight."

Leigh looked at the fish doubtfully. As proud as she was of it, it was hardly big enough to feed one, much less two. She was relieved when Matt caught six more and added them to the string where her fish floated in the surf.

That night, they spread their blanket on the beach and gathered driftwood for a fire. Then they sat watching the flickering colors of the fire while their fish cooked over it. When it was done, they sat cross-legged, eating hungrily, laughing at each other's ravenous appetites.

When every last bite of the fish was consumed, they lay back on the blanket and gazed at the stars above them, feeling a contentment that came from something much deeper than a full stomach. Matt pulled Leigh into his arms.

Lying there in their warm circle, she listened while he pointed out the constellations to her, telling her the mythological tales behind them. Leigh loved the sound of the deep timbre of his voice. Even more, she enjoyed his laugh, for with her head on his broad chest, she could hear it rumbling up long before it reached his lips.

Matt made love to Leigh that night on the blanket on the beach. Leigh made no objection. To her, it seemed so right under the twinkling stars, with the soft breeze caressing her naked flesh as tenderly as Matt's hands and lips, and the sound of the surf in her ears, mingling with Matt's murmured words of endearment and their moans of pleasure.

Nor did she object when he rolled the blanket around them, saying in a drowsy voice, "Let's sleep here tonight, kitten. In each other's arms, with the stars to protect us."

When Leigh awakened in the morning, the eastern horizon was a slash of silver across the dark sky. She watched, fascinated, as the sky turned from silver to orange streaked with vivid pinks, and then to blood red.

"Matt, look at the sunrise," she whispered, longing to share this magnificent sight with him.

"I know," he whispered back, already watching over her shoulder.

They watched the spectacular sunrise with breathless wonder, both feeling as if nature was performing this colorful panorama just for their eyes. And when it was over and the sun was a golden orb in the blue sky and the water was sparkling as if covered with millions of glittering diamonds, they walked in silence, hand in hand, back to the cabin, still awed by what they had witnessed.

That afternoon, Matt sat watching Leigh as she fed

bread crumbs to the sea gulls, the wind whipping her hair and skirt around her. Matt's feelings for her amazed him. He couldn't get enough of her, looking at her, touching her, hearing her voice, being with her. He watched as she threw a piece of bread high in the sky and laughed as the flock of birds dove for it. He felt that strange emotion stirring again, swelling, growing, and then bursting within him. Matt felt as if he had been hit by a bolt of lightning as the sudden realization dawned on him. The emotion was love. He loved her, this small, fragile, beautiful woman who was his wife. For a moment, he soared with happiness and then, remembering that she didn't love him, was dashed to earth.

He looked at her thoughtfully. Was it possible to make someone fall in love with you? More than anything in this world, Matt wanted Leigh to love him as much as he loved her. Could he woo her at this late date? He had heard of couples falling in love after marriage. Did she already feel something for him? Surely, a woman couldn't give herself as completely, as totally, as Leigh had last night, without feeling something more than just desire. The beginnings of love, maybe? For the time being, he decided, he would say nothing of his love for her. Leigh was unpredictable. If he spoke too soon, there was no telling what her reaction might be. She might back off or, worse yet, laugh at him.

When Leigh ran back up the beach to him, Matt was waiting for her with open arms. She was stunned by his fierce embrace.

Several days later, Leigh watched as Matt worked on his sand castle. He had been at it all morning, and now it stood almost as tall as he. She marveled at his patience and perseverance.

She sat back, admiring him as he worked. It was

still hard to believe that this beautiful man was her husband. Even more surprising was how well they had gotten along since their marriage. What had happened to the arrogant, domineering man Matt used to be? She found she was enjoying his company, not just his love-making. She relished being around him, watching him, and listening to his deep voice and rich laughter. Was it just that they were married now, and she no longer felt she had to fend off his advances? Had that kept her tense and constantly on guard? Whatever, she was finding marriage to Matt much more delightful than she had ever dreamed it could be. And maybe, with time, they could build something of this union that had started out more as a business arrangement than a marriage.

Matt stood back and admired his castle. "What do you think?" he called.

Leigh rose and walked up to the sand castle, circling it slowly. For some perverse reason, she suddenly had an urge to destroy it. Without even thinking, she picked up a piece of driftwood and threw it at the castle, completely spoiling it. Shocked at her own rash action and fearing Matt's reaction, she shrieked and ran down the beach.

Matt took off in hot pursuit, calling, "You're going to pay for that!"

But Leigh was no longer worried. She heard the laughter in Matt's voice. She continued racing down the beach, running in the wet sand where the surf washed up on the beach, the wind whipping her hair and skirts around her, laughing, with the sound of Matt's deep laughter in her ears.

He caught her, but Leigh twisted away, laughing, to run a few more feet. Matt took a flying tackle, grabbing her around the hips and tumbling them both into the surf. Leigh came up sputtering, crawling toward the beach, still bent on escape. When she was almost out of the water, Matt caught her again, rolling her to her back and straddling her.

Leigh lay on her back on the wet sand, still panting from her mad dash down the beach, the water softly swirling and ebbing around her hips and legs. She looked up at Matt. His dark eyes were glued to the front of her blouse. She glanced down and realized that Matt could see her breasts through the thin, wet material. "No, Matt. Get off me," she said in a weak voice.

Matt said nothing. Instead, he raised her blouse and bent, kissing her breasts softly, then licking the salt water away. Leigh tingled all over.

He raised up, unbuttoning his breeches with one hand, then wiggled out of them and kicked them away.

"Not here, Matt. Not here in broad daylight," Leigh objected.

"Hush, sweet," he whispered, lying beside her and pulling her into his arms. He smoothed back her wet hair as he kissed the water from her eyelashes, then bent to lick it from her lips. His mouth captured hers, kissing her deeply, his lips and tongue tasting of salt. Leigh heard a roaring in her ears that had nothing to do with the surf breaking around them.

He slowly inched off her blouse and skirt, raining ardent kisses over her as his hands stroked her wet, silky skin. He rolled her to her side facing him, bending her knee to rest high on his hip, and then slipped into her in one smooth thrust. His lips locked on hers as he began his movements, slowly back and forth, like the ebb and flow of the water around them, a movement as ancient as the sea itself.

Then they were both oblivious to the fluffy clouds racing across the sky above them. They didn't hear the roar of the surf around them or feel the water tugging at their legs. The lovers had become a part of the sea itself, riding on their own wave of rapture, swelling, building higher and higher, holding at the crest, and then crashing over the brink, swirling in a sensation so powerful it threatened to drown them.

And when they surfaced from the depths of their experience, they lay gasping and clutching one another while the water washed over them, soothing them. Finally, Matt leaned over Leigh, pushed back her wet hair, and kissed her tenderly. He ached to tell her he loved her. Instead, he smiled and said, "That will teach you to destroy my sand castles."

That evening when they returned to the cabin, their meal was waiting for them and, as usual, still warm. Leigh had been amazed at the variety of their meals: bouillabaisse; a delicate cheese soufflé; crusty fried shrimp served with a hot, spicy sauce; baked fish, swimming in a delicious white sauce; and stuffed crabs. The meals were always accompanied with fresh baked bread: brioche, sour dough, French, *pain ordinaire*, or *pain de seigle*, a bread made of rye flour.

Leigh bit into a crusty piece of bread, saying, "I think your hermit is really a leprechaun."

Matt looked up and frowned. "A leprechaun?"

"Yes, a leprechaun."

"What in the hell is a leprechaun?"

Leigh grinned, saying, "Sure an' ye'll not be tellin' me ye've never heard of a leprechaun?"

Matt grinned back and said, "No, I haven't, my fine Irish lass. Suppose you enlighten me."

"The leprechauns are what we Irish call the little people. They're little men with short legs and stocky bodies. They usually have long gray beards, bushy eyebrows, and twinkling blue eyes. But they always have pointed ears and magical powers. They're very shy and hard to catch. It's said if you can catch a leprechaun, he has to give you his pot of gold."

Matt smiled, saying, "A very fetching fairy tale."

"But it's not a fairy tale!" Leigh objected. "Leprechauns are real."

Matt laughed.

"There really are leprechauns. Both my mother and Uncle Sean said so."

"They were just joshing," Matt answered, his eyes twinkling with amusement.

Leigh glared at him, saying hotly. "No, they weren't. It's true! Leprechauns really exist, and they do have magical powers!"

"Come on, Leigh," Matt replied in an exasperated voice. "You don't actually believe there are little men with long gray beards, pointed ears, and magical powers running around, do you? Besides, the hermit couldn't be Irish."

"And why not?" Leigh snapped.

Matt laughed, saying, "An Irishman who cooks French cuisine as good as any French chef?"

"A leprechaun can do anything he wants to! I told you he has magical powers. Haven't you ever thought it almost uncanny the way the hermit knows what time we're going to eat? Why, most of the time, we don't even know that ourselves."

"That's just a coincidence, Leigh," Matt said, dismissing the subject.

Leigh sat back sullenly. She didn't care what Matt said. She knew leprechauns really existed.

Two days later, when they walked into the beach house, they were surprised to see the hermit standing there. The little man looked startled. But he certainly wasn't any more stunned than Matt, who stared at the stocky, little man in total disbelief. The hermit looked exactly as Leigh had described a leprechaun, right down to the pointed ears.

Without a word, the hermit was away in a flash. Matt turned to face Leigh, an astonished look on his face. She stood, arms folded across her chest, a smug, I-told-you-so smile on her face.

The days drifted by. Matt and Leigh passed their time beachcombing, sunbathing, swimming and fishing in the surf, and exploring the sand dunes. They talked, teased, laughed, and made love.

Leigh was amazed at the different moods of Matt's lovemaking, sometimes with laughter, sometimes slow and leisurely, sometimes with a fierceness that thrilled and excited her, and sometimes with such exquisite tenderness and sweetness that Leigh was left with tears stinging her eyes from the wonder of it. At these times, Matt would kiss away her tears, whispering endearments.

Their last day on the beach, they ignored the storm that was rapidly approaching over the gulf. They both hated to give up their warm, sandy domain. Not until the last minute, when the wind was already gusting around them and threatening to rip the clothes from their bodies, did they make a mad dash for the beach house.

They ran, with the wind whipping their hair around their faces and lashing at their bodies, as jagged, blue-white lightning streaked and thunder crashed about them. Then, the rain came in torrents, drenching them to the skin in seconds.

Leigh was terrified to be out in the open in the storm. She still had not recovered from her fright from the horrible storm at sea aboard the *Avenger*. And even though Matt's arm was around her protectively, her heart raced with fear.

Suddenly, Matt stopped and whirled her around in

his arms, his mouth crashing down on hers in a fierce kiss.

Leigh tore her mouth away, saying, "No, Matt! Not here!"

"Yes, here! Now!" Matt said in a rasping voice. He wrestled her down to the wet sand and pinned her with his big body. His mouth covered hers, forcing her lips apart, his tongue seeking, demanding, tasting the honeyed sweetness of her mouth, mixed with salt. His love-making was fierce, bordering on savagery, as he took her with a passion as unbridled and tumultuous as the storm around them. And despite her earlier terror, Leigh answered him with a wild excitement of her own, frenzied, matching his powerful thrusts, urging him on, clawing at his back and nipping at his broad shoulders. And when they reached that peak, they climaxed with a violence that surpassed the storm itself, as they heard a roaring in their ears, saw the white-hot flashes of light, and felt the earth shake beneath them.

And then, they lay trembling uncontrollably in each other's arms, both deeply shaken by the experience, totally oblivious to the wind and rain lashing at their bodies. Suddenly, Leigh began to cry, as deep soul-racking sobs tore at her throat and tears coursed down her cheeks to mix with the rain.

Matt picked her up, carried her into the cabin, wrapped her tenderly in a blanket, and held her in his lap, rocking her and soothing her with muttered endearments, until her sobs finally diminished.

"You didn't hurt me . . . That's not why I'm crying . . ." Leigh mumbled between sobs. "It's just that . . . that . . ."

"Ssh, sweet, I know. I felt it too," Matt whispered. He hugged her tightly, saying in a rush of words, "Oh, kitten, you're the only woman I've ever felt this way about. I can't get enough of loving you. I want to love you under the stars, under the warm sun, in the moonlight, in the rain, in every possible place and in every possible way."

If Leigh had listened carefully to Matt's words, she would have realized he was telling her that he loved her. But she was still too shaken by the experience to notice.

The next day as they packed to leave, they were both quiet and withdrawn. Leigh looked down at the table and saw a pile of gold coins on it. She looked at Matt, her eyes questioning.

"That's for the caretaker," Matt said.

"I thought you paid him in advance."

Matt grinned sheepishly. "I did. That's for our leprechaun's pot of gold."

As they drove away, Leigh looked back at the beach and cabin wistfully. It had seemed to be a magical place, filled with enchantment. Was that the leprechaun's influence, or had Matt bewitched her himself? She thought it was probably a good thing that they were leaving. She feared that she was beginning to fall in love with her new husband, and that would never do, because Matt didn't love her.

When Leigh and Matt returned to New Orleans, Grandmère noticed the change in Matt. His stolen glances at Leigh were no longer hungry, but full of love, having an almost pleading look that tore at Grandmère's heart. She was surprised that he was the first to recognize his love. She had expected it to be Leigh. And even more puzzling, Leigh seemed to be totally unaware of his feelings. Hadn't he told her he loved her? And if not, why? Grandmère shook her head and firmly reminded herself that she had sworn not to interfere in their affairs anymore.

During that week, Matt was busy outfitting and

restocking the *Avenger* and was rarely at home. Leigh discovered that she missed him terribly, and as the day of his departure grew nearer, she was filled with dread at the thought of it.

The night before he sailed, Matt's lovemaking was fierce, urgent, filled with desperation. When it was over, he buried his face in her hair. Smelling its sweetness and feeling her soft body against his, he couldn't hold back the words any longer. They tumbled from him as if torn from the depths of his soul. He whispered in her ear in an agonized voice, "I love you, Leigh. Oh God, I love you so much!"

Leigh heard his words, and her heart soared with happiness. But then, she remembered other words Matt had once said, *"Men often say things they don't mean in the heat of their passion."* A tear of disappointment rolled down her cheek. She said nothing.

Chapter 19

Once the *Avenger* was safely out to sea, Matt paced the deck, his thoughts again on Leigh. Had she not heard his proclamation of love, or had she heard and refused to answer because she didn't love him back? He was wounded deeply, not just his male pride, but something much deeper. Over the next few days, he agonized.

I was a damned fool, he thought bitterly. I should have wooed her, courted her from the very beginning. Instead, I rushed in, arrogant and totally insensitive, forcing her to be my mistress. No wonder she doesn't love me. Well, I can't expect to win her love in one short month. It will take much longer than that to regain her trust and respect. He looked toward the heavens and vowed, by God, I'll have Leigh's love, completely and totally—even if it takes me the rest of my life to earn it!

Knowing that he couldn't begin to fulfill his vow until the war was over, Matt set his energies to ending it as quickly as he could. Over the next two months, he stalked the Caribbean with a vengeance, taking one prize after the other. The *Avenger* became the scourge of British shipping in the area, and soon

Matt's reputation as the Sea Wolf was as well known in the Caribbean as it had been in the English Channel earlier in the war.

But as the *Avenger* swept back and forth in search of prey, Matt became aware that something was brewing, something big. More and more often, they sighted heavily protected British convoys. Matt knew from his experience in the channel that these were troop transports. An invasion was being planned. But what was their target, and when would they strike?

He hailed down the first American ship they saw and asked if they had heard any rumors. It was then that he learned of the British attack on Washington, under the Command of Brigadier General Robert Ross, and the burning of the Capitol. Matt was shocked by the news. Would the British victory lengthen the war? If so, for how long? Years, maybe?

The captain of the American merchantman had also noticed the increase in military convoys. According to him, scuttlebutt had it that the British planned to attack New Orleans and thereby gain control of the Mississippi River.

In the following days, Matt hailed down two more ships, one another American privateer, the other a French brig. They both had heard the same rumor: New Orleans was the target.

Now Matt paced the deck with a new worry. New Orleans was virtually defenseless. Except for Fort St. Phillip and Fort Bourbon, south of the city on the Mississippi River, there were no other fortifications. And those two small forts could offer no opposition to an invasion force the size the British were amassing. To make matters worse, there was no American army in Louisiana. In fact, Matt had no idea where the nearest American army might be. New Orleans was an isolated city.

And if the British were successful in their invasion, they wouldn't leave as they had done in Washington. No, the whole purpose of capturing the city would be to control the Mississippi, American's only lifeline, now that the Eastern Coast had been totally blockaded.

Another thing that plagued Matt was who would be in command of the British invasion force? Under the firm, stern command of General Ross, there had been no rape or pillage during the Washington invasion, other than the burning of the Capitol. But Ross was dead, killed by an American sniper during the British retreat from Baltimore. Would the British invasion force be under the command of a man like Cockburn, the British officer responsible for the infamous rape, murder, and destruction in the upper Chesapeake Bay in the Spring of '13?

Matt continued to pace. If he went back to New Orleans, he would be risking his ship's being trapped in that port by the British blockade until the end of the war. Or worse yet, if the British invaded and captured the city before he could get back out, the *Avenger* would be confiscated. But Leigh was in New Orleans. He had to protect her, if not getting her out by sea, then at least away from the city. His decision was made. He turned the *Avenger* back.

Matt had pushed his ship and crew before, but never as hard as he did on that wild race back to New Orleans. He made the trip in record time. Having no idea when the British were going to attack, he was relieved when he approached the Mississippi delta and saw no British troop convoy anchored in the surrounding gulf.

As he tacked his way up the Mississippi to New Orleans, Matt noted the absence of any new fortifications or breastworks. When they entered the port, business seemed to be going on as usual, the port crammed with ships and river barges being loaded and unloaded. Was it possible the people of New Orleans didn't even know of the impending attack, he wondered. But surely, with so many ships coming and going, they must have heard the rumors.

Before Matt left the *Avenger*, he announced to the crew that there would be no shore leave, not even overnight. They would take on fresh water and supplies and then leave. He was not going to take any chances on getting the *Avenger* trapped in New Orleans.

As Matt drove through the city, he again noticed the lack of fortifications or preparations for battle. But his excitement at seeing Leigh again crowded out his puzzlement.

When he reached the town house, he jumped from the carriage and strode rapidly through the courtyard, then up the stairs, taking them two at a time. He rushed to their bedroom to find it empty. Then he walked through the corridors, opening doors and calling "Leigh? Where are you?"

He heard Grandmère's voice calling from the salon, "Matthew? Is that you?" Of course, that's where they are, he thought, his heart racing with anticipation.

He stepped into the salon and looked around. Then he saw Grandmère, sitting with one leg up on a stool, her ankle in a heavy splint. "My God, what happened to you?"

"*Mon dieu*, like a silly old woman, I broke my ankle," Grandmère replied.

Matt noticed her pale face and pained look. "Is it serious?" he asked with concern.

"*Non, non*, Matthew. It is just a little break. The doctor says I'll be back on it in a few weeks. But what are you doing here in New Orleans? I had not expected you back so soon."

"And I wouldn't have been back either, if it hadn't been for the British planning to attack New Orleans. Haven't you people heard the news?"

"*Oui*, we've heard," Grandmère replied indifferently.

"And nothing is being done about it?" Matt asked in a shocked voice.

"*Non*, something is being done. The American government is sending General Andrew Jackson with a big army. We are expecting them to arrive any day now."

"I mean, isn't anyone building fortifications, breastworks?"

"*Non*—the fools! *Mon dieu!* Half the Creoles don't believe the rumors, the other half say New Orleans is American now, let the Americans defend it."

"They're not rumors, Grandmère. The British are going to attack New Orleans. The only question is when? Thank God, I got here before they did. That's why I'm here, to get you and Leigh out of New Orleans."

"Leave New Orleans? *Non!*"

"Grandmère, the British are going to attack this city. You can't stay here!"

"*Non*, Matthew, I'll not leave. I didn't run when Admiral Cochrane attacked and captured Martinique, and I'll not run now. The British won't harm an old woman with a broken ankle."

"Grandmère! This whole damned city may be turned into a battleground! If you won't come with Leigh and me on the *Avenger*, at least go to Twelve Oaks, or better yet, to one of your friends' plantations farther back in Louisiana."

"*Oui*, perhaps I will. We'll see."

What was wrong with her, Matt thought. She

seems so distracted. "Well, I guess now I'll have a devil of a time convincing Leigh to leave you." He looked around, saying, "By the way, where is she?"

Grandmère turned deathly pale. "She is gone," she said, almost whispering.

"Gone where? Visiting? Shopping?"

Grandmère took a deep breath before answering. "*Non*, Matthew. She has gone to England."

Matt couldn't believe his ears. He stared at Grandmère in disbelief, then said in a low voice, "What did you say?"

"I said she has gone to England. To find her father."

"Gone to England? But why? I promised her I'd take her after the war was over!"

"Oh, Matthew, after you left, the news came of the burning of Washington. Then the rumors, the talk! Everyone was saying the defeat would lengthen the war, that it might last as long as the War for Independence, as much as five or six more years. And the more everyone talked, the more upset Leigh became. *Mon dieu!* I should have guessed, but I thought she was worried about you."

Matt said nothing. He just stared at her.

"Matthew, if I had known what she was planning, I would have locked her in her room. But as I said, I thought she was just anxious about you. Then I broke my ankle, and the doctor kept me heavily sedated for a few days. That's when she left. My maid found the letter the next day in her room."

"Letter? She left you a letter?"

"*Oui*. She wrote she was going to England to try and find her father. She said she was sorry, but she couldn't wait any longer, she felt she had to go. Oh, Matthew, you can read it yourself. You can tell by the way it's written, that she was distressed, that she was not herself."

"I don't want to read her damned note!" Matt said angrily. "What I want to know is where in the hell did she get the money for the passage?"

"*Oui*, I wondered that too. I hired investigators. They found the pawn shop where she had sold her pearls."

"She sold her pearls? She sold my wedding present to her?" Matt asked in an outraged voice.

"*Non*, just the earrings, not the necklace. But don't worry. I bought them back. I knew you would be furious. The investigator also discovered what ship she sailed on. It was a French ship bound for London. They say the captain of the ship is a respected man, a stern disciplinarian and known to run a good, tight ship." She sighed deeply. "I found some comfort in that." She looked up at Matt, her eyes pleading forgiveness, saying, "I feel I have let you down terribly."

"No, Grandmère. I know how unpredictable Leigh is. Don't blame yourself," Matt answered, barely unable to control his fury.

Matt paced the floor, thinking, yes, she is unpredictable—and deceitful! She had been sitting back all this time just waiting for the opportunity to bolt. She doesn't give a damn about me. No, she goes running off to find her father, a man she has never seen in her life, a man who may not even exist. To hell with me, and to hell with her marriage vows! She even had the audacity to slap me in the face by selling my wedding gift to her. Yes, my first estimation of her was correct. She is deceitful. And what a damned fool she has made of me, following her around like some lovesick puppy. Well, she won't make a fool of me again! Never again! But, dammit, she's my wife! And by God, she's going to honor her marriage vows!

He turned and walked angrily to the door. Grandmère was alarmed at the fierce look on his face. "*Sacre-bleu!* Where are you going?" she called.

"To England, goddammit!" Matt roared. "To fetch my wife!"

Chapter 20

To Leigh, the trip across the Atlantic to England seemed to take a lifetime. The monotony of sailing day after day with nothing to do but stare at the sky and open sea only added to her restlessness. During the entire crossing, only two other ships were sighted. The first was a foul-odored slaver, a long twenty-four cannon mounted on a turntable between her two masts. Then, when they reached the north Atlantic, with its long gray rollers, a whaler was sighted, its superstructure of brick enclosing the try pots on her mid-deck. The ship passed so close to them, Leigh could smell the gurry, the odor of old blood and whale oil that permeated the wood of the ship.

When they finally reached the English Channel, Leigh could barely contain her impatience for the trip to be over. Then they were forced to wait until high tide to sail up the Thames River to London, fifty miles upstream.

Leigh was astonished when they reached the port of London. She had seen the ports at Boston, Charleston, and New Orleans, but they were nothing compared to the size of this port. Great docks, deep artificial lakes, were surrounded by wharves for miles and miles down the wide Thames. As the gates closed behind them, trapping the water from high tide, Leigh stood and gazed at the different foreign flags fluttering above the ships: French, British, Spanish, Dutch, Swedish, Portuguese, Russian, Greek, and a score or more of national flags that she didn't recognize. One flag was conspicuous in its absence, the American Stars and Stripes. She wondered how long it would be before another American ship sailed into this port.

Could the war really last for another five or six years? It had been the speculation on that probability that had sent Leigh on her precipitous search for her father. That, and the dream.

As the talk of the probability of the war being lengthened by the British victory in Washington swirled around her, Leigh had become more and more disturbed. The thought of delaying her search for her father for years was more than she could endure. It was more than just curiosity about the man who had fathered her. Having never known a father, she felt that a part of her was incomplete, never developed for lack of the opportunity to know the other half of her heritage, which left a void within her. She hungered to fill that void, and, like all hungers, it only grew with the passage of time. Then, she had the dream.

She had dreamed that her father was dying and was calling for her. His face had been a vague blur, but the rest of the dream had been shockingly real, so real she had awakened sobbing. The dream had haunted her. For days, she had paced. She had no idea how old her father was. For all she knew, he could have been much older than her mother. But old age and death did not necessarily go hand in hand. Hadn't her mother died young? The fear that she was running out of time to find her father had compounded her hunger for him. She had finally decided to go to England. She would delay no longer.

Leigh felt remorse that she had slipped away from Grandmère while her guard was down. And she wouldn't have left, had not the doctor assured her the broken ankle was not serious. She wished she could have told the old lady her plans, explained why it was so important to her to go now instead of waiting. But she knew Grandmère wouldn't have approved and, therefore, would have gone to any lengths to stop her from going without Matt.

She also regretted having to sell her earrings. Knowing nothing about jewels, she had been shocked to find out their value. Matt had spent a small fortune on his wedding gift to her. If only he had left her money, instead of authorizing his bank to pay for any purchases she made or debts she incurred during his absence. But he hadn't, and she had been forced to sell her earrings for cash. Thankfully, she had not had to sell the necklace, too.

No, money would be no problem now. She still had enough left to pay for her return trip and keep her for several months, if necessary. But she really didn't expect finding her father would take that long, not now that she had found the solution to her dilemma.

When Leigh had left New Orleans, she still had no idea of how she was going to find her father, only that she had to find him. And then, as sometimes happens in life, the solution had come out of the blue. She remembered a friend of her mother's who had come into a sudden, unexpected inheritance from the woman she had served in England before she had married and emigrated to America. Leigh's mother had been amazed that the barrister who was handling the will had managed to track her friend down in another country, and after twenty years had passed since her employment. Surely, if a barrister had the means of tracing people for inheritance purposes, one could help her find her father.

But Leigh's solution presented its own problems. She was reluctant to tell a lawyer the truth, fearing that he would hesitate to help her, knowing that she was illegitimate and thinking that her father might prefer to remain unknown. As yet, she hadn't thought of a likely story to tell the barrister.

After Leigh had disembarked and climbed into the coach that would take her to the hotel, she asked the coachman to drive past the Houses of Parliament first, curious to see the place where her father had spent so much of his time.

They crossed over one of the many bridges that spanned the Thames to the north side of the river, and as they drove through London, Leigh was amazed at the size of the city. No city in America could compare to it. She had heard that London's population was well over a million, an astronomical number to her. She couldn't imagine a million of anything, much less people.

While Leigh was impressed with the size of the London and its huge limestone, Gothic buildings, she found the city gloomy. The buildings were covered with a thin layer of accumulated soot, and a thick cloud of smoke hung over the city, so thick the sun couldn't penetrate it. As a result, the city had a grimy look about it. She compared it to the crystal-clear air and bright sunshine of New Orleans and felt a wave of homesickness.

As they drove down Whitehall, Leigh barely scanned Westminster Abbey, with its flying buttresses. St. James Palace she completely ignored. She wasn't interested in where the king and queen of the

United Kingdom resided. Her eyes were glued to the House of Lords. Inside that building, her father had walked, talked, perhaps even laughed. Could he possibly be there right now? A thrill ran through her.

On impulse, she cried to the coachman, "Stop the carriage! I just want to take a closer look."

She climbed from her coach and stood on the steps of the building for a long time, staring at it, as if she were trying to will her father to step before her eyes. Then, realizing what she was doing, she laughed at herself. Even if he were to walk right past you, you wouldn't know him, she reminded herself.

The gray-haired old guard standing by the entrance watched Leigh curiously. Not many people showed such interest in the Parliament buildings, particularly not with the famous Westminster Abbey and St. James Palace standing right beside them. But this beautiful young woman seemed to be fascinated with the House of Lords.

He walked up to Leigh and asked, "Would you like to look inside?"

Leigh was stunned by his question. Could anyone go inside? She wouldn't think so. Surely, sightseers would be distracting to the lords. She stammered, "No—no thank you. I wouldn't want to disturb them at their work."

The old guard's brow wrinkled even more. "Disturb whom?"

"Why, the lords, of course," Leigh replied.

The old man smiled and said, "There is no one in there now, young lady. Parliament recessed the first of September. They won't be back until January. Would you like to take a peek?"

See the place where her father worked? Yes, she would like that very much. She smiled and replied,

"Oh, yes, if it's not too much trouble."

She followed the guard and waited while he unlocked the door, her heart racing with excitement. She stepped into a massive room, its ceiling towering high above her. Rows of long bench seats, upholstered in plush velvet, stood at each side. At the end of the room, the throne sat on a raised dais, covered with an ornate Gothic-carved wooden canopy. High on the walls above the throne were huge arched windows, fitted with beautiful stained glass. The room was hushed, filled with a quiet dignity.

Leigh stood gazing at the room in awe. Almost reverently, she touched the plush velvet on one of the benches. Had her father sat here? Had he stood in this very spot and addressed his fellow peers? A feeling of pride filled her.

The old guard stood back, pleased with the young woman's reaction. So many people thought the abbey and palace beautiful and awesome. Personally, he preferred the House of Lords, for in this room lay the true power and majesty of the United Kingdom, not in the palace across the street. The old king, crazy George, hadn't known what was going on for years. And that son of his, traipsing around in his fancy clothes and acting more like a tomcat than a prince, wasn't much better.

Leigh smiled gratefully at the old man and said, "Thank you for showing it to me."

He nodded and grinned. It had been a pleasure to show the House of Lords to someone who really appreciated it.

Leigh walked back to the coach and climbed in. As they drove away from the government buildings, another coach passed them. Leigh's eyes caught the coat of arms painted on the coach's door as the vehicle sped by. A glimmer came into her eyes as her quick mind began to plot the story she would tell the barrister.

Leigh was in the office of a prestigious law firm the next morning. After she had been led into a dim, musty-smelling office, and seated, the barrister, sitting behind the desk, asked, "Now, how may I be of service to you, Miss—'?"

The barrister's calling Leigh "miss" was no oversight on the man's part. Leigh had deliberately left her wedding band off that day, afraid that the lawyer would wonder why she wasn't letting her husband handle this business if he knew she was married.

"Miss O'Neal," Leigh answered. For a moment, she hesitated, and then, swallowing nervously, said, "I'm hoping that you can find a certain man for me."

Just the faintest hint of surprise crossed the barrister's lean face before he quickly hid his reaction to Leigh's words. "I'm sure we can, Miss O'Neal. Our firm hires people for that specific purpose. Of course, we'll need some information from you first." He pulled a piece of paper closer and picked up a pen, saying, "Now, if you'll just give me the man's name."

"That's the problem. I don't know his name," Leigh answered.

This time the man couldn't hide his look of surprise.

"You see," Leigh continued, "many years ago, before my father emigrated to America, he was attacked by footpads here in London and robbed. My father tried to resist and was badly beaten. A young man came to his rescue and chased the footpads away. Then he put my father in his coach and carried him to the nearest doctor. He even paid the doctor for his services before he left. The stranger saved my father's life."

As she talked, Leigh watched the barrister's face closely to see how he was reacting to her tale. He was leaning forward, apparently engrossed in her story. So far, so good, Leigh thought.

Encouraged, Leigh continued. "Throughout his life, my father always wondered who the man was. He kept telling himself that he would come back to London some day and try to find the man to thank him. Perhaps, he would have—if he hadn't had a sudden heart attack. Before he died, he made me promise to come in his stead."

When Leigh finished, the lawyer sat back and frowned. "Then you have no idea what this man's name was?"

"No."

"What about the doctor who took care of your father? Didn't he know?"

"No, I'm afraid not. My father asked him."

The barrister shook his head, saying, "Miss O'Neal, I don't know how we could possibly find this man with no name to go by."

"I do have something that may be of help," Leigh said.

"Oh? What?"

"My father said he knew the man was a nobleman, because he heard the coachman address him as m'lord, when they were lifting my father into the man's coach. My father also distinctly remembered seeing a coat of arms on the coach's door before he lost consciousness."

The barrister's head snapped up at this information. "A coat of arms? Did your father remember what it looked like? We might be able to identify the stranger from that."

It was all Leigh could do to hold down her excitement. "Yes, my father remembered it very clearly. He

418

said it was a gold falcon on a crimson background."
She leaned forward, her look hopeful, asking, "Do
you recognize that insignia?"

"No, I'm afraid not. The nobility have hundreds of
coats of arms, many of them similar. However, with
this information, we may be able to narrow it down to
a few possibilities. Will that do?"

A few possibilities, Leigh thought in dismay. This
was going to be more complicated than she had
thought. She had hoped for much more but, at least,
it was a start. "Yes, I suppose it will have to. How
soon can you have the information?"

"I think we can have it by tomorrow morning. Why
don't you come back then?"

The next morning, Leigh waited anxiously in the
barrister's office for the man to join her. What if she
had guessed wrong, she thought. What if the emblem
on her father's signet ring and his coat of arms
weren't the same? What if there wasn't any coat of
arms with a gold falcon on a crimson background?
Maybe, she should have told the lawyer the truth. By
the time the barrister entered the small office, Leigh's
nerves were stretched taut.

The barrister sat down behind his desk, looking
very stern and businesslike, making Leigh still more
apprehensive. Then he smiled, saying, "We were more
fortunate than I anticipated. There were several coats
of arms with falcons on them, but only one with the
colors you described, a coat of arms that dates back
to King Richard the Lion-Hearted. I've written the
lord's name on a piece of paper and his London
address. I've also included the location of his country
estates."

The barrister handed Leigh a sealed envelope.
Leigh fought down the urge to tear it open and look
at the name. In as calm a voice as she could manage,

she said, "Thank you," and rose from her chair.

"I'm glad we could be of service to you," the barrister replied, coming to his feet.

After Leigh had paid the man, she rushed from the office. Standing on the sidewalk outside the building, she tore open the envelope and unfolded the piece of paper in it. The name seemed to leap out at her. It read: Lord Leigh Stanford. She stared at it in disbelief.

Leigh remembered Matt once saying something about her name, that Leigh was a man's name. Her mother had named her after her father. There was no doubt in her mind that this Lord Stanford was the man she was seeking. She had found him! She had found her father!

Her hand shaking with excitement, she quickly read the title behind the name, the Earl of Gloucester. Her father was an earl? My God!

She read further and saw the London address. Whirling, she hailed the first public coach she saw.

Thirty minutes later, Leigh stood before a gray stone town house in Cavendish Square. What if her father wasn't in London? she thought. With Parliament not being in session, he could well be at one of his country estates. But surely, there would be someone in residence here. A caretaker perhaps. They could tell her where to find him.

Taking a deep breath to fortify herself, she walked up the steps and knocked on the door with the heavy brass knocker.

A tall, gray-haired butler opened the door, looked down his nose at Leigh, and said in a haughty voice, "May I help you?"

Ignoring her trembling legs and racing heart, Leigh said, "May I speak to Lord Stanford, please?"

The butler's eyebrows rose in disapproval. "Your

ame, please?"

Name? What name should she give? Certainly not
her married name. That would have no meaning to
her father. "Tell him Miss O'Neal would like to speak
to him."

The butler looked at her with distaste and said
coldly, "Do you have an appointment, miss?"

"Why, no," Leigh blurted.

He looked down his thin nose at her and said,
"You can't speak to his lordship without an appointment. Come back tomorrow when his secretary is
here."

He started to shut the door, but Leigh stopped him.
"No, I can't wait until tomorrow," she cried. "This is
personal. I need to see him now!"

"My dear, young lady," the butler said in an arrogant voice, "I just told you no one speaks to his
lordship without an appointment."

After all she had gone through to find her father,
Leigh wasn't about to be put off one more minute,
and certainly not by some pompous butler. She
pushed the door open and rushed past the man.

The astonished butler caught her arm and pulled
her back, saying, "Here now, miss, you can't come
barging in here like that!"

"I've got to see his lordship!" Leigh screamed.
"Now!"

"Masters? What's going on out there?" a deep
masculine voice called from down the hall.

"Now see what you've done?" the butler hissed to
Leigh before he called back, "Nothing that I can't
manage, m'lord."

My lord? That was her father's voice? Leigh's eyes
were glued on the doorway from where the voice had
come.

The butler's fingers dug into Leigh's arm as he

pulled her back to the door, saying, "Now, out with you, miss, before I'm forced to set the constables on you."

"No!" she screeched, twisting from the butler's grasp and running toward the room her father occupied.

The butler caught her inside the doorway of the room. They tussled.

"My God, Masters!" Lord Stanford cried. "What are you doing to that young lady?"

The red-faced butler pushed Leigh behind him, saying, "She doesn't have an appointment, m'lord. I told her to come back tomorrow to see your secretary, but she just barged in!"

Leigh stepped from behind the butler, saying, "Please, Lord Stanford, I have to talk to you."

The butler started to push Leigh back, but Lord Stanford said in a low, tight voice, "No, Masters. Leave us."

The butler looked dismayed. "But m'lord—"

"I said leave us," Lord Stanford repeated firmly.

"Yes, m'lord," the butler replied stiffly. He gave Leigh a heated look and left the room.

Leigh had been staring at the tall, dark-haired man who was her father. His hair was streaked with gray at the temples, and Leigh thought him terribly handsome and distinguished-looking. Except, her dream must have had some foundation after all. He looked very pale.

Suddenly, Leigh was appalled at her own behavior. Goodness, what must he think of me? Pushing my way in and acting like some hoyden. She smiled nervously, saying, "I'm sorry to disturb you like this, Lord Stanford, but I had to talk to you. You don't know who I am but—"

"I know who you are," Lord Stanford interrupted

422

n a hushed voice. "When I saw you standing there, I thought it was my Meagan. Then I saw your eyes — ny eyes." His look was penetrating. "You are my daughter, aren't you?"

Leigh couldn't believe her ears. She had expected to have to explain herself, offer him the ring as proof. She had steeled herself to be prepared for rejection, to be denied. Instead, he had accepted her on sight. The shock was too much for her. Suddenly, she burst into tears.

Lord Stanford pulled her into his arms, and Leigh clung to him, sobbing against his broad shoulder as if she had known him all her life. When she finally composed herself, she mumbled, "I'm sorry. It's just that — that I was afraid you would deny me."

"Deny you?" Lord Stanford said in an incredulous voice. "Deny my own daughter, my own flesh and blood, the daughter of my beloved Meagan? No, my child, I'd never do that." He lifted her chin gently, saying, "But I must admit, I'm terribly shocked. You see, all these years, I've believed your mother to be dead."

"You thought she was dead?"

"Yes. I took her and your uncle to the dock myself. I booked passage for them on the *North Hampton*. The ship went down in the north Atlantic with no survivors." He shook his head in bewilderment, saying, "I still don't understand."

Leigh smiled. "I think I can explain that. I once asked my mother about her trip from England to America. One of the things she told me was that they didn't take the first ship they had booked passage on. My uncle didn't like the looks of that ship. He changed their passage to another ship that sailed later that day. But I don't think my mother knew the first ship had sunk. At least, she never mentioned it."

423

Lord Stanford sighed deeply, saying, "All thes[e] years, I've been blaming myself. I thought I had sen[t] her to her death. What a relief!"

He led Leigh to a couch. Before he sat in the chai[r] across from her, he asked in an anxious voice, "An[d] your mother? Did she marry?"

Leigh could see the pain in his eyes. At tha[t] minute, she knew this man had loved her mothe[r] deeply, still did. She smiled, saying, "No, she neve[r] married. She had plenty of opportunity to, but sh[e] said she never loved any man but you."

Lord Stanford couldn't hide his excitement. "The[n] where is she? Did she come with you? Is she i[n] England?"

Leigh hated to break the news and said as gently a[s] possible, "No, she didn't come with me. She die[d] almost a year ago."

The look of happiness drained from Lord Stan[-]ford's face with her words. "Died? Of what?"

"There was a tumor," Leigh murmured.

He slumped into the chair, leaning forward, hi[s] head buried in his hands for a long time. Finally, h[e] looked up and said in a bleak voice, "At least, I didn['t] send her to her death, as I believed all these years[.] His eyes drifted over Leigh's face. "And she left me [a] part of her, a beautiful gift." He shook his head[,] saying, "I still can't believe I have a daughter."

Leigh smiled and nodded, saying, "I know how yo[u] feel. I didn't know I had a living father, either, unt[il] my mother told me when she was dying. She mad[e] my uncle promise to bring me to you."

Lord Stanford jumped to his feet. "Of course! Ho[w] stupid of me. Sean brought you. Is he outside?" H[e] turned and walked to the door, saying, "Why didn['t] he come in?"

"No, Lord Stanford," Leigh cried, "Uncle Sea[n]

didn't bring me."

He turned, a confused look on his face. "But you said—"

"He was bringing me to England when he was killed during a storm at sea," Leigh interjected.

"Killed?" Lord Stanford said in a shocked voice. "Sean is dead too?"

"It's a long story," Leigh said in a sad voice. "Please, sit down. This may take a while."

After Lord Stanford had sat down, Leigh told him of her mother's death, what she had told her about him, and of her uncle's promise to her mother and his reluctance to bring her to him. She related how she had disguised herself as a boy and stowed away on Matt's privateer, how her uncle died, and how her disguise was discovered. She mentioned nothing of Matt forcing her to be his mistress. She didn't want her father to know anything of that disgraceful part of her life. She was very vague about her marriage. She finished by telling him about her dream, her trip across the Atlantic, and how she had found him.

Lord Stanford was amazed at her story. That she had gone through all that to reach him touched him deeply. "It's incredible. You didn't even know my name? All you had was my ring?"

"Yes."

"And your husband was at sea when you left? Won't he be frantic when he returns and finds you gone?"

Leigh flushed, thinking, No, he'll be furious. She smiled, saying, "I am hoping to be back in New Orleans before he returns from sea, Lord Stanford."

"No, please, don't call me that, at least not when we're alone. Call me father, and I'll call you . . ." His brows furrowed. "I don't even know your first name."

"It's Leigh."

"Leigh?" her father asked in a surprised voice.

"Yes, my mother named me after you. Do you mind?"

"Mind? My God, no! I can't tell you how much it pleases me."

Leigh glanced at the clock on the mantel. Goodness, she had been here for hours. She rose, saying, "I didn't realize it was getting so late. I'd better go back to the hotel."

"Go back to the hotel? Then you won't stay here with me?" her father asked in a disappointed voice.

"But how could I?" She flushed, saying, "I mean, wouldn't it be awkward with your wife here and all?"

"Leigh, my wife doesn't live here. We've been separated since before your mother left for America. In fact, my wife no longer lives in London. She resides at one of my country estates."

"You and your wife are separated?"

He frowned. "Didn't your mother tell you why I sent her away? Didn't she tell you my wife tried to kill her? Not once, but twice!"

"Kill her?" Leigh gasped.

Lord Stanford's face flushed with anger. "Yes, my wife tried to kill your mother, but she was clever about it. She hired killers, so I could never prove her part in it. The second attempt on your mother's life was almost successful. I knew my wife would try again. It terrified me, so I sent your mother away to protect her. You can't possibly think I would continue to live with my wife after she had done that?"

"I didn't know about that. I never knew why my mother left."

He smiled sadly, saying, "No, I see you didn't know. I hate to think what your opinion of me must be. An older, married man, with a son, a Lord of the Realm." His look was intense. "But Leigh, I didn't seduce your mother. It wasn't a casual love affair. We fell deeply in love. And I didn't betray my wife's love, either. We had never loved one another. It was an arranged marriage. I had married because it was expected of me. I had an obligation to produce an heir to carry on the family name and inherit my title. My wife was a beautiful woman from a prestigious family. A satisfactory match, I thought. It wasn't until after we were married that I discovered how devious, selfish, and cruel she was."

"You have a son?" Leigh asked in surprise.

"Yes, and from the minute he was born, my wife has been obsessed with him. Unfortunately, he's turned out just like her, cold and totally ruthless. It was this obsession, this fierce protectiveness over my son, that provoked the attacks on your mother's life. My wife couldn't have cared less if your mother loved me, or that I loved her. She didn't care a whit about me. All she cared about was my title and wealth. She knew Meagan, herself, was no threat. She knew I would never divorce her and bring that kind of scandal down on my family. But she was terrified that Meagan might bear me a child, a child that I would acknowledge publicly. She was determined that her son would share nothing with another. It wasn't enough that he would inherit the title and the majority of my estates by rights of primogeniture," he said in a bitter voice. "She wanted it all for him, my title, my lands, my money, everything."

Lord Stanford rose and paced the room for a few minutes. Then he turned, saying, "I find myself torn." He took Leigh's hands in his, looking deeply into her eyes, saying, "Do you realize how much I long to acknowledge you publicly? Shout to the whole world, look at this beautiful, warm woman! She's my daughter, and how proud I am of her! But I don't dare, Leigh, for fear of what my wife would do if she knew of your existence. I just can't take the risk, any more than I could with your mother. It would be too dangerous for you."

His wife would try to have her killed? A shiver of horror ran through Leigh. She glanced at her father's agonized face, and her heart melted with love for this man. "I didn't come here for you to acknowledge me publicly, Father. I don't want to be your heir. All I ever wanted was for you to want me—to love me."

Lord Stanford pulled her into his arms in a fierce hug. "Oh, my child, I do want you, and you'll always have my love, all of it." He looked down and smiled ruefully. "For what it's worth."

Leigh smiled back, smiling, "It's worth everything to me."

"Then you will stay with me? I realize I can't have all your love, that I can't keep you forever. After all, you do have your husband. But you will stay for a while?"

Leigh sighed blissfully. "Oh, yes, I'll stay," then she added, "for a while."

For the next several weeks, Leigh and her father were constant companions. They took long rides through London as he showed her the sights. One day was spent picnicking at Hyde Park and another touring the Tower of London—a grim, ancient fortress with enormously thick walls and thirteen towers, used to house political prisoners. There, Leigh saw the Yeomen Warders—the tower guards—dressed in their Henry VIII coats, ruffs, and beefeater hats.

One day, they drove past the Admiralty building. As her father pointed it out to her, Leigh paid particular interest to the building with its three huge domes. She noticed it was heavily guarded. Had that been true the night Matt broke into its offices and stole the navy's secret papers? Or had it only been since then, that it had been heavily guarded? She sat back, amazed at her husband's audacity.

Lord Stanford took Leigh shopping at the Bond Street shops, to the theater and opera, and to dinners at many of London's finest restaurants. He introduced her to his friends and colleagues as a distant relative visiting in London, using her married name, Mrs. Matthew Blake, in case his wife should hear any rumors. That way, she would never associate Leigh with the woman whom she had felt had been a threat to her son's inheritance.

One evening, Lord Stanford had several of his colleagues in for dinner. Leigh served as hostess. During the meal, he sat watching her proudly, his eyes filled with love.

After the meal was over and most of his guests had departed, his best friend pulled him aside, saying, "Your daughter is a beautiful, charming woman. I don't wonder at your pride in her."

Lord Stanford's head jerked up in surprise. "My daughter? How did you know?"

His friend chuckled, saying, "Stanford, your eyes are identical. Besides, anyone can see how proud you are of her." He laid his hand on the earl's shoulder, saying, "But be careful, my friend. You don't want your wife getting suspicious."

From then on, Leigh and her father spent most of their time at home.

One evening, as they sat before the fire in the library, Lord Stanford looked across at his daughter. He found it hard to believe how much he had enjoyed the last few weeks with her. She had given him a new lease on life, a reason for living, other than his work. She had told him everything of her childhood and life in Boston, sharing all her little fears and hopes and dreams, so that Lord Stanford felt that he had shared those years with Leigh and her mother, and a lonely, empty gap in his life had been filled.

But while she had been very open to him about that, she had told him very little about her husband and marriage, almost as if she were hiding something from him. He sensed there was something wrong there and waited patiently, hoping that as she came to trust him she would confide in him. The thought that his daughter might be unhappy made him ache for her. He longed to help for, more than anything in this world, he wanted her happiness.

He finally decided to bring the subject into the open, saying softly, "You've told me very little about your husband, my dear. I've come to the conclusion that he must be cross-eyed and bow-legged."

Leigh's breath caught in her throat, surprised at her father's question. What could she say? That she had disliked Matt at first because of his arrogance and domineering attitude? That she had feared his strange magnetism until he had taught her passion? That she had married him because of this physical attraction and his promise to help her find her father? Her father would think her a wanton. And how could she admit to her father that Matt had married her because he wanted her, not because he loved her? And she could never begin to explain her feelings toward Matt now, feelings that she herself was confused and bewildered by.

She smiled nervously and said, "No, my husband is a very handsome man." She hesitated, trying to collect her thoughts, then said, "His family owns a shipyard and shipping company in Charleston. Matt owns several ships of his own and was captain of one of them before the war. I've already told you about his home in New Orleans, where we were married, and of course, you know he's a privateer." Leigh flushed in embarrassment at this last statement. Goodness, what must her distinguished father think of her, married to a man who was almost a pirate?

Lord Stanford frowned at her evasive answer. Then he smiled, saying, "Ah yes, your husband is one of those bold, ingenuous privateers. An amazing breed of men, your American privateers. Men with courage, aggressiveness, endurance, and initiative, mixed with a spirit for gambling and danger and remarkable seamanship." He chuckled, saying, "I once heard one of my colleagues refer to your privateers as America's secret weapon."

Leigh was shocked. Her father sounded almost as if he admired the privateers. "Certainly, you can't approve of privateering?" she asked in an outraged voice.

The earl's dark eyebrows rose. Was this the problem with her marriage? Leigh didn't approve of her husband being a privateer? He answered in a carefully, measured voice, "Approve? No, my dear. No more than I approve of war. But war is an ugly fact of life, Leigh, and, along with it, destruction. Rather, let's say I'm resigned to it. And privateering is an accepted method of war in our world today, and has been since the fifteenth century. It's a particularly effective weapon when a country is too small or poor to maintain a large navy. Its purpose is to harass the enemy's shipping, make a nuisance of itself, so that the enemy will sit up and take notice of the smaller country's demands. And from that standpoint, your American privateers have excelled in this war. Do you realize that your privateers, alone, have taken over thirteen hundred prizes, to say nothing of the ships they have ransomed, ships they have let go with the promise that their owners will pay money for them not being destroyed?"

Leigh stared at him in disbelief. "You sound as though you admire them."

"I believe in giving credit where credit is due, my dear. I'm afraid my country seriously underestimated the seamanship of your young men, both your navy and your privateers. Not only have they proved to be an embarrassment to the British navy, the most powerful the world has ever known, but we in England are beginning to feel the pinch. Insurance rates at Lloyds are so high that most shipping firms and owners can't afford them. And no man is foolish enough to send a ship to sea without it being insured. As a result, our trade is down drastically. Now, stop and consider, my dear. England is an island. Half of our food and almost all of the raw materials needed for our industry are imported. Our merchants are clamoring that there's not enough goods to sell. Many of our mills have been forced to close for lack of raw materials. Just recently, Parliament received a petition for an armistice signed by sixty thousand textile manufacturers and employees."

Leigh was astonished at her father's words. Matt had said virtually the same thing, and she had scoffed at him. Now she was finding out that what he had predicted was coming true. A new respect for her husband crept in. She said, "Then you think the war will end soon?"

"I certainly hope so. And the news from Belgium seems to be pointing in that direction. In my opinion, it's a war that should never have happened in the first place."

Leigh's patriotism flared. "President Madison had to declare war. You had no right to impress our seamen and interfere with our trade."

Lord Stanford smiled, secretly admiring her spirit.

"You are right, my dear, we didn't. But let me point out something. We British were involved in a life-and-death struggle with the biggest tyrant the world has ever known. And make no mistake about it, Leigh. Napoleon didn't just want Europe. He wanted the whole world. The war completely drained our country of its young men. Given a choice between fighting with Wellington on the Peninsula or joining the British navy, almost invariably, the young men chose Wellington. That left the navy with only the press gangs and impressment to fill its need for men. And we needed our navy badly, not only to blockade the French ports, but to transport everything across the channel. It's difficult to fight a war across water. The French had a decided advantage from that standpoint. It's always easier to maintain supply lines over land than water."

Leigh couldn't believe her ears. "Then you do think you had the right to impress our seamen?"

"No, Leigh, I was just trying to point out our position. I fought impressment and interruption of your country's trade from the very beginning, along with others in Parliament. We felt that just because we were fighting for our rights as free men, didn't give us the right to deny others their freedom of choice. Unfortunately, we were in the minority. But even at that, we had just revoked our orders-in-council when we discovered your country had already declared war. If we had moved a little faster, or your government a little slower, this war would never have happened."

Every time impressment was mentioned, Leigh's blood boiled. She kept remembering Matt's younger brother. She said in a bitter voice, "And would invoking your orders-in-council have stopped your navy from impressing our seamen?"

433

Lord Stanford frowned, saying, "You have a good point there, Leigh. I'm afraid our Admiralty has gotten out of hand. Instead of being a servant of our people, it's become too powerful. There are some of us in Parliament who feel it was our Admiralty's high-handed methods that pushed us into this war. We're concerned and determined to put it back in its proper place. Fortunately, our members are growing."

Leigh suddenly felt ashamed of herself. She couldn't blame her father for the war. Apparently, he had done everything in his power to prevent it. "I'm sorry. It's just that I feel very strongly about impressment."

"As does your President Madison. In fact, the question of impressment is the only thing holding back peace negotiations. Your president won't yield and, unfortunately, neither will our cabinet. I guess you Americans and we British are too much alike. We're both a proud and stubborn people."

Proud and stubborn. The words reminded her of Matt. Unknowingly, she smiled.

"Why are you smiling?" her father asked.

"Something you said reminded me of my husband."

"Oh?"

"Yes, I'm afraid he has a tendency to be domineering and very stubborn."

Lord Stanford wasn't particularly surprised. He wouldn't have expected an American privateer to be meek and mild-mannered. Was that the problem with their marriages? They were both too strong-willed? Having come to know Leigh over the past few weeks, he realized that his daughter could be stubborn herself.

Lord Stanford studied his daughter thoughtfully. She was a high-spirited, young woman. It would take a strong man to handle that much woman. But if that strength was tempered with love . . . He said, "Your husband must love you very much."

Leigh was taken completely by surprise. She blurted, "No, he doesn't love me."

Lord Stanford frowned. He could see himself marrying to fulfill an obligation, but he couldn't imagine a fiercely independent privateer doing such a thing. "Then why did he marry you?" he asked.

Leigh blushed and averted her eyes, saying, "Because he desired me. You see, to him I'm just another possession. He may be proud of me, want me, but he doesn't love me."

Again, Lord Stanford wasn't surprised. His daughter was a beautiful, desirable young woman. And a passionate one, he suspected. He could well understand her husband wanting her. He wondered if Leigh realized how close wanting a woman and loving a woman could be. There was a fine line between the two, so fine one was often mistaken for the other, so fine a man could easily cross from one to the other. And there wasn't a man alive who hadn't wanted before he loved. At least, not to his knowledge.

He also doubted that Leigh's husband considered her only a possession. He had noticed her expensive clothing and the exquisite pearl necklace. Somehow, he couldn't see a man spending so lavishly on something he considered a possession.

"And why did you marry him?" he asked bluntly.

Leigh was aghast. She couldn't possibly tell her father that she had wanted Matt, desired him just as much as he desired her. She hedged, saying, "For security, I suppose. Doesn't every woman want a man to take care of her, protect her?"

If any other woman had given that answer, Lord Stanford would have accepted it, but he couldn't see his strong-willed, independent daughter marrying for security and protection. He strongly suspected his daughter was in love with her husband and too proud to admit it.

He sat back and pondered over what his daughter had said. Just as he suspected, Leigh was troubled with her marriage. If she had told him her husband was cruel to her, mistreated her, he would have interfered in her behalf. But it seemed to him, the trouble was more a misunderstanding between the two. He thought it a shame her husband had to go back to sea so soon after their marriage. He sensed that all the young couple needed was a little time to work out their differences.

Chapter 21

"Goddamn you, Matt! Why do you have to be so stubborn and pigheaded? Of all the stupid, idiotic, crazy stunts you've pulled, this one takes the prize," Kelly yelled.

"I don't recall asking your opinion, Mr. Kelly. It's none of your goddamned business what I do! Now, get the hell out of my cabin!" Matt yelled back.

The argument had started when Matt returned to the *Avenger* in New Orleans and told Kelly of Leigh's flight and of his intention of going after her. It had continued the entire trip across the Gulf of Mexico and the broad Atlantic, Kelly trying to talk Matt out of it, Matt clinging stubbornly to his plan. Now, as the *Avenger* rocked in a craggy hidden cove off the coast of Cornwall, Kelly was getting frantic.

"Matt, for God's sake, be reasonable. The lass will come home. There's no need for you to go tearin' off after her like a ragin' bull. My God, man, what if the British catch you? Hell, they'll hang you!"

Matt glared at Kelly. "I told you this is none of your damned business. Butt out, mister!"

"Then, Godalmighty, let me go instead," Kelly persisted. "I know London just as well as you do. I'll find her and bring her back. At least, if I get caught, all they'd do is throw me in prison. Hell, I'd probably be exchanged in a couple of months."

"Goddammit! Leigh is my wife, and I'm going after her. If I'm willing to take the risk of getting my neck stretched, it's my business!" Matt's black eyes bored into the first mate, glittering dangerously. "Now, put the longboat over the side, Mr. Kelly."

"Matt, listen —"

"That was an order, Mr. Kelly," Matt interrupted in a low, steely voice.

Kelly looked at the determined look on Matt's face, his clenched jaw. He knew he had lost. "Aye, Cap'n," he replied tightly, then turned and stomped from the room, slamming the cabin door behind him.

A few minutes later, when Matt walked up to the rail, Kelly was staring at the darkened, deserted beach. "How are you goin' to get to London, anyway? Walk?" the first mate said in a disgusted voice.

Suddenly, the whole thing struck Matt as funny. And to think Kelly accused *him* of being stubborn. Hell, his first mate never gave up. He chuckled, saying, "I'm sure I can find someone to give me a ride to London. I understand these Cornishmen will do anything for the right amount of money. I'll also butter a few palms before I leave, so the villagers will be willing to turn a blind eye to the foreign ship anchored in their cove."

Kelly nodded sullenly.

Matt grinned and clapped the older man on the shoulder, saying, "Come on, Kelly. I don't look like the captain of an American privateer, do I? Who's going to recognize me?"

Kelly looked at Matt. In his cutaway coat, cravat, breeches, and high polished boots, he looked just like any British gentleman. And Kelly knew he could imitate the British accent perfectly. He glanced up at his golden hair, thinking, But dammit, I wish he had dyed that hair. "Aye, I suppose not," he admitted grudgingly.

"You'll keep a sharp eye out for British patrols?" Matt asked.

"Goddammit, if you don't trust me, why don't you stay here and let me go instead," he snapped.

Crafty, old sea dog, isn't he, Matt thought. He smiled, saying, "You know damned well I'd trust you with my life. You remember the signal?"

"Hell, yes, I remember! What do you think I am, a three year old? Watch at midnight for a flash of three lights. Wait five minutes, then another flash of three lights. Then I put down the longboat."

Matt started to climb over the rail. Straddling it, he said calmly, "Oh, by the way, Kelly. If I'm not back in a month, sail without me. You'll find papers in my cabin turning the captaincy and ownership of the *Avenger* over to you.'

Fear clutched at Kelly's heart. "Matt—"

"That's an order, Mr. Kelly," Matt interjected in a stern voice.

Before Kelly could object, Matt had scrambled down the Jacob's ladder to the longboat. Kelly watched as the boat was rowed to shore. He had a bad feeling about this. "Crazy, damn fool," he muttered, blinking back tears.

Three days later, Matt stood in front of John Rogers's house. Rogers, a fellow American, had been a lifelong friend and had acted as his father's shipping agent before the Blake's London shipping office had closed. He had lived in London for the past ten years, and if anyone could find the man Matt was looking for, he knew John could.

When Rogers opened the door and saw his old

friend standing there, his usually florid face turned pale. "My God, Matt! What in the hell are you doing here?" Before Matt could answer, he pulled him into the house, then quickly looked both ways down the street and shut the door.

Matt laughed, giving John a hearty slap on the back, saying, "That's a hell of a way to greet a friend you haven't seen in over three years."

"Christ, man! Are you crazy? What are you doing in England? Don't you know there's a warrant out for your arrest here?"

Matt's look sobered. "Yes, I know."

"Well, come on back to the library. I don't know about you, but I need a drink."

John and Matt walked down the hall to the back of the house. Matt towered over his husky friend by a good six inches. Looking down at him, Matt thought John hadn't changed since they had been boys together back in Charleston. He still had the same boyish, freckled face and errant lock of red hair over his forehead. He remembered the scrapes he and John had gotten into as boys. Matt had instigated them, but John had always been an eager partner.

After both men were seated with their drinks, John shook his head and said, "Godalmighty, Matt! You've pulled some crazy, reckless stunts in your life, but breaking into the Admiralty? What in the hell got into you? Spying is no laughing matter."

"I wasn't really spying, John. I'm not a spy for any country. You know that. I just stole some papers I was interested in."

"Well, I'm afraid the Admiralty doesn't look at it that way!" John snapped.

Matt frowned, saying, "I'm sorry, John. Did they give you a bad time?"

"No, not really. They came and searched the house. Asked a lot of questions and made a lot of threats. After a couple of weeks, I guess they finally realized I didn't know any more about it than they did." He grinned, his blue eyes twinkled. "Hell, Matt, it's not that I mind you getting me in that scrape. You've been doing that since we were boys. But you could have forewarned me. They came busting in on me and my lady friend that night. It was downright embarrassing!"

Matt chuckled and said, "Sorry, John, but I'm afraid I was in a bit of a hurry."

"I'll bet you were," John said wryly. He sat back and studied his friend, then said, "You know you've racked yourself up quite an impressive record." He chuckled, saying, "Did you know they call you the Sea Wolf?"

Matt nodded his head in acknowledgment, then sat forward, his look intent. "I didn't come here to discuss the war, John. I'm here on business, and I need your help."

The humor disappeared from John's eyes. "I didn't figure you dropped in for a social call," he said dryly. "What can I do for you?"

"I'm looking for a man. All I know is he's a lord and once had a signet ring with a gold falcon on a crimson background on it. Do you think you could find out his name and address for me?"

A lord? Was Matt planning another crazy stunt? "My God, Matt, you're not thinking of kidnapping a member of Parliament, are you?" John asked in a horrified voice.

Matt chuckled, saying, "No, John, all I want to do is ask the man some questions about—about a mutual acquaintance." Matt didn't want John to know

441

about Leigh. He was too proud to let his friend know his wife had run off to find a man she wasn't even sure existed.

"Who's the mutual acquaintance?" John asked curiously.

"Someone you don't know," Matt replied tightly.

John knew his friend well enough to know when to back off. He had heard that warning tone in Matt's voice often enough. "All right, Matt. I'll put one of my investigators on it right away. Shouldn't take long."

Matt rose from his chair, saying, "When should I check back with you?"

"Check back with me?" John asked in a surprised voice. "Where are you going?"

"I thought I'd find an inconspicuous hotel and get a room."

"Like hell you will! You'll stay here with me."

"I don't want to cause you any more trouble, John."

"Then stop arguing with me. Hell, Matt, I'd feel a lot safer with you staying here than wandering around out there." He grinned. "Knowing you, there's no telling what kind of rumpus you might get started."

"What about your servants?"

"The only servant I have is an old lady that comes in every afternoon to straighten up and cook my evening meal. There's a room up in the attic she doesn't even know about. You can hide up there when she's around."

Matt smiled, saying, "Thanks, John."

"Hell, stop acting like an ass! You know damned well you'd do the same for me."

In his usual, efficient manner, John had the information Matt wanted by the next night. He walked into the library where Matt was sitting, saying, "The man you're looking for is Lord Leigh Stanford, the Earl of Gloucester. He has a town house over on Cavendish Square." He handed Matt a piece of paper. "Here's the address."

"Leigh?" Matt asked in surprise. "Did you say his name was Leigh?"

"Yeah. What's the matter? Don't you think he's the man?"

"Oh, he's the man all right," Matt answered, recovering from his surprise that Leigh had been named after her father. "Did your man happen to say if Lord Stanford was in London or not?"

"He should be," John answered. "According to my investigator, he lives in London all the time. Seems he and his wife have been separated for twenty years or more."

Matt's golden eyebrows rose at this information, an expression John didn't miss. Damn, he sure wished he knew what Matt was up to. He said, "I have another piece of information you may be interested in. It seems the earl is one of America's staunchest supporters in Parliament. According to my man, he's fought against this war from the very beginning."

Matt wondered if the investigator had said anything about seeing a young lady with the earl. "Did he say anything else?"

"No, that's all," John replied. "Was there something else you wanted to know?"

"No, this is fine," Matt said, holding up the piece of paper. He turned, picked up his coat, and slipped it on.

"You're going right now?" John asked.

"Yes. My best chance of catching the earl at home with probably be in the evening," Matt replied, trying to hide his excitement.

"Will you be back?" John asked.

"Not if I find what I'm looking for." He frowned, saying, "If not, I'll need the services of your investigator again."

Matt headed for the door with John beside him. Then he turned and said, "Can I ask one more favor of you, John?"

"Of course. What is it?"

"Have you a map showing the coastline of England?"

"Yeah, right over here." John reached into his desk drawer and handed the map to Matt.

Matt spread the map out on the desk, studied it for a minute, and then pointed his finger, saying, "See this cove on the Cornish coast?"

John nodded.

"Well, that's where Kelly is waiting with the *Avenger*. If you should hear of me being arrested, would you go down there and tell Kelly I said to get the hell out of there? I told him if I wasn't back in a month to set sail. But knowing that stubborn old cuss, he'd sit there forever before he'd sail without me."

Fear for his friend's life welled up in John. Trying to appear calm, he said, "Sure thing, Matt. What's the signal?"

Matt explained the signal. Then the two men walked to the door. Matt offered his hand to John. His friend gripped it in a bone-crushing grasp, saying, "For God's sake, be careful, man."

Matt grinned, saying, "Stop worrying, John. You and Kelly are beginning to sound like two old women. I have no intention of getting caught. I have plans for the future."

An hour later, Lord Stanford was sitting in the library alone, Leigh having retired early that night. He heard the knock on the door and, curious to know who was calling at this time of the night, rose and peered down the darkened hallway.

As the butler opened the door, the earl saw Matt's imposing figure and heard his deep, authoritative voice ask, "Is Lord Stanford in?" No one had to tell the earl who this man was. His masculine, commanding presence filled the foyer. Without a doubt, Lord Stanford knew this was Leigh's privateer.

Hoping to avoid another hassle with his butler, Lord Stanford called, "Show the gentleman in, Masters."

Matt got a glimpse of the earl before he stepped back into the library. What he saw impressed him — a tall, dark-haired, distinguished-looking man, a man who radiated dignity.

When Matt stepped into the library, the earl smiled and offered his hand, saying, "Well, Captain Blake, I must admit I'm surprised to see you here."

Matt was stunned. "You know who I am?"

"Of course, I do. Leigh has told me all about you."

"Then she's here?" Matt asked in surprise.

The earl didn't miss the brief, but profound, look of relief on Matt's face. That look, plus the conviction that no man was foolish enough to risk prison for a mere possession, told him everything. The captain obviously loved his daughter. Had the man realized he had crossed that fine line between wanting and loving?

"Yes, Leigh's here," Lord Stanford answered. "She traced me down through my coat of arms, with the help of a barrister —" He chuckled — "and the help of a rather inventive tale." Lord Stanford smiled warmly, saying, "I feel I should apologize for my daughter, Captain. I'm sure you must have been frantic when you discovered she had left New Orleans and come to England, right in the middle of a war. I'm afraid Leigh is rather impetuous. But then, I suppose you know her well enough to know that already."

His daughter? Then he had acknowledged her. "She showed you the ring?" Matt asked.

"That wasn't necessary. I knew Leigh was my daughter the minute I saw her. She looks exactly like her mother, except for my eyes, of course." The earl turned, saying, "Have a seat, Captain. I'll fix us a drink."

Matt sat down, feeling stunned. Things were moving too fast for him. Not only had the earl apparently accepted Leigh with wide-open arms, but he acted as if he had known Matt all his life. He hadn't expected this warm a reception. In fact, Matt hadn't really expected to find Leigh at the earl's home.

"What will you have?" Lord Stanford asked. "I have Scotch, bourbon, and brandy."

"Scotch, sir," Matt replied.

As the earl handed Matt his drink, he said, "I can't begin to tell you what having Leigh here these last few weeks has meant to me. I didn't even know she existed. She's brought a new meaning to my life."

For the first time since his marriage, Matt feared losing Leigh. What if she chose to remain with her father, this man who obviously idolized her? His fear led to anger. "Why in the hell didn't she wait for me to get back from sea? I promised her I'd bring her here after the war."

Oh, an angry young man, the earl thought. Well, he couldn't blame him. Any man would be upset to come home and find the woman he loved was missing. "I'm sorry, I wasn't aware of that. But I think I can answer your question. It seems Leigh had a dream that I was dying. She panicked. And I don't think she really meant to upset you. She planned to be back in New Orleans before you returned from sea."

Leigh had planned to return before he got back from sea? Sneak in and out, hoping he would never know of her deception? But now that her father had accepted her so warmly, would she balk at returning with him? Goddammit, no! She was his wife! He said in an angry voice, "I've come to take my wife home!"

Lord Stanford acted as if he hadn't even noticed Matt's anger. He replied in a calm voice, "I assumed that's why you are here. As a matter of fact, I'm glad you came. Frankly, I didn't like the idea of her traveling back to America alone, and unfortunately, with Parliament due to reconvene in a few weeks, I'm not in the position where I can leave England right now, or I'd accompany her back myself."

Matt was becoming frustrated. He was finding it hard to stay angry. The earl's calm and agreeable manner was totally disarming him. For the first time, he realized the power of diplomacy.

Lord Stanford continued. "As much as I have come to love Leigh, I realize I can't keep her with me. Her place is with you, her husband."

My God, does he read minds too, Matt thought in dismay.

"I understand you're a privateer?"

Matt's head shot up. How much had Leigh told her father about him. Did the earl know he was the Sea Wolf, that he was wanted for spying? He was suddenly very aware of his position. He was the enemy. Was all this talk about being glad to see him and sending Leigh back with him just a play for time? Had the butler already gone for the authorities?

"Relax, Captain," the Earl said softly. "I wouldn't do anything so foolish as to turn you in. You're here for personal reasons, not political. Besides, you're my son-in-law, and I would never do that to Leigh. But I'm afraid I used the wrong term. I should have said 'sea captain'."

Then he didn't know about the spy charge, Matt thought. Surely, if he knew that, he would feel obligated to turn him in, regardless of his relationship to Leigh. But Matt was still wary. He said in a terse voice, "Yes, I'm a sea captain."

"I was wondering if you could give me a little advice?"

"Advice?" Matt asked in a surprised voice.

"Yes. I was thinking of investing in shipping after the war. Personally, I think overseas trade is going to mushroom. But frankly, I don't know a damn thing about ships and shipping. I must warn you, however, that I intend to invest in British shipping. As a member of Parliament, I feel that is only right. These long years of war have drained us. My country is going to need all the economic stimulus it can get. So maybe you'd prefer not to advise me, since I'd be a competitor."

Matt's admiration for the earl rose another notch. Not only was he a far-sighted businessman, but a true patriot. Most men would have put profits before country. He began to relax, saying, "I agree with you, sir. I, too, anticipate overseas trade will soar." He smiled, saying, "I think there'll be enough business to go around. What did you want to know?"

As Lord Stanford and Matt talked, the earl assessed the young captain. His whole purpose in starting the conversation had been to gain time to do just that. Matt was doing his own evaluation of the older man. Both were impressed. But Matt was anxious to see Leigh, and his eyes repeatedly drifted to the doorway.

Seeing his look, Lord Stanford said, "I'm ashamed of myself for taking up your time. Naturally, you're anxious to see Leigh."

"Yes, I am," Matt admitted, feeling his heart quicken in anticipation.

As they climbed the stairs, Matt wondered what Leigh had told her father about them. Obviously, she hadn't told him how he had forced her to be his mistress before their marriage. For this, Matt was grateful. The earl may be a lord and a gentleman, but Matt didn't doubt for one minute that he could be a formidable foe if the occasion warranted it. And apparently, she hadn't told her father about Matt bribing her to marry him, since the man knew nothing of Matt's promise until tonight. He got the impression that the earl thought everything was fine between them. Had Leigh painted a rosy picture of a perfect marriage to her father? And was he supposed to play the part of the loving, devoted husband? He would be damned if he would!

"When will you leave?" Lord Stanford asked.

"Tomorrow," Matt answered in a firm voice, his look determined.

"As much as I hate to see Leigh go, I agree. Coming to England at this time is risky business for you. The sooner you get out of the country the better."

Matt frowned, once again feeling as if he had been disarmed, but suddenly he became very angry at all Leigh had put him through.

449

They stopped before a door, and the earl knocked, calling softly, "Leigh, are you still awake?"

Leigh opened the door a minute later. At the first sight of Matt, her eyes lit up with happiness. "Matt!" Then she saw the furious look on his face and paled, saying, "What are you doing here?"

Lord Stanford saw the brief look of happiness in Leigh's eyes. That was enough for him. At that minute, he knew the two loved each other. Now it was time for them to discover it. "I'll be going now. I'll see you two in the morning."

Leigh watched her father walking away with dismay. Was he going to leave her to face Matt's anger alone?

Matt saw Leigh's look and his jealousy flared. "Aren't you going to invite me in, dear wife?" he said in a low, angry voice. "Or do you prefer your father's servants hear everything we have to say?"

Leigh backed away from the door. She had never seen Matt this furious. As soon as she shut the door, she said, "I can explain, Matt."

"I don't want to hear any of your damned explanations or lies," Matt snapped. He grabbed her arm roughly, saying, "And finding your father by yourself doesn't change anything. You're still my wife, dammit, and by God, you're coming back with me—tomorrow!"

She would have to leave tomorrow? But she was just getting to know her father. Why did it have to be so soon? And wouldn't her father be offended if they left so abruptly? "Matt, we can't leave tomorrow. My father would be hurt if we just rushed off."

The fact that she was worried about her father's feelings only fueled Matt's jealousy and anger. "Goddammit, woman, I said tomorrow!" Matt roared.

450

So the honeymoon was over, Leigh thought bitterly. He was back to being the arrogant tyrant. She jerked her arm away from Matt's grasp and walked to the closet. As she started to pull her trunk from it, Matt shouldered her aside to pick it up. "I can get it myself," she snapped.

"Like hell you will!" he snapped back. He lifted the heavy trunk and placed it in the middle of the bed. Then he slouched in an overstuffed chair and watched moodily as Leigh packed.

Matt was totally frustrated as a mixture of emotions boiled in him: anger, jealousy, fear, and desire. Dammit, why did she have to be so beautiful? Now, as the heat rose in him, he realized there was no way he could ever be around Leigh and ignore her. Despite everything, he still desired her. Well, dammit, she was his wife. It was her duty to submit, he rationalized. And by God, he would exercise his rights!

The minute she had closed the trunk, Matt lifted it from the bed. To Leigh's dismay, he started undressing. She stared at him.

"Well, what are you waiting for? Get your clothes off and get in bed," he said in a cold voice.

It was one thing for Matt to seduce her, overpower because he desired her. It was quite another to be taken in anger, as a form of punishment, or even worse, to be coldly used just to satisfy his lust. She would tolerate neither. She raised her chin and looked him straight in the eye, saying, "No."

"No?" Matt's black eyes glittered with anger. "Have you forgotten you're my wife? I have my rights!"

Leigh's own anger was rising. "Rights? What rights? The right to use your wife like a prostitute to satisfy your appetite? To use sex to punish her? No, Matt, I won't let you do it!"

451

"You'll do what I tell you to!" Matt yelled.

"You go to hell!" Leigh screamed back.

Matt jerked her into his arms as his mouth came down on hers in a possessive, brutal kiss. His hands bit into the soft, sensitive skin of her shoulders. Leigh struggled, kicking and clawing. Finally, she managed to bite his lip, tasting his blood before he jerked away.

The sudden pain brought Matt to his senses. He released her abruptly and stood back, wiping his mouth with his fingers. He stood looking down at the blood on them in disbelief.

Leigh glared at him, still panting from the struggle. "I'll go back with you, Matt. But if you ever try to force me again in anger, or use me like a *thing*—I'll kill you!"

Leigh turned and walked into the dressing room. When she returned much later, Matt was on the far side of the bed, his back to her. They slept that night on the same bed. As for the distance between them, the bed could have been as wide as the Atlantic Ocean.

When Lord Stanford saw Leigh and Matt the next morning, their faces drawn and pale, he knew, if anything, their relationship had deteriorated. And when it came time to say good-bye to his daughter and she threw herself in his arms, hugging him tightly and crying, he wondered if he shouldn't insist she stay with him. Then he looked over her shoulder and saw Matt's face. He had never seen such raw pain, such obvious misery and remorse. He knew then that whatever had happened the night before, Matt regretted it with all his soul. He remembered the pain he had felt when Meagan walked out of his life and couldn't submit the young man to that.

Gently, he pushed his daughter back, saying, "Now

452

now, my dear, this isn't the end of the world. As soon as the war has ended, I intend to come visit you."

"You do?" Leigh asked in a half-sob.

"Of course. You don't think now that I've found you, I'll let you walk out of my life, do you? I intend to keep close contact. And we'll both write often." The earl turned and looked directly at Matt, saying, "I assume, I'll be welcome?"

Matt sensed the earl was giving him a second chance. For this, he was grateful. He answered, "Of course, you're welcome, sir. Any time."

Watching their coach drive away a few minutes later, the earl thought, I can only pray to God I've done the right thing.

The drive down the coast toward the cove where the *Avenger* lay was a trial for both Leigh and Matt. They were both subdued, each staring out of his respective window, both lost in their dark thoughts.

Matt had never been so miserable in his life. Once his anger, fueled by his jealousy of Leigh's father, had cooled, he realized that he had almost totally wiped out any hope of winning Leigh's love. What had gotten into him? He had almost raped his own wife. Again, he had rushed in like a damned fool, letting his passion rule his reason, destroying everything he had so carefully built on their honeymoon, shattering all his hopes and dreams for their future. Would he ever be able to put the pieces together again?

Leigh's emotions were more tangled. She was torn at having to leave her father, and yet she had not wanted to be left behind by Matt, either. Strangely, even after what had happened last night, she wanted to be with him. If only his anger had been motivated by love, instead of possessiveness. And was this how their marriage would be for the rest of their lives?

Each ignoring the other? She longed to fill the gap, say let's start all over, but her pride and fear of rejection held her back.

Again, fate intervened. The coach hit a deep rut in the road, shearing off the back wheel, and as the coach lurched violently, Leigh was thrown against the wall, hitting her head against the hard wood and temporarily losing her consciousness.

Immediately, she was in Matt's arms, as he called frantically to her, "Leigh, Leigh!"

In a daze, she looked up to see Matt's pale, stricken face. She mumbled, "What happened?"

Matt hugged her fiercely, saying, "Oh, kitten, thank God, you're all right. I've never had such a fright in my life. If anything had happened to you . . ."

Leigh was as stunned by Matt's words and concern as she was by the blow to her head. Why, he does care about me, not just my body, but me, she thought with amazement. She pushed away, saying, "I'm all right, Matt. It just stunned me."

Matt's eyes searched her face. "You're sure?"

"I'm sure."

"Here, let me look at your head." He gently pushed the hair back from her forehead and saw the swollen, red spot. "My God, you could have been killed," he said in a shaky voice.

Leigh remembered that this was the man who had nerves made of steel, a man who could stand on the deck of a ship during a raging battle or a fierce storm and never lose control. And yet, he was obviously shaken to the core by her small accident. Could he possibly care that much?

At that minute, the door was jerked open by the coachman, saying, "I'm sorry, sir. The coach hit a rut and threw a wheel."

"You goddamned fool! My wife could have been killed!" Matt roared.

The coachman's eyes flew to Leigh, his look horrified. "No, I'm all right," Leigh assured him. She laid her hand on Matt's arm, trying to calm him, saying, "Matt, it was an accident. Coaches are always throwing wheels. You know that. Believe me, I'm fine. I just tapped my head."

Matt glared at the coachman. The man shuffled his feet nervously under that hot look. The coachman stammered, "I'll—I'll help you get out of the coach. Then—then I'll go back to the village we just passed through and borrow a coach to bring you back in." He looked at Matt and winced, fearing the angry man's reaction to his next words. "But I'm afraid I can't get this coach fixed before nightfall, sir. We'll have to wait till tomorrow to continue our trip."

"Tomorrow?" Matt yelled.

The poor coachman just about jumped out of his skin. "Aye, sir. I'm sorry, sir."

"Is there an inn in the village?" Leigh asked.

"Yes, madam," the coachman answered, watching Matt warily. "A nice inn. And I'll pay your bill, sir, since it was my fault," he added quickly.

Matt had recovered from his fright. "That won't be necessary. Just help us out of this damned thing."

An hour later, the coachman drove up before the inn in the borrowed coach and held the door as Matt and Leigh alighted. "I'll have the coach fixed and ready to leave first thing in the morning, sir," the coachman said.

Matt nodded curtly and guided Leigh into the inn. As they walked up the stairs to their room, Matt, still concerned for Leigh, didn't notice the two sailors

455

sitting in the adjoining pub and drinking ale.

One of the sailor's eyes widened in disbelief when he saw Matt. Then he nudged his companion, saying in a low voice, "Look at that man goin' up the stairs."

The second sailor looked up at Matt. His eyes narrowed in recognition.

"Do ye think it's him?" the first sailor asked.

The second sailor's look turned ugly. "Aye, 'tis him, all right. I'd not forget that bastard." He rose, saying, "Come on!"

His friend's face paled. "You're not thinkin' of takin' on the Sea Wolf by ourselves, are ye?"

"Hell no! You think I'm looney? No, we'll go to the Admiralty in London. Let that son-of-a-bitch find out what it's like to rot in prison for a change!"

When Leigh and Matt reached their room, Matt said, "Don't you think you should lie down and rest?"

Leigh had been pleased with Matt's concern at first, but after an hour of being treated as if she were a delicate piece of crystal, she was a little irritable. Why did he always carry everything to extremes? She bit her tongue to keep from snapping at him. "No, Matt. I'm fine, believe me."

She walked to the small mirror over the dresser and looked into it. She could barely see the small bruise on her forehead, but her hair looked a mess. She had better redo it before they went down to dinner, she thought, pulling the long pins from it.

Matt took off his coat and cravat, then tossed them on a chair. He peered out the window and saw the gray fog drifting in. "It's getting foggy," he commented.

Leigh laughed, saying, "That doesn't surprise me. It seems that England is either smoky or foggy." She sat on the stool before the dresser and began to brush her long hair, saying with a sigh, "I've missed New Orleans' fresh air and sunshine."

Matt was pleased with her statement. He turned; his breath caught at the lovely sight of Leigh brushing her long hair. He walked to the bed and sat, watching her with admiration.

Through the mirror, Leigh saw Matt's look. For a minute, she tensed. Then seeing he was content to just look, she relaxed and continued brushing. She wasn't aware when Matt rose and walked over to her.

"Let me," Matt said softly, holding his hand out for the brush.

Leigh's head jerked up in surprise. Without thinking, she handed the brush to him. She watched him warily through the mirror, but as he brushed her long hair, she began to relax, thinking that she loved to have someone brush her hair, a luxury she had never known until Grandmère's maid insisted on it. The feel of the brush sliding down her long tresses soothed her, leaving her feeling relaxed and drowsy.

After a few minutes, Matt said, "You know, the crew still argue over what color your hair is, brown with red highlights, or red with brown."

Leigh smiled. It had been a long time since she had thought of the crew. "How is everyone on the *Avenger*?"

"Fine."

"And Kelly?"

Matt chuckled. "Ornery and stubborn as ever."

"Cookie?"

"Same grouchy, old man." Matt grinned, saying, "You know, the man I assigned to help him complained so bitterly about the work, that now I have to rotate the crew through mess duty to keep peace. I think they've come to respect the old man more. Of

457

course, that doesn't stop them from making their smart remarks about his cooking."

Leigh smiled, knowing that Cookie would be hurt if the crew didn't harass him. "And Lucifer?"

Matt's look was thoughtful. "I think he's mad at me. Every time he comes in the cabin, he just sits and glares at me."

Leigh laughed, saying, "It must be your imagination."

"No, it's not my imagination. I think he blames me because you're not there. He misses you, Leigh."

Matt stopped brushing. Their eyes met and locked in the mirror. "We all miss you," he said softly.

Leigh's heart raced. She held her breath as Matt put the brush down and stepped around in front of her. Gently, he tilted her chin, looking deeply into her eyes, saying, "But I miss you the most."

Slowly, Matt lowered his head and kissed her lips, softly, almost tentatively. When she made no effort to resist, he pulled her to her feet and cupped her face in his big hands, kissing her forehead, her eyelids, her nose, her lips, in a flurry of soft, sensuous kisses. Matt raised his head and saw the frantic pulse beat in her throat. He frowned, then said, "Are you afraid of me?"

Leigh felt that familiar warm, weak feeling wash over her. "No."

His words came in a rush, as if the floodgates of his soul had been opened. "Oh, Leigh, can you forgive me? I was a damned fool last night. I feared you would want to stay with your father, and I was crazy with jealousy." He buried his face in her hair.

Leigh knew how much those words cost a man as proud as Matt. Her arms folded around his broad shoulders in forgiveness. He groaned and scooped her up, carrying her to the bed. When he reached it, he hesitated, looking down at her with questioning eyes.

"Yes, Matt," Leigh sighed.

Exaltation rose in Matt. He struggled to hold back his excitement and impatience. He laid her gently on the bed, lay himself beside her, and kissed the soft column of her neck and below her ear, whispering in a ragged voice, "Oh, kitten, I've missed you. God, how I've missed you!"

His fingers fumbled at the buttons on her bodice, trembling so badly he couldn't manipulate the tiny buttons. He groaned in frustration, "Damn!"

Leigh smiled and pushed his hands away, undoing the buttons while Matt watched with hushed expectancy. And when she was bared to him, his warm eyes feasted on her creamy breasts. He mumbled, "beautiful, so beautiful." His arms tightened convulsively around her as he buried his face in those soft mounds, kissing them softly, his tongue teasing and circling, until his mouth covered one throbbing peak. Leigh moaned, pulling him closer.

Leigh was on fire, her blood pounding in her ears. Suddenly, she couldn't stand their clothes between them. She tore at them with impatience, demanding, frenzied. And not until they were both stripped, warm skin pressed against warm skin, did she sigh in contentment.

They were both hungry for the feel and taste of each other as their hands and lips roved, exploring intimately, rediscovering each other's secrets, until they were both quivering in a heated pitch of excitement.

Trembling, Matt rose over her. His warm lips brushed her breasts and nibbled at her shoulder before they covered her lips in a deep, penetrating, searching kiss that seemed the suck the breath from her lungs. And when he plunged into her, fusing them together, filling her eager, throbbing body with his hard, pulsating maleness, Leigh clutched at him, crying out with sheer happiness.

Then he was moving inside her, at first slowly and sensuously, then boldly, urgently, masterfully, their bodies rocking in that ancient rhythm, their hearts pounding in unison, as he swept them upward, surging and dipping, until they were teetering at the zenith, trembling with anticipation. And with one powerful, deep thrust, they were soaring into space, hurled into oblivion as the stars and universe exploded around them and their souls splintered from their bodies and merged in a union of their own.

After they slowly drifted back to earth, Matt bathed her face in soft kisses, whispering husky endearments. Leigh sighed in deep contentment and buried her face in the crook of his tanned neck, kissing the damp skin there and tasting his saltiness. Locked in each other's arms, they drifted off to sleep.

Matt was the first to awaken. He looked about the darkened room and then gently untangled himself from Leigh's arms. He rose, lit the lamp, and looked down at his sleeping wife, thinking that he had never dreamed it possible to love someone so much. He bent and tenderly covered her with the sheet.

He walked to the window and looked out at the inky darkness. A quick, furtive movement caught his eye. Then he noticed another, and another. His senses alerted, he moved to the window at the opposite corner. Again, he saw the movements. As one of the figures dashed across the yard below him and briefly passed through a shaft of light from a window, Matt saw the uniform.

Alarmed, he raced to the door and, opening it just a crack, peered over the landing to the floor below him. Already, the marines were entering the inn. He closed the door and leaned against it. Trapped! He was trapped!

Had the earl betrayed him? Turned him in after all? No, he wouldn't do that. Besides, he had no way of knowing they had stopped at this inn because of the accident. It had to have been someone in the inn itself, someone who recognized him, for they had stopped nowhere else. He was a damned fool! Why hadn't he paid attention? His eyes flicked to Leigh on the bed. How ironic, he thought bitterly. Just when he thought he could win her love, after all. Now, time had run out for him.

His concern for Leigh overrode all else. Quickly, he searched his coat and found the pencil and paper. He sat on the bed and scribbled a name and address on it. Then he shook her, calling softly, "Leigh, wake up!"

Leigh awakened and looked about her in a daze, muttering, "What's wrong?"

"Listen to me," Matt said in an urgent voice. "The inn is surrounded. There's no way I can escape. I've been caught."

Caught? What was he talking about? Then suddenly, Leigh remembered that Matt was a wanted man in England. If caught, he would go to prison. No, not prison. He would be hanged! She refused to accept the horror of it. She sat up, saying, "Maybe, it's not you they are looking for, Matt. Maybe, there's a highwayman hiding in this inn."

"No, Leigh, those aren't constables out there. They're Royal Marines, the navy's soldiers."

"Maybe they're looking for a deserter."

"No, Leigh. There must be twenty marines out there. It's me they're after." He smiled and said in a bitter voice, "Well, sweet, it looks as though you're finally going to get rid of me."

Leigh gasped.

"Now, listen," Matt said in a firm voice. "They mustn't know you're my wife. Do you understand?"

"But they wouldn't do anything to me," Leigh objected.

"Have you forgotten that I'm the Sea Wolf and wanted for spying? They have a double reason for hating me. There's no telling what they'd do to you if they knew you were my wife."

"They wouldn't hurt a woman."

"Wouldn't they? Goddammit, Leigh, this is the British navy! Have you forgotten what they did to my brother?"

Leigh's eyes widened at Matt's words. If they would impress a twelve-year-old boy, commit him to virtual slavery, what would they do to the wife of the Sea Wolf, their hated nemesis and spy?

Matt took her hand and placed the piece of paper in it, saying, "This is the name and address of a friend of mine in London. Tell him I said to take you to Kelly. He knows where the *Avenger* is anchored. He'll get you out of the country."

Leigh was staring off into space, still lost in the horror of what was happening.

Matt shook her roughly, saying, "Dammit, Leigh, listen to me! We don't have much time. Did you hear what I said? Go to my friend in London. He'll help you."

"But I can't leave you!" Leigh cried.

"Goddammit, Leigh, this is no time to argue.

462

lease, do what I'm asking you," he said in an gonized voice.

Then Matt heard the creak of a floorboard outside heir room. He flipped the sheet back and covered Leigh's body with his own, smothering her cry of urprise with his mouth. A second later, the door rashed open and five marines rushed into the room.

Matt raised his head, bellowing, "What the hell?"

He turned his head and saw the marines, their nuskets pointed menacingly at him. Feigning surrise, he stared at them in open-mouthed disbelief.

A naval officer stepped into the room, smiling mugly. "So, Captain Blake, we meet again."

Matt's eyes narrowed in recognition. The same astard that had caught him in the Admiralty office hat night, he thought. He glared at the man, saying, Yes, we meet again." He glanced at the marines. But it seems the odds are a little more in your favor onight."

The officer smirked. "It seems we caught the Sea Wolf red-handed, men." Then glancing meanfully over Matt's naked body, he added, "Or rather, barerssed." The marines guffawed.

Matt clenched his teeth and climbed from the bed, quickly jerking the sheet up over Leigh's naked body. He reached for his breeches and pulled them on while he marines watched him warily.

The officer's eyes were locked on Leigh, who lay cowering, the sheet pulled up to her chin. "Who's the woman?" he snapped.

Matt shrugged, saying in an indifferent voice, "Who knows? I didn't bother to ask her name. She's ome doxy I picked up in London this morning."

"Is that true?" the officer asked Leigh.

Over the officer's shoulder, Leigh could see Matt's

dark eyes boring into her, as if willing her to confirm his lie. Her mind raced. If she told them the truth they might put her into prison. And if she was in prison, she couldn't help Matt.

"Answer me!" the officer demanded.

"Sure an' I'd not be knowin' the big bloke's a highwayman. Do ye think I'm daft?" Leigh answered

The British officer glared at her.

"Ye'll not be arrestin' me, too, will ye, constable? be just a poor workin' girl!" she wailed.

Constable, the officer thought with outrage. Why the stupid slut didn't even know the difference between a constable and an officer of the Royal Navy He looked at her more closely. Not bad looking for a doxy. In fact, he wouldn't mind sampling some of that himself. And he would be damned if he would pay for it!

Matt saw the look on the officer's face and knew what he was thinking. He ached to slam his fist in that leering bastard's face. Fear for what might happen to Leigh after he was taken away prompted him. He had to distract the officer. He laughed harshly, saying, "Forget it, fella. After she's had a real man, she wouldn't want your puny, little thing."

The officer whirled, his fist smashing into Matt's mouth. Matt staggered back from the blow, and Leigh screamed. The officer's eyes glittered with hatred. "You and I still have a personal debt to settle Captain." He turned, saying to the marines, "Tie him up. I want him delivered to my office before you take him to prison." Then he strode angrily from the room.

Two of the marines moved cautiously toward Matt "Wait a minute, gentlemen," Matt said in a casual voice. "You wouldn't want me to leave without pay-ing the little lady first, would you?"

The marines hesitated, then nodded, stepping back.

Matt pulled a bag of coins from his coat pocket and walked over to the bed, tossing the bag in Leigh's lap. He leaned forward, his eyes slowly drifting over her face, as if he was trying to memorize each feature. Then he looked at her with a look so intense, so profound, that Leigh knew he was telling her with his eyes what he didn't dare say with his lips—"I love you." Then he smiled and said softly, "Good-bye, kitten. You're one hell of a woman."

Leigh choked back a sob as tears stung her eyes.

Matt turned, slipped on his shirt and boots, and offered his wrists to one of the marines. As he tied them, the marine smirked and said, "She's a good piece, huh, Cap'n?"

Matt forced himself to grin and reply, "The best I've ever had. But let me warn you, she's expensive. Very expensive."

The marine's look turned to disappointment. Dammit, he wished marines weren't so poorly paid. He led Matt from the room, the four marines following, their muskets still aimed at the American.

Just before they pushed him through the door, Matt glanced back for one last look at the woman he loved.

Chapter 22

Long after Matt had been taken away, Leigh cried bitter tears. Why had it taken her so long to realize she was in love with him? Why had they both been so stubborn and held back that declaration? Now, it was too late.

She remembered the day on the *Avenger* that she had vowed revenge on Matt. It seemed her vow had come true. If she had waited until after the war for him to bring her to England, he would have never been captured. She had brought her husband to his death. To make matters worse, he thought she would be glad to be rid of him. He would die never knowing that she loved him.

No, I won't let him die, Leigh vowed fiercely. I won't let them hang him! Somehow, someway, I'll get him out of prison. No one, not even the high and mighty British navy, is going to take my love from me!

Early the next afternoon, Leigh was standing in front of the London address Matt had given her. As the door opened to her knock, Leigh saw the red-headed man standing before her. "Are you John Rogers?" she asked.

John was surprised to see the beautiful, young woman standing on his doorstep. His eyes slid over her admiringly. This is my lucky day, he thought. Smiling his most charming smile, he said, "Yes, I am. What can I do for you, miss?"

Why, he's flirting with me, Leigh realized with outrage. She bristled and snapped, "I'm not a miss! I'm *Mrs.* Matthew Blake."

John frowned. What in the hell was going on here? He knew Matt wasn't married.

"Matt told me to come to you," Leigh said.

Was this some kind of a trick? Did the Admiralty know Matt was in London and was trying to trick him into betraying him? "I'm afraid I don't know any Matthew Blake," John said coldly.

"Don't know him?" Leigh said in a shocked voice. "But he told me you'd help me."

"You must be mistaken."

"I couldn't be mistaken! He wrote your name and address down himself." Leigh fumbled in her reticule and pulled out the scrap of paper Matt had given her. She handed it to John, saying, "He told me you would take me to the *Avenger*."

John looked down at the paper. That was Matt's handwriting all right, he thought. He would know that scrawl anywhere. He frowned in puzzlement.

"Please, you've got to help me. Matt has been arrested!" Leigh cried in an agonized voice.

John's head snapped up. "Arrested? When?"

"Last night," Leigh replied, fighting back fresh tears. "They surrounded the inn we were staying at. Before Matt was taken away, he told me—"

Leigh wasn't able to finish her sentence. John's hand flew out and jerked her into the house. Slamming the door, he glared down at her, saying, "By God, this had better not be a trick."

468

"Trick? What makes you think it's a trick?"

"Because Matthew Blake isn't married." John snapped.

"Yes, he is. We were married last summer in New Orleans."

"Then why didn't he tell me about it a few days ago when he was here?" John asked in a suspicious voice.

Matt was here a few days ago? Did this man help him find her father? She imagined the reason Matt didn't tell his friend of his marriage was because he was ashamed to admit he had a wife foolish enough to go searching halfway across the world for a man whose name she didn't even know. But Leigh didn't have time to explain everything now. "Please, you've got to believe me," she pleaded.

"If you got married in New Orleans, then you should know the name of his uncle's plantation." He leaned forward, menacingly, saying, "Let's see you answer that one!"

Leigh beamed. "His uncle's plantation is named Twelve Oaks."

John drew back, a surprised look on his face.

Leigh's eyes glittered as she continued, "He has another uncle in New Orleans who owns a shipping office. His town house is in the Vieux Carré. He has a French grandmother who lives in Martinique, except she was in New Orleans when we were there. His first mate's name is Kelly and he has a black cat—"

"All right!" John interjected. "I believe you."

Leigh sighed in relief, "Oh, thank God." She rushed on, saying, "Mr. Rogers, you've got to take me to the *Avenger* right away. I've got to get to Kelly and the crew. They won't let them hang Matt. They'll come and break him out of prison. I know they will."

Break him out of prison? Hell, this woman was even more reckless than Matt! "Whoa, lady, slow

469

down," John said. "In the first place, just how far do you think two hundred American sailors would get before someone got suspicious? In the second place, the Admiralty will be expecting just some crazy stunt like that and be waiting for them. At the first sign of an attack, they'd probably shoot Matt."

Shoot Matt? Leigh turned pale; her knees buckled.

John caught her before she fell, supporting her, saying, "I'm sorry, I didn't mean to frighten you. Here, come into the library and sit down."

After Leigh was seated in a chair, John poured two brandies and handed one to her. Leigh sipped at it, but even the warm liquor couldn't melt the icy knot of fear in her stomach.

John paced the floor thoughtfully, then turned, saying, "No, the best way is to work from the inside out."

"What do you mean?"

"Bribe the guards to let Matt escape."

"Can you do that?" Leigh asked in surprise.

"Mrs. Blake, you can do anything if you have enough money." He turned and looked at her, saying, "How much do you have?"

"Money?"

John nodded.

Leigh frowned in concentration. "Well, I have about four hundred pounds and Matt gave me a purse before they took him away that had another three hundred in it."

John rubbed his chin thoughtfully. "I could probably scrape up another thousand on such short notice. But I don't think seventeen hundred pounds is going to be enough."

"I have a valuable pearl necklace I could sell."

John shook his head, saying, "I doubt it. The economy in England is pretty bad right now. No one buying jewels. Even if you could sell it, you'd only get a fraction of what it's worth."

Leigh was becoming frightened again. "How much do you think we'll need?"

"I don't know for sure. I've never bribed anyone out of prison before."

"You've never done this before?" Leigh asked in horror. "Then how do you know who to contact?"

"Don't worry about that," John said calmly. "I have an investigator who can find out the right contacts. He knows all kinds of underworld characters."

"Do you really think it would take more than seventeen hundred pounds?"

"Yes, I do. We not only have to bribe the guards, but pay silence money to all the contacts in between. And I'd imagine their price will be high. After all, Matt is no small fish. I'll put my investigator on it right away. We should know the exact amount by tomorrow. By the way, what prison did they take Matt to?"

Leigh was stunned by the question. She had never thought to ask. "I don't know," she answered in dismay.

"Don't worry about it," John assured her. "My investigator will find that out, too. But I think we'd better have that money raised by tomorrow morning. If I know the Admiralty, they're not going to waste any time getting that noose around Matt's neck. He's escaped them too many times in the past."

"How much time do you think we have?" Leigh asked in a weak voice.

"Not over forty-eight hours, I'd guess."

Matt could be dead in two days? For the first time in her life, Leigh felt faint.

"I have some friends I might be able to borrow the

471

money from," John said.

A sudden thought occurred to Leigh. "No, I thin
I can raise the difference. I know someone who'
loan me the money."

"Who?" John asked, curious.

"I'd rather not say," Leigh answered tightly.

"Can he be trusted to keep his mouth shut?"

"Yes, he can be trusted," Leigh answered confi
dently.

John shrugged. "Just so we have it by morning.

"I'll have it here by morning," Leigh assured him

After Leigh had left, John stood, wondering whom
she planned to borrow the money from. Whoever i
was, he hoped Matt's wife was correct about his bein
trusted to keep his mouth shut. Otherwise, he and sh
would both land up in prison. Was she going to th
mutual acquaintance Matt had mentioned? And wh
hadn't Matt told him he was married? And where di
the earl fit into all this? Dammit, he sure wished h
knew what was going on. He would go crazy trying t
figure this one out!

Lord Stanford was shocked when his daughte
walked into his library. She looked terrible. Had sh
left her husband after all?

Before he could say a thing, Leigh threw herself i
his arms, crying, "Oh, Father, you've got to help me!

"Yes, yes, of course, I will," the earl answered
smoothing her hair. He lifted her tear-streaked face
saying, "But what in the world happened, child?"

"Matt has been arrested," Leigh sobbed.

"Arrested? When? Where?"

"Last night, at the inn where we were staying
Someone must have recognized him and went to th
Admiralty. They took him away!"

"Here, here, child," he said in a soothing voice
"It's not all that bad. I'm sure I can pull some string

472

and have him exchanged with the next group of prisoners of war. Why, he'll probably be out in a few months."

"They're going to hang him!" Leigh cried.

"No, child. We don't hang prisoners of war," Lord Stanford said patiently.

"You don't understand. They arrested him for spying!"

The earl's face blanched. "Spying? What in God's name are you talking about?"

Leigh forced herself to remain calm. "I'm afraid I haven't told you everything about Matt, Father. Have you ever heard of the Sea Wolf?"

The earl's dark eyebrows rose. "The most notorious American privateer of the war? The man who has taken more British prizes than any other? Yes, I've heard of him. But what does he have to do with this?"

"Matt is the Sea Wolf."

Lord Stanford was stunned speechless.

Leigh continued, saying, "At the beginning of the war, Matt broke into the Admiralty building and stole some important papers, information about convoys' supplying Wellington. That's why the Admiralty wants him for spying."

Her father frowned. "I know nothing about a break-in at the Admiralty offices, or any theft of papers. Are you sure of this?"

"Yes. The navy kept it quiet. They didn't want anyone to know they had been so careless."

Lord Stanford scowled. It was one thing to keep information from the public in time of war to prevent panic. It was quite another to withhold information from the government.

"But, Father, Matt's not a spy. He's not an agent for any government. He did it for personal reasons, to get revenge on the British navy. He may be a thief,

473

but he's not a spy."

"Personal revenge on the navy?"

"Yes." Leigh's voice was bitter. "Several years be
fore the war, Matt's younger brother, Mark, wa
impressed by the British navy. He was only twelv
years old, a mere boy. Matt tried to stop them bu
they shot him and he almost died. Matt's father cam
to England to try to get the boy released, but th
Admiralty denied the whole thing. Matt thinks Marl
is dead by now, and he blames himself. He swore t
get revenge on the British navy. That's why Matt ha
been such an extraordinarily successful privateer. Thi
war is his means of getting personal revenge."

"You say the boy was just twelve? The navy tool
him by force?" Lord Stanford said in an outrage
voice. "Who did this? Do you know the name of th
officer?"

Leigh was taken aback by the question. Sh
searched her memory. Then she remembered wha
Matt had told her. "Yes, Matt said the officer's nam
was Benjamin Coke."

The earl carefully filed the name away in his head

But Leigh's concern was for her husband. "Oh
Father, I can't let them hang Matt! It's all my fault
He wouldn't have come to England if it hadn't beer
for me." She broke into tears, sobbing, "I can't le
them hang him. I love him."

The earl thought it a shame that it took somethin
this tragic to bring her to her senses. He took her ir
his arms and comforted her while she cried, wonder
ing what he could do to get Matt out of this mess

Finally, Leigh looked up and said, "Father, I nee
money. Will you loan it to me?"

"Money?"

"Yes. Matt has a friend that may be able to brib
Matt out of prison. But his friend says it will take

lot of money, and we don't have enough."

Lord Stanford frowned. Loaning Leigh money to help a man accused of spying escape from prison bordered on treason. Surely, there must be something he could do within the limits of the law. "Leigh, let me go to the Admiralty and find out what's going on. After all, I do have a little influence. Perhaps, I can arrange a pardon, or perhaps, get the charge changed to theft."

"But if you can't—"

"Please, my dear," Lord Stanford interjected. "Give me a chance, at least. I'll know by nightfall where we stand."

There was nothing Leigh could say. She nodded.

"You look exhausted, child. Go upstairs and rest until I come back."

Leigh was exhausted. She fell asleep the minute her head hit the pillow. When she awakened, it was dark, and her father had still not returned. She paced her room anxiously long into the night.

When her father finally returned and entered her room, an angry look on his face, Leigh cried, "What did you find out?"

"They have him all right. He's being held in the Tower of London. And they've already held the trial." He scoffed, saying in a bitter voice, "If you can call that travesty a trial. It was a farce. My God, he didn't even have a counselor! And they tried him in an Admiralty court!" He paced angrily, saying, "The whole damned thing is totally illegal. Out-and-out murder, as far as I'm concerned. The goddamned bastards! Who in hell do they think they are? We have a judicial system in this country, and it's not the Admiralty!"

Leigh was shocked. She had never seen her father angry, much less furious. And they had already held the trial! "When will he be sentenced?" she asked in a trembling voice.

The earl looked at his daughter's pale face and trembling lips. He instantly regretted his loss of control. As justified as his anger was, it certainly wasn't helping her. He fought his anger down and said gently, "I'm afraid they've already sentenced him."

"When . . . when . . ." Leigh couldn't finish the question.

"He's to be hanged at dawn the day after tomorrow. But don't give up yet, child. How much money did you say you needed?"

"Then you will help us?"

He sighed deeply and sat down in a chair opposite her. "If there was any other way I could get Matt freed, I would. I would have preferred doing it within the law. If Parliament were in session, I could demand an immediate investigation. But they aren't. I tried to see the Prime Minister, but he's gone to his country estate for a few days. The same for the Prince Regent. I couldn't even track down the Lord of the Admiralty, not that he and I are friends. As for the king, that poor old man doesn't even know his own name. So with the Admiralty pushing it through so fast, I have no other choice. I won't stand by and watch a man be murdered — any man! And until that man has had a fair trial, that's what I consider it."

"But won't the Admiralty suspect your involvement in Matt's escape?"

"Undoubtedly, they will. Particularly after I vented my wrath so openly. But they won't be able to prove a thing. Fortunately, I keep large sums of money on hand. There won't be any incriminating, large bank withdrawal to explain. Matt's friend won't know where you got the money from, and even if he did, I doubt that any accusations would come from that end. I'm sure he's protecting himself as well. And if he's working through underworld channels, as I suspect he is, the Admiralty will find it impossible to track the money back to either of us. No, Leigh, the Admiralty may strongly suspect my involvement in Matt's escape, but they won't accuse a member of Parliament without proof. Not even they would dare that."

The next morning, Leigh was back at John's house with the money. As she handed it to him, she said, "If it's not enough, I can get more."

John's eyebrows rose, but he said nothing.

Because Leigh did not want John to know of her father's involvement, she waited at John's house for news of the developments. The day was agony for her as hour after hour passed by and John didn't return.

When he finally walked in that evening, he looked haggard. He sat wearily on a chair, saying, "It's all been arranged."

Leigh sat down across from him, weak with relief. "When?"

"Tomorrow morning at three o'clock."

"Isn't that cutting it awfully close? He's to be hanged at dawn," she said apprehensively.

"I know. Personally, I'd prefer earlier. That will only leave him a two-hour headstart. But the guards specified the time. They said the prison would be its quietest at that time of the morning, and therefore, the least likely time for discovery."

"Where do we meet him?"

John's eyebrows rose. "We?"

Leigh raised her chin stubbornly, saying, "Yes. I'm going with you."

John took one look at the determined look on her face and decided not to argue. "They'll deliver him to

477

the street on the side of the fortress that faces the Thames, the fourth gate down. There'll be a coach waiting right down the street. The coachman is in on it, too. He'll drive you and Matt to the Cornish coast. That is all part of the arrangements."

"When do we leave?"

"About two in the morning. We want to be sure and be there in time."

Leigh rose, saying, "Then I'll be here at one-thirty."

"I can pick you up," John replied.

"No, that won't be necessary," Leigh answered firmly.

After Leigh had left, John wondered who had loaned her the money. Whoever it was, she was protecting him. Well, the less he knew, the better, he decided.

When the guard came and shook Matt in the middle of the night, with a curt, "Come on, mister," Matt assumed he was being taken for one last beating before the hanging. He almost welcomed the distraction. Anything was better than the torment he had been going through, lying in the dark cell and thinking of Leigh.

As the guard led Matt down the damp limestone stairs and through the maze of darkened corridors, Matt noticed the absence of guards. Where were they tonight, he wondered. Off sleeping some place or playing cards? When the guard turned down a new corridor, Matt became suspicious. This wasn't the way to the room where they had taken him to beat him earlier. What was going on?

As the guard bent and unlocked the manacles at Matt's ankles and then at his wrists, Matt knew something was up. Had they gotten worried about that farce of a trial? Yes, he decided, that must be it. It would be much safer to have him shot while trying to escape. That way, there could be no backlash if an investigation was ever made into his death.

The guard opened the gate and, without a word, shoved Matt into the street outside. Matt stumbled on the wet, slippery cobblestones, then straightened, expecting to feel the musket ball slamming into his body. When nothing happened, he frowned. What did they want him to do, run? Well, he would be damned if he would give them the satisfaction of shooting him in the back!

"Matt, over here," a husky voice whispered urgently.

Matt's golden head shot up. Hell, that sounded like John's voice. He turned his head in the direction the voice had come from and squinted into the fog rolling off the river. A shadowy figure stood in a darkened niche of the old fortress.

"What in the hell's the matter with you, man?" the voice asked.

That *was* John's voice. My God, he was free! He had never expected that. In a daze, he walked toward his friend.

When the shadowy figure turned into two, Matt gasped, "Leigh! What in hell are you doing here?"

Leigh choked back tears of happiness. "Getting my husband out of jail," she answered in a shaky voice.

"You arranged this?" he asked in an incredulous voice.

"No, John arranged it," Leigh answered, wishing he would stop asking questions and kiss her.

"That's right, Matt," John said with a big grin, "but your wife raised the money for the bribes. Dammit, man, it's good to see you!" he said, clapping him heartily on the back.

Matt winced and groaned in pain.

"What's wrong, Matt?" Leigh asked anxiously. She stepped closer, peering at his face, then gasped. One eye was black and blue, almost swollen shut. His face was covered with bruises and abrasions, his lips puffy, the lower lacerated at one side. "My God, they beat you!"

"Yeah, the bastards had to get their last licks in," Matt answered bitterly.

"How dare they! I'll kill them!" Leigh cried.

"Shh, sweet," Matt said softly. "I'm all right. I've taken worse beatings than this in tavern brawls."

"It was that damned officer that arrested you, wasn't it?" Leigh raged. "I hate him! I'll kill him!"

"Leigh, why are you so upset?" Matt asked. "I told you, I'm all right."

"Why am I so upset?" Leigh sobbed. "Because they beat the man I love, that's why!"

Matt wondered if the beatings had damaged his hearing. He lifted Leigh's chin and saw the tears streaming down her cheeks. His breath caught. "What did you say?" he asked in a husky whisper.

"I said I love you, you big ape!" Leigh sobbed.

"Oh, God, kitten," Matt moaned as he pulled her into his arms. His lips covered hers in a warm kiss. It hurt like hell, but he wasn't going to let that stop him.

When the kiss became more impassioned and Matt pulled Leigh even closer, John looked about nervously. "Hey, break it up, you two. Have you forgotten where we are? You're not out of this mess yet."

Matt broke the kiss and grinned at him over Leigh's shoulder. "All right, boss-man. What's next on the agenda?"

"There's a coach right down the street," John answered. "It will take you to the *Avenger*."

Matt frowned, saying, "Aren't you going with us?"

"No."

"But the Admiralty will suspect you right off. They'll come down hard on you, John."

"They haven't got a damned bit of proof," John answered. "And I've got an alibi for tonight."

"An alibi?"

John glanced at Leigh and flushed, saying, "There's a little lady that's willing to swear I was with her all night. I even made a point of making sure there are plenty of witnesses that saw me go to her room last night and won't see me come back out until late this morning."

"Come out late this morning?" Matt asked.

John grinned, looking like a mischievous, little boy. "I crawled out through the window." Then he frowned, saying, "I only hope I can crawl back in. You know, Matt, you've got to stop getting me into these scrapes." He patted the small paunch on his stomach. "I'm getting too old for this foolishness."

Matt and Leigh laughed. John grinned and clasped Matt's hand, saying, "Good luck, Matt. See if you can't stay out of trouble for a while." He glanced at Leigh, saying, "And congratulations on your marriage. You're a very lucky man to have Leigh."

"Thanks, John, for everything," Matt answered.

John nodded and turned, disappearing into the fog. As he walked away, he thought, So her name is Leigh? The same as the earl's. Could she be his daughter? And was he the man she had borrowed the money from for the bribes? Then he scoffed at himself, thinking, No, he couldn't be the man. Not an earl. Not a member of Parliament. It was just a coincidence.

As Leigh and Matt hurried toward the coach at the end of the street, another coach turned the corner and drove toward them. Matt pulled Leigh against the wall of the fortress. They stood pressed against the damp stone, holding their breath, hoping the thick fog and shadows would conceal them.

The coach stopped right beside them. "Leigh?" Lord Stanford's voice called from the window.

Matt stood in stunned silence. Leigh sighed in relief and rushed to the coach, saying, "What are you doing here, Father?"

He opened the coach door, saying, "Get in, both of you. You'll have a much better chance of getting through the navy's roadblocks in this coach. The marines may stop us, but I don't think they'll search inside."

"But, Father, you said yourself the Admiralty might suspect you," Leigh objected. "They may watch for your coach."

The earl grinned. "I know they might put out word to watch for my coach, my dear. But look at the door."

Leigh glanced down at the door. She had never seen the coat of arms on it in her life. This wasn't her father's coach.

Lord Stanford laughed at his daughter's stunned look. "I borrowed this coach from a good friend. I told him mine was broken down and I needed to visit one of my estates for a few days. I don't think the marines are going to search the coach of every member of the House of Lords. If they did, can't you just imagine the lords' outrage at having their coaches searched for an American spy?"

Leigh laughed, but Matt frowned, saying, "Thank you, sir, but I don't want to get you involved in this mess."

"He's already involved, Matt," Leigh said. "What did you think I meant when I said the Admiralty might suspect him? And where do you think I got the noney to pay the bribes?"

Matt looked at her in shock.

"And he's right about the coach," Leigh continued.
As soon as they discover your escape, they'll be after
s. Oh, please, darling, don't argue."

"What about him?" Matt asked, nodding to the
rl's coachman. "Can you trust him?"

"Tom is my coachman," Stanford answered. "He's
een in my service for thirty years, and I'd trust him
ith my life."

Matt was still reluctant, but Leigh urged him into
e coach. The earl called to his coachman, "Tom, go
ll that coachman up there he won't be needed after
ll."

A few minutes later, the other coach rumbled off.
s it disappeared, the earl said, "If you two don't
ind, I think I'll join Tom up on top for a while. This
g is giving me a chill in my bones, and if I know
om, he's got a bit of something up there to warm me
p."

Neither objected. They knew he was giving them
me time to themselves. Before he stepped down
om the coach, Lord Stanford asked Matt, "Which
rection should I tell my coachman to take?"

"Toward the Cornish coast," Matt answered.

The earl smiled and said ruefully, "I should have
nown."

After the coach pulled away, Matt drew Leigh into
is arms and carefully laid her head on his shoulder.
eigh snuggled up to him. They sat in silence,
rapped in a warm haze of happiness. Then Matt
ulled her tighter and groaned in her ear, "What a
irty trick."

"What?" Leigh asked.

He managed a lopsided grin. "I've got the perfect
pportunity to make love to you, and I'm too damned

sore to even move."

"Oh, Matt," Leigh cried, pulling away. "I'm sorry, completely forgot about your being hurt."

"Come back here," Matt said in a husky voice. " may be too sore to make love to you, but I'm damned sure going to hold you."

Leigh settled back in, saying, "We'll have lots o time to make love."

Matt chuckled, saying, "Forever won't be lon; enough for me." Then he hugged her tightly, saying "Oh, kitten, I love you so much. Didn't you guess?'

"I think I was too busy trying to keep you from knowing I loved you." She sighed, saying, "We'v both been too stubborn and proud."

A minute later, Matt chuckled again. "Now what' so funny?" Leigh asked.

"With two stubborn parents like us, I hate to thin of what our children are going to be like."

Leigh smiled. "They'll be wonderful," she said Just like you, she thought as she dozed off.

The earl climbed back into the coach at dawn and for the first time, got a good look at Matt's face. "M God! What happened?"

"They beat him!" Leigh said angrily.

"But why?"

Matt shrugged. "For old time's sake, I guess."

The earl had heard rumors of the navy beatin; their prisoners. But this was the first time he ha actually seen the results of such a beating. He wa shocked. The unnecessary brutality fueled his ange at the Admiralty even more. He vowed he would ge an investigation into the navy's sadistic actions if was the last thing he did.

The coach hit a bump in the road, and Mat winced, holding his side. The earl frowned and said "Are you injured there, too?"

Matt nodded. "One of them kicked me a couple of times. I think I might have a few cracked ribs."

"Why didn't you tell me that?" Leigh demanded.

Matt shrugged again.

Leigh glared at him, then said, "Father, will you help him get that shirt off?"

As her father helped Matt remove his bloody shirt, Leigh shimmied out of one of her petticoats and tore it into strips. Then she and her father bound Matt's chest tightly. As they wrapped the bandages around him, the earl noticed the scar on Matt's chest. His anger flared again.

When they had finished, Leigh asked, "How does it feel?"

"I can't breathe, but it feels wonderful," Matt answered.

They stopped early that morning at an inn. While Matt crouched on the floor, hidden beneath Leigh's voluminous skirts, the coachman went in for a picnic basket and a bucket of iced champagne. The ice went on Matt's swollen face; the champagne was used to cleanse his cuts. They all laughed about the rumor the innkeeper was probably already spreading about the drunken nobleman, who stopped and bought champagne at eight o'clock in the morning.

Three times that day, they were stopped at roadblocks. Each time, Matt crouched on the floor, hidden under Leigh's spread-out skirts. True to her father's prediction, as soon as the marines saw the coat of arms on the coach's door, they were waved through.

The last time Matt came out from under Leigh's skirts, he grinned devilishly and whispered in her ear, "I think I'm getting well, kitten. If I have to go down there one more time, I'm going to ravish you right here, father or no father."

Leigh blushed furiously and hoped that her fath[er] hadn't heard her husband's outrageous remark.

It was dark the next day when their coach rumbl[ed] past the small Cornish village. They were all elate[d] knowing that Matt's escape was virtually secur[e]. After the coach had stopped on the steep cliff abo[ve] the cove where the *Avenger* was anchored, Ma[tt] looked down at the earl's expensive clothing and fi[ne] boots, saying, "You're sure you want to come dow[n] sir? It's going to be a rough climb down and an ev[en] worse climb back up."

"I'm going to see this through to the very end," t[he] earl answered. Then he laughed, saying, "I haven['t] had this much excitement in my entire life."

It was a long, tedious climb down the jagged, roc[k] cliff. When they reached the beach, Matt's ey[es] searched the cove. In the inky darkness, he could s[ee] no sign of the *Avenger*. A new fear rose in him. Wh[at] if they had been sighted and captured while he w[as] gone?

"Are you sure they're out there?" Leigh ask[ed] apprehensively.

"We'll find out in another hour," Matt answere[d] trying to hide his own anxiety.

It was cold on the open beach with the wi[nd] coming off the water. They huddled behind an ou[t] crop of big rocks, shivering, wishing that they cou[ld] build a fire, but knowing that they didn't dare.

When it was almost midnight, Matt picked up t[he] coach lantern and said to Leigh's father, "I hate to [do] this, sir, but may I borrow your coat?"

Lord Stanford nodded and slipped it off. Ma[tt] dropped the coat over the lantern while he lit it an[d] then climbed to the top of the rock with the lante[rn] still covered. "Tell me when it's midnight," he said [to] Lord Stanford.

When the earl called the time, Matt lifted the coat ree times, flashing three quick lights. Five minutes ter, he repeated the signal. Then he blew out the ntern and jumped down from the rocks, saying, Now, we wait."

The next fifteen minutes seemed like a lifetime as e three stood on the beach and strained their eyes to the darkness, the cold wind whipping their othes around them. Matt, with his keen eyesight, as the first to spy the longboat. "There she is!" he ied.

Leigh couldn't see a thing. "Are you sure?"

Matt laughed, saying, "I'd know Kelly's ugly mug ywhere."

Leigh and Matt turned to tell Lord Stanford good-e. He smiled, saying, "I've been saving this as a st-minute surprise. Call it a belated wedding esent, if you like. I went back to the Admiralty uilding and made a few inquiries. Your brother is ive, Matt. He's on a frigate patrolling the Indian cean. His ship is due back in England in three onths. I can guarantee he'll be released."

Matt could hardly believe his ears. "How in the orld did you manage that, sir? My father used all s influence and didn't get anywhere."

"While I have no influence with the Admiralty, yself, I do have acquaintances who do," the earl nswered. "Several of these men owed me debts or vors I've never bothered to collect on — until all this me up. I don't think I could have gotten you leased, Matt, without going to higher authorities, t I was able to exert enough pressure to get your other released. I'll personally see that he gets back fely to you."

Matt blinked at the sudden moisture filling his es. "I don't know what I can say, sir. What can I ever do to repay you for all you've done?"

"There is something you can do," the earl sa
softly.

"What, sir?"

Lord Stanford looked at Leigh warmly, sayin
"Take care of my daughter. Love her totally, cor
pletely, for the rest of your life. Love her as I nev
had the chance to love her mother."

Matt pulled Leigh closer to his side and look
down at her lovingly. "You don't have to ask tha
sir." Smiling, he turned back to the earl, saying, "I'
turning in the *Avenger*'s letter of marque as soon a;
reach New Orleans. My personal war is over. If I
any more fighting in this war, I'll join the navy."

"I doubt if the war will last much longer," the e;
replied. "Another month or two, at the most."

"And you'll still come to visit?" Leigh asked ar
iously.

"Yes, as soon as the war has ended and I've gott
my affairs straightened out. Perhaps, Matt's broth
and I will be able to make the trip together."

The good-byes were quickly said. Then Matt a;
Leigh ran down the beach, hand in hand, to t
approaching longboat. As the boat was beache
Kelly jumped from it and hugged them both fierce
saying, "God, am I glad to see you two." He glanc
up and saw Lord Stanford standing farther up t
beach. "Who's he?" he asked Matt.

"A very good friend. Leigh's father," Matt a;
swered. "I'll tell you about it later. Right now, let's {
the hell out of here!"

Later, as the *Avenger* skimmed across the wave
running before the wind, her sails snapping and h
rigging humming, Leigh and Matt stood on the dec
watching the English coastline disappear. Ma
slipped his arm around his wife, pulling her ba

488

against him. Leigh laid her head back against his broad shoulder and, for a minute, stood luxuriating in the feel of being in the warm, protective circle of his arms.

Then she turned and looked up at him, a mischievous glint in her eyes, an impish smile on her face. "Is it true what you told my father? You'll give up your pirating ways?"

"Privateering, kitten," Matt corrected her for the hundredth time. "Yes, it's true. The *Avenger* has taken her last prize." Then he smiled, saying, "But I really can't regret my privateering. If I hadn't done it, I would have never captured my most precious prize."

"Oh? And which prize was that?" Leigh asked curiously.

Matt's dark eyes caressed her face warmly, lovingly, before he answered, "You, my love."

Epilogue

On Christmas Eve, 1814, six days after the *Avenger* sailed from the coast of England, the Treaty of Ghent was signed. But because of the slow communications of that day, the war continued, both on land and at sea.

The Battle of New Orleans was fought on January , 1815. The most decisive American victory of the war was fought two weeks after the peace treaty was signed. But the Battle of New Orleans was not the last battle of the War of 1812, as commonly believed. The war at sea continued long afterwards.

While Bonaparte raised his ugly head and started another war in Europe and Stephen Decatur was fighting America's newest war against Algiers in the Mediterranean, the *Peacock*—still under the command of Lewis Warrington—fought doggedly at the old war, totally unaware that the war had ended. On the last day of June, 1815, six months after the peace treaty had been signed, the *Peacock* fought the last battle of the War of 1812. On that day, off the coast of Java, Warrington captured his last prize. Ironically, her name was the *Nautilus*, an American ship that had fallen into British hands three years before at the beginning of the war.

Three months later in New Orleans, Leigh gave birth to a lusty, golden-headed son, his eyes as blue as the Caribbean. She took one look at her son and promptly named him Matthew Blake III. Three nights later, two doors down from where her golden-haired, blue-eyed great-grandson had been born, Grandmère died in her sleep, joining her beloved *capitaine*. The maid who found her the next morning remarked that she must have died peacefully—for she was found with a happy smile on her face.

FOR A DELECTABLE READ
Try Zebra's Historical Romances

LOVING FURY (1820, $3.95)
by Phoebe Conn

By day Angelique's mother forced her to dress and act as a child, but by night she met the dashing Diego Aragon. Diego was determined to discover who his mysterious temptress was. He swore he'd make her pay for teasing him and turn his suffering into *Loving Fury*.

WILD HEART (1786, $3.95)
by Virginia Brown

Stolen away from her family, Amanda feared for her life. But the bandit leader El Leon awakened in her a longing that reached down to her toes, making her want to tame her reckless *Wild Heart*.

YANKEE'S LADY (1784, $3.95)
by Kay McMahon

Rachel lashed at the Union officer and fought to flee the dangerous fire he ignited in her. But soon Rachel touched him with a bold fiery caress that told him—despite the war—that she yearned to be the *Yankee's Lady*.

CRIMSON ANGEL (1783, $3.95)
by Penelope Neri

No man had any right to fluster Heather simply because he was so impossibly handsome. But before she could slap the captain for his impudence she was a captive of his powerful embrace.

PASSION'S GOLD (1781, $3.95)
by Nancy Kovats

Molly Lewis headed west searching for gold—but instead found Hugh Everett and lost her heart. But Hugh was a man haunted by his past and determined to control his own destiny. He had to have Molly just one, shattering night with *Passion's Gold*.

Available wherever paperbacks are sold, or order direct from the Publisher. Send cover price plus 50¢ per copy for mailing and handling to Zebra Books, Dept. 2064, 475 Park Avenue South, New York, N.Y. 10016. Residents of New York, New Jersey and Pennsylvania must include sales tax. DO NOT SEND CASH.

TANTALIZING HISTORICAL ROMANCE
From Zebra Books

CAPTIVE CARESS (1923, $3.95)
Sonya T. Pelton

Denied her freedom, despairing of rescue, the last thing on Willow's mind was desire. But before she could say no, she became her captor's prisoner of passion.

EMERALD ECSTASY (1908, $3.95)
by Emma Merritt

From the moment she arrived in Ireland, Marguerite LeFleur heard the stories of the notorious outlaw. And somehow she knew that it would be him who would teach her the heights of passion.

LOUISIANA LADY (1891, $3.95)
by Myra Rowe

Left an orphan, Leander Ondine was forced to live in a house of ill-repute. She was able to maintain her virtue until the night Justine stumbled upon her by mistake. Although she knew it was wrong, all she wanted was to be his hot-blooded *Louisiana Lady*.

SEA JEWEL (1888, $3.95)
by Penelope Neri

Hot-tempered Alaric had long planned the humiliation of his hated foe's daughter. But he never suspected she would become the mistress of his heart, his treasured, beloved *Sea Jewel*.

MIDNIGHT THUNDER (1873, $3.95)
by Casey Stuart

The last thing Gabrielle remembered before slipping into unconsciousness was a pair of the deepest blue eyes she'd ever seen. Instead of stopping her crime, Alexander wanted to imprison her in his arms and embrace her with the fury of *Midnight Thunder*.

Available wherever paperbacks are sold, or order direct from the Publisher. Send cover price plus 50¢ per copy for mailing and handling to Zebra Books, Dept. 2064, 475 Park Avenue South, New York, N.Y. 10016. Residents of New York, New Jersey and Pennsylvania must include sales tax. DO NOT SEND CASH.

THE ECSTASY SERIES
by Janelle Taylor

SAVAGE ECSTASY (Pub. date 8/1/81)   (0824, $3.50)

DEFIANT ECSTASY (Pub. date 2/1/82)   (0931, $3.50)

FORBIDDEN ECSTASY (Pub. date 7/1/82)   (1014, $3.50)

BRAZEN ECSTASY (Pub. date 3/1/83)   (1133, $3.50)

TENDER ECSTASY (Pub. date 6/1/83)   (1212, $3.75)

STOLEN ECSTASY (Pub. date 9/1/85)   (1621, $3.95)

Plus other bestsellers by Janelle:

GOLDEN TORMENT (Pub. date 2/1/84)   (1323, $3.75)

LOVE ME WITH FURY (Pub. date 9/1/83)   (1248, $3.75)

FIRST LOVE, WILD LOVE
(Pub. date 10/1/84)   (1431, $3.75)

SAVAGE CONQUEST (Pub. date 2/1/85)   (1533, $3.75)

DESTINY'S TEMPTRESS
(Pub. date 2/1/86)   (1761, $3.95)

SWEET SAVAGE HEART
(Pub. date 10/1/86)   (1900, $3.95)

Available wherever paperbacks are sold, or order direct from the Publisher. Send cover price plus 50¢ per copy for mailing and handling to Zebra Books, Dept. 2064, 475 Park Avenue South, New York, N.Y. 10016. Residents of New York, New Jersey and Pennsylvania must include sales tax. DO NOT SEND CASH.